Susanna Gregory was a police  an academic career. She has serv during seventeen field season taught comparative anatomy a

She is the creator of the Matthew Bartholomew series of mysteries set in medieval Cambridge and the Thomas Chaloner adventures in Restoration London, and now lives in Wales with her husband, who is also a writer.

Also by Susanna Gregory

The Matthew Bartholomew series
A Plague on Both Your Houses
An Unholy Alliance
A Bone of Contention
A Deadly Brew
A Wicked Deed
A Masterly Murder
An Order for Death
A Summer of Discontent
A Killer in Winter
The Hand of Justice
The Mark of a Murderer
The Tarnished Chalice
To Kill or Cure
The Devil's Disciples
A Vein of Deceit
The Killer of Pilgrims
Mystery in the Minster
Murder by the Book
The Lost Abbot
Death of a Scholar
A Poisonous Plot
A Grave Concern
The Habit of Murder

The Thomas Chaloner series
A Conspiracy of Violence
Blood on the Strand
The Butcher of Smithfield
The Westminster Poisoner
A Murder on London Bridge
The Body in the Thames
The Piccadilly Plot
Death in St James's Park
Murder on High Holborn
The Cheapside Corpse
The Chelsea Strangler
The Executioner of St Paul's

SUSANNA GREGORY

A
WICKED
DEED

sphere

SPHERE

First published in Great Britain in 1999 by Little, Brown and Company
First published in paperback in 2000 by Warner Books
This edition reissued in 2017 by Sphere

3 5 7 9 10 8 6 4 2

A CIP catalogue record for this book
is available from the British Library.

ISBN 978-0-7515-6939-1

Typeset in Baskerville and Omnia by
Palimpsest Book Production Limited,
Falkirk, Stirlingshire
Printed and bound in Great Britain by Clays Ltd, Elcograf S.p.A.

Papers used by Sphere are from well-managed forests
and other responsible sources.

MIX
Paper from
responsible sources
FSC® C104740

Sphere
An imprint of
Little, Brown Book Group
Carmelite House
50 Victoria Embankment
London EC4Y 0DZ

An Hachette UK Company
www.hachette.co.uk

www.littlebrown.co.uk

To Sarah Atkinson

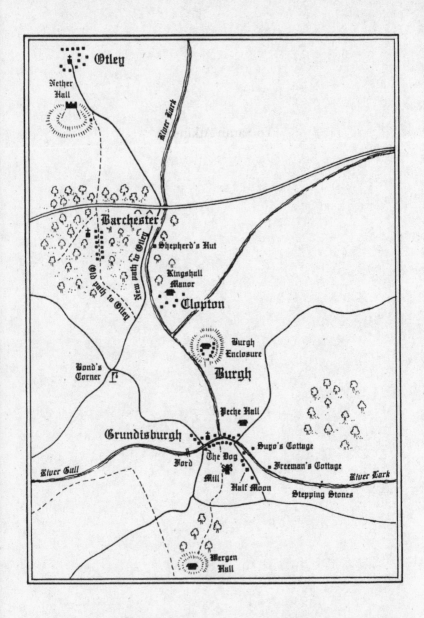

PROLOGUE

Suffolk, April 1353

TWIGS SLASHED AT ALICE QUY'S FACE AND ARMS AS SHE raced through the undergrowth, certain that the dog that chased her would bring her down at any moment. She tripped over a tree root, tumbling head over heels down a leaf-strewn slope, until coming up hard against the trunk of an old beech. She could not see the dog, with its small glittering eyes and its shaggy white coat rippling as it moved, but she knew it was behind her. She scrambled to her feet, sobbing in terror, and ran towards the river.

She knew she should never have come to the woods that night. It was true that she had been well paid, and that the money would help to buy the new cow her family needed, but money would be no use to her if the huge dog that snapped and slathered at the top of the slope were to catch her: she could not spend the gold coins that jangled in the purse at her waist if she were dead. She glanced behind, aware that the animal was beginning to gain on her, loping through the woods in a deceptively unhurried gait that was faster than anything two legs could achieve.

She had heard stories in the village about the massive white dog that haunted the abandoned plague village of Barchester. It was known to be a ferocious beast, given to tearing out the throats of its victims, and it was said that even to catch sight of the thing was sufficient to set a person on the road to doom and disaster. Alice Quy tried not to think about it, forcing herself to concentrate on where she stepped as she reached the River Lark, and waded across it, falling headlong as the cold water that surged around her legs slowed her down. Gasping for breath and dashing the droplets from her eyes, she splashed through the shallows on the other side, and began to force her way through the trees on the opposite bank.

Suddenly she was out of the woods that surrounded Barchester, and was at the edge of the neat strip-fields that belonged to Roland Deblunville, the lord of the manor whose land abutted on to that of her own village of Grundisburgh. She knew what would happen if he caught her trespassing on his land and trampling his ripening barley, but she did not care. Her only concern was to escape the white dog, the hot breath of which she could almost feel on the back of her neck, as she left the trees and began sprinting across the ploughed earth.

It was a dark night, and the moon was obscured by a thick covering of cloud. She stumbled over one particularly deep furrow and fell, grazing her elbows and knees on the stony soil. Terrified, she clambered upright and plunged on, too frightened to look behind to see if the dog were still in pursuit. The ground was becoming more uneven, and she fell again almost immediately. This time, she did not rise, but lay on the ground, weeping with fear and exhaustion.

Gradually, as she lay motionless on the cold earth, her breathing began to return to normal, the thudding of her heart subsided, and the blind terror began to recede. She had escaped! Scarcely daring to believe her good luck, she slowly relaxed her tensed muscles, and sat up to peer around her in the blackness. She could see nothing in the dark, but it seemed as though her prayers had been answered, and that the dog had abandoned the chase and allowed her to live another day. Almost dizzy with relief, she climbed unsteadily to her feet, and started to stumble away from Master Deblunville's land before he or his men caught her.

She had not taken more than a few faltering steps when she heard a noise behind her. Heart pounding again, she looked around her wildly, trying to penetrate the velvety blackness to see what it was. She could see nothing, but the sound was there sure enough – soft, slithering footfalls as someone or something inched its way toward her, slowly and carefully, like a wolf stalking its prey.

Was it the dog that approached her so stealthily? Or was it one of Deblunville's guards, slinking up behind a trespasser on his lord's lands? Alice Quy was almost at the point where she did not care. She started to run, but her legs were too weak to carry her, and she fell on to her knees. The slithering sound was closer now. Desperately, she tried to crawl, oblivious to the sharp stones that cut into her hands and legs.

It was hopeless. She could hear breathing now, slow and even. She was almost paralysed with terror, and collapsed in a heap on the ground, shuddering uncontrollably and aware that the footsteps were coming closer and closer. And then something reached out and touched her shoulder.

Alice Quy found she was unable to do so much as flinch: fright had finally paralysed her, like a deer caught in the light of a hunter's flaring torch. She felt herself rolled on to her back. She did not look at her captor, but gazed up at the black sky with eyes that were fixed and dilated with fear.

Two weeks later
It had been a busy day for James Freeman, the butcher. Lady Isilia from Wergen Hall had sent him two pigs to be slaughtered, and the landlord of the Half Moon had bought a sheep that needed gutting in order to feed the rough group of men who had been hired to weed the village's ripening crops. And in a couple of weeks' time there would be the Pentecost Fair with its feasts – the butcher was always inundated with

work for that. The Pentecost Fair was the highlight of the village's year, a much-loved occasion that was eagerly awaited by everyone after Easter. The villagers were not expected to work from Saturday to Monday – an almost unheard-of luxury in a time when labour was scarce and landlords demanding – and there would be music, dancing and feasting. But James Freeman was not interested in the Fair this year, because he knew he would not live the two weeks to enjoy it.

Lethargically, he hacked at a sheep leg bone with his meat cleaver, muscles bunching under his bloodstained shirt. He saw his wife watching him with an odd mixture of pity and wariness. He had tried hard to pretend that he was not afraid of what might happen, but they had known each other since childhood, and he sensed she had not been deceived by his blustering attempts to shrug off the inner fear that gnawed at him day and night. How would he die? he wondered, as he raised the cleaver again. Would his hand slip as he butchered an animal, severing some great vein so that his life blood would drain away? Would he choke over his food one night for no apparent reason? Would he stumble as he walked along the road, and be crushed under the wheels of a passing cart? He shuddered, and pushed such thoughts from his mind, aware that his wife was coming toward him.

'Do not think about it, James,' she said, seeing in his face what was going through his mind. 'If you do not think about it, it might not happen.'

They regarded each other sombrely, both knowing her words were meaningless: James Freeman would be dead within a few days just as surely as would the pig that blithely awaited execution in the yard outside.

He summoned a wintry smile and looked away. 'Alice Quy tried not to think about it, but look what happened to her. We all thought she had escaped when she returned from Barchester that night, but she died – just as I will.'

'No, James,' protested his wife, although he could not but

help notice that her voice lacked conviction. He knew that, as far as she was concerned, he was already dead. He also knew that she had started to look to her future without him, and he had seen her flirting with Will Norys, the pardoner.

Still, Freeman thought, if she married Norys at least he could go to his grave knowing that she would be properly looked after. Being a widow was not easy in rural Suffolk, and the pardoner's trade had been booming since the plague – everyone wanted forgiveness for sins when no one knew when the pestilence might strike again. Norys would provide her with all she could want, and she would not be forced to eke out the rest of her life in miserable poverty, stewing animal skins and nettles to eat, like some widows.

'I am hungry,' he said, not comfortable with the way she looked at him – like she might the lepers from the nearby hospital, who still breathed and walked even though a requiem mass had already been said over their rotting, living bodies. 'Is the meal ready?'

She shook her head. 'But it will be by the time you have finished with this sheep.'

She started to leave the butchering shed, to make her way to the house at the top of the garden, but then hesitated, her eyes fixed on the sharp cleaver that dangled from his hand. As if she thought it might be the last time she would see him alive.

'Be careful, James.'

He watched her walk away, before turning his attention back to the carcass that lay on the bench in front of him. He was about to raise the chopper to continue his work, when he became aware of a shadow in the doorway. Thinking it was only his wife, checking to make sure he did not do something foolish, he did not look up, but started to chop through the sheep's thigh bone with rhythmic, precise blows.

By the time he realised that the shadow was not his wife, it was too late. He felt a hot, burning sensation somewhere in his head, and then blackness claimed him.

CHAPTER 1

Suffolk, May 1353

ATTHEW BARTHOLOMEW, DOCTOR OF MEDI-
cine and fellow of Michaelhouse at the
University of Cambridge, lay on his stom-
ach in the long grass at the side of the road, and waited.
The only sounds were the twittering of a lark from high up
in the clouds and the muffled voices of the men who lurked
in the deep ditch opposite. One of them gave a low laugh,
and Bartholomew thought he heard the faint metallic clink
of a sword or a dagger that tapped against a stone. Next to
him, his book-bearer, Cynric, tensed suddenly and pointed
down the trackway to their left. A small cart was creaking
towards them, a ramshackle affair on wheels of different
sizes, drawn by a listless horse with bony withers.

The men in the ditch had seen it, too, and fell silent
as it rumbled closer. With mounting horror, Bartholomew
realised what was about to happen. Dried leaves rustled as
he eased himself up on to his elbows, preparing to shout a
warning to the man who drove the cart. Cynric grabbed a
handful of his tabard and jerked him down again, shooting
the physician a look of disgust, appalled that he would
compromise their own safety to help a stranger who was
probably doomed anyway.

The cart was almost on them, wooden wheels protesting

in irregular squeaks and groans as they jolted across ruts that had been baked hard by the early summer sun. The driver, a skinny, undersized man wearing a bell-shaped hat of straw and a rough homespun tunic, was taking fruit to be sold at the market in Ipswich, and a sorry offering of wizened apples, carefully hoarded from the previous year's crop, rolled around in the back with hollow thumps.

With ear-splitting yells, the men exploded from the ditch, and had surrounded the cart before the driver guessed what was happening. The horse pranced in terror at the sudden noise, and the cart tipped, sending its cargo bouncing across the road. The petrified driver did not wait to hear the robbers' demands, but scrambled off the cart, and began to race back the way he had come. He tore his purse from his belt as he fled, and hurled it behind him, an astute move that distracted the robbers just long enough to allow him to be out of arrow range when they saw he was escaping.

While the thieves argued over the meagre contents of the purse and unharnessed the frightened horse from the cart, Bartholomew and Cynric eased further back into the scrubby undergrowth and watched them. There were five in all, a rough-looking group of men, who wore shabby clothes and whose faces were masked by bandages. Had they not looked so well-fed and healthy, Bartholomew might have supposed they were lepers, hiding their ravaged features from the world with only their eyes showing through the swaths of dirty grey-brown linen. Three sported hose and jerkins that had probably once been of fine quality, suggesting to Bartholomew that the attack on the would-be apple-seller was not their first ambush of travellers along the Old Road that linked the prosperous city of Ipswich to the Suffolk coast.

Since the black days of the plague, which had carried away a third of the country's population, roadside robbers were becoming increasingly common. Some were simply desperate people who had learned that preying on travellers was an easier and quicker way of earning a loaf of bread than toiling in the fields for pitifully low wages. Others, like the five who argued over the apple-seller's pennies, were more professional, perhaps veterans from King Edward's army, who believed England owed them more than a life of labouring on the land after their great victory over the French at the Battle of Crécy in 1346.

'They will have to attack someone else tonight,' whispered Cynric to Bartholomew, as he watched the squabble become more acrimonious. 'There will not be enough in the apple-seller's purse to satisfy them, and that pathetic nag will not fetch much at the market.'

'Then what shall we do?' asked Bartholomew in a low voice. 'We need to use the road, but it will be dark soon, and if they do not hesitate to attack travellers in daylight, I dread to think what they might be like at night.'

Cynric shrugged. 'They will not stay here in case the apple-seller fetches the Sheriff's men – they will move further down the road. Therefore, we cannot go on or we will walk right into them, and it is too late to return to the last village we passed.' He grimaced and glanced at the road, an ancient trackway that ran as straight as the path of an arrow for almost as far as the eye could see. 'The highways of England are no place for honest men after dusk these days.'

'So, we cannot go on and we cannot go back,' concluded Bartholomew. 'What do you suggest we do? Stay here?' He looked around with a distinct lack of enthusiasm. While he did not mind sleeping under the stars, particularly when the weather was dry and warm, he did not relish the idea of doing so while there was a ruthless band of outlaws prowling nearby.

'We will take that path that leads north,' whispered Cynric promptly, pointing to a gap in the trees to the left. 'The village of Otley should be a mile or two that way, if my memory serves me right.'

Bartholomew climbed to his feet, anxious to be away from the road before darkness fell. The sun had already set, disappearing in a blaze of gold-red, and the first stars were pinpricking the sky. His travelling companions – three other Michaelhouse Fellows and three students – had been left with the horses a short distance away, bundled to safety when Cynric first became uneasy about the deep ditch to one side of the road, and the low mutter of voices that only he had heard.

But Bartholomew's haste made him careless, and there was a sharp snap as a twig broke under his foot. Cynric cast him a withering look, and quickly tugged him down again as the robbers immediately fell silent. With horror, Bartholomew saw them draw short swords and move toward the undergrowth in which he and Cynric hid. One gestured to the others and they began to fan out, creeping like shadows through the bushes and trees. Cynric poked Bartholomew in the ribs and indicated that he was to move to his right, away from where the other scholars were waiting to be told whether it was safe to continue their journey. When Bartholomew glanced around, the Welshman was nowhere to be seen, having melted away into the foliage as though he had never been there at all.

Trying to tread lightly, Bartholomew threaded his way through the woods, wincing as leaves crackled under his feet. Then, a triumphant yell told him that he had been spotted. He risked a quick glance backward, and saw one of the men racing toward him, sword held high above his head. Abandoning stealth, Bartholomew turned and ran, crashing through twigs and brambles that scratched his face and tangled themselves around his feet as he went. The medicine bag, which he always wore looped over his shoulder, snagged on branches, slowing him down. He did not need to look behind again to know that the robbers were gaining on him.

He ran faster, breath coming in ragged gasps, stumbling as his foot caught on the root of a tree. The undergrowth was becoming more dense, so that it was harder to move in a straight line, and he knew it was only a matter of time before the robbers drew close enough to hack at him with their swords. With a strength born of desperation, he raced on, trying to force a final spurt of speed in the vain hope that his pursuers might give up the chase if he were able to increase, even slightly, the distance between them.

He saw a silvery glint as something dropped into the ferns ahead of him. One of the robbers had thrown a dagger, aiming to bring him down before they wasted more energy in tearing through the scrub. A distant part of Bartholomew's mind supposed it was the sight of his heavy bag that made them so determined: they were not to know it contained only salves, potions and a few surgical instruments, none of which would be of much value, even to the most destitute of thieves. He plunged into the ferns where the knife had fallen, but they were tangled and thick, and he tripped almost immediately, sprawling forward on to his hands and knees.

He saw the dagger on the ground, and snatched it up as he struggled to his feet to face his pursuers. There were three of them. They slowed when they saw he was run to ground, and began to spread out, making it difficult for him to watch them all at the same time. One of them feinted to his left, while another darted behind him. Even through their bandaged faces, Bartholomew could sense they were grinning, confident that they would make short work of him and make off with the contents of the intriguing leather bag that bulged at his side.

Suddenly, one of them dropped to his knees, clutching his upper arm. An arrow protruded from it, and for an instant all three robbers and Bartholomew did nothing but stare at it in surprise. Then the stricken outlaw gave a tremendous shriek of pain and fear that almost, but not quite, drowned out the hiss of a second quiver that thudded into the ground at the feet of one of his companions. Leaving the injured man to fend for himself, the other two promptly fled, smashing through the scrubby vegetation every bit as blindly as Bartholomew had done. The wounded man staggered to his feet and followed, leaving Bartholomew alone.

'Never run into a place you cannot escape from, boy,' said Cynric admonishingly, as he stepped out from behind a tree, still holding his bow. 'I have told you that before.'

'It was not intentional,' said Bartholomew, rubbing a shaking hand through his hair. 'What happened to the other two thieves?'

'Run off down the Old Road like a pair of frightened rabbits,' said Cynric, fingering his bow as he glanced around him. 'We should leave here before they regroup and come after us again.'

On unsteady legs, Bartholomew followed Cynric through the woods to the small clearing where they had left their Michaelhouse colleagues. The Franciscan friar, Father William, sat with his two students – Unwin and John de Horsey – under a spreading oak, reading from a psalter in an unnecessarily loud voice. The third student, Rob Deynman, was minding the horses, while the Cluniac, Roger Alcote, who as Senior Fellow considered himself to be in charge of the deputation, paced impatiently in the centre of the glade. Lastly, Brother Michael lounged comfortably with his back against a sturdy tree-trunk, his jaws working rhythmically and the front of his black Benedictine habit sprinkled with crumbs.

With the exception of Michael and Cynric, none of the Michaelhouse scholars were travelling companions Bartholomew would willingly have chosen. In fact, he had not wanted to make the journey at all, preferring to remain in Cambridge with his patients and students. But the Master of the College had been adamant, and Bartholomew had been given no choice but to join his colleagues for the long trek to the village of Grundisburgh in east Suffolk, to the home of Sir Thomas Tuddenham. This knight had generously offered to give Michaelhouse the living of his village church, and the scholarly deputation was to draw up the deed that would make the transfer legal.

The gift of the living of a church – especially one in a wealthy village like Grundisburgh – was something greatly valued by institutions like Michaelhouse. Not only would it provide employment for their scholars – because owning the living meant that they could appoint whomever they liked as village priest – but if it chose Michaelhouse could pay that priest a pittance to act as vicar, while pocketing for itself the lion's share of the tithes paid to the church each year. Such gifts were therefore taken seriously, and the large deputation from the College was not only to pay tribute to Tuddenham's generosity, it was also to ensure that the transfer was completed so meticulously that no future Tuddenham could ever try to claim it back.

'Well?' asked Michael, looking up from the crust of a pie he had been devouring. 'Was Cynric right? Were there outlaws on the road waiting to rob us of our meagre belongings? Or have we been lurking in this miserable hole all evening for nothing?'

Bartholomew flopped on to the grass next to him, and rubbed his face with hands that still shook. 'You know Cynric is always right about such things, Brother. He thinks we should stay in Otley tonight, rather than continue along the Old Road.'

'But I wanted to be in Grundisburgh by this evening,' objected Roger Alcote, with a petulant scowl. 'Tuddenham was expecting us to arrive there three days ago. He has been most generous in giving Michaelhouse the living of his village church, and it is ungracious of us to arrive so much later than we promised.'

'He will understand,' said Bartholomew tiredly. 'It is a long way from Cambridge to Grundisburgh, and the roads are dangerous these days.'

Alcote was not in a mood to be placated. 'Cynric said the journey would take five days at the most, and we have been travelling nine already,' he complained.

'That was because we spent so long in that disgracefully luxurious Benedictine abbey at St Edmundsbury,' said Father William, favouring Michael with a disapproving glower. The austere Franciscan claimed to despise anything vain or worldly, although Bartholomew had noticed that he had declined none of the Benedictines' generous hospitality, despite roundly condemning them for their wealth and comfort.

' "Disgracefully luxurious",' mused Michael, his green eyes glittering with amusement as he tossed the remains of the pie crust over his shoulder into the bushes. 'I found it rather primitive, personally. Particularly when compared to my own abbey at Ely.'

'We can travel the last few miles to Grundisburgh at first light tomorrow,' said Bartholomew quickly, before Michael could goad the humourless Franciscan into an argument. He glanced up at the sky. 'But we should leave here now if we want to reach Otley before it is completely dark.'

'Well, do not just sit there, then,' snapped Alcote impatiently, thrusting the reins of Bartholomew's horse at him. He put his head on one side in the way that always reminded the physician of a bad-tempered hen, and fixed him with his sharp, pale eyes. 'We would have been in Grundisburgh by now if your servant had not been so nervous. We have been loitering in this wretched place for hours waiting for the two of you to come back.'

'Lead on, Cynric,' said Michael, as he swung himself up

into his saddle with surprising ease for a man of his immense girth. 'Let Matt and Roger stay here and argue about outlaws if they will, but take me to a decent inn where I can enjoy a good meal and a soft bed.'

'You have not stopped eating since we left Cambridge,' remarked Father William critically, looking around for his donkey. The brawny friar refused to ride anything except a donkey, loftily maintaining that to mount a horse, like the others, would be succumbing to earthly vanity. The animal that had been provided, however, was one of the smallest Bartholomew had ever seen, and the friar's feet touched the ground on either side as he rode.

'Enough,' said Bartholomew, as he saw Michael's eyes narrow, a sure sign that the monk was assessing which of several pithy replies that doubtless came to his quick mind would most antagonise the sanctimonious friar. 'There are five outlaws at large, and we should not be here when they pull themselves together and come back seeking revenge.'

Cynric nodded fervent agreement, and began to lead the way through the undergrowth toward the Old Road. The others followed, while Bartholomew, still uneasy that the robbers might yet be skulking in the deepening shadows, brought up the rear. He rummaged in his medicine bag for the small knife that was part of his surgical equipment, and kept twisting around in his saddle so that he could see behind him. Cynric crossed the Old Road, before heading up the path that wound through the darkening woods to the north.

The evening air was still, and smelled of grass mixed with the richer scent of sun-baked earth. The scholars had been lucky on their travels – the ground had been hard and dry, and there had been none of the struggling through morasses masquerading as roads that Bartholomew had encountered on other journeys. Even so, he was tired. It had been several years since he had ventured so far outside Cambridge, and he had forgotten quite how exhausting travelling could be.

Memories of his days as a graduate student at the University of Paris came flooding back to him, when he had traipsed miles through France, Italy and Castile with the Arab physician with whom he had chosen to study. While his fellow students learned their medicine in dimly lit halls, Ibn Ibrahim had taken Bartholomew with him as he rode far and wide to tend interesting cases. But Bartholomew had been younger then, and Ibn Ibrahim's enthusiastic discourses on healing had taken his mind off the miseries of the journey. Not surprisingly, Alcote's complaining and William's dogmatism had done nothing to alleviate the boredom and discomfort as the scholars had ridden eastward into Suffolk.

Bartholomew stifled a yawn, looking from side to side into the now impenetrably black bushes that flanked the path. Something rustled and he tensed, anticipating another attack, but it was only a blackbird rooting about in the dried leaves for grubs. It fixed him with a bright yellow glare before flapping away, twittering in alarm.

Ahead of him, he could hear Alcote and William arguing about something, their voices growing louder and louder as each tried to put forward his own point of view without listening to the other. Michael rode behind them, and Bartholomew could see his plump shoulders shaking with mirth as he listened. Knowing Alcote's mean-mindedness and William's uncompromising opinions, Bartholomew could well imagine why Michael was finding their ill-tempered exchange amusing, but he was still too shaken by his encounter with the robbers to feel much like being entertained by his colleagues' bigotry.

Horsey and Deynman began to sing 'Sumer is icumen in', and Michael, never averse to a little impromptu music, switched his attention to providing a bass part. He tried to persuade the third student to join in, but Unwin declined and fell back to ride next to Bartholomew.

'Did you sleep easier last night?' Bartholomew asked him, still peering behind at the darkened track. He thought he saw something move, and was on the verge of shouting for Cynric when a pair of amber eyes blinked at him, and he realised it was only a fox.

The Franciscan student-friar gave a strained smile. 'A little. The draught you gave me helped, but I will only be better once we reach Grundisburgh and I know what is expected of me.'

'Grundisburgh already has a parish priest, and it might be years before he dies or retires and you have to take over his duties,' said Bartholomew, not for the first time since the Master of Michaelhouse had announced that he had chosen the studious Unwin to become Grundisburgh's next vicar.

In order to express to Tuddenham that his gift was truly appreciated, the Master had appointed Michaelhouse's most brilliant student to the post of priest-elect of Grundisburgh. He reasoned that not only would Unwin learn the parish's ways before taking up office permanently, but the villagers would be assured that Michaelhouse intended to take its obligations seriously, and would provide them with the best the College could offer. Bartholomew had been surprised when Kenyngham had selected Unwin to serve as Grundisburgh's vicar-elect: an excellent student he might be, and there were few who could best him in a theological debate, but he was far too timid and unworldly to make a good priest for a large rural parish.

'I know I shall have time to learn from the present incumbent,' said Unwin, shoving a thumb that had already been gnawed raw into his mouth. 'But supposing I am not what Grundisburgh expects? What if they want a more . . . ?' He faltered, chewing on his thumb in agitation. '. . . A more charismatic priest?'

Then they would be disappointed, thought Bartholomew. The diffident, bookish Unwin was one of the last people who could be considered charismatic. He did not even look inspiring. Although barely twenty, his fair hair was already thinning, and his pale blue eyes were weak and watery from reading in bad light. He stooped, too, and had a peculiar habit of looking over people's shoulders when addressing them, instead of meeting their eyes. Although Bartholomew knew this resulted from shyness, those who knew him less well invariably considered him shifty. And shiftiness was not a character generally sought after in a parish priest.

He smiled encouragingly. 'You can always confine yourself to saying masses for the plague-dead until you feel confident enough to take on other duties.'

Unwin brightened. 'I had not considered that.' He pulled his thumb from his mouth, and smiled thoughtfully. 'I will not have to hear confessions that will shock me, or deal with adulterers, thieves and sinners if I am praying for the souls of the dead, will I?'

He lapsed into silence, leaving Bartholomew more certain than ever that a less scholarly and more practical student might have better served Grundisburgh's pastoral interests.

It was not long before the acrid smell of wood-fires added their pungent aroma to the scent of late evening, and Cynric called out that they were nearing Otley. Dominating the village was a castle, comprising a compact bailey ringed by a palisade of sharpened posts, a stone house with a reed-thatched roof, and a grassy motte topped with a wooden watchtower. The bailey gates stood open, and a flurry of activity indicated that the owner had recently returned from a hunt. Dogs milled around the legs of the stable boys who rubbed down the sweating horses, and scullions spirited away a dead stag for butchering.

A heavy-set guard, with a bushy beard and one of the filthiest boiled-leather jerkins Bartholomew had ever seen, had stopped Cynric and was asking his business in Otley. Impatiently, Alcote jostled the Welshman to one side, and began to berate the guard for daring to question the representatives of the University of Cambridge in so abrupt a manner, adding darkly that the villagers of Otley should consider the state of their immortal souls for hunting on a Holy Day.

'Hunting is no more wicked on the Feast Day of St John the Evangelist than is travelling,' retorted the guard immediately, eyeing Alcote with dislike. 'You are sinning just as much as we are.'

Alcote's head tipped to one side. 'But we are on God's sacred business,' he announced, wholly untruthfully, given that the journey was being undertaken solely because Michaelhouse wanted the living of Grundisburgh church. 'You only seek to gratify your greedy appetites with fresh venison.'

Bartholomew saw Brother Michael raise his eyes heavenward, and then hurry to intervene before Alcote's arrogant self-importance could have them escorted out of the village and thrown back on the perils of the Old Road for the night.

When Bartholomew looked behind him for Unwin, he was alarmed that the student-friar was nowhere to be seen. Leaving Michael to negotiate with the guard, he turned his horse and rode back the way he had come, straining his eyes in the darkness to try to see whether the Franciscan was still loitering on the track. There was no sign of him. Perplexed, he returned to the others, wondering whether the terrifying notion of becoming a parish priest had finally caused Unwin to flee once and for all.

With some relief, he eventually spotted Unwin emerging from one of the outbuildings in the castle bailey. He was closely followed by a knight dressed entirely in black, whose bald head gleamed whitely in the gloom. The knight suddenly reached out and grabbed Unwin's arm, so fiercely that the friar all but lost his balance, and whispered something in his ear to which the friar nodded. Bartholomew frowned, puzzled by the exchange. What was Unwin doing in the bailey talking to a knight? As far as he was aware, Unwin had never been to Suffolk before, and knew no one in the area – and he was certainly not the kind of man to go exploring alone.

'What was that about?' he asked curiously, as Unwin rejoined him.

Unwin shook his head. 'Nothing,' he muttered, glancing behind him in a way that could only be described as furtive. 'Where are the others?'

'Explaining to the guard who we are,' said Bartholomew, regarding the friar doubtfully, perplexed by his odd behaviour.

'There is no need for that,' came a booming voice, so close behind them that it made Unwin start backward and frighten his horse. It was the knight in black. 'Use your wits, Ned: here are monks, friars and men in scholars' tabards. It is obvious that these are the scholars from Cambridge – Sir Thomas Tuddenham has been expecting them over at Grundisburgh for the last three days.'

The guard acknowledged him with a sloppy salute, and gestured that the scholars were to pass into the village.

'I am Sir Robert Grosnold, lord of Otley Manor,' said the black knight grandly. He was powerfully built, with dark beady eyes and no neck, and his black leather armour gave him a rather sinister appearance, accentuating the whiteness of his hairless pate. He gestured to the stone house in the bailey. 'This is Nether Hall, granted to me by the King himself in recognition of my bravery at the Battle of Crécy in 'forty-six.'

'I see,' said Bartholomew, uncertain what else he could say.

'Great day for England, that,' continued Grosnold with unconcealed pride. 'And I was there.'

Bartholomew nodded politely, still wondering what had induced Unwin to slip away from his companions to the out-house in the bailey with the boastful lord of Otley Manor.

'You should not have been travelling this late,' Grosnold went on, when Bartholomew did not seem inclined to indulge in military small talk. 'We have had wolvesheads on the Old Road recently.'

'We saw them,' said Bartholomew. 'They chased us into the woods near the Otley path, but ran away when my book-bearer injured one of them with an arrow.'

Grosnold was startled. 'It seems you University men are not the gentle priests Tuddenham is expecting. Archery is an unusual skill for a scholar's servant to possess, is it not?'

'Cynric was a soldier once,' explained Bartholomew.

'Like me, then,' said Grosnold, deftly seizing the oppor-tunity to turn the subject back to fighting matters. He looked Bartholomew up and down disparagingly, taking in his darned and patched clothes, neatly trimmed black hair and clean hands. 'But you are no warrior, I see.'

'I am a physician,' said Bartholomew.

Grosnold was unimpressed. 'You are tall and strong: you should not have wasted such a fine physique by sitting around in dark rooms with dusty scrolls and ancient monks with no teeth.'

Was that how the people of rural Suffolk saw scholarship? Bartholomew wondered, not sure how to reply. He need not have worried: Grosnold had already lost interest in the conversation and was hailing his guard, ordering him to escort the scholars to the village inn.

'I will need my stars read in a few days,' Grosnold announced, as Bartholomew and Unwin began to walk away. 'I might summon you to do it, if you are lucky, physician.'

'I do not give astrological consultations,' said Bartholo-mew, trying not to be irritated by the man's presumption. He might have added that he did not believe that the stars made the slightest difference to a person's health, and that he considered studying them a complete waste of his time, but he had learned that few people agreed with him, and that some even regarded his opinions as anathema. It was nearly always prudent to keep his views to himself.

'Rubbish,' said Grosnold. 'All physicians read their patients' stars. I shall send for you when I am ready.'

'He can send for me all he likes,' muttered Bartholomew to Unwin, as they walked toward the inn. 'But I am not messing around with pointless astrological consultations.'

'Perhaps he will forget,' said Unwin, casting a nervous glance to where the black knight stood at the gate of his manor, yelling orders to scurrying servants at a volume sufficient to wake the dead.

'Have you met him before?' asked Bartholomew, still intrigued by the fact that Unwin had been in the bailey with Grosnold. 'What were you doing in his house?'

Unwin shook his head in the darkness. 'Nothing. We have never met before.'

Bartholomew let the matter drop. He was tired and aching from a long day in the saddle, and wanted nothing more than a straw mattress in a quiet room. Welcoming lights shone gold from the village inn, and, with relief, he handed the reins of his horse to Cynric and went inside.

The following day dawned clear and cool, and dew was thick on the ground. Bartholomew woke early, feeling refreshed, and joined Father William and two elderly local women in celebrating prime in the small, dark church. After a breakfast of watered ale and cold oatmeal, he sat on a bench in the pale light of the rising sun and talked to the taverner while he waited for the others. Eventually, they were ready, and he led the way out of Otley, following the landlord's directions to the village of Grundisburgh. They passed Grosnold's fortified manor house, but the gates were closed, and the guard, the top of whose metal helmet could be seen glinting above the palisade, was sound asleep.

The sun shone through the leaves of the trees, making dappled patterns on the grassy path. To one side, bluebells and buttercups added a splash of colour to the sludge of brown, rotting leaves from the year before, and to the other, a stream sparkled silver as it meandered south. The only sounds, other than birdsong, were the occasional clink of a harness and the gentle thud of horses' hooves on the turf. A butterfly danced across the path and then was gone, while a group of rabbits, probably escapees from some nobleman's warren, darted down a sandy hole with flicks of their white tails as the horsemen approached. Bartholomew took a deep breath, laden with the scent of warm, damp earth. He closed his eyes, relishing the feel of the sun on his face and the peace of the countryside.

'Suffolk is a godforsaken place,' grumbled Michael, riding next to him and glancing around disparagingly. He wore a wide-brimmed black hat to shade his face from the sun, and his skin was alabaster white against his dark Benedictine habit. Strands of lank brown hair dangled limply from under the hat, already wet with sweat, despite the cool, early-morning air. 'I have never been anywhere so dismal.'

'I suppose you miss the stench of the King's Ditch in Cambridge?' asked Bartholomew. 'Or the pleasure of strolling along the High Street, with its piles of offal, sewage and dead animals?'

Michael shot him an unpleasant look. 'At least it is good town filth,' he said. 'Not like this vile, endless scrub, and these miserable, tree-infested pathways that stink of grass. But look at Roger Alcote! He sits in his saddle like a ploughboy!'

'You have pointed that out already – several times,' said Bartholomew mildly. He was not in a position to comment on Alcote's equestrian abilities since, according to Michael, he rode even less elegantly than did the Senior Fellow, and even their long friendship had not protected him from Michael's scathing criticism about it over the last few days.

'And that Franciscan is just as bad,' Michael continued contemptuously, shifting his disdain from Alcote to William on his long-suffering donkey. 'He looks like a peasant astride a pig!'

Since there was some truth in Michael's observation, Bartholomew was unable to suppress a smile. 'You are in a fine mood today. Are you ill? Did you overeat again last night?'

'No, I did not overeat!' snapped Michael. 'I am just weary of this interminable journey. Do you know, the only one other than me who has the slightest grace is that Rob Deynman.' He looked over his shoulder to where Deynman and his two fellow students dawdled behind them. Seeing the obese monk glance backward, Deynman quickly slipped something out of sight and assumed a guileless expression. Michael's eyes narrowed suspiciously.

'Coming from such a wealthy family, Deynman could probably ride before he could walk,' said Bartholomew to distract him. Like Michael, the students were bored by the long journey, and Bartholomew had been impressed, but not particularly surprised, when they had devised a way of playing illicit games of dice as they rode.

'Deynman will never make a physician, Matt,' said Michael, fixing the uneasy student with a stony glower. 'I cannot imagine why you persist in trying to teach him.'

'You know very well why I continue to teach him, Brother,' said Bartholomew, 'since it was you who made the arrangements. The extortionate fees his father pays for his tuition keep Michaelhouse in bread and ale for at least half the year.'

'Rock-hard bread and sour ale,' spat Michael, forgetting Deynman's suspicious behaviour as he found something else to grumble about. 'And this journey had better be worth all this hardship and discomfort. If I find I have travelled sixty miles on a scrawny nag, just so that the College can own the living of a pig-pit of a parish, I shall have serious words with the Master.'

'This has nothing to do with the Master,' said Alcote, overhearing and reining back so that he could join in the conversation. 'It was my doing that Sir Thomas Tuddenham offered us the living of Grundisburgh's church. I hope you will remember that, Brother.'

'I certainly will,' muttered Michael bitterly. 'And all I can say is that if this living does not swell the College coffers beyond my wildest dreams, there will be hell to pay.'

'Grundisburgh is a very wealthy parish,' said Alcote. 'It has about two hundred occupants, most of whom pay annual tithes to the church. These will provide Unwin with a respectable stipend, and there will be enough left over for the College to make even the greediest Fellow happy.' He treated Michael to a nasty smile, head on one side in his bird-like way.

'I do not see why we had to come here at all,' Michael continued. 'If Tuddenham feels as much admiration for Michaelhouse as you claim, then he should have travelled to Cambridge to prepare the deed, not had us traipsing over the country after him. We are still in the middle of term, and I have teaching to do.'

'Then you should not have volunteered to come, Brother,' said Alcote coldly. 'None of you should. It is for me, as Senior Fellow, to oversee the writing of this deed – the advowson, as it is called – and it has nothing to do with anyone else.'

'It has a lot to do with Unwin,' Bartholomew pointed out. 'Once Tuddenham signs the advowson giving Michaelhouse the church, we will go home, but he will have to stay.'

'This is a superb opportunity for Unwin,' argued Alcote.

'He will train to be the vicar of a wealthy parish that will be his one day. What more can a young man ask?'

'I expect he would ask to stay in Michaelhouse and study,' said Bartholomew. 'He does not want to be a village priest.'

'Has he told you that?' asked Michael, surprised.

'He does not need to,' said Bartholomew. 'Have you not noticed how he has grown steadily more terrified the farther we have come from Cambridge?' He saw Alcote frowning, and hurried on. 'He will try his best – he is too obedient a friar to do otherwise – but the thought of being a parish priest does not appeal to him.'

'Then that is just too bad,' declared Alcote. 'He is our most promising student, and Tuddenham must be rewarded for his generosity by being given the best Michaelhouse can offer.' He glanced disdainfully at his companions, particularly at Bartholomew's frayed cuffs and threadbare tabard, and brushed an imaginary speck of dust from his own expensive robe.

Alcote had taken orders with the Cluniacs, once he had realised that life as a monk in the University could be comfortably lucrative. Previously, there had been a brief and unsatisfactory allegiance with the Carmelites. But it had been the Cluniacs who had best satisfied Alcote's requirements: they were an Order strong enough to promote him in University circles, but one that would leave him to his own devices as long as regular donations to the Mother House continued to swell its coffers.

'What will Tuddenham think when he sees the shambolic deputation the Master of Michaelhouse has dispatched?' Alcote went on. 'A fat Benedictine, an eccentric physician, a huge Franciscan on a tiny mule, a servant who is more soldier than book-bearer, and three disreputable students, one of whom is destined to be his parish priest, but who would rather be doing something else. What was the Master thinking of?'

'I suspect he was thinking of the peace he would have, once rid of a few troublemakers,' shot back Michael. 'He is weary of your constant criticism. Meanwhile, William is becoming so obsessed with being the University's next Junior Proctor that he is beginning to make a serious nuisance of himself with the Chancellor; young John de Horsey is here to ensure his friend Unwin does not flee his duties; Rob Deynman is still in disgrace over that nasty business regarding Agatha the laundress's teeth; and Matt's dalliance with the town's most beautiful prostitute means that the Master had a very good reason for wanting *him* out of Cambridge!'

'Just a minute,' began Bartholomew, horrified. 'I have never—'

'I heard about that,' said Father William smugly, his timely entry into the conversation indicating that he had been listening all along. 'Disgraceful! If I were Master, I would insist you took major orders, and become a friar or a monk, like the rest of us, Matthew. That would put an end to unseemly lechery with harlots. And I am not obsessed with becoming Junior Proctor, by the way. I have just made it clear in certain quarters that I would accept such a post if it were offered to me.'

'And you are here to keep us all in order, I suppose,' said Alcote, sneering at Michael. 'You can spy for the Master, just as you spy for the Chancellor and the Bishop.'

'The Master wanted *me* here to make sure the College was not cheated,' said William, before Michael could reply to Alcote's accusation, which was just as well, given that there was more than a grain of truth in it. Michael was not only the University's Senior Proctor and a valued member of the Chancellor's staff, he was also a trusted agent of the Bishop of Ely.

'God sent a terrible plague to warn us against the deadly sin of greed,' William ranted on, 'yet every monk in the country still hankers after power and wealth. Michaelhouse's interests would not be secure with only monks to watch over them.'

Monks and friars were invariably at loggerheads – friars denounced the contemplative lives of monks as selfish and cosseted, and monks objected to friars working in the community and involving themselves in human affairs. William despised the avaricious Alcote, and did not approve of Michael's growing influence in the University; in turn, Alcote was repelled by William's grimy, unkempt appearance, and Michael had no time at all for the friar's bigotry.

'God did not send the plague,' said Bartholomew, to avert a row. 'It just happened.'

There was a shocked silence, during which Bartholomew received a sharp kick from Michael. With a sinking heart, the physician realised that, far from preventing an argument, he had just managed to precipitate one. William drew himself up to his full height, almost losing the donkey from underneath him as he did so.

'Are you suggesting that God is not all-powerful?' he demanded hotly. 'Do you propose that other agents are equally able to cause such devastation in the world?'

'It seems to me that is exactly what he is suggesting,' said Alcote, as keen to promote dissent as Bartholomew was to stop it. 'He is a heretic!'

'He is nothing of the kind,' said Michael before Bartholomew could say anything in his own defence and make matters worse. 'And now is not the time for theological debate: we have arrived.'

So engrossed had they been in bickering that they had entered the village before realising they had done so. It was tiny, comprising no more than two parallel rows of shacks bordering the path. Behind the houses was the village church, a small, low building that squatted on its rise almost malevolently. Its glassless windows were dark slits in grey walls, and there was ivy growing up the tower. The village was as silent and as unsettling as the grave.

'This must be Barchester, not Grundisburgh,' said Bartholomew, looking around at the lonely houses and overgrown gardens. 'The taverner told me about Barchester this morning. Apparently, only one of its inhabitants survived the plague, but she drowned herself in the river last winter. It has been abandoned ever since.'

'Is that her?' asked Deynman in an unsteady voice. Bartholomew looked to the house where the student was pointing and saw an expanse of skirt with a shoe at the end of it, just visible under the cracked piece of leather that served as a door. The physician dismounted and took a step forward.

'No!' cried Michael suddenly, his voice shockingly loud in the silent village. He grabbed Bartholomew's shoulder. 'The Death may still lurk in this place, Matt. Leave her! If she drowned herself last winter, you can do nothing to help her now.'

'It cannot be the woman who drowned,' said Bartholomew reasonably. 'How could she have moved here from the river, if she were dead?'

His colleagues, to a man, crossed themselves vigorously.

'I have heard of these places,' said Cynric, looking around him uneasily. 'The spirits of those not granted absolution haunt them, and their screams of torment ring out each midnight.'

'That is superstitious nonsense, Cynric,' said Bartholomew firmly, refusing to allow his book-bearer's vivid imagination to unnerve him.

'It is truth, boy,' said Cynric with conviction. 'If you were to come here at the witching hour, you would hear them.'

'Well, that is no tormented spirit,' said Bartholomew, nodding at the bundle of clothing in the doorway. 'But it may be someone needing help.'

'I do not like this at all,' said Alcote, looking around him as though he expected to see the plague-dead rising up and rushing out of their houses to lay ghostly hands on him. 'It is sinister!'

Bartholomew handed the reins of his horse to Cynric, and walked through the nettles and weeds to the house where the skirt and shoe lay.

Aware that Michael was right, and that the house might still contain the decomposing bodies of unburied plague victims, Bartholomew picked up a stick, and used it to ease back the piece of leather that hung in the doorway. He gave a sigh of relief when he saw the skirt and shoe were nothing more than that – discarded clothes that had fallen in such a way as to appear as though someone was inside them.

As the daylight filtered into the house's single room, Bartholomew noticed it was surprisingly intact for a place that had been abandoned four years before. But, he thought, as he looked around, perhaps it had belonged to the woman who had killed herself, and had therefore only been left to decay for a few months. There was a table in the centre of the room with some carrots on it, black and shrivelled and with a knife lying next to them, as if their owner had been preparing a meal before she left, never to return. Cold, dead ashes lay in the hearth, stirring slightly in the draught from the doorway, and a rusting metal pot nestled among them.

Something glittered on the ground near the threshold, and Bartholomew crouched to look at it. It was a shiny new penny, still copper-bright from the mint, and not the dull brown of most of the coins of the realm. He turned it over in his fingers, and saw the date was that of the current year – 1353.

Bartholomew was puzzled. Coins did not remain clean for long, and he could only suppose that someone had dropped it recently. He turned his attention to the skirt and shoe. Both were free of dust and leaves, and the skirt was relatively clean. Neither could have been there for more than a few days at the most. He stood up. Doubtless some passer-by had dumped the old clothes there, and dropped the penny at the same time. Regardless, it was nothing to warrant him wasting any more of his time, and certainly no one needed his medical skills.

He made his way back to where his colleagues waited for him. Alcote moved away as he approached, holding a large pomander to his nose. It was not the first time the pomander had made its appearance on the journey: Alcote was terrified of the plague returning, and he invariably had the thing clasped to his face the moment they entered a village or a town. It was stuffed with cloves, bayleaves, wormwood and – if the students were to be believed – a little gold dust mixed with dried grasshoppers. Alcote had used it during the pestilence, and attributed his survival to its efficacy, although Bartholomew suspected that him locking himself away in his room had more to do with his escaping the sickness than the mysterious assortment of ingredients in the now-filthy pomander.

'There was nothing there,' he said in answer to his colleagues' anxious looks.

'Was the hovel full of skeletons?' whispered Deynman fearfully. 'Victims of the plague?'

Bartholomew shook his head. 'No, just some old clothes.'

Michael looked at the skirt and shuddered, memories of the plague in Cambridge surging back to him. There were villages all over England like Barchester, where the plague had struck particularly hard, either killing every inhabitant or driving the few survivors away to seek homes elsewhere. To Michael, the deserted settlements were eerie, haunted places where, as Cynric had suggested, he imagined he might hear the cries of the dead echoing from their hastily dug graves if he listened long enough.

'What was that?' Unwin exclaimed suddenly.

'What?' asked Deynman, twisting in his saddle to look around. 'I saw nothing.'

'Something white,' said Unwin, pointing off into the trees. 'A massive white dog.'

'Probably a stray,' said Bartholomew, mounting his horse with an inelegance that made Michael wince. 'There have been lots of strays since the plague.'

'Strays do not live in deserted settlements,' said William knowledgeably. 'They live near villages and towns where there is rubbish to scavenge.'

'Perhaps it buried a bone here,' said Bartholomew without thinking.

The others regarded him, aghast. 'That is an unpleasant suggestion, Matt,' said Michael eventually. 'I thought you said there were no skeletons here. Do you really think that dead villagers were left here to rot, and to be eaten by the wild beasts of the forest?'

'Come on,' said Alcote, spurring his horse forward decisively. 'This place has an evil air about it, and whatever secrets are here should be left well alone. The wild dog Unwin saw has gone now, and we should leave before it comes back and tries to savage us all.'

'It was a horrible thing,' said Unwin with a shudder. 'Huge, and with a dirty white coat.'

'Perhaps it was a wolf,' said Deynman, easing his horse after Alcote. 'My brother told me that there are wolves in this part of the country.'

'Listen,' said Michael softly, as the others rode away. 'It is completely silent here. The birds are not singing, and even the wind has dropped, so that the trees are as still as stones. It is almost as if the souls of the dead *are* walking here, inhabiting these houses and drifting along these paths.'

No one heard him, and Michael found himself alone in the main street. Not wanting to be left too far behind, he urged his horse into a trot, so that he could ride next to Bartholomew.

'Are you ill?' Bartholomew asked, noting the monk's pale face in concern.

Michael shook his head. 'These eerie Death villages unnerve me, Matt. This is the fourth we have seen since we left Cambridge.'

'You sound like Cynric,' said Bartholomew, surprised by the monk's uncharacteristic sensitivity. 'When you consider how many people died of the plague, it is no wonder that there are so many abandoned settlements. But that is no reason to give your imagination free rein.'

'There speaks the man of science,' said Michael. 'Always with a practical explanation to offer.'

'Better a practical explanation than believing all that rubbish about tormented souls,' said Bartholomew. 'But the plague has gone now, and we should look forward not back.'

'But it has not gone, Matt!' said Michael with sudden vehemence. 'There are abandoned hamlets everywhere; there is livestock still unattended and roaming wild; there are disused churches wherever you look, because even if there are congregations, there are too few priests alive to serve them. And people talk about it all the time – either as we are doing now, or just as a reference point – "before the Death" or "after the Death". It is here with us now, just as much as when it was killing us with its deadly fingers.'

Bartholomew could think of nothing to say, suspecting the monk was right, but unwilling to admit that the most devastating and terrifying episode in their lives still had the power to affect them so deeply. They rode in silence. Michael's bad temper had become gloom, while Bartholomew thought about the friends and colleagues he had lost to the Death. Then he recalled the people he had met since, particularly the beautiful prostitute, Matilde. He glanced behind him to make sure the students could not hear.

'The Master did not really send me to Suffolk because of Matilde, did he? I can assure you he had no cause.'

Michael chuckled softly, grateful to be thinking of something other than the pestilence. 'I can assure you he did. Ever since your fiancée abandoned you for a wealthy merchant a couple of years ago, you have done nothing but make a nuisance of yourself among the town's women.'

'I have not!' objected Bartholomew, startled by the accusation. 'I—'

'Do not try to deceive me, Matt. I have known you too long, and I have seen the way you look whenever Matilde speaks to you. Then there was that Julianna.'

'That Julianna set her sights on Ralph de Langelee, as well you know,' said Bartholomew tartly. 'And she and I have never had the slightest liking for each other.'

'I wonder what Langelee is doing now that Michaelhouse's four most senior Fellows are away,' mused Michael, changing the subject abruptly. 'It would not surprise me if he took advantage of our absence somehow. Perhaps we will find that we have a new Master by the time we return.'

'I wish Julianna *had* persuaded him to marry her,' said Bartholomew. 'Since Fellows of Colleges are not permitted to marry, it would have been an excellent way to rid ourselves of him without the need for violence.'

'Funny you should mention that,' said Michael. 'I heard a rumour that a certain ceremony involving those two took place recently in Grantchester Church. So far, I have been unable to verify it, but I can assure you I will look into the matter most carefully when we return. We do not want that belligerent lout as our next Master.'

They had not travelled far before they reached a crossroads, where the others waited for directions to Grundisburgh. Bartholomew's attention, however, was on something else.

Gibbets were commonplace at crossroads, and the one near Grundisburgh was a stark wooden silhouette against the sky, comprising a central post with two arms, one of which had a corpse dangling from it. But it was not the sight of a hanged criminal that caught Bartholomew's eye – he had lost count of the number of felons he had seen along the way, who had been executed and whose remains had been displayed to serve as a deterrent for anyone else considering breaking the law – there was something unusual about the body that made him want to take a closer look. First, the hands were not bound as was usual, but hung loosely at the sides; and second, the corpse was fully clothed. Ignoring William's gusty sigh of irritation, and Alcote's vocal revulsion at the physician's unseemly interest, he dismounted and made his way to the foot of the gibbet.

It was high, and the hanged man's feet swung near Bartholomew's shoulders. The shoes were of good-quality leather, with strong, almost-new soles, and a pair of gleaming silver-coloured buckles. The hose were made of soft-woven red wool, and the shirt was of fine linen, although the cuffs were beginning to fray. A handsome blue doublet embroidered with silver thread, and a thick belt, from which dangled a bejewelled dagger, completed the outfit. There was plenty of wear left in the garments, while the dagger would have fetched a good price, so why had no one relieved the corpse of them? Such items were usually considered the perks of the hangman's trade, and to find clothes so casually abandoned in these times of acute need was curious to say the least.

As Bartholomew looked upward, a flicker of movement caught his eye. At first he thought he had imagined it, but when he looked harder he saw it again. The hanged man's mouth had moved: he was still alive!

'He is still breathing!' Bartholomew yelled, making his

colleagues jump. He grabbed the hanged man's legs, trying to lift him to relieve the pressure around the throat. 'Help me, Michael!'

'What are you doing?' asked Alcote, watching him in horror. 'Leave him alone, Matthew, and come away before you land us all in trouble.'

'He is alive!' Bartholomew shouted, struggling to bear the man's weight. 'Cynric, cut the rope! Quickly!'

Cynric hesitated, but then moved forward. Before he could act, Michael intervened, raising an imperious hand that stopped the Welshman dead in his tracks.

'He is a convicted felon, Matt,' said the monk firmly. 'You cannot go cutting down criminals whenever you feel like it. You are likely to end up swinging next to him.'

'He is not a criminal,' Bartholomew gasped, desperately trying to support the body. 'Or, at least, he has not been lawfully executed. The hangmen would have taken his clothes had they been legally employed to kill him, and they have not.'

'Perhaps the nature of his crime was too heinous,' said Alcote with a shudder. 'Come away from him, before someone sees what you are trying to do.'

'Cynric!' pleaded Bartholomew.

The Welshman glanced uneasily at Michael, but then stepped towards the gibbet. He climbed up it before anyone could stop him, and sawed quickly through the rope. Bartholomew staggered as the body was suddenly freed and its weight dropped on to him. He laid the man down in the grass and loosened the noose, peering into the face for any signs of life. With a raw, rasping sound, the man drew breath.

'This is outrageous!' exclaimed Alcote, watching Bartholomew work. 'I am not staying here to be charged with helping a felon evade justice!'

He grabbed the reins of his horse and waved them,

expecting the animal to know which way he wanted to turn. When nothing happened, he gave it a sharp slap on the hindquarters that made it trot down the right-hand track in agitation. Michael motioned for the students to go with him – it was not safe for a man to travel alone – and dismounted with a sigh.

'You will be the death of me,' he mumbled to Bartholomew under his breath. 'I very much doubt whether the Bishop of Ely's authority will carry much weight here. We are likely to be hanged for tampering with the King's justice first, and questions asked after.'

William watched Alcote disappearing down the road with the students at his heels, and it seemed as if he would follow. Instead he raised one leg to let the exhausted donkey go free, and went to stand next to Michael, breathing heavily to signify his disapproval of what Bartholomew had done.

'You have endangered us all by interfering with the course of justice,' he said angrily to the physician. 'This is not Cambridge, you know. There is no friendly Sheriff Tulyet here to look the other way while you break the law.' He paused in his tirade. 'Well? Will he live?'

Bartholomew shook his head. 'I think his neck is broken.'

While William dropped to his knees and began intoning prayers for the dying in a voice loud enough to wake the dead, Bartholomew put his ear to the stricken man's mouth, listening to the faint rustle of breath that whispered there. Whether he was conscious of what was happening to him, Bartholomew could not tell. His eyes were half open, but were dull and glazed. There were blood clots around his lips, and his face was a deep red, suggesting that his death was as much due to strangulation as to the damaged vertebrae.

'Padfoot.'

Bartholomew looked sharply at him, but his breathing had faltered into nothing. He was left wondering whether he had imagined the man uttering a word with his dying breath, or whether the barely audible syllables were simply involuntary contractions of the tongue as the life went out of him. With William bellowing at his side, it had been difficult to hear much anyway. He sat back on his heels, puzzled.

'Now what?' asked William, finishing his prayers, and looking at the dead man in concern. 'Do we put him back as we found him?'

'I hardly think so!' said Michael, raising his eyebrows in horror. 'What if someone sees us?'

'It cannot be any worse than someone seeing us now, having cut him down,' retorted the friar. He sighed irritably, sketching the sign of the cross on the dead man's forehead, mouth, chest and hands. 'There, I have finished. Now we should follow Alcote's example, and leave while we still can. I do not want to be granting absolution to anyone else today, particularly if it is one of us.'

'This is all very odd,' said Bartholomew, still kneeling in the grass next to the dead man. 'His neck seems broken, yet his purple face suggests he died of strangulation.'

'Your interest in this sort of thing is most unnatural,' said Michael with a shudder. He reached out and plucked at Bartholomew's tabard, urging him to stand up.

'And whose fault is that?' demanded Bartholomew, shaking him off. 'Who is it who has dragged me into all sorts of unsavoury investigations for the University, and forced me to learn about murder and suicide?'

'Murder?' echoed Michael, gazing down at the dead man in dismay.

'Suicide?' asked William, equally shocked. 'I sincerely hope you are wrong, Matthew! I have just granted this man absolution, which suicides are not entitled to have.'

'This man has not been murdered,' said Michael firmly, recovering quickly from his shock. 'And he has not committed suicide, either. He has been executed perfectly lawfully for some crime.'

'Then why have his executioners not remained here to ensure he died?' demanded Bartholomew. 'Why did they not take his belongings? Why did they not tie his hands and feet, as is common practice among hangmen? And look at the clothes he is wearing. This is no common thief, but a man of some wealth.'

'Men of wealth are just as liable to be punished under secular law as are common thieves,' said Michael pompously.

'It looks to me as though someone strung him up and he started to choke,' said Bartholomew, his attention still fixed on the corpse that lay in front of him. 'Look at how his fingernails have been broken as he struggled to tear the noose away from his throat, and how the blood has clotted around his lips. Then, I imagine, his killer tugged on his feet to snap his neck.'

'I have seen people doing that,' said William, nodding. 'When I was with the Inquisition in France, we had occasion to dispense with a number of heretics. If the drop did not kill them instantly – and it seldom did – their friends would jump on their legs to put them out of their misery.'

Bartholomew and Michael stared at him. 'For a man of God, you have some nasty tales to tell, Father,' said Bartholomew.

William regarded him coolly. 'Hardly worse than you enthusing over whether a man has died from a broken neck or suffocation, Doctor. Now, I suggest we leave this poor sinner where he is, and head for Grundisburgh before Alcote tells anyone what we have been doing.'

'You mean, just leave him here?' asked Cynric, appalled. 'We are not heathens to leave our dead for the carrion birds.'

'Someone will be back for him,' said William. He started to walk toward his donkey, which saw what was coming and began to back away. 'It will just look as though the rope has snapped naturally, and deposited him on the ground.'

He captured his mount, and they began circling each other in a curious dance-like motion, showing that William was as determined to sit on the beast's back as the donkey was to avoid it. Meanwhile, Michael took Bartholomew's arm and pulled him to his feet with surprising strength for a man so fat and unhealthy. He brushed dead leaves from the physician's black tabard, and slapped the reins of his horse into his hand, glancing nervously up and down the trackway as though he expected a vengeful throng from the local Sheriff to bear down on them at any moment.

'Just lead the thing,' he snapped to William, still embroiled in the war of wills with his donkey. 'The poor animal is exhausted; you are far too large for it.'

Deciding it was less undignified to yield to the donkey's wishes than to continue chasing it in ever-faster circles, William began to walk toward the path Alcote had taken.

'Not that way,' said Cynric, watching Bartholomew hop with one foot in the stirrup as he struggled to mount a horse that was every bit as mobile as William's donkey. 'The right-hand turn leads to Ipswich; we need to carry straight on.'

William gave a wolfish grin, revealing large, strong brown teeth. 'It was kind of you to share that information with Alcote, Cynric. He has taken the wrong path.'

'Will he be safe?' asked Michael anxiously. 'He has all our money.'

'There is another village three miles down the Ipswich road,' said Cynric, displaying remarkable memory for a man who had travelled to Suffolk only once, some twenty years before. 'He can ask for directions there. The diversion will not take him too far out of his way.'

'And it will be pleasant to escape his company, even if only for a little while,' said William, smiling with glee. He hauled his donkey toward the Grundisburgh path, but the animal did not want to be led by the friar, either, and there began an angry duet of brays and curses.

'God's teeth!' exploded Michael, as he watched Bartholomew continue to do battle with his horse. 'Am I completely surrounded by imbeciles? Hold the reins near the bit, man! Cynric, help him, or we shall be here all day.'

He wheeled his own horse around and headed for the track Cynric had indicated, leaving the others to follow.

'You should not have interfered,' said Cynric, as he trotted next to Bartholomew.

'But it is bad enough seeing people die because my medicine cannot help them, without seeing them die because someone else has decided they should not live.'

'It is no good theologising with me, boy,' said Cynric primly. 'I am just a simple soldier who follows the law as well as he can. And the law does not look kindly on travellers rescuing criminals.'

'I know,' admitted Bartholomew wearily.

'And soldiers try not to leave bodies lying around without a decent burial,' continued Cynric, turning to give William a look of disapproval. 'So neither should scholars. It is not proper.'

'I agree,' said Bartholomew. 'But someone will be back for him soon – to collect his fine clothes and dagger, if nothing else.'

'I was looking forward to arriving in Grundisburgh,' said Cynric gloomily. 'I have heard that they celebrate a three-day Fair, and it will be starting today. But there is nothing like a dying man to turn gaiety into ashes.'

'Fairs are heathen occasions,' gasped William breathlessly, as he bolted past them on the donkey he had finally managed to mount, and that was repaying him by galloping furiously along the track, grimly resisting his attempts to restrain it. 'They are events celebrated by heretics!'

'Nothing like a fanatical Franciscan to turn gaiety into ashes, either,' said Bartholomew, as the friar and his donkey disappeared around a bend ahead of them.

CHAPTER 2

THE PATHWAY TO GRUNDISBURGH WOUND DOWNWARD, and soon the scholars emerged in a pleasant, shallow basin, surrounded on all sides by gently rolling hills. The fertile valley bottom had been cleared of its scrub for farming, and neat, thin strips showed where crops of wheat and barley had been sown. It was rich land, with sandy soil that was far easier to plough than the clays to the north. The distant hillsides were dotted white with sheep, while the trees that marked the parish boundaries were still sprinkled with the pinks and creams of late blossom. In the morning sunlight, set against a clear, pale blue sky, the scene that stretched before them was one of peace and prosperity.

It was not long before Grundisburgh's Church of Our Lady came into view. Initially, Bartholomew thought it unattractive: its flint tower was squat and sturdy, and only just taller than the pitched nave roof, while the main body of the building had narrow lancet windows punched into it, like arrow-slits in a castle. Yet the more Bartholomew looked, the more he appreciated its stark simplicity, and the timeless, brutal strength of the Norman belfry. It stood at the heart of the village, overlooking a swath of grass that formed a pleasant green, dwarfed by towering elm trees in which rooks cawed.

The green provided the villagers with communal grazing land, and straddled both sides of a shallow brook. There were no bridges, and the paths that met in the village centre dipped down to three muddy fords. Willow-tree branches cascaded to the water's edge, offering cool, shady spots away from the glare of the sun. Opposite the church was a line of reed-thatched wattle-and-daub houses, some of which had smoke seeping from their chimneys as meals were prepared. The homely scent of burning wood mingled with rich soil and cooking food.

Michael was waiting for him in front of the church, smiling, while Father William pursed his lips in disapproval. Cynric had been right; the Pentecost Fair was in full swing. It centred on the green, which thronged with people, some sitting in groups under the trees, others gathered near a makeshift stage on which four enthusiastic musicians played energetic reels on a rebec, two pipes and a drum.

Near the church a pole had been erected, and children were skipping around it holding strips of coloured material. Bartholomew imagined the pole was supposed to end up neatly wrapped in the cloth, but the children were having far too much fun for anything so organised, and pelted round the tottering pillar at a speed that had most of them reeling with dizziness. Shrieks of laughter and the admonishing tones of an ignored adult drifted across the green. Someone darted forward as the pole began to list to one side, and rapidly became entangled in the children's gaudy bands. His struggles to extricate himself made the pole more unstable than ever and in a shower of dirt the bottom flicked upward so that the whole thing toppled to the ground, and delighted children ran to fling themselves on top of it.

Bartholomew dismounted and stood next to Michael, content to watch the villagers at their revels for a while, before seeking out the generous Sir Thomas Tuddenham. Michael's attention, however, was elsewhere. Bartholomew saw his keen gaze firmly fixed on a line of trestle tables, almost invisible under mounds of food – pyramids of bread loaves; a huge, golden-crusted pie surmounted by an oddly shaped pastry bird; a vat of something that looked like saffron custard; massive platters of meat delivered by a team of women who chattered noisily as they hacked up two roasted sheep; and a mound of brown-shelled eggs that stood higher than a man was tall. Bartholomew had not seen as much food in one place – including the market at Cambridge – since before the plague.

'Right,' said Michael, rubbing his hands as he assessed the quality of the fare with a professional eye. 'We should make ourselves known before this feast starts, so that we can join in.'

Away to one side was a smaller table, covered by a spotless white cloth that was almost dazzling in the bright sun. Behind it sat a man, fifty or sixty years of age, with bristly grey hair, who wore a handsome blue capuchin and matching hose, and a shirt that was almost as brilliantly white as the tablecloth. He wore a somewhat fixed smile as he watched the children's antics with the pole, revealing some of the longest yellow teeth Bartholomew had ever seen. His seat of honour led Bartholomew to suppose he was Sir Thomas Tuddenham, the lord of Grundisburgh manor, and the man who was to give Michaelhouse the living of his church.

Tuddenham had a woman on either side of him. The one to his right was elderly, and had almost as outstanding an array of amber fangs as did Tuddenham; Bartholomew assumed she was his mother. She had kindly eyes that went in slightly different directions, and her creased, walnut-brown face was framed by a wimple that had seen better days – no longer crisp and white, but cream-coloured and worn. Her shabby brown dress, offset by an unashamedly ostentatious brooch, suggested that she cared nothing for appearances, and set more store in personal comfort.

The woman to the left was young and had raven-black hair that cascaded down her back, topped by a simple, but delicate, bronze circlet. Her dress was deep green, and the way it glittered as it caught the sun indicated that it had been shot through with gold thread. She turned to whisper something to Tuddenham, laughing as she did so. Bartholomew realised she could be no more than twenty. He found himself staring at her in admiration; with the possible exception of Matilde, he thought he had never seen a woman quite so lovely.

He was still gazing at her when Tuddenham noticed the three scholars standing at the edge of the green. His fixed smile became genuine, and he strode forward to greet them, his kinswomen in tow. William gave Bartholomew a sudden jab in the ribs, although whether it was because Michael was introducing him to Tuddenham, or because his inquisitor's nose had detected a hint of inappropriate admiration for Tuddenham's wife, Bartholomew could not tell.

Tuddenham held his hands apart, palms upward, to indicate they were welcome, and presented them with an impressive display of his dental armour to underline the sentiment.

'At last!' he cried with pleasure. 'I was beginning to believe you would never come. I expected you days ago.'

'Our arduous journey took us a good deal longer than we anticipated,' said Michael, blithely omitting reference to the three-day sojourn at St Edmundsbury Abbey. 'The roads are fraught with danger, and thieves and murderers lurk in every village.'

Bartholomew regarded him uncertainly. With the exception of the previous day the journey had been tediously uneventful – mainly due to Cynric's skill in avoiding situations that might have proved unsafe.

'Well, it is most gracious of you to come all this way to accept the living of my church,' said Tuddenham sincerely. 'Especially since it seems there was considerable risk to yourselves.' He turned to gesture to the elderly woman who stood at his side. 'My mother, Dame Eva, once visited Cambridge. She is looking forward to hearing news of it during your stay here.'

'It will be my pleasure, madam,' said Michael, favouring her with one of his courtly bows.

'And this is my wife, Lady Isilia.' Tuddenham smiled at the scholars' surprise as he introduced the dark-haired woman. 'You think Isilia is too young to have a husband my age. She is my second wife – my first was taken by the Death, as were my three sons.'

'A sad, but common, tale,' said Michael. 'There is not a soul in the kingdom who has not lost someone he loved to the pestilence.'

'But your wife is with child,' said Bartholomew, whose training as a physician meant he noticed such things. He smiled at her. 'So you may yet have sons to inherit your estates.'

Tuddenham nodded. 'My current heir is my nephew, Hamon. He is overseeing the Pentecost Fair celebrations at my other manor this morning. I own two manors, you see: this one, and one just over those trees. I allow Hamon to run the smaller of the two, to gain experience for managing both in the future.'

'Our estates will not prosper under the rule of that young oaf,' said Dame Eva with sudden feeling. 'My husband – God rest his soul – spent all his blameless life building these lands into something worth having, but Hamon will destroy everything in weeks with his weakness and foolery if you are rash enough to entrust them to him.'

Tuddenham sighed, and Bartholomew suspected that the argument was not a new one. 'You malign the lad – there is some good in him. But I have no choice: Hamon is the only male Tuddenham in his generation to have escaped the Death.'

'But he will not inherit over my children,' said Isilia, smiling reassuringly at her mother-in-law. She slipped her arm through that of her husband, and addressed Bartholomew. 'Poor Thomas has been so long without children of his own that he still cannot believe that he is to be a father again.'

Tuddenham smiled, rather sadly. 'My wife is right. It is strange for a man at my stage in life to be contemplating fatherhood again, but the plague changed all that.'

'Is that why you are giving us the living of the church?' asked Michael. 'Bestowing a gift on our College to ensure the heavens look favourably on your unborn child?'

Since the plague, such benefactions had become increasingly common as the wealthy sought to put themselves in God's favour by making donations of land and money to the Church or a College. There was nothing like a brush with death to make people generous.

Tuddenham considered. 'In a sense, I suppose. But Isilia's dowry included land at Otley, and it is because of this that I am able to donate the church to Michaelhouse. Speaking of which, shall we make a start on drafting out the deed that will make the living legally yours?'

'What, now?' asked Michael, taken aback, and looking meaningfully at the food-laden tables.

Tuddenham did not seem to notice the monk's reluctance. He beamed and rubbed his hands together enthusiastically. 'Why not? I have always believed in getting on with things. Did you bring the licence from the King that will allow me to grant you the advowson?'

'We did,' said Michael. 'It was signed in Westminster on the sixth day of May, so you can legally pass the living of the church to Michaelhouse any time you like.'

'Good, good,' said Tuddenham, still rubbing his hands. 'And then you can write my will for me, and act as my executors after I die?'

'I understand that is part of the informal agreement you made with Master Alcote when you first discussed this matter,' said Michael, his eyes still fastened on the food. 'Our College has some excellent lawyers, and acting as your executors will be the least we can do to show appreciation for your generosity.'

'Do not talk about deaths and wills on such a day,' protested Isilia, clutching at her husband's sleeve. 'It is the first day of the Pentecost Fair, and we should be feasting and enjoying the music, not talking about boring old deeds and legal rubbish.'

'Quite so, madam,' said Michael quickly.

'No time like the present for these matters,' said Tuddenham, as if they had not spoken. 'Did you bring your own writing materials, or shall I send for some?'

Dame Eva stepped forward and rested a frail hand of bones and soft skin on her son's shoulder, shaking her head indulgently. 'Really, Thomas,' she said, affectionately chiding. 'I know you are anxious to have the deed signed and sealed as soon as possible, but we should not forget our manners. Our guests must be weary after their travels. Tomorrow will be soon enough to start.'

'Thank you for your consideration, madam,' said Michael graciously. 'We are indeed tired.' He eyed the food tables again. 'And hungry.'

With clear disappointment, Tuddenham dropped the subject of the advowson, and gestured that the scholars should sit on a bench, while he called for a servant to bring them ale. When it arrived, Isilia poured it into pewter cups. It was warm from the sun, and tasted sour and strong. As she handed him his, Bartholomew found himself gazing at her again, admiring her delicate beauty. He blushed when she glanced up and caught him. Unabashed, she gave him a patient smile that suggested she was used to such responses, and then politely turned her attention to Michael's account of their journey, flagrantly exaggerated to ensure Tuddenham would fully appreciate the gesture the Michaelhouse men were making by undertaking such a long and dangerous mission.

*   *   *

Listening to the conversation with half an ear, Bartholomew sipped his ale and began to relax, grateful that the journey was at an end at last. All they needed to do now was to draft the advowson – which might take as long as several days, if Tuddenham's personal affairs were complex – and then go home. He pushed the dull prospect of legal documents from his mind, and turned his attention to the merrymaking on the green.

The villagers seemed in high spirits, something that had been conspicuous by its absence in most of the settlements they had passed since leaving Cambridge. The plague had hit rural England hard, and many people, tied by law to the lord of the manor in which they were born, were no longer able to scrape a decent living from the land. To see folk well fed and adequately clothed, and even with spare pennies to squander on the useless trinkets that a chapman was hawking on the green, was a pleasant and unexpected change.

Bartholomew's teaching, his patients and his half-finished treatise on fevers seemed a long way away as he watched Grundisburgh's villagers celebrate their Pentecost Fair. Some of the younger people were dancing to the musicians' furious music, skipping and weaving around each other playfully, and calling for others to join in. Bartholomew was about to yield to the persistent demands of one pretty flaxen-haired girl and be her partner in a jig, when a sharp cry from Dame Eva made him glance at her in surprise.

'Barchester? You came through Barchester?'

The old lady and Isilia exchanged a significant glance, and Isilia shifted closer to her mother-in-law, as if for the comfort of physical contact. Michael, who had been about to describe the clothes in the otherwise deserted village, regarded them uncertainly, while Bartholomew's golden-headed maiden backed away hurriedly at the mention of the plague village, and ran to find another man with whom to dance.

'That was the way the path ran,' said Michael, watching the girl leave with unmonklike interest. 'Have we done something wrong? Trespassed unknowingly on someone's land?'

'Barchester belongs to no one,' said Isilia, in a hushed voice.

'No one would have it,' added Dame Eva, crossing herself vigorously.

'Actually, it stands on *my* land,' said Tuddenham, a touch impatiently. 'Near the boundary with Otley. It was abandoned after the plague, and all sorts of silly stories have grown up about it. The only people who visit it these days are travellers, like you, who do not know that the locals use the new track to the east, to avoid it.'

'It is a village that the plague destroyed,' whispered Isilia, her eyes wide as she moved closer still to Dame Eva. 'It is a haunted place, and no one from around here would set foot in it under any circumstances.'

'Nonsense, my dear,' said Tuddenham. 'It is just like any other of the plague villages in the shire – a poor, sad place that the Earth is slowly reclaiming.'

'It is one of the gateways to hell,' announced Dame Eva uncompromisingly, crossing herself again. 'Only the damned willingly go there – in the darkest hours near midnight, in order to commune with the Devil.'

'There was nothing to be afraid of,' said Michael, not entirely truthfully, since, by his own admission, the village had unnerved him. 'Matt even looked in one of the houses, and there was nothing amiss.'

'You went into a house?' asked Isilia, aghast. She flinched away from Bartholomew, as though his very presence might prove contaminating. 'You touched a threshold?'

'I looked inside,' said Bartholomew. 'There was nothing

sinister or terrifying there – just a few old vegetables on the table, and some clothes in the doorway.'

Dame Eva and Isilia exchanged more frightened glances. 'They must have been Mad Megin's clothes,' said Dame Eva. 'She drowned herself last winter because Barchester sent her insane.'

'She drowned herself because she was a lonely old woman who had lost her family and friends,' explained Tuddenham impatiently. 'You see how these stories become exaggerated? Megin was the only Barchester resident not taken by the pestilence, and one of our villagers – Tobias Eltisley, the landlord of the Half Moon – found her floating in the river just after Christmas.'

'He buried her in Barchester's churchyard,' said Isilia fearfully, 'and it is said that she leaves her grave each night to wander the village, calling for her loved ones.'

'A sad tale indeed,' said Michael brusquely, never a man much interested in local stories and folklore. 'But we escaped from Barchester unscathed to arrive here in one piece.'

Tuddenham smiled reassuringly at his nervous women-folk, and nodded to the festivities on the green. 'Let's not discuss Barchester while the Fair is in full swing. You arrived at an opportune time, gentlemen. At sunset, we will all eat the food the villagers have provided to mark the Fair's beginning; on Monday, I, as lord of the manor, will provide the feast that marks the end of the celebrations. It is a tradition that goes back many years.'

'It does not seem to be a *religious* occasion, Sir Thomas,' observed Father William, eyeing the villagers reprovingly. 'It looks more like pagan revelry to me.'

'Roger Alcote took the wrong turning at the crossroads,' said Michael quickly, changing the subject before the fanatical friar could antagonise their benefactor. 'But he should be here soon.'

Tuddenham was concerned. 'It is not wise for a man to be travelling alone these days. Outlaws are as numerous as the stars in the sky along the roads to Ipswich.'

'He is not alone,' said Michael to allay his fears. 'The students are with him.'

'Students?' asked Tuddenham uneasily. 'How many Michaelhouse scholars did you bring?'

'We are seven, plus our servant, Cynric,' said Michael.

Dame Eva raised her eyebrows. 'That is quite a deputation,' she remarked bluntly. 'We were expecting Alcote, a scribe and the lad who will be our priest when Master Wauncy retires. We had no idea that to draft an advowson would require seven scholars. No wonder honest men avoid the law when they can – it promises to be an expensive business!'

'Mother, please!' said Tuddenham, embarrassed. He smiled unconvincingly at Michael. 'It is true that we were not anticipating such a number, but you are all welcome, nonetheless.'

The number of scholars to visit Grundisburgh had been a matter of fierce debate at Michaelhouse's high table for several weeks before their departure. If too few people went, it would appear as if the College did not appreciate the magnitude of Tuddenham's generosity; if too many went, the knight might feel his hospitality was being imposed upon. At the same time, none of the Fellows, with the sole exception of Alcote, wanted to go themselves, but none of them trusted him to draft out the deed without taking the opportunity to negotiate a little something for himself – either to the College's detriment or to prey on Tuddenham's kindness.

In the end, the Master had made a unilateral decision, and had dispatched William and Bartholomew to monitor the avaricious Alcote, and Horsey to keep the nervous Unwin company. Deynman had been an afterthought, to remove him from harm until the temper of Agatha, the College laundress, had cooled over the business regarding her teeth. Michael, meanwhile, had been seconded to the deputation by the Chancellor, to see whether Tuddenham's generosity might be further exploited in the University's interests.

Michael smiled ingratiatingly at Tuddenham. 'Master Kenyngham dispatched not only his four most senior Fellows to acknowledge your handsome gift, but three of his finest students.'

Bartholomew winced, hoping Tuddenham would not embark upon any lengthy discussions with the woefully unacademic Rob Deynman. There was not another student in the entire University who was in Deynman's league for atrocious scholarship, and even after three years of painstaking care and effort on Bartholomew's part, Deynman remained as cheerfully ignorant as on the day he had arrived.

'And is one of these fine students Unwin?' asked Tuddenham, flattered, and treating Michael to a display of his long teeth. 'The man who will become our new priest when the old one retires?'

'Yes,' said Michael. 'Unwin is keen to make your acquaintance as quickly as possible.'

'Excellent,' beamed Tuddenham, rubbing his hands together again. 'This is all working out most agreeably.'

It was pleasant sitting in the sun and watching the revelry on the green. At noon, the sun became so warm that Bartholomew, drowsy from the ale, fell asleep, and did not wake until well into the afternoon. He looked around for his colleagues, and was disturbed to hear that Alcote and the students had still not arrived. He considered going to look for them, but Cynric did not seem to share his concern, suggesting that Alcote must have stopped for a meal at an inn along the way, and that they should give him a little longer.

While he had been asleep, a colourful awning had been erected over the Tuddenhams' table, and Michael sat under it, regaling the knight and his family with stories of life in Cambridge, while devouring a plate of cakes that had been set in front of him. Seeing him awake, Isilia came to fill Bartholomew's cup with yet more ale. To avoid being caught staring at her again, he studiously watched some jugglers on the green, only looking at her when she left, to admire the way her green dress clung to her slender hips.

When she had returned to her seat, Tuddenham took Michael's arm, and led him to where Bartholomew leaned comfortably against the sun-warmed stones of the church-yard wall. William joined them, not wanting to be left out of any interesting discussions. Tuddenham glanced furtively at his wife and mother, both now conveniently out of earshot, and then turned his attention to the scholars.

'Now you have taken some ale and slept a while, can you make a start on the advowson?'

'Tomorrow would be better,' said Michael, regarding the notion of immediate labour without enthusiasm. 'We will be rested, and less likely to make mistakes that will later need to be rectified.'

Bartholomew agreed. Keen though he was to return to Cambridge, advowsons were invariably complicated documents, and mistakes made early in the proceedings usually resulted in delays later.

'He wants to get rid of us as quickly as possible,' said William to Bartholomew, in a whisper that Tuddenham would have to have been deaf not to hear. 'I said seven scholars was too many.'

'Then perhaps a little wine might help,' said Tuddenham to Michael, beckoning to his wife to bring some. 'Ale is no drink to stimulate the brain.'

When Isilia presented her guests with the wine, the goblets proved to be enormous, and Bartholomew did not know how he would finish his, as well as the ale, without becoming drunk. He need not have worried: Michael downed most of his own in a single gulp, and then furtively switched vessels with the physician in the hope that he would not notice.

Isilia sat next to Bartholomew and refilled the cup in front of him, while Father William – no more in the mood for writing legal texts that evening than Michael and Bartholomew – invented a host of spurious reasons why work on the advowson would be better undertaken the following day.

Isilia frowned thoughtfully before addressing Bartholomew. 'Grundisburgh Church is a very rich living. Why did Michaelhouse appoint a student to be a priest, rather than a Fellow like you?'

She smiled at him, green eyes dark against her white skin, and Bartholomew's hand shook, spilling wine on his tabard.

'Unwin is a deeply religious, compassionate man and a fine scholar,' he said, choosing his words carefully. Although Michaelhouse was delighted to possess the living, none of the Fellows much relished the notion of being banished to deepest Suffolk to act as parish priest. That was something to be foisted on students, who were not in a position to argue about it.

She regarded him quizzically. 'I would expect most friars to be deeply religious, compassionate men.'

Bartholomew wondered how she had arrived at such a conclusion. It was certainly not one that applied universally to friars from somewhere like Cambridge, where membership of a strong Order like the Franciscans or the Dominicans was often seen as the best path to earthly, rather than heavenly, power.

Isilia continued. 'But you make Unwin sound dull. A

"deeply religious, compassionate man and a fine scholar". Is there nothing more interesting to say of him?'

Bartholomew suspected there was not, and personally considered the Franciscan something of a nonentity – unlike his friend John de Horsey. Horsey was tall and striking, with amber eyes and smooth nut-coloured hair. He was also quick-witted, amusing and popular, and would have made a far better priest for Grundisburgh than the timid Unwin.

'So, you are a physician?' she asked conversationally, when Bartholomew did not reply. 'That must be an unpleasant occupation.'

'At times,' Bartholomew admitted. 'But it can also be very rewarding. For example, physicians are not usually called to childbirths, but a number of women have asked me to attend them since the plague took so many of the skilled midwives. Delivering a healthy baby is very satisfying.'

'Oh,' said Isilia, clearly scraping the recesses of her mind for something intelligent to say. 'These are merchants' and landowners' wives, I imagine? You must meet some interesting people.'

'Actually, they are usually the town's poor. The landowners' and merchants' wives can afford to pay the high fees of the two surviving midwives.'

'I see,' said Isilia, trying hard to mask her distaste. 'But do these women not object to having a man present at such a time? I would.'

'Most of them are so desperate, they would not care if I were a dancing bear, as long as I helped them. Unfortunately, the shortage of experienced midwives has led to a number of unscrupulous women pretending to be qualified when they are not. They concoct dreadful potions that they say will hasten labour or deliver a boy-child rather than a girl, and they often make the mother ill.'

'How dreadful,' said Isilia. Bartholomew did not see the

desperate glance she cast at Dame Eva in the hope that she might be extricated from the disagreeable discussion.

'I caught one feeding a paste of crushed snails, sparrows' brains, red arsenic and wormwood to her patient, telling her it would prevent fevers,' he continued, warming to his theme. 'It killed the unborn child and gave the mother a terrible bleeding . . .'

'I hardly think descriptions of your dealings with pregnant peasants is a suitable topic of conversation for Lady Isilia, Matt,' said Michael, gallantly coming to her rescue. 'You should tell her about your expertise with horoscopes instead.'

'Really?' said Isilia, suddenly interested as Bartholomew shot the monk a withering look. 'Then you must cast mine and that of my unborn child. And I will introduce you to Master Stoate, the village physician. He, too, loves astrology.' She hesitated. 'Although I am certain he will not want to talk about pastes made of snail brains and crushed sparrow.'

'I am not very good at horoscopes,' said Bartholomew firmly, wanting to nip that notion in the bud before he became inundated with requests for astrological consultations. Predicting courses of treatment for continued good health from the movements of the heavenly bodies was a time-consuming and tedious business if it were to be done accurately, and Bartholomew was determined not to waste his time on it.

Isilia seemed as though she would insist, but Michael interrupted with a spiteful chuckle. 'Here comes Alcote at last. I was beginning to think we had succeeded in losing him completely.'

'Is that *him*?' Isilia asked with sudden hope in her voice, astrology and Bartholomew instantly forgotten as a tall student-friar strode towards them. 'Is that Unwin, our next priest?'

'That is John de Horsey, madam,' said Michael, trying to hide his amusement at the yearning in her voice. 'Unwin is behind him.'

There was no mistaking the bitter disappointment on Isilia's face when she saw that the comely John de Horsey was not the long-awaited Unwin. To her credit, she rose and went to meet the unprepossessing friar with good grace, offering him wine and a seat in the shade, although Bartholomew noticed that Horsey was given the better place and the larger cup. Scurrying behind the students came Alcote, who contemptuously brushed aside Isilia's polite greeting, and made straight for Tuddenham.

'Someone should tell Alcote that spurning the lovely wife of our benefactor is not the best way to gain that benefactor's good auspices,' remarked Michael, unimpressed by Alcote's display of poor manners. 'That man's dislike of women is unnatural.'

'He is a monk, Brother,' Bartholomew pointed out. 'He is supposed to be uninterested in women. As are you.'

'As a monk, I love all my fellow men and women with equal fervour, although I find women far easier to love than men.' Michael nudged Bartholomew in the ribs, and nodded to where Isilia was listening with rapt attention to something Horsey was saying. 'Handsome John de Horsey is her first choice, but she would settle for you, with your black curls and vile stories of childbirth, over the dull Unwin. He does not interest her at all.' He took another gulp of Bartholomew's wine.

'You do talk nonsense sometimes, Brother,' said Bartholomew. He yawned. Even the small amount of wine he had managed to drink before Michael took it all was making him sleepy again.

'Isilia is a very attractive lady,' Michael continued. 'Although I can see I do not need to tell you that. You spilled half my wine while you were ogling her.'

'I did not,' said Bartholomew, wishing the monk was less worldly in his observations.

'I expected to find you hanged,' muttered Alcote unpleasantly to Bartholomew, apparently having decided that a cup of wine was more urgent than toadying to Tuddenham. He flopped on to the grass next to them. 'And Michael, William and Cynric with you. Next time you want to rescue cut-throats, do it when you cannot drag other Michaelhouse scholars into the mire, too.'

'Keep your voice down,' warned Michael irritably. 'Or it will be *you* responsible for having us all clapped in irons for tampering with gibbets. And where have you been? You should have been here hours ago.'

'No thanks to you,' snapped Alcote. 'You let me take the wrong road on purpose. But it all worked out rather well, as it happened. I met a group of travellers who had been attacked by robbers, and one of them lay dying. He paid me a shilling for writing his will, and another two to say masses for him at the shrine of St Botolph at St Edmundsbury on our way home.'

Bartholomew regarded him in disgust. 'You took money from a dying man?'

Alcote shrugged. 'Why not? And do not be sanctimonious with me, young man. Physicians make their living by charging dying men for their services.'

'It is not the same,' objected Bartholomew.

Alcote overrode him. 'If God had not wanted me to make a profit today, he would not have let me take the wrong road. Now, what about this felon you freed from the noose? Did you save the man? Can we all sleep less soundly in our beds tonight, because you released a convicted criminal to continue a life of villainy?'

'For a man of God, you have a very cold soul,' said Bartholomew, regarding the Cluniac with dislike. 'Where is your compassion?'

'My compassion is reserved for those who deserve it,' said Alcote haughtily. 'And what I do with it is none of your business.'

'And what I do with mine is none of yours,' retorted Bartholomew.

'That must be Walter Wauncy, Grundisburgh's current parish priest,' interrupted Michael, gesturing with his goblet to a tall, cadaverous-looking man wearing the habit of an Austin canon, who was coming from the direction of the church. 'No wonder poor Isilia's hopes were high for a handsome young friar. What with Sir Fang on the one hand, and a priest who looks three days dead on the other, she must be absolutely desperate to set her fair eyes on something pleasant. Even plain Unwin has to be an improvement on the menfolk here.'

'I hope you are not encouraging her to lascivious thoughts, Brother,' said Alcote primly. 'It would be most improper.'

Michael regarded him with a hurt expression. 'I am distressed that you should think such things of me, Roger. I was merely commenting on the variety within God's creation.'

They stood politely as the Austin approached. Bartholomew had seldom seen anyone look so unhealthy, and wondered whether Unwin might find himself vicar of Grundisburgh sooner than he anticipated. Wauncy was gaunt to the point where he appeared skeletal, and there were dark rings under his yellowish eyes. His head seemed uncannily skull-shaped, accentuated by the fact that he was almost completely bald except for a short fringe of hair at the back and sides. Out from this surged a pair of enormous ears that turned a blood-red colour when the sun was behind them.

'I am delighted to meet you,' said the priest in a graveyard whisper to the scholars. 'You must forgive my lateness in greeting you. I have been saying masses for the dead all day.'

'What is the going rate for masses in these parts?' asked Alcote conversationally. 'In Cambridge we can only charge a penny, because it is a place with more than its share of priests, but I have heard that people pay handsomely where clerics are less numerous.'

'I charge a fourpence,' said Wauncy superiorly. 'Otherwise I would have all the village's poor after me to pray for their dead, and I can barely manage the demand imposed by the wealthy.'

Alcote was impressed. 'I can see Unwin will make a tidy fortune here, and will have plenty to spare for his old College.'

'Have you travelled far today?' asked Wauncy.

'From Otley,' said Alcote. He shuddered. 'A shabby place that smells of pigs, quite unlike this charming village, Master Wauncy.'

'Then you must have lain in bed a long time this morning,' said Wauncy, a note of censure in his deep voice. 'Otley is no great distance from Grundisburgh, yet I hear you have only just arrived.'

'We stopped at the crossroads to pray for the soul of the poor man who was hanged there today,' said Alcote, before anyone could stop him.

Bartholomew exchanged a weary glance with Michael. Not only was Alcote's claim a brazen lie but it was imprudent in the extreme to mention the hanged man when they might yet be in trouble for cutting him down.

Wauncy looked blank. 'What hanged man?'

'The criminal who was hanged at the crossroads today,' pressed Alcote. 'On the gibbet.'

'The gibbet at Bond's Corner?' asked Wauncy, looking from Alcote to Michael in confusion. 'But no one has been hanged there for weeks.'

A wave of rough laughter from a group of men sitting under a willow tree gusted towards them, as a pig made off with a loaf of bread belonging to a man who was determined to have it back. A fierce tussle ensued, after which the pig emerged victorious with the larger piece. Bartholomew, Michael and Alcote stared at Wauncy, who gazed back in confusion.

'I can assure you, gentlemen,' said the parish priest, 'no one has been hanged on the gibbet at Bond's Corner since Easter. Are you sure about what you saw?'

'It was a man wearing a blue doublet embroidered with silver thread,' said Alcote impatiently. 'And a fine white shirt, and shoes that looked new. He had not been there for long. Matthew thought he might even still be alive. He was not, of course, and we made no attempt to interfere with the King's justice by cutting him down.'

Michael closed his eyes. 'That man is beyond belief,' he muttered to Bartholomew. 'Talk about incriminating himself.'

'Or worse still, incriminating us,' Bartholomew whispered back.

'But no one was hanged there today,' insisted Wauncy. 'We do not hang people during the Pentecost Fair. It would spoil the festivities.'

'It looks as though you were right after all,' said Michael in a low voice to Bartholomew. 'The man was not executed legally, or people would have known about it. What a curious turn of events!'

Seeing Alcote did not believe him, Wauncy beckoned Tuddenham over. The knight had been cornered by Father William, who was regaling him with one of his rabid diatribes on heresy. Clearly relieved by his timely rescue, Tuddenham came toward them, hauling his wife away from the handsome Horsey as he passed. Bartholomew did not blame him. Horsey might well be a friar in major orders, and forbidden physical relations with women, but so was Michael, and Bartholomew was certain the fat monk was no more celibate than was Matilde the Prostitute.

'Our guests claim there was a man hanging on the gibbet at Bond's Corner today,' said Wauncy to Tuddenham. 'I have just informed them that is not possible.'

'Wauncy is right,' said Tuddenham, surprised. 'No one has been sentenced to the gibbet for at least six weeks.'

'Well, someone was hanging there,' said Michael.

Tuddenham shrugged, bemused. 'I cannot imagine what has happened. I will send my steward to find out as soon as the festivities are over.'

'Do you not think he should go now?' suggested Michael. 'If you say no one has been lawfully hanged on your gibbet, then the man we saw was *un*lawfully executed, and a murder surely merits immediate investigation?'

Tuddenham was clearly torn: the feast was about to begin, and it was already late in the day, with the sun casting long shadows across the green. Yet he did not want the scholars to consider him a lax landlord, who turned a blind eye to violent crimes committed on his land. After a moment, he sighed and agreed to look into the matter in person. He yelled to a servant, who was trying to prevent a group of children from stealing boiled eggs from one of the tables. 'Siric! Saddle up a couple of horses. I have business at Bond's Corner.'

Siric hurried away to do his master's bidding, reluctantly leaving the eggs unsupervised. The children, however, hesitated to take advantage of the situation: Dame Eva was watching them with her bright, intelligent eyes. But, within moments, one leathery eyelid had dropped in a conspiratorial wink, and the children's dirty faces broke into gap-toothed grins. Clutching their booty, they scampered away while Dame Eva turned her attention to making polite conversation with Father William.

'This corpse you found was probably that of an outlaw,' said Tuddenham. 'It has not been unknown for travellers to catch would-be thieves on the road, and then dispense their own justice rather than wait for the Sheriff. I am sure the body belongs to none of my villagers – they are all here, enjoying the fair.'

'The dead man wore a fine dagger,' said Alcote, who invariably noticed such things. 'It was gold with an emerald in the hilt, and there was also a belt decorated with silver studs.'

The colour drained from Tuddenham's face, and his jaw dropped. Isilia rushed to his side, and helped him to sit on the wall, while Dame Eva abandoned William and came to stand next to him, laying a motherly hand on his shoulder and peering into his face in flustered concern.

'Are you unwell, Thomas?' she asked, alarmed. 'Shall I summon Master Stoate? Perhaps Doctor Bartholomew can bleed you, or give you a potion?'

'A gold dagger with an emerald?' whispered the knight, clutching at Isilia's hand. 'And a belt with silver studs?'

Alcote nodded triumphantly. 'You do know that a man was hanged there!'

Tuddenham seemed appalled at that notion. 'I know no such thing, Master Alcote! Are you certain this man was dead?'

'Who was dead?' cried Dame Eva, bewildered. 'What has happened, Thomas?'

'The man was dead according to our physician,' Alcote replied, ignoring her and gesturing to Bartholomew. 'Although he has some peculiar theories about health – for example, he believes people should wash their hands before they eat.'

'How very odd,' mused Walter Wauncy. 'But what of this hanged man? Are you sure he was not some lad playing a joke on you by pretending to be dead?'

'He was dead,' said Bartholomew, wishing Alcote would keep his nasty opinions to himself. 'But it seems you know him from his dagger. Who was he?'

Tuddenham exchanged a glance with Wauncy, and hesitated. It was Wauncy who spoke.

'You must understand that we cannot be certain until we see the body, but there is only one man near here who owns anything as frivolous as a gold dagger and a silver-studded belt. But he has not been sentenced to hang. All this is most distressing!'

'Especially for the man on the gibbet,' Michael pointed out. 'But who is it who owns this distinctive gold dagger?'

Tuddenham swallowed hard. 'My neighbour from the manor of Burgh – Roland Deblunville. I saw him wearing it at the Lord Mayor's Feast at Ipswich last year. None of my other neighbours have the funds to waste on such frippery.'

'Does this mean that someone has hanged Deblunville?' asked Dame Eva, bewildered.

Tuddenham leaned forward and rubbed his hands across his face, while she patted his shoulder in a distracted sort of sympathy. Isilia's face was unreadable as she stood behind her husband. After a moment, the knight looked up at his priest.

'Wauncy, you know what will be said if Deblunville really is hanging at Bond's Corner?'

Wauncy nodded. 'But we should ascertain the facts before we leap to conclusions, Sir Thomas. We will ride to Bond's Corner immediately, and try to find out what has happened.'

'What will be said?' asked Michael, interested.

Wauncy gnawed on his lip uncertainly, while Tuddenham stared at his boots and did not reply.

'They will find out sooner or later, Thomas, regardless of whether Deblunville is dead or alive,' said Dame Eva practically. 'Your feud with the wretch is not exactly a secret.'

Tuddenham sighed. 'You are right. I just did not want

our guests to be burdened with what is just a silly border dispute.'

'It is a good deal more than that,' said Dame Eva. She looked at the Michaelhouse men. 'This villain – Roland Deblunville – has been invading almost every aspect of our lives recently. When we go to Ipswich, he is there selling his goods at absurdly cheap prices, so that it is difficult for us to trade ours; when sheep go missing from our meadows, they are always last seen near his fields; and he even purchased that lovely length of peach-coloured satin I had been saving to buy for Isilia since Christmas.'

'I will find her something else,' said Tuddenham tiredly.

'What does he want peach satin for anyway?' said Dame Eva, shaking her head. 'He must have seen me admiring it, and bought it out of sheer spite.'

Tuddenham's eyebrows drew together angrily at that notion. 'Then I shall ensure his satin will pale beside the piece Isilia shall have. He will not win that battle!'

It seemed a petty state of affairs, but Bartholomew knew only too well how quickly little aggravations could escalate into serious quarrels in isolated communities. He had seen men kill and be killed for far less than a length of peach-coloured satin.

'You must wonder what you have wandered into,' said Tuddenham, with a strained smile. 'Please allow me to explain. As I have mentioned, there are two manors in Grundisburgh parish, both of them mine. Deblunville's manor borders my estates, and he claims that Peche Hall – where my nephew Hamon lives – is on his land.'

'So?' asked Michael. 'Boundary disputes are common all over the country. Take your case to the county assizes at Ipswich, and let the lawyers decide the outcome.'

Tuddenham fixed him with a determined look. 'The case is clear-cut, Brother: I do not need to pay lawyers to tell me I am right. The land near Peche Hall is mine. It came to me from my ancestor Hervey Bourges, who was granted it by the Conqueror himself. Hervey's daughter founded our fine church, and her sons built Peche and Wergen halls. My family's roots are as deeply entrenched in this village and its land as are these ancient buildings themselves.'

'If the case is so clear-cut, then why does Deblunville press his claim?' asked Michael. It was a reasonable question, but not one that Tuddenham seemed inclined to answer directly.

'The man is an opportunist. He came into possession of Burgh by marrying a woman twice his age – and she died within a week of the happy event in very suspicious circumstances. So, Deblunville is a young man with a tidy fortune, and a burning ambition to make himself one of the wealthiest and most powerful men in the county.'

'I see,' said Michael noncommittally. 'But you have not yet told us what it is that people will say when they hear Deblunville has been hanged.'

'The gibbet is on my land,' said Tuddenham flatly. 'People will say I had him killed.'

'No!' cried Isilia, appalled. 'No one would say such a vile thing.'

'I agree,' said Michael. 'You would hardly string him up on your own gibbet if you intended to dispense with him. Any rational man wanting to commit murder would be a little more circumspect.'

'But we do not know that murder has been committed,' Wauncy pointed out. 'Or even that it is Deblunville who is dead. We know only that the scholars saw a body on the gibbet with a dagger that might or might not belong to him. We should not speculate further until we have the facts.'

'And we are not the only ones to have trouble with Deblunville,' Tuddenham continued, apparently unwilling to end the conversation before he had completed his list of gripes. 'Robert Grosnold of Otley has had cattle stolen by him, while John Bardolf of Clopton lost his daughter.'

Michael frowned. 'What do you mean by "lost" exactly?'

Tuddenham glanced prudishly at his wife and pursed his lips. 'Suffice to say that Janelle's marriage prospects are not what they were.'

'You mean she is with child?' asked Michael. 'And you believe Deblunville to be the father?'

'I would not have put it so bluntly myself,' said Tuddenham primly, regarding his wife with such concern that Bartholomew wondered if he might clap his hands over her ears to prevent her from overhearing such ribaldry. 'Deblunville offered to marry her, but that would make him Bardolf's heir. Bardolf was agreeable to the match at first – he said the damage had already been done, and he needed to make the best of the situation – but Grosnold, Hamon and I reminded him how Deblunville's first wife had come to a sudden and unexpected end once he had no more use for her, and Bardolf prudently changed his mind.'

'The sooner we satisfy ourselves that our guests have been mistaken, and that Deblunville is safe in his fortress like a spider in its web, the sooner we can return to enjoy this feast the villagers have provided,' said Wauncy practically. 'Come, Sir Thomas. We should leave now.'

'And if they are not mistaken?' asked Tuddenham uncertainly. 'What then?'

'Then you have two hundred people who will attest that you were at the Fair all day, and not hanging a man at Bond's Corner,' said Wauncy soothingly. 'Including your priest.'

Isilia looked uneasy, and Dame Eva took her hand reassuringly. 'I told you it was only a matter of days before Deblunville would die after he saw – well, you know what he saw,' she said, looking at Tuddenham and Wauncy accusingly. 'You did not believe me, but now who is right?'

'Not that superstitious nonsense again!' sighed Tuddenham.

'You cannot simply ignore these things and hope they will go away,' said Dame Eva firmly. 'Deblunville saw ... that thing, and now he is dead. Just as I told you he would be.'

'It is wrong to place your faith in superstitions,' said Wauncy sternly. 'I have told you that before.'

'Maybe he saw the evil of his ways at the Pentecost celebrations, and was so overcome with remorse that he hanged himself,' suggested Isilia hopefully.

'That does not sound like Deblunville,' said the old lady. 'He is too convinced of his personal worth to take his own life. He is more likely to hang every lord of the manor he can lay his vile hands on, and steal their lands and titles for himself.'

'What exactly did he see?' asked Michael, intrigued by the turn the discussion was taking.

'Nothing,' said Tuddenham before Isilia or Dame Eva could answer. 'My mother merely refers to an old country yarn from these parts. There is nothing to it but superstition.' He looked reprovingly at the women, daring them to contradict him.

'Oh,' said Michael, immediately losing interest. He was never particularly keen to hear about local customs and folktales, preferring current intrigues and scandals to ancient ones. 'Some evil spirit haunts the roads near here, I suppose?' he added politely, when he saw Dame Eva look disappointed by his response. She seemed kindly enough, and Michael, who approved of old ladies who turned a blind eye to hungry children stealing eggs, did not want to hurt her feelings.

'If you like fairy tales, I will tell you some this evening,' said Tuddenham, not altogether pleasantly. 'But we should not be here chatting while Deblunville might lie dead. Siric! My horse!'

He strode away, his priest scurrying at his heels. Dame Eva and Isilia went to sit in the shade again, where the old lady was solemnly presented with a daisy chain by a small child with egg yolk around her mouth.

'This Deblunville sounds quite a character,' remarked Michael in an undertone to Bartholomew. 'It is a pity he is dead – I would have liked to meet him.'

'Whenever someone is described to me as "quite a character", it usually means that he has some offensive or unappealing quality about him that is being passed off as entertaining,' replied Bartholomew, watching Siric bridle Tuddenham's horse. 'Experience has taught me that I nearly always do not like him. Will you go with Tuddenham to the gibbet?'

'We both will,' said Michael. 'And it will be as much to ensure that we have not unwittingly left some clue regarding our role in all this, as to see justice done.'

Once Tuddenham had made the decision to ride to Bond's Corner, there was a flurry of activity. Cynric saddled Bartholomew's horse, and then started to prepare his own mount, which was munching the buttercups that grew among the grass by the churchyard. Bartholomew stopped him.

'There is no need for you to come, Cynric. Stay here and keep an eye on William. He has been drinking wine too fast for his own good, and you know what he can be like if he becomes intoxicated. We do not want him regaling Lady Isilia with tales of the Inquisition.'

'She would probably prefer them to tales of childbirth, boy,' said Cynric, smiling. He looped the reins of his pony over the church gate. 'Are you sure you do not need me? These are dangerous roads to travel, and it will be dark soon.'

'I will be safe enough with Tuddenham,' said Bartholomew. They looked to where the knight was donning a metal helmet and a boiled leather jerkin, and buckling a sword belt around his waist. 'Although it looks to me as though he thinks he is heading for the battlefields of France, not some part of his own manor.'

'That is probably because he knows a lot more about this place than you do,' said Cynric. 'And all the more reason for me to come.'

'It is probably just for show,' said Bartholomew. 'Anyway, I am perfectly capable of looking after myself.'

Cynric's snort of derision was drowned by Michael's exclamation of disgust as he watched Bartholomew climb on the low wall that surrounded the churchyard, and leap on to his horse's back in a way that made the animal rear and kick in shock. The monk himself swung into his saddle with the ease of a born horseman.

'This affair has an unsavoury feel to it,' said Bartholomew, following him as he rode across the green. 'It seems village life is not so different from the University – all petty feuds and enmity.'

'Yes,' said Michael gleefully. 'I thought I was going to be bored in this rural desert, but matters are definitely looking up: we have three lords of the manor united against the fourth, who is an opportunist and who did away with his elderly wife; we have some curious folktale that the ladies believe has some relevance to this Deblunville's demise – assuming it was Deblunville we found; and we have suspects galore as to who wants him dead.'

'Just a moment, Brother,' said Bartholomew, alarmed. 'This is not Cambridge, and you have no legal authority to start probing around in all this. If one of these lords really has dispensed with a hated rival, you would be well advised to stay clear of the whole business.'

'Where is your spirit of enquiry and thirst for the truth?' asked Michael playfully. 'Come on, Matt! This might prove interesting.'

'That is not what the Master will think if you interfere with these people and return to Michaelhouse without the advowson,' warned Bartholomew.

'Tuddenham is a nobleman,' said Michael. 'He will not renege on his promise to give us his church simply because we are curious.'

'He might consider doing exactly that if you start investigating a murder he may have committed, or that involves his neighbours or his nephew.'

'So you believe we should start to draw up the deed tonight, then?' said Michael, nodding thoughtfully. 'That is prudent thinking, Matt. Once we have it, we can do what we like.'

'That was not what I meant at all,' sighed Bartholomew. 'Anyway, if Grundisburgh is as seething with intrigue and murder as you seem to hope, then Michaelhouse should decline anything Tuddenham offers. We do not want the good name of the College besmirched by tainted gifts.'

'Rubbish,' said Michael. 'Most gifts to the University are tainted in some way or another. No one gives out of the goodness of his heart, you know. There is always some catch.'

'The advowson of Barrington church is ours, and that does not have any unpleasant catches,' said Bartholomew.

Michael gave a short bark of laughter. 'In that case, why do you think it took four years for Michaelhouse to get the grant executed once the licence had been issued? Negotiations, Matt! Surely you must have noticed that all the priests we have appointed have been personal friends of the Bishop of Ely, who just happened to decree its appropriation? Or did you consider that pure coincidence?'

Bartholomew *had* considered it pure coincidence, and the thought that some nepotistic mechanism was at work behind the scenes had never crossed his mind. 'Well, the advowson of Cheadle, then,' he said, thinking of the second of Michaelhouse's four properties. 'No friends of the Bishop have been appointed there.'

'Indeed not,' said Michael. 'But some of the income generated by that transaction is "donated" to the Guild of Weavers, the leader of which pressed the lord of Cheadle manor to grant it to us in the first place.'

'And Tittleshall?' asked Bartholomew weakly. 'Was that not a simple act of generosity made by a grateful student to his former College, as we are always informed on Founder's Day?'

'Of course not,' said Michael scornfully. 'That was given to us because the said student, now a powerful lawyer in Westminster, tampered with one of the nuns at St Radegund's Priory while he should have been reading his *Corpus Juris Civilis*. It was the price he had to pay the then Master of Michaelhouse not to make his misdeeds public.'

'I see,' said Bartholomew, disgusted and disillusioned, as he often was when he talked to Michael about the affairs of the University and its Colleges.

'The only one of our four advowsons that is straightforward is the one that grants us St Michael's Church in Cambridge, given to us by our founder. But even that is not entirely without strings – we are obliged to say a set number of masses for his immortal soul each year, and you know what a nuisance that can be when we are busy.'

'So why do you think Tuddenham is granting us Grundisburgh?' asked Bartholomew doubtfully. 'Do you believe it is to ensure the health of Isilia's unborn child, as you asked him, or is there another reason – such as to atone for an incestuous relationship with his mother, or in anticipation of his murder of Deblunville?'

'You have a nasty imagination, Matt,' said Michael, giving him a sidelong glance. 'But this advowson is important to us. It will make us the third richest College in Cambridge, with only King's Hall and Clare above us. Would you sacrifice such power on mere principle?'

'Yes, probably,' said Bartholomew. 'And if Tuddenham

has his own reasons for granting us the advowson, I would like to know what they are before we accept it. If some of his land is in dispute with his neighbour, this church might not be his to give.'

'I checked that at St Edmundsbury Abbey,' said Michael comfortably. 'I saw copies of documents proving beyond the shadow of a doubt that Tuddenham is the lawful recipient of the church tithes here. However, I did see deeds that indicate that his claim on the eastern side of his manor – his nephew's land – is not entirely clear cut.'

Bartholomew shook his head in awe. 'So that is why you spent so long closeted away with the Abbot. I should have known you were up to something. William was under the impression you were praying to atone for your greed at the inn the night before. I thought that sounded unlikely.'

'I do not have time to waste on false confessions,' said Michael loftily. 'But you are right to ask what prompts Tuddenham to make this offer to Michaelhouse. He has no connection to the College, and it is a most generous gift. However, a country knight like Tuddenham will not best two of the finest legal minds in the country – mine and Alcote's. Do not look astonished, Matt: Alcote is very astute when it comes to business matters. How do you think he has become so wealthy?'

'So much for leaving intrigue and treachery in Cambridge,' said Bartholomew with a sigh.

Michael nodded cheerfully. 'I was beginning to think I had wasted my time with this journey. Now I hear you voicing your usual complaints about the deception and plotting that comes naturally to most people, and I am beginning to feel quite at home.'

'I am glad to hear it,' said Bartholomew flatly.

He shifted uncomfortably in his saddle. The sun was hot and red as it sank over the horizon, and he was thirsty from drinking Tuddenham's warm ale and strong wine.

He dismounted, and went to a brook that bubbled along the side of the road for some water. It was clean and clear and tasted of river weed, quite different from the brown-coloured, peaty stuff he drank in Cambridge with its occasionally sulphurous taste that he preferred not to think about.

A blackbird sang sharply in the tree above his head, while another answered from further away. In the shadows, a kingfisher flitted brilliant blue as it dropped almost silently into the bubbling water and emerged in a flurry of droplets with a minnow in its beak. The wind hissed gently through the trees, twitching the leaves and bending the long grass and nettles that grew along the bank. It smelled sweet, flowers mingled with the earthy scent of rich earth.

It was peaceful by the stream, and Bartholomew did not feel inclined to leave it in order to go to the body of a man who had probably been murdered. He sat in the grass and waited for his horse to finish drinking, watching it take great mouthfuls of water with loud slurping sounds. The blackbird continued to call, while on the opposite side of the brook a bright male pheasant strutted and pranced, trying to attract the attentions of a dowdy hen.

Finally, feeling he could delay no longer, he took the reins of his horse and led it up the hill toward the crossroads. Tuddenham and Wauncy stood together, while Michael poked about near the foot of the gibbet in the dying light. From the stony expressions of the knight and the priest, Bartholomew sensed that something was amiss.

'Are you sure about this?' asked Wauncy in a tone that was not entirely friendly. 'I have heard that the scholars of Cambridge have a reputation for savouring fine wines.'

'Are you implying we were drunk?' asked Michael coldly, pausing in his prodding to favour the priest with the expression normally reserved for students who tried to lie to him.

Wauncy clearly was, but he folded his hands together and

forced a smile. 'All I can say is that you must have been mistaken in what you thought you saw. Look around you, Brother. There is no hanged man here now. And from what I can see, there never was.'

CHAPTER 3

'I CAN ASSURE YOU, SIR THOMAS, THAT THERE WAS A man hanging at Bond's Corner yesterday morning,' said Michael firmly. 'Someone must have returned after we left, and taken the body away.'

Tuddenham was clearly sceptical. He gestured to Siric to refill the scholars' goblets, but Bartholomew noticed that the steward was being more cautious with the portions than he had been the previous day. Michael noticed, too, and was not amused.

It was the day after the mysterious disappearance of the corpse on the gibbet, and the scholars and Tuddenham's household were sitting at a large table in the knight's handsome two-storey manor house of Wergen Hall, which stood about a mile to the south of the main village. Outside, a moat and two sets of earthen banks provided basic protection against attack, although these had apparently been added when Roland Deblunville moved to the neighbouring village of Burgh, and had nothing to do with the continuing wars with the French.

Wergen Hall's main chamber was a pleasant room with brightly painted window shutters that had been thrown open to the golden morning sunlight. Hand-woven tapestries adorned the walls, depicting hunting scenes and a rather alarming vision of Judgement Day in scarlet and emerald, which Isilia told them had been sewn by Dame Eva while her husband was on a pilgrimage to the Holy Land many years before. The rafters above it were stained black with decades of smoke from fires burning in the central hearth, while the wooden floor had been liberally sprinkled with dried grass and fragrant herbs.

Bartholomew considered the oddly empty scaffold of the day before, as Michael continued to try to convince a disbelieving audience that he had not been drunk. With Tuddenham and his priest Wauncy looking on, Bartholomew had knelt in the grass below the gibbet and inspected it closely. Some of the blades were flattened where the body had lain, although with four horses trampling about it was flimsy evidence at best. He had presented Tuddenham with the rope Cynric had cut, but the knight claimed it had been left from the previous hanging. Bartholomew had discovered only one other thing: in the fading light, something had glinted dully, and he saw it was one of the silver studs from the belt the dead man had worn. Tuddenham shrugged, unimpressed, and pointed out that it might have been there for weeks, and provided no incontrovertible evidence that Deblunville had been hanged there earlier that day.

It had been an uncomfortable ride back to Grundisburgh. Tuddenham was clearly relieved that the scholars had been mistaken, but was not pleased that he had been dragged away from the Pentecost Fair on a wasted errand. His priest, meanwhile, hinted darkly about the widely known penchant of Cambridge scholars for strong wines. As far as Bartholomew was concerned, the timely disappearance of the corpse added credence to his initial claim that the hanged man had been murdered, while Michael fretted about whether the incident would make Tuddenham rethink his intention to grant the advowson to Michaelhouse.

Michael need not have been concerned. As soon as they entered the grassy courtyard of Wergen Hall, the knight had asked yet again whether they were inclined to begin sifting through the pile of deeds that needed to be read before the advowson could be drafted. Michael pounced on the opportunity – uncharacteristically declining an invitation to attend the villagers' feast on the green – and summoned Alcote so that they could begin immediately. The rest of the evening was spent painstakingly sorting through the mass of scrolls and deeds that proved Tuddenham's legal ownership of various plots of land and buildings.

Michael and Alcote, with William and Bartholomew helping, toiled well into the night, working in the unsteady light of smoking tallow candles. Eventually, eyes stinging from the fumes and from the strain of reading poor handwriting in the gloom, they were obliged to sleep where they sat, hunched over a trestle table piled high with documents, because all the best places by the fire had been taken by Tuddenham's servants hours before. The scholars were woken, stiff and unrested, before dawn the following morning by Tuddenham himself, eager to know how much progress had been made.

Later, over a breakfast of hard bread and salted fish, during which the usual topics were aired – it was indeed mild for the time of year, the scholars had heard that the Pope had died the previous December, and food prices had risen alarmingly since the plague – Dame Eva turned the conversation to the mysteriously absent hanged man. Tuddenham pursed his lips, reluctant to resurrect a subject he considered closed, but the old lady persisted, claiming she was concerned that the outlaws on the Old Road might have dipped south on to Tuddenham land.

As she spoke, Bartholomew wondered how old she was. Although she possessed almost all her long yellow teeth and her eyes were bright and alert, she seemed so small and frail that he thought a gust of wind might blow her away. But elderly though she might be, she was astute and far too wary of her neighbours to make light of the odd disappearance of a corpse on her son's manor. Given the seemingly precarious state of his relationship with Deblunville, Bartholomew thought her concerns were probably justified, and that Tuddenham would do well to pay heed to her.

'The hanged man was about thirty years of age,' said Alcote, looking up from where he was prising the bones from his herrings with a delicate silver knife, 'with brown hair and a red face.'

'He had a red face because he had been suffocated,' Bartholomew pointed out. 'I cannot imagine it was that colour in life.'

Tuddenham raised silvery eyebrows. 'It is not much of a description, gentlemen. Can you recall nothing else about him? Did he have any marks or scars?'

'Not that I saw,' said William. 'He was just an ordinary sinner.'

'And you are certain he was dead,' said Walter Wauncy, chewing slowly and deliberately on a piece of bread, as if he imagined his teeth might drop out if he were too vigorous. 'Because dead men do not cut themselves down from gibbets and walk away.'

'How can you be sure of that?' asked Isilia, her green eyes round and sombre as she regarded the cadaverous priest. 'Strange things have been happening here since the Death.'

'Not *that* strange!' said Tuddenham, with a bemused smile. He shook his head at his mother. 'Have you been telling her silly tales again?'

'Do not mock things you do not understand, Thomas,' said the old lady sharply. 'Isilia is right: strange things have happened here since the Death.'

She exchanged a glance with Isilia, and they instinctively moved closer together as if for protection. Bartholomew noticed that the old lady's gaudy brooch had been exchanged for a heavy gold cross, which she clutched at with bird-like fingers.

'But dead men do not walk,' intervened Michael firmly,

never a man to exercise patience with superstition. 'The solution to all this is perfectly clear: someone removed the body after we left.'

'Why would someone do that?' asked Wauncy, tearing off a fragment of crust with bony fingers and cautiously placing it in his mouth. 'If the man were dead, why bother to spirit the corpse away?'

'To claim his jewels and dagger, of course,' said Alcote impatiently. 'And to steal his clothes.'

'But that does not explain why the whole body disappeared,' said Michael. 'A thief would have stripped the corpse where it lay, not removed the whole thing.'

'It is more likely that the body was stolen to prevent an investigation into its death,' said Bartholomew. 'It is difficult to solve a murder when there is no corpse.'

'True,' said William, anxious to join in the conversation and demonstrate his deductive skills – skills he hoped Michael would report to the Chancellor when they returned to Cambridge, and that would see him appointed as the University's Junior Proctor. 'But it seems that the killer was interrupted before he had finished his business. When Matthew cut the body down, the man was still alive – just for a few moments. We—'

He jumped suddenly, and leaned down to rub his shin. Michael glared at him, while Bartholomew felt his heart sink.

'You cut down the body of a man who might, for all you knew, have been lawfully executed?' asked Tuddenham, shocked. Isilia and Dame Eva exchanged a look of horror, and Wauncy shuddered. 'That is scarcely a wise habit, gentlemen!'

'Professional hangmen do not abandon their victims before they are dead,' said Bartholomew curtly, deciding there was little point in denying what they had done. 'It was clear this man had not keen killed legally.'

'Nor do hangmen abandon their victims' clothing,' added Michael. 'They usually consider those part of their payment. As Matt says, there was something peculiar about the man's death, and we sought only to avert a possible miscarriage of justice. We were right: whoever we saw die was not executed after a fair trial.'

'Perhaps he took his own life,' said Wauncy, still chewing slowly. 'And then, when you saved him, he just walked away, seeing his rescue as an act of divine intervention.'

'He was dead,' said Bartholomew firmly. 'I am a physician – I know a corpse when I see one.'

'But there are certain illnesses and potions that make a man appear to be dead when he still lives,' observed Wauncy. 'I have heard stories where grieving families were delighted to discover that a loved one was not dead after all.'

Bartholomew had been wrongly accused of misdiagnosing a dead man in the past, and was not prepared to let it happen again. 'His neck was broken, so he could not have walked away even had he wanted to. And he was not breathing. The only plausible explanation to all this is that someone took the corpse away, so that it would not be found.'

Tuddenham scratched his scalp through wiry grey hair, and gave a heavy sigh. 'I can see this business has distressed you, and I sense you will not give your full attention to my advowson until it has been satisfactorily resolved.'

'That is not true,' began Alcote hurriedly. 'This incident is wholly unimportant to us—'

Tuddenham raised a hand to silence him. 'I am a fair and law-abiding man, and I shall do all in my power to investigate this affair. I will send my steward, Siric, to Peche Hall later this morning to tell my nephew Hamon to meet me near the river with six armed men.'

'Do not involve that oaf!' advised Dame Eva with feeling. 'He will do more harm than good with his short temper and lack of common sense.'

Tuddenham overrode her. 'Meanwhile, Master Wauncy can ride to our neighbours – Grosnold at Otley and Bardolf at Clopton – and tell them what has happened. Then, while Master Alcote and Father William remain here to work on my advowson, Doctor Bartholomew and Brother Michael will ride with us to visit Deblunville, so that we can satisfy ourselves, once and for all, that nothing terrible has befallen the man.'

'But today is Sunday, Sir Thomas!' protested Wauncy immediately. 'I have masses for the dead to say . . .'

'You seem to do nothing but say masses for the dead these days,' said Tuddenham accusingly. 'It is just as well Unwin will soon be able to help you, since you spend far more time with your deceased parishioners than your living ones.'

'The plague-dead need my prayers,' said Wauncy in a superior tone of voice. 'They will never escape from Purgatory without them.' He gave Tuddenham a sepulchral look that was about as comforting and friendly as a greeting from the Grim Reaper. 'All mortals should take heed: unless they wish to spend an eternity in Purgatory, they should leave a decent endowment so that masses can be said for their sinful souls.'

'And at fourpence a mass, the endowment needs to be decent indeed!' muttered Michael under his breath.

'Say your masses later, Master Wauncy,' said Tuddenham. 'This morning you will tell Grosnold and Bardolf that I plan to visit Deblunville today.'

Wauncy was unrelenting. 'I do not believe that is wise, Sir Thomas. Deblunville will not take kindly to a dozen soldiers from neighbouring manors appearing on his doorstep unannounced – particularly if one of them is Hamon. You know they do not like each other.'

'And who can blame Deblunville,' mumbled Dame Eva. 'Hamon is an ill-mannered lout.'

'According to our guests, Deblunville is not a man we

need be concerned about again,' said Tuddenham. 'With the exception of saying masses for his soul, of course. Let us hope he has left a suitable endowment.'

'But there is no real evidence that it was Deblunville the scholars saw,' objected Wauncy. 'They cannot know him because they have never met him.'

Tuddenham nodded. 'Nevertheless, I will satisfy myself that Deblunville is alive, and that one of my neighbours has not grown weary of his black deeds and taken the law into his own hands.'

'But what about the Pentecost Fair?' asked Wauncy desperately, wringing his skeletal hands. Bartholomew regarded him thoughtfully. Did the priest have hidden reasons for not wanting Tuddenham to visit Deblunville, or was his agitation genuinely the thought of losing the opportunity to earn fourpences for his masses?

'The villagers do not need you or me to enjoy the Fair,' said Tuddenham dryly. 'In fact, I imagine you will find they will welcome relief from our watchful eyes for a few hours.'

'Very well,' said Wauncy stiffly, in the tone of a man who still feels he is correct. He reached bony hands behind his head and drew his cowl over it, so that his skull-like face was in shadow. The whiteness of his skin and the metallic glitter of eyes from deep inside the hood was the stuff of which nightmares are made, and Bartholomew wondered whether the priest deliberately cultivated his death's-head look in order to remind people of their own mortality, so that they would be sure to put money aside to pay him for his prayers when they died.

Tuddenham treated the scholars to a flash of his long teeth. 'As soon as we return, having satisfied ourselves that Deblunville is alive, I will recommence work on the advowson with you.'

William glanced up from his salted fish disapprovingly. 'It

is Sunday, Sir Thomas. We men of God do not sully a Holy Day by labouring.'

'But the advowson is God's work,' Alcote put in quickly. 'While Bartholomew and Michael resolve this business concerning your neighbour, I will continue work on the deed.'

Tuddenham was pleased. 'Good, good. I want it ready as soon as possible.'

'You seem very keen to have the deed completed,' observed Alcote. 'I do hope the reason is not because the Master sent too many scholars and you feel we are an imposition on your hospitality.'

Tuddenham shook his head. 'I can assure you that is not the case, Master Alcote. But you were doubtless uncomfortable here in my hall last night, so I shall secure you more spacious quarters today or tomorrow. Tobias Eltisley at the Half Moon runs a clean and respectable establishment – you would be better with him than here. And, as regards my advowson, I have long wanted to make a gift to a foundation like Michaelhouse; I am simply impatient to see my hopes come to fruition, nothing more.'

He displayed his teeth again, and left to give orders to his steward. Bartholomew watched him go, not sure that he was telling the truth. As far as he could tell, Tuddenham was not a man who particularly encouraged scholarship, and Bartholomew was growing increasingly suspicious of the unseemly speed with which Tuddenham wanted matters signed and sealed. Was it because he genuinely wanted to share his fortunes with 'a foundation like Michaelhouse', or was it to encourage the saints to give Isilia a healthy boy-child? Or was there a darker reason behind Tuddenham's desire to relinquish his property – a reason that necessitated some very expensive atonement?

Later that morning, with Michael and Bartholomew in tow, Tuddenham cut across the fields to meet his neighbours at the boundary between Grundisburgh and Deblunville's manor of Burgh. Larks twittered in the air high above them, black specks in the blue sky. In the distance, a cuckoo called, reminding Bartholomew of his happy childhood at his brother-in-law's home just outside Cambridge. It was difficult to believe he was chasing vanished corpses on such a fine day, while the birds were singing and the azure heavens were flecked with fluffy white clouds.

By the time they reached the river a number of armed men were waiting, along with the lord of Otley, who was clad entirely in black armour and sat astride an ugly charcoal-grey destrier. His bald head was hidden by a bucket-shaped helmet, and he carried a monstrous two-handed sword. His attire seemed a little excessive for visiting a neighbour, but Bartholomew suspected that there were not many occasions that called for such finery, and that Grosnold probably tended to seize any opportunity that arose, appropriate or otherwise.

'Who is that, the Prince of Wales?' asked Michael of Bartholomew, regarding the curious figure in amusement, and referring to the penchant of King Edward the Third's eldest son for black armour.

'That is Sir Robert Grosnold,' said Bartholomew, smiling. 'We met him in Otley two days ago, remember? He must like that colour.'

Grosnold nodded a greeting to Bartholomew, and Tudden-ham gestured to a younger man who stood at his side, introducing him as Hamon, his nephew and heir.

Bartholomew regarded Hamon with interest. Like his uncle, he possessed a formidable array of long teeth, although Hamon's were whiter. He was sturdily built, with short brown hair that had been carefully slicked down for the Pentecost Fair, and his well-honed sword and battered shield contrasted oddly with what were clearly his best clothes. He was in his mid-thirties, although a life spent outdoors had given him a leathery complexion that had aged him beyond his years.

'I have been overseeing the festivities at Peche Hall,' he explained in a thick local accent. 'But I was planning to come to meet you as soon as they were over – a visit by scholars from Michaelhouse has been the talk of the village for weeks.'

'You are too kind,' said Michael, bowing. 'And I am sorry we should meet in circumstances such as these.'

'You mean finding Deblunville dead?' asked Grosnold bluntly. 'Believe me, Brother, that would add a little extra zest to our celebrations! Deblunville is not a popular man around here.'

'So I understand,' said Michael. 'It seems he is surrounded by people who do not like him.'

'It is all his own doing,' said Hamon. 'The moment he arrived at Burgh two years ago to marry poor Pernel – she was a widow old enough to be his grandmother and he seduced her into marrying him with his viperous tongue – he started to make enemies. He tried to claim Peche Hall was on his land, and then he diverted the stream that we use to water our cattle to run his mill.'

'And I am certain it was he who stole my bull to breed with his cows,' added Grosnold. 'Not to mention offering my free-men higher wages during last harvest, so that they all went to work for him and I was obliged to hire labour from outside.'

'And then, of course, there was poor Bardolf's daughter, Janelle,' said Tuddenham, pursing his lips. 'That was a terrible business.'

Hamon's wind-burned face became angry, and he turned away abruptly, fiddling with his horse's reins with his back to everyone.

'The lass who carries his child?' asked Michael.

Wauncy nodded, and Bartholomew saw Hamon gave his horse's harness a vicious tug. The animal flinched.

'She would have made a fine match for any of the lords around here,' said Grosnold. 'But who will take her now that she is carrying Deblunville's bastard?'

'No one would have taken her anyway,' said Tuddenham. 'She is pretty, but she is a shrew.'

Hamon spun round, breathing hard. His uncle waved an admonishing finger at him. 'It is about time you ceased to hanker after that woman, Hamon. Even before she gave herself so willingly to Deblunville she would not have made you any kind of wife. Now, where is Bardolf?'

Wauncy, who was supposed to have fetched him, shrugged. 'His house was empty, and all his villagers were drunk without him there to keep them in order. I could not find him.'

Bartholomew and Michael exchanged a glance. 'I know what you are thinking,' said Michael in a low voice. 'I hope you are wrong.'

'That Bardolf murdered Deblunville and then fled?' asked Bartholomew. 'If so, then I recommend we leave Grundisburgh today – without the advowson, if necessary – before the whole area erupts in a frenzy of revenge killings.'

'We can manage this perfectly well without Bardolf,' said Grosnold to Tuddenham. 'He is probably off with his sheep – the man is obsessed with the beasts these days.'

'Only since Deblunville stole some of them,' said Tuddenham. 'But time is passing. Let us solve this mystery as quickly as possible, so we can all return to our Pentecost Fair celebrations. I resent spending time away from them because of Deblunville.'

Grundisburgh's eastern parish boundary marked the division between Tuddenham's and Deblunville's manors, and was formed by the River Lark, a meandering stream that wound down from the higher land to the north. Trees hugged the banks on both sides, but there was a clearing where the river was shallowest that had evidently been used as a ford in more friendly times. The ground on the far side rose in a gentle slope to a crest. On it stood a church with a flint tower, while behind was a series of ramparts leading to a haphazard collection of shabby wooden buildings.

'That is Deblunville's "stronghold",' said Grosnold disdainfully. 'He thinks that trifling wooden palisade and that little knoll will keep his enemies at bay. I fought at the Battle of Crécy, next to the Prince of Wales, and those defences would not pose much of an obstacle to a professional soldier like me.'

He raised his right arm, military fashion, to indicate that they were to cross the river. It was deeper than it looked, and murky water lapped around his knees as he led the way, holding his sword above his head. The others sloshed after him and cantered up the slope that led to Deblunville's encampment. First they passed the church, a silent, dour building, with a substantial lock on the door and closed shutters on the windows. It looked to Bartholomew the kind of place that would have armies of spiders in every corner and desiccated flies on the sills. There were mounds in the graveyard, and a few rough wooden crosses. In one corner, under an ancient yew tree, was a much larger knoll and Bartholomew did not need a local to tell him that this was where Burgh's plague-dead had been buried. They had been lucky: in Cambridge, there had been too many dead to bury in the churchyards, and pestilence victims had been tossed into pits dug outside the town gates.

'St Botolph's,' said Michael, looking at the church. 'The Abbot of St Edmundsbury told me about this church. It was named for the saint whose bones once rested nearby.'

'Yes,' said Bartholomew. 'I read that the relics of St Botolph used to be in a chapel near here, until the monks of St Edmundsbury came one night and stole them for their abbey.'

'The monks did not steal them,' said Michael defensively. 'They merely removed them from a place where they were all but forgotten, and placed them in a fine chapel where they would be freely available to the populace as a whole. Hundreds of people come to pay homage to those bones each year. Would you deny them that privilege?'

'You Benedictines certainly stick together,' said Bartholomew, laughing. 'Why not let a little village keep its relics? Why do they all have to be in great abbeys and monasteries?'

'The monks had the permission of King Canute to remove them from here to St Edmundsbury,' protested Michael. 'It was all perfectly legal.'

'Then why, according to the historical documents I read, did they choose a dark night to do their "removing"? Why not come in the daytime and ask nicely?'

'Asking nicely gets you nowhere in this life,' said Michael, regarding Bartholomew as though he were insane. 'If you want something, you just have to take it.'

'And this is the philosophy expounded by the Benedictine Order, is it? No wonder all your monasteries are so rich!'

'The relics of one of England's most venerated saints should not be left to rot in some godforsaken settlement on a road that leads to nowhere,' said Michael testily. 'St Botolph deserves to be somewhere splendid.'

'Did the Abbot tell you about the golden calf, too?' asked Bartholomew, seeing he would not be able to make the monk see his point of view, and disinclined to waste his energies in pointless debate.

'No,' said Michael curiously. 'What was it? Some sort of pagan idol the villagers made to replace their lost bones?'

'A statue of a cow was also in the chapel, but the monks missed it when they "removed" St Botolph's bones. This statue was said to have been made of solid gold, and was thought to have been of great value. The villagers were afraid the monks would come back and "remove" that, too, so they buried it for safekeeping. And there it remains to this day.'

'You mean there is a lump of solid gold buried here somewhere?' asked Michael, looking around him as though he imagined he might see a glittering hoof protruding from the ground.

Bartholomew nodded. 'So the legend says. It is supposed to be near the chapel.'

'And where is the chapel?' demanded Michael keenly. 'I might set Cynric to a little digging if we have time.'

'You will do no such thing,' said Bartholomew, surprised that Michael, who was usually scornful of such tales, believed this one. 'If you want to root about for gold, you can do it yourself; you are not to use Cynric. Anyway, with no relics to house, the chapel gradually fell into disrepair and collapsed. No one knows exactly where it stood. It was all a very long time ago.'

'Before the Conqueror came, according to the Abbot,' agreed Michael. 'But how do you know all this? You said you had never been here before.'

'I read it in the Abbey while you were checking up on Tuddenham. Did you visit the monks' library? It has all of Galen's works, plus two copies of Honeien ben Ishak's *Isagoge in Artem Parven Galeni*. And there were treatises by Theophilus, Nicholas and even Trotula.'

'How fascinating,' said Michael dryly. 'Now, about this calf . . .'

'And there were texts by great Arab philosophers, like Averroes and Avicenna, including little-known commentaries on Galen that I have never read before,' continued Bartholomew enthusiastically, not to be deterred by Michael's apathy. 'One of them suggested a cure for Anthony's Fire that I intend to try on my next patient who is afflicted with that disease, and a—'

'There are flowers around the door of the church,' interrupted Michael. 'How very quaint. I thought this was just another one of those depressing decommissioned places that does not have enough of a congregation to keep it going. Look, Matt! Blue and yellow things.'

'Violets and oxlips,' said Bartholomew, glancing at them absently. 'And in one of the Greek translations of the Arab surgeon Albucasis, there was a technique for incising fistulae that—'

'You will end up in trouble with the Guild of Barbers again if you persist in practising surgery,' warned Michael. 'You are a physician, not a surgeon, and you are not supposed to chop and slice people about.'

'And you are a monk, not a lawyer, but you still study deeds and writs and haggle over legal details,' Bartholomew retorted.

Michael inclined his head. 'Point taken. But let's not talk about such things as incising fistulae. Most men would be discussing horseflesh, or how the beautiful Isilia rates against the exquisite Matilde, not stolen bones and lancing boils. There must be something wrong with us, Matt.'

Close up, Deblunville's encampment was better fortified than Grosnold had led them to believe. There were parallel ditches surrounding a rectangular outer bailey, while a second set of ramparts and a neat palisade of sharpened stakes defended an inner bailey. At the heart of the complex was a row of huts and a low motte topped by a timber building.

They had not taken many steps towards it, when Bartholomew heard the unmistakable clicks of crossbows being wound. He stopped dead in his tracks and looked around him wildly, hoping that Deblunville's men were not trained to shoot first and discuss visiting hours later. Tuddenham dismounted, and raised his hands in the air to indicate that he held no weapon. He did, however, have a hefty broadsword strapped to his waist, as well as at least two daggers that Bartholomew could see, not to mention Grosnold, six alert archers and Hamon, who breathed heavily in anticipation of violence like a trapped boar.

'We come in peace,' Tuddenham declared in a loud, confident voice. He gestured to Michael and Bartholomew. 'These are scholars visiting from Michaelhouse at the University of Cambridge. They claim to have seen a man hanged at Bond's Corner yesterday, and, since all our villagers are accounted for, I felt obliged to ensure that Burgh's people were similarly safe.'

No one answered.

'If it was Deblunville we saw dead on the gibbet, he is unlikely to come out to greet us now,' Michael whispered to Bartholomew. 'And his people will be leaderless.'

Receiving no response, Tuddenham started to move forward again. He stopped short when an arrow thudded into the ground at his feet. He looked at it quivering, and took several steps back. He was prevented from taking several more only by the fact that Grosnold was in his way.

'I have already told you that we have not come with any hostile intention,' he said, his voice tight with anger. 'I demand to speak to Deblunville immediately!'

More silence greeted him, and he turned to Michael and Bartholomew in exasperation. 'You see what the man is like? He will not even speak in a civilised manner. I have had enough of this nonsense. If he is dead, then all I can say is good riddance! Hamon, lead the way home.'

'Wait!'

It was a woman's voice that came from the outer ramparts. There was a pause, and then a figure appeared, climbing lithely on to the top of the bank. A hand grasped firmly around one of her ankles suggested that someone in the ditch behind did not share her confidence in her balancing skills and was trying to ensure she did not fall. For the second time in two days, Bartholomew found himself gazing in admiration at a woman. This one was small and delicate, with corn-fair hair knotted into a thick plait that reached almost to her knees. Even from a distance, he could see her eyes were a startling blue and that her cheeks were pink and downy, not brown and weathered from too much sun. She wore a dress of fine peach-coloured material that shone in the sun as she moved.

'My God,' breathed Tuddenham. 'There is my poor Isilia's piece of satin. I wondered why Deblunville wanted that.'

'Who is she?' asked Bartholomew, unable to tear his eyes away from her.

A clatter to one side made him jump. Hamon had dropped his sword, and was standing open mouthed as he stared at the woman on the earthwork.

'It is my Janelle!' he cried in anguish. 'Deblunville has taken her hostage!'

Tuddenham's little army, Bartholomew and Michael all continued to stare at the small figure standing on the earthen bank. Hamon took several steps forward, as though he would race up and snatch her away, but an arrow snapped into the grass to one side of him and he faltered, standing helplessly with his hands dangling at his sides. Tuddenham and Grosnold were shocked into silence, while Walter Wauncy's expression was unreadable.

'Janelle!' cried Hamon in despair. 'Has Deblunville harmed you? I will kill him if he has!'

'Of course he has not harmed me!' she snapped. 'I am carrying his child! Why should he want to harm me?'

In Bartholomew's experience as a physician, a woman carrying a child was not necessarily cause for a man to celebrate, and he had attended several patients where prospective fathers had decided to prevent an unwanted birth by attempting to dispatch the mother.

Janelle ignored Hamon and addressed Michael, whose distinctive habit marked him as a Benedictine monk. 'Please forgive our wariness, Brother, but not all visits from Grundisburgh and Otley over the past two years have been friendly.'

'Watch your tongue, Janelle!' said Tuddenham sternly. 'And what are you doing here anyway? Have you been abducted? Do not worry, we will soon have you safely home.'

'Of course I have not been abducted,' said Janelle scornfully. 'I came here of my own free will. Roland Deblunville and I were married yesterday in St Botolph's, just after dawn. Did you not notice the wild flowers around the church door?'

'No!' cried Hamon in horror. 'You cannot have done!'

'That is preposterous!' exploded Tuddenham. 'You have no right to wander off and marry the first man you encounter. What will your father say?'

'Ask him,' said Janelle defiantly. 'He is here, in the house. He attended our wedding, and is delighted that hostilities between his manor and Roland's are finally at an end. Now we can devote our energies to something more meaningful than perpetuating silly squabbles – such as making our farms more profitable.'

'No wonder Bardolf did not answer our summons and all his villagers were drunk,' muttered Grosnold. 'The man was busy marrying off his only daughter to the greatest scoundrel in Suffolk.'

'Perhaps this is not such a terrible thing,' suggested Wauncy carefully. 'At least the child will be born in wedlock.'

'Of course it is a terrible thing!' shouted Tuddenham. 'And never mind the wretched brat! What about us? What will Hamon do when Deblunville inherits Clopton from Bardolf and becomes the most powerful landowner north of Ipswich?'

'Hamon will have your two manors,' snapped Grosnold,

pulling off his heavy black helmet to reveal a head criss-crossed with red marks where it had rubbed. 'It is I who will be vulnerable. My cattle will never be safe now!'

'No self-interest here, Matt,' whispered Michael to Bartholo-mew. 'At least our colleagues at the University are a little more subtle in their ambitions and desires.'

'Janelle!' yelled Hamon heartbrokenly. 'What have you done?'

'Well, *I* do not believe you married Deblunville!' yelled Grosnold to Janelle after a moment's reflection. 'You are just making mischief. Your father would never betray us in so foul a fashion.'

'And why should allowing his daughter to marry the man she loves be an act of betrayal?' demanded Janelle. 'It is my business who I marry, not yours. You had no right to attempt to prevent it in Lent, and you have no right to claim you have been betrayed now. It is none of your affair!'

'Your father has been cruelly misled!' shouted Tuddenham. 'He has been misguided by that beast who seduced you. I will talk to him and we will have this marriage annulled. These Michaelhouse men are scholars – they will find a way to put an end to this vile union.'

'We do not have the authority to meddle with that sort of thing,' said Bartholomew in alarm, afraid that Michael might agree to help for the sake of the advowson.

'My colleague is correct,' said Michael, to Bartholomew's relief. 'You will need to apply to a bishop for that.'

'We will apply, then,' determined Grosnold, ramming his helmet on his head again. 'I will show Deblunville that we mean business. I will not have my neighbours' women married off with gay abandon.'

'We should ascertain that Deblunville is still alive first,' said Wauncy thoughtfully. 'Janelle was married at dawn yesterday, but the scholars claim they saw a man wearing

Deblunville's dagger hanging on the gibbet by mid-morning. She may already be a widow.'

Hamon's eyes lit with sudden hope, and Grosnold nodded keenly.

'Perhaps you will allow us to question this lady,' said Michael, sensing that if Deblunville was still alive he might not stay that way long, given his neighbours' reaction to his choice of bride. 'She can harbour no ill-feelings towards a harmless Benedictine monk.'

'Then you do not know her,' said Grosnold with feeling. 'That is no lady, that is a vixen!'

'She is an angel,' whispered Hamon, gazing across at her. 'And Deblunville has poisoned her innocent mind.'

Grosnold gave a snort of derisive laughter. 'Lust has made you blind, Hamon. She has never possessed an innocent mind!'

Hamon stepped towards him threateningly, but Tuddenham pushed his nephew away. The young knight was strong enough to have taken exception to this rough treatment, but he yielded to his uncle's stern glare, and stalked away to stand sulkily with the archers. Grosnold clicked his tongue, and shook his head in disapproval at Hamon's behaviour.

'May I offer you my congratulations, madam?' called Michael. 'Please accept the prayers of a humble monk for a happy and fecund union.'

'It is already fecund,' muttered Tuddenham. 'That was the problem.'

'I would like to speak to your husband,' Michael continued. 'Is that possible?'

'Why?' demanded Janelle. 'So that Hamon's archers can shoot him down in cold blood as soon as he makes an appearance? I do not think so!'

'Madam!' said Michael, sounding suitably shocked. 'I am a man of God and abhor violence. I came here only so that I could be assured of your husband's safety.'

'And how do I know I can trust you?' she demanded. 'You have come to Grundisburgh solely to see what you can inveigle out of Tuddenham for your College.'

Bartholomew looked down at his feet so no one would see him smiling. She was astute, and would not easily become a victim of Michael's smooth charm.

'Hardly inveigle, madam,' said Michael, offended. 'I am here on God's business, not my own. I do not know your husband, so cannot wish him harm. I desire only a few moments of his time.'

Janelle appeared to waver. Michael opened his mouth to add more, but then hesitated, and Bartholomew knew the monk was uncertain what else to say. If it had been Deblunville they had found hanging on the gibbet, and his expensive dagger suggested it was, then there were gentler ways of informing Janelle that she was a widow the day after she became a bride than howling across a field that someone had murdered him.

'Please,' Michael called. 'Allow me and my colleague to come a little closer, and we will discuss this rationally. You can see we carry no weapons.'

'All right, then,' she conceded after a moment's thought. 'But walk slowly, and no tricks! I have archers with arrows aimed at Grosnold, Hamon and Tuddenham. Their lives depend on you being exactly what you say you are.'

'Let's go home,' said Tuddenham, plucking at Grosnold's chain-mailed sleeve. 'We came here out of neighbourly concern, and we do not have to play silly games with that harlot.'

'Just give us a few moments,' said Michael. 'Remember that if Deblunville is dead, all your actions now will be reconsidered later, if you become a suspect for his murder. Standing here while we go to talk to her will say more for your innocence than if you leave.'

Tuddenham glanced at Wauncy, who indicated with a

shrug of his skeletal shoulders that the logic was sound.
With a gusty sigh, the knight waved his hand to indicate that
Michael and Bartholomew should move forward. Wisely, he
led his nephew some distance away, where the younger man
would not be tempted to undertake some rashly conceived
rescue mission.

'Come on, Matt.'

Assuming that no mere physician would dare to disobey
the imperious tone of Michael, the University of Cambridge's
Senior Proctor and valued agent of the Bishop of Ely, the
monk began to walk toward Janelle, holding his hands above
his head. Unhappily, Bartholomew followed, anticipating an
arrow slicing through him at every step.

With misgivings that grew with each passing moment,
Bartholomew moved closer to the ramparts. Michael was
a monk, and even the most lawless of men were usually
loath to harm men of God, lest they pay for it in the fires
of hell. But Bartholomew – although he had taken minor
orders that meant if he committed a crime he would be tried
under canon, rather than secular, law – was no priest, and he
imagined that Janelle's archers would not hesitate to kill him
if they felt threatened. He swallowed hard, wondering how a
pleasant journey to a pretty part of rural Suffolk had ended
with him at the mercy of hidden archers and a pregnant
woman in peach-coloured satin.

'That is far enough.'

With relief, Bartholomew stopped short of the first rampart. Closer, Janelle was even more attractive, although she
was also older, than his initial impression had suggested.
From Tuddenham's description of her careless pregnancy,
he had imagined her to be in or near her teens, like Isilia,
and her fair hair and delicate figure had made her appear
childlike from a distance. But it was no child that glared
down at him from her vantage point. It was a woman in
her late twenties with a no-nonsense face and a determined

expression in her eyes. He forced himself to look away, knowing it was not wise to admire other men's wives openly when there were crossbows and arrows trained on him from all directions.

Michael spoke in a low voice, trying to be gentle. 'I hope you will forgive me mentioning such unpalatable matters, madam, but as we rode past Bond's Corner yesterday we found a man hanging on the gibbet. My colleague here did all he could to revive him, but it was too late. His neck was broken, and he breathed his last as we gave him absolution.'

'You are right – that is not the kind of tale I like to hear,' said Janelle. 'Who was he? And why have you come here, at considerable risk to yourselves, to tell me about it?'

'This hanged man was wearing a blue doublet sewn with silver thread, a fresh white shirt and new shoes. He also wore a studded belt, and there was a jewelled dagger at his side.'

'I wondered what had happened to those,' came a man's voice from behind the wall. A moment later, a head poked up next to Janelle's ankles. 'I am Roland Deblunville, gentlemen. I assume you believe your hanged man was me?'

Judging from Tuddenham's agitated pacing, he was not comfortable with the notion of his guests disappearing inside Deblunville's enclosure. Hamon simply sat on the grass with his head in his hands, while Walter Wauncy leaned over him and whispered bleak words of comfort. Grosnold slouched against the trunk of a tree, his lips moving in agitation as he muttered to himself all the things he would do to Deblunville, if the opportunity came his way. But Tuddenham need not have worried. Bartholomew and Michael were invited only to the small barbican, and not the house, so that Deblunville could speak to them without needlessly exposing himself to his neighbours' archers.

From all he had heard of Deblunville, Bartholomew had anticipated a great hulking figure with a bristling black beard, missing teeth and plenty of scars. Deblunville, however, was not much taller than his elfin wife; he had a mop of fine, fair hair that flopped boyishly when he walked, and had no scars at all that Bartholomew could see. Only the lines around his eyes and one or two strands of silver in his beard suggested he was no youngster. And he was most definitely not the man who had been hanged on the gibbet.

'I am sure Tuddenham has explained to you that relations between us are not all they might be,' said Deblunville, with a spontaneous grin that revealed small, white teeth. 'And I am also sure that he insists it is all my fault.'

'Is it?' asked Michael.

Deblunville gazed at him for a moment, before throwing back his head and laughing. Michael exchanged a furtive glance with Bartholomew, not at all certain what was funny. His wife certainly was not amused: she raised her eyes heavenward and folded her arms, presenting quite a formidable figure for one so slight.

'I imagine I am totally to blame, Brother,' said Deblunville, still smiling. 'According to Tuddenham, I am a wife-killer, rapist and land-thief. However, go to the courts in Ipswich, and you will see documents that show *I* am the legal owner of the land near the river that Tuddenham says is his. He even built himself a house there – Peche Hall – to try to strengthen his claim. But he will live to regret spending his money, because I *will* have what is rightfully mine.'

'Tuddenham said Peche Hall was an ancient house, not one he raised himself,' said Michael.

Deblunville waved a dismissive hand. 'There was an old house there, but he pulled it down and built a new one. Peche Hall is a modern mansion – go and see it for yourselves.'

'But there *was* an old house there,' pressed Michael, 'so he was telling the truth.'

'In a manner of speaking,' said Deblunville, leaning against the rampart and chewing on a blade of grass. 'But take your fine Benedictine robe. If I were to replace all the old material and sew it with new thread, would it be an old garment or a new one? You are intelligent men – you can see that it would be a new one. That is what Tuddenham did with Peche Hall.'

'No, the issue is not quite so straightforward, my son,' said Michael patronisingly. 'And the analogy you posed has room for considerable debate. But we did not come here to argue about houses and land – we are simple scholars and know little of such matters. We came to—'

'Simple scholars?' interrupted Deblunville, his blue eyes glittering with merriment. 'I am sure you will haggle long and hard, and with every ounce as much lawyerly skill as that crafty Walter Wauncy when you negotiate for the living of Grundisburgh's church.'

'I am sure Wauncy will appear a mere novice when compared to Brother Michael of Cambridge,' said Janelle, appraising the monk coolly. Bartholomew was sure she did not intend the remark to be complimentary.

'Perhaps,' said Michael with a faint smile. 'But we did not come here to discuss our advowson, either. I am relieved to see you fit and well, Master Deblunville, but how do you explain the fact that your clothes and dagger were on a corpse? Have you lost them? Have you missed a member of your household, who might have borrowed them and been killed instead of you?'

'That is a sobering thought,' said Deblunville. 'I noticed the clothes were missing a few days ago, but I merely assumed I had misplaced them.'

'Do you know of anyone who might have taken them?' asked Michael.

Deblunville shook his head. 'No, and I am certain no one is missing from my household. Usually, the people of Burgh are scattered all over my estates, tending the sheep. But we are still celebrating our wedding day, and all the villagers have gathered here to wish me well.'

'And to drink your wine,' added Janelle dryly.

Deblunville laughed and, as she smiled back, Bartholomew could well understand what had captured the man's heart. The harsh lines around her mouth softened and her eyes lost something of their piercing, forceful quality. He wondered how she had stayed unmarried for so long, particularly given that Hamon clearly adored her and the Tuddenhams were a powerful force in the area.

'What clothes have you missed, exactly?' Michael asked.

Deblunville tore his attention away from Janelle, and scratched his head. 'A blue doublet and red hose that belonged to my father. They have always been too big for me, and I seldom wear them. There was also a dagger – purely ornamental and so blunt it would not slice through warm butter. You will understand when I say such a weapon is of no use to me, given that I have neighbours who want me dead. I always carry something a little more practical. It is not real gold, by the way, just gilt. But it looks good, and I know my neighbours are jealous of it, thinking it to be valuable. They are foolish men, Brother, and they covet foolish things – like a dagger with no cutting edge.'

'When was the last time you could say, with absolute certainty, that these things were in your possession?'

Deblunville shrugged. 'I really do not know. I missed the doublet when I went to church last Sunday. I wanted to wear it so that I could keep this one clean for my wedding. Before that, I could not say when I last saw it. The same goes for the dagger.'

'And you have no idea why a man wearing your clothes

and knife should be hanged on the gibbet at Bond's Corner?' queried Michael.

Deblunville shrugged again. 'None at all. I can give you a list of a dozen men – all lords of manors and their henchmen – who would dearly love to see me dead. The only thing I can suggest is that someone stole my belongings and was rash enough to wear them. He was then mistaken for me and paid the price.'

'For a man who has so many enemies, including one who may well believe he has killed you, you seem remarkably calm about all this,' observed Michael.

Deblunville raised his eyebrows. 'What else can I do? I am not a man to skulk in his house like a frightened cat, and there is nothing I can do about the way my neighbours feel about me. All I can do is go about my business, and ensure I never travel anywhere alone or unarmed.'

'Well,' said Michael, preparing to leave. 'Please accept my congratulations once more. I am delighted to find you not a corpse but a bridegroom.'

'Nicely put,' said Deblunville. He turned to Bartholomew. 'You are a physician?'

Bartholomew nodded. 'But I do not conduct astrological consultations,' he added quickly, before he was invited to provide a horoscope for the bridal couple.

Deblunville looked taken aback. 'That is a peculiar thing for a physician to say. Your colleagues are usually desperate to get patients alone for an expensive afternoon with their charts.'

'Well, I am not,' said Bartholomew shortly.

'No matter,' said Deblunville. 'I had a fairly lengthy consultation last week with Master Stoate, Grundisburgh's physician. I needed to know whether yesterday was a good time to marry, and Stoate assured me it was, because Jupiter is ascendant. He seems to have been correct.'

'But, more importantly, yesterday was convenient for me,'

Janelle pointed out. 'It would not have mattered whether Jupiter had dropped out of the sky, you still would have wed me then.'

Bartholomew gazed at her with open admiration. Here was a woman after his own heart, who cared not a fig for the mysterious movements of the heavenly planets, and was certainly not prepared to allow them to rule her life.

'Do you need my colleague's services for anything?' asked Michael. 'If not, we had better return to Tuddenham before he tries to attack you. He is becoming increasingly agitated, and I do not want our discussion to jeopardise the advowson.'

'I am sure you do not,' said Deblunville, winking at the monk. He turned to Bartholomew. 'Janelle is with child, and she has been feeling sick in the mornings. Stoate said the feeling would pass when Jupiter became ascendant over Mars, but he miscalculated. She is not feeling better at all.'

'How long?' asked Bartholomew.

'The sickness?' Deblunville shrugged. 'Two months.'

'About three weeks,' Janelle corrected.

'Well, it seems like two months,' grumbled Deblunville.

'And when did you know you were pregnant?' asked Bartholomew.

Janelle shot an imperious glance at Michael, and declined to answer until the monk had sauntered out of hearing, pretending to inspect the revetted walls of the embankment. 'I noticed . . . matters were not all they should be at the beginning of Lent.'

'That was when I first tried to marry her,' announced Deblunville. 'I thought we might avoid a scandal if we did it straight away. Unfortunately, Tuddenham put an end to that, although how he, of all people, discovered Janelle was pregnant, I cannot imagine.'

'Mother Goodman, probably,' said Janelle carelessly. She explained to Bartholomew. 'She is the only midwife in these parts, and not much escapes her eagle eyes. She has an uncanny talent for spotting a pregnancy – sometimes she knows it before the mother herself.'

'She sounds as if she knows her business.'

'She does,' said Janelle, 'but she is fiercely loyal to Tuddenham, and I cannot call on her now that I have married Roland. She might slip me some wormwood, and that would be the end of the child.'

'You had better arrange to have it in Ipswich, then,' said Bartholomew. He considered, thinking that a woman of her age might well have had children from a previous liaison. 'This will be your first child, will it?'

'Of course it will!' exploded Deblunville angrily. 'We were only wed yesterday.'

'Being unmarried does not prevent women from having babies,' retorted Bartholomew curtly. 'Unfortunately for most people, including you it seems, it does not work that way.'

Deblunville drew breath to argue, but then conceded the point. 'The boy will be Janelle's first child. We will name him Roland, after me.'

'And what if it is a girl?' asked Bartholomew. 'They make appearances from time to time, too, you know.'

Deblunville looked as though that thought had not crossed his mind.

'It will not be a girl,' said Janelle firmly. 'I have already prayed to St Margaret of Antioch about that, and she will see I have what I want.'

'I see,' said Bartholomew, wondering whether even a saint would have the audacity to turn a deaf ear to the forceful requests of an expectant mother like Janelle. 'But about this sickness. Did Master Stoate prescribe anything for you?'

She nodded. 'He said I was of a choleric disposition, and so I should drink poppy juice and pennyroyal three times a day for as long as Mars remained ascendant, and then switch to betony in mint water when Jupiter became ascendant.'

Bartholomew tried not to show his alarm. Betony and pennyroyal were herbs often used to end unwanted pregnancies, and if Janelle had been taking Stoate's concoction three times a day, she was lucky not to have lost the child already.

'I would recommend you do not take any more of that,' he said carefully. 'Try cumin in milk, if you like, but the feeling will pass soon anyway.' Although whether Jupiter or Mars was ascendant had nothing to do with it, he thought to himself. All midwives knew that queasiness in the mornings eased off by the end of the third month of pregnancy, and whatever planet happened to be dominant in the sky made not the slightest bit of difference.

'I should really examine you,' he said. 'To make certain there is nothing other than the child that is making you ill.'

'What do you mean?' said Deblunville uneasily. 'Examine her with what?'

'I will check the rate of her pulse, test for areas of tenderness around her chest and stomach, and perhaps inspect her urine,' said Bartholomew. 'There is nothing to be alarmed about.'

'Is that what they do in Cambridge, then?' asked Deblunville doubtfully. 'I was told that was an odd part of the country. All right, very well, then. Carry on. Do what you will.'

'Here?' asked Bartholomew, glancing at Deblunville's archers, who had Tuddenham fixed in their sights, and at Michael, who was leaning against the revetment, humming softly to himself.

'Why? What is wrong with here?' demanded Deblunville.

'I usually conduct these examinations somewhere a little more private,' said Bartholomew. 'And not usually with half the male members of the household watching.'

'You mean you want my wife to go into some chamber alone with you?' asked Deblunville, aghast. 'What kind of physician are you?'

'Just let me measure her pulse rate, then,' said Bartholomew, aware of Michael's barely concealed amusement. He reached out and grabbed Janelle's wrist, trying to block out Deblunville's nervous exhortations to be careful, so that he could count the steady beat in her hand. It was the contention of the Greek physician Galen that subtle variations in pulse rates revealed a great deal about a person's health. Janelle's was rather fast for a person of her size, so he made her sit on the ground while he felt it again.

After a while, during which Deblunville sighed and paced impatiently, and Bartholomew's knees grew cramped from crouching, the physician stood. He was not entirely satisfied that all was as it should be, but Janelle claimed there was nothing wrong except the sickness and she was becoming restless with his ministrations.

'Grind cumin leaves, and mix them in milk sweetened with honey. It sounds unpleasant, but it will not taste as bad as the concoctions Stoate prescribed. Perhaps someone could read to you while you drink it.'

'Read?' asked Janelle, exchanging a dubious look with her husband. 'Read what, exactly?'

'Anything you like,' said Bartholomew. 'A book of hours or some poetry. Anything.'

'We have a list of recipes somewhere,' said Deblunville, thinking hard. 'Will that do?'

'Well, no, not really,' said Bartholomew, bemused. 'The object is to take her mind off her sickness, not to make her feel worse by reciting lists of food.'

'I have the legal documents pertaining to my ownership of the manor,' said Deblunville, scratching his head. 'How about them?'

'Well, perhaps reading was not a good idea,' admitted

Bartholomew. 'But maybe someone could tell her some stories.'

'What kind of stories?' asked Deblunville suspiciously. 'Religious tales from the Bible? Or the kind that I hear in taverns?'

'Something in between, I suppose,' said Bartholomew. 'As I said, the point is to take her mind off feeling ill. Can you not make something up?'

'I expect I could,' said Deblunville, casting a perplexed look at his wife. 'This is a peculiar sort of consultation. Are you sure you are a physician?'

'He is the most senior physician at the University of Cambridge,' said Michael grandly, from where he had been listening. 'And he has something of a reputation for his unorthodox but sometimes effective cures.'

'I see,' said Deblunville. His elfin face broke into a sunny smile. 'I suppose we are just used to Master Stoate's ways, and not these modern methods. We will try your potion, Doctor.'

'Good,' said Bartholomew. 'But you should come to see me if it does not work. There are other remedies we can try.'

'I have no money with me to pay you,' said Deblunville apologetically. 'But perhaps you would take this instead.'

He rooted around in his pocket, and handed Bartholomew an irregularly shaped ring made of some cheap metal. It was far too large to be worn comfortably, and far too ugly to warrant the trouble. Bartholomew was often offered peculiar things when patients found themselves unable to pay for his services, but the items usually had some value or use – food, candle stumps, scraps of parchment, needles, pots, even nails. But he did not wear jewellery, and he did not want Deblunville's cheap-looking trinket.

'Please,' he said, returning it. 'Consider the advice a wedding gift.'

'I insist,' said Deblunville, pressing it into his palm. 'It might not look much, but there are men in Ipswich who would pay handsomely for one of these.'

'In that case,' said Bartholomew, trying to pass it back to him, 'it is far too valuable, and you should keep it for your unborn child.'

'I have another for him,' said Deblunville. 'This is a spare.' He gave a sudden grin. 'I see you do not understand, Doctor. You think I am passing you a worthless bauble. This is a cramp ring.'

'I see,' said Bartholomew, trying to sound appropriately grateful. 'But I would not wish to deprive you of it.'

Janelle shook her head in disgust at his response. 'He has no idea what you are giving him,' she informed her husband. 'He does not even know what a cramp ring is.'

Deblunville looked surprised. 'I thought everyone knew that. They are rings made from the metal handles of coffins. It is common knowledge that such rings prevent cramps.'

'Of course,' said Bartholomew, who had not been party to this generally accepted fact, and was now rather repelled by the heavy object that lay in his hand. 'But you might need it yourselves.'

'There were four handles on my last wife's coffin,' said Deblunville cheerfully, 'so I had four rings made. One for me, one for Janelle, one for the boy and one for you.'

Bartholomew thought quickly. 'But you may have other children after this one. You should keep this for them.'

'There will be other coffins before they come along,' said Deblunville generously. Janelle shot him an uncomfortable glance. 'Do not worry about us, Doctor.'

'Thank you,' said Bartholomew, seeing he was stuck with it, whether he wanted it or not. He put it in his medicine bag, and turned to Michael. 'We should go before Tuddenham thinks we are bartering for the living of Burgh church, as well as Grundisburgh's.'

They took their leave to rejoin Tuddenham, who turned to Grosnold with relief when he saw his guests emerge unharmed. Meanwhile, Hamon was sullen, sitting astride his horse, and casting resentful glances to the rampart where Janelle had stood.

'So,' said Tuddenham as the scholars approached. 'You have seen Deblunville alive and well, and shamelessly ignoring the wishes of his neighbours regarding his marriage with Janelle. Whoever you saw hanged was not him, and so we will say no more about this unpleasant business.'

'What did they tell you about their union?' asked Walter Wauncy, walking with Michael as he went to collect his horse. 'Did they tell you why they saw fit to antagonise their two most powerful neighbours and wed?'

'They did not need to,' said Michael. 'It seemed to me that they had a liking for each other. And Janelle is a determined lady – I imagine she usually gets what she wants, and she wanted Deblunville. The pregnancy merely hastened matters.'

As they rode, Tuddenham and Grosnold regaled Bartholomew and Michael with a further list of grievances suffered at the hand of Deblunville, while Hamon lagged behind with the archers. By the time Hamon peeled off to return to Peche Hall, the sun was beginning to dip, sending long evening rays across the fields, and deepening the shadows under the trees.

The following day was as lovely as the previous one, with pink rose fading to pale blue as the sky lightened. The Michaelhouse scholars began work on the advowson in earnest, now that Tuddenham had shown Deblunville to be alive and well – and a missing hanged man of unknown identity was, after all, none of their business.

Tuddenham ordered a table to be moved near a window, and then threw open the shutters so that light flooded into the shady interior of the main hall. Bartholomew's heart sank when box after box of documents was brought for their perusal, his hopes of a short stay at Grundisburgh quickly evaporating when he saw the amount of work that drafting the deed would entail.

Wauncy, who had an interest in his lord's affairs that far exceeded the pastoral, arrived to help, and Bartholomew watched his bony fingers pick through the writs like a demon selecting souls to torment. While Alcote, who had placed himself in charge, assessed the more important items with Michael, Bartholomew and William were relegated to determining who owned different parts of the church at varying points of its history – a tedious and complex business that did not interest Bartholomew in the slightest. The students fared worse still, and did nothing but run silly errands for Alcote or sharpen his pens – although Bartholomew was relieved that Deynman was kept well away from anything important.

At noon, trestle tables were assembled for the midday meal, which comprised bean stew, barley bread and strong ale. Tuddenham's neighbour from Otley, Robert Grosnold, joined them, listing the disadvantages to himself of Janelle's marriage in a voice sufficiently loud to prevent all other conversation. He wore a black cotte and matching hose, so that Bartholomew began to wonder whether his entire wardrobe was that colour. After the meal, Grosnold and Tuddenham retired to the solar to indulge in further defamation of Deblunville's character with Wauncy, while the Michaelhouse scholars returned to the advowson.

A little later, when Bartholomew was numb with boredom, Isilia came to inform them that it was almost time for the feast that marked the end of the Pentecost Fair, and invited them to attend. Alcote hesitated, eyeing the formidable pile of documents that still required his attention, but Michael had flung down his pen and was rubbing his hands in greedy glee before the others could do more than blink their tired eyes.

Tuddenham was not pleased that his wife wanted to take the scholars away from his advowson, but accepted that he could not withdraw the invitation once it had been extended. Mounting a sturdy horse, he led the way along the woodland path that led from Wergen Hall to Grundisburgh village, with Grosnold riding behind; Isilia, Dame Eva, Wauncy and Alcote in a small cart; and William, Michael and Bartholomew bringing up the rear with the students.

When they arrived at the village green, people were sitting in groups on the grass talking in low, resentful voices. Because Tuddenham had been griping with Grosnold about Deblunville, he was late to arrive for the feast, and the villagers were not happy. Lined up under the trees, and defended by three nervous men with drawn swords, were the trestle tables, once again laden with food – platters of meat and fruit, a huge cheese, waist-high baskets of bread and a cauldron of steaming broth. Bartholomew was impressed, but Michael shook his head dolefully, claiming that many people would still be hungry at the end of the day.

'But there is enough here to feed King Edward's army,' objected Bartholomew.

Michael regarded it critically. 'There are two hundred people in Grundisburgh, so this food will not go far. It seems to me that the villagers did a good deal better two days ago, when they provided their own feast.'

In the centre of the green, Grundisburgh's children had been herded into a reluctant group to sing songs, while a group of men were engaged in a half-hearted tug of war over one of the fords, all of them more interested in the guarded food than in any other activities. Meanwhile, a baby on the opposite side of the green shrieked in delight as an adult in an amber cotte tossed him into the air and caught him again. The shriek turned to a startled howl when the man's second attempt was not so successful, and the baby fell to the ground. Women rushed to soothe the resulting screams of outrage and shock; the clumsy man slunk away quickly.

'I should return home,' said Grosnold, surveying the scene critically. 'My steward is presiding over Otley's feast, but he is overly indulgent. Last year there were two rapes and a murder because I left him in charge.'

'And you think Cambridge seethes with unrest,' muttered Michael to Bartholomew.

'We will discuss this shameful matter of Janelle's marriage again tomorrow,' said Tuddenham to his neighbour. 'I will visit you in the morning.'

The black knight nodded and, jamming a hat on his head, he spurred his horse across the village green. Obediently it thundered forward, causing people to scramble out of the way of its pounding hooves. Women screamed, and there was a huge crash as it knocked over one of the tables, sending hard-boiled eggs and bread bouncing across the ground. Bartholomew watched aghast, and looked at Tuddenham, expecting to see some anger at the cavalier manner in which his neighbour treated his villagers.

'Fine beast that,' said Tuddenham, observing it with an experienced eye as it ploughed through a small group of nuns. 'Grosnold certainly knows his horses!'

He strode to the canopied bench that had been set up for his family, and clapped his hands together. There was an instant, anticipatory hush among the people.

'Please,' he said, gesturing to the surviving trestle tables. 'It is my privilege, as lord of the manor, to provide this feast to mark the end of our Pentecost Fair.'

Bartholomew was not sure whether Tuddenham intended to say anything else, and it was irrelevant anyway. What happened next could only be described as a stampede. People leapt to their feet, and dashed to the tables in a solid mass of bodies. Hands reached, snatched and grabbed, and the mountains of food were reduced to molehills within moments. Children foraged desperately on the ground among the milling feet for the scraps that had been missed, while the old and the slow did not stand a chance. Bartholomew ducked backward to avoid a three-way fist fight that broke out over some kind of pie, while William only just managed to escape being drenched by the vat of broth that toppled over during the affray.

To one side, someone was broaching barrels of ale. The sweet smell of the fermented drink mingled with wet grass, as people jostled and shoved to try to reach it. Bartholomew saw there was not a villager in the seething crowd who had not brought some kind of drinking vessel, although there were many who would not see them filled. The ground seemed to be receiving most of it.

'My God!' breathed Alcote, standing next to Bartholomew and watching in horror. 'I have seen better manners in a pack of animals.'

'That went well,' said Tuddenham, rubbing his hands, and nodding towards the empty tables. 'The villagers do so enjoy this particular festival. It is always a raging success.'

'Did you manage to grab anything?' Michael asked Bartholomew as they walked away. 'I got a handful of meat and three eggs.'

'You did well, then,' said Bartholomew, not surprised that the monk had emerged from the mêlée with something, but astonished that he should enter it in the first place. 'I did not even try. It was all over before I realised it had started.'

'It was rather sudden,' agreed Michael. 'You can have one of my eggs. Or maybe you can ask someone to swap something edible for that bit of coffin in your pocket. Cramp ring, indeed! This place is most odd, Matt. The sooner we return to the normality of Cambridge, the better. There, at least, your patients usually pay you with something practical.'

Bartholomew peeled the hard-boiled egg as they walked,

appreciating the fact that Michael, who had eaten very little all day, was being unusually generous in sharing his spoils. 'This business with the hanged corpse is odd. I suppose we shall never know what all that was about.'

Michael shook his head, his mouth full of roast lamb. 'Some thief stole Deblunville's clothes, and was probably mistaken for him by one of his many enemies. I suspect we interrupted the killer, who then waited until we had gone, crept out and spirited the corpse away, so that no one could investigate further.'

Bartholomew thought about it. 'But the man who died was quite large. How could he have been mistaken for Deblunville, who is small? It is not as if the attack took place in the middle of the night.'

Michael waved a piece of meat dismissively. 'I doubt these lords of the manor do their dirty work themselves. They probably hired some louts to do it for them – louts who did not know Deblunville personally.'

'But that explanation assumes that the lords gave the killers a description of Deblunville's clothes, and Deblunville himself told us they were not ones he wore very often,' said Bartholomew, finishing the egg, and wishing Michael would share his meat.

'Well, as you said yourself, we will probably never know the answer to all this, so it is best you put it from your mind.'

Bartholomew supposed he was right, and sat on the low wall that encircled the pleasant garden of the Dog, the inn that looked across the village green. Michael lounged next to him, finishing his meat and holding forth about the accuracy of his prediction that the food provided for the Fair's grand finale was inadequate to feed the whole village.

Bartholomew listened with half an ear, his mind wandering from the hanged man to Janelle's morning sickness. He saw Tuddenham ensure that the attentions of his wife and mother were on the activities on the village green, and then seek out Alcote to present him with a handful of pens and a sheaf of parchment. The fussy scholar was escorted to one of the empty food tables and invited to sit, while Tuddenham peered over his shoulder as he began to write. Even at the Pentecost Fair finale, the advowson was not to be neglected, apparently.

Time passed, the sun set and Bartholomew began to feel drowsy. He asked Michael where he thought they might sleep that night – Tuddenham had mentioned moving Michaelhouse's scholarly deputation from the floor of Wergen Hall's main chamber to one of the village's two inns, where he said they would be more comfortable. Bartholomew did not much care – one straw pallet was very much like another, although he hoped one would be made available reasonably soon. He had found sitting in one place all day, reading and writing, far more tiring than teaching or visiting patients.

Michael opened his mouth to reply, when frantic shouting caught their attention. Thrusting his way through the crowd that still hovered around the ravaged food tables came John de Horsey, the handsome student-friar whom Isilia had mistaken for Unwin. He was breathless, and his eyes were wide and staring.

'Whatever is the matter?' asked Michael disapprovingly. 'You are making a dreadful spectacle of yourself.'

'It is Unwin,' Horsey gasped, trying to steady the trembling in his voice. 'I think he is dying!'

CHAPTER 4

BARTHOLOMEW PUSHED HIS WAY THROUGH THE MILL-ing villagers, splashed through the ford, and ran as fast as he could to the church. Michael panted behind him, while Horsey urged them to hurry. The door to the church was closed, and Bartholomew struggled to open it, his haste making him clumsy with the heavy latch. It clanked ajar and he shot inside.

Like many parish churches, Our Lady's of Grundisburgh was shadowy and intimate, its narrow windows admitting little of the fast-fading light of day. It smelled of the beaten earth that formed the floor of the nave, of the old cobwebs that hung like tendrils of mist from the wooden rafters of the roof, and of cheap incense. Wooden benches were placed at the back for those not able to stand during masses, and a single tallow candle burned on the altar at the eastern end. The walls were covered with paintings, some of them crudely executed with a good deal of black and red, others more delicate, like the one of St Margaret wearing a wimple and touching a hand to her heart.

'Over here!' yelled Horsey, grabbing Bartholomew's sleeve and hauling him toward the chancel. 'He is here.'

Unwin lay face down in front of the altar. Unlike the nave, the chancel had been paved with patterned tiles, and blood seeped from under Unwin to form a smooth black pool across them. Bartholomew felt for a life-beat in the student's neck, but there was nothing. He hauled him on to his back, and put his ear against Unwin's chest, straining to catch the muffled thud of a beating heart.

'Is he dead?' demanded Michael. 'What killed him? What happened?'

'Michael!' snapped Bartholomew, covering one ear to listen. 'I cannot hear.'

'Hear what?' shouted Michael. 'Is he dead?'

'He must be dead,' said Horsey in a horrified whisper. 'Look at the blood!'

Bartholomew snatched a candle from the altar, prised open one of Unwin's eyes, and passed the candle back and forth near it, looking for some movement that would tell him there was still a spark of life left. The eye was flat and glassy, like that of a landed fish. He balled his fist, and gave the student a hefty thump in the middle of the chest, following a procedure his Arab master had taught him to make the heart start again.

The door clanked, and Father William entered at a run with Alcote and Deynman behind him.

'What has happened?' the friar demanded. 'I saw you three race in here as if the Devil was on your heels.' He stopped when he spotted Unwin lying on the floor, and drew in his breath sharply. Alcote and Deynman stood next to him, gaping in shock as they saw the prone student and the blood on the tiles.

Bartholomew tore open his bag and fumbled for the phial of foxglove juice he carried there. In large amounts the plant was a deadly poison, but it was possible to use a little to stimulate a heart into working. He lifted Unwin's head, and poured some of the colourless liquid into his mouth, although his face had the pale, waxy look that suggested death had already won the battle.

Bartholomew thumped the student's chest again, and put his own face near Unwin's mouth, hoping against all odds to feel the warmth of breath against his cheek. There was not even the slightest whisper.

'He has gone, Matt,' said Michael, touching the physician

gently on the shoulder. 'He was dead before we arrived.'

'Not yet,' muttered Bartholomew. He poured a few more drops of the foxglove into Unwin's mouth, willing him to swallow them and start to breathe again.

'It is over.' Michael tugged at Bartholomew's tabard to pull him away. 'We were too late.'

Bartholomew shrugged him off, thumped Unwin's chest a third time, and then listened. The only sounds were the distant, angry voices of villagers arguing over food on the green, William's prayers for the dying, and Michael still panting from his run. Bartholomew sat back on his heels, and felt for a life-beat in Unwin's neck for the last time. The skin was still warm, but there was no pulse under his fingers. He rubbed a hand through his hair and looked up at Michael in despair.

'Let him go, Matt,' said the monk softly. 'You have done all you can. Now it is our turn.'

Horsey moaned and dropped to his knees, taking one of Unwin's hands and cradling it to his chest. Michael crouched next to him and chanted a requiem, his strong baritone echoing around the church, while Father William began to anoint the body and grant it absolution. William, like many priests, believed that the soul remained in the body for a short time after death, and that giving a corpse absolution would help with the soul's journey to wherever it was bound. Alcote's reedy tenor joined in Michael's dismal dirge, while Horsey wept silently.

Bartholomew moved away and sat with his back against one of the pillars, watching his colleagues. He was suddenly reminded of the plague, when dying people were far more grateful for the absolutions and masses of Michael and William than any feeble, useless treatments Bartholomew had to offer. So engrossed was he in his morbid thoughts that he was not aware that Michael had finished his prayers until he was tapped smartly on the shoulder.

'I need you to tell me what happened to him,' said the monk. He peered at Bartholomew in the gloom. 'What is the matter? You are as white as snow.'

'I wish I could have done more to help him,' said Bartholomew, scrubbing tiredly at his face with fingers that felt clammy and cold. 'And that poor man at the gibbet. I am not used to losing two people in such quick succession – at least, not since the plague.'

'Their hour had come,' announced William, in a voice that was kinder than usual. 'You did all you could to snatch them back, but even your heretic medicine cannot cheat Death of his prey.'

Bartholomew supposed William was trying to be comforting, but to be reminded of his own mortality as well as the limits of his medical knowledge was not particularly consoling.

'Come on,' said Michael, holding out a hand to pull the physician to his feet. 'We are all shocked by this, but we must try to understand what happened. Was Unwin stabbed? There is blood everywhere.'

Reluctantly, Bartholomew went to look at the dead student. One sleeve was soaked with blood, and there was more of it on his stomach. Bartholomew knelt, and used one of his surgical knives to make a slit in Unwin's habit. Below the ribs there was a puncture wound about the width of two fingers. Bartholomew probed it carefully. It looked deep, certainly deep enough to kill him.

'Stabbed,' he said in answer to Michael's query, although the amount of blood and the gash should have made the cause of death obvious, even to a monk.

'By someone else?' asked William, somewhat indignantly. 'He was murdered?'

'I suppose so,' said Bartholomew. 'In my experience, most people driving knives into their own stomach use two hands – only one of Unwin's is bloodstained. And the weapon seems to have disappeared.'

'So,' said William, when a quick search of the church failed to locate any knife or other sharp instrument, 'we can conclude that someone murdered him, because had he killed himself the weapon would still be here?'

Bartholomew nodded.

'But why?' demanded Alcote crossly, as though the murder of Unwin was a personal affront to his dignity. 'Is it something to do with you cutting down that hanged man, do you think? Was it a villager who does not want Michaelhouse to be granted the advowson? Or was it just that someone did not like the look of Unwin for their parish priest?'

No one could answer him, and they stood in silence around the dead student, looking down at him helplessly.

'How did you come to find him?' asked Michael of Horsey. 'He is still slightly warm, and so has not been dead for long. Were you with him? Did you see anyone else in the church?'

Horsey shook his head, tears glistening on his cheeks. 'After the spectacle of that food frenzy, Unwin said he wanted to pray for the people who would soon be under his care. I think he was deeply shocked by their behaviour. I should have gone with him to the church, and then this would not have happened.'

'You cannot know that,' said Bartholomew gently. 'How long was he in the church before you came to find him?'

Horsey shook his head, distressed. 'Not long. I was listening to Lady Isilia talking about her husband's sheep. Sheep! While some vicious killer was slaying poor Unwin in a church!'

'Easy,' said Bartholomew, sensing Horsey was about to become hysterical. 'So what made you decide to come to look for him?'

Horsey swallowed. 'Unwin is my closest friend, and I know he is terribly anxious about his future responsibilities here.

I felt I should be with him, so I excused myself to Lady Isilia, and came to find him. There was no one else here – the church seemed empty. Then I saw him lying on the floor, and all that blood . . . I just ran to fetch you. I thought you might be able to save him.'

The last part held the hint of an accusation, and Bartholomew winced. But once a knife or a sword had been thrust deep into a man's innards, there was very little that could be done to save him. Vital organs were ripped and punctured and they could not be repaired. If the damage did not kill him, the resulting infection would. Bartholomew's Arab teacher had told him it was possible to suture organs, and that the victim might live to tell the tale, but Bartholomew had seen him try many times on battlefields, and never with success. Bartholomew's attempts to start Unwin's heart with punches and foxglove were as futile as had been Ibn Ibrahim's struggles to mend the slippery intestines of injured soldiers.

'Why is one sleeve drenched in blood?' asked William. He answered his own question. 'I suppose he fell on to his arm, and it leaked out from his stomach wound.'

'No, he was lying just as you found him,' said Horsey shakily. 'Both arms were above his head, and he was resting on his face.'

'He must have been moved, then,' said Michael, frowning. 'I noticed both arms were stretched above his head before Matt moved him, and yet the blood on his sleeve must mean that he lay in a different position immediately after his death. I can only conclude that he was killed elsewhere, then brought to the chancel.'

Bartholomew pushed up Unwin's sleeve, and pointed to a small gash near the elbow. 'It looks as though he was injured defending himself, but the fatal wound was the one to the stomach.'

'But we have not answered Roger's question,' said Michael,

rubbing his chins thoughtfully. 'Why should anyone kill Unwin? He has not been here long enough to make enemies, surely?'

'Unlike Roger himself,' muttered William, eyeing Alcote with dislike. He spoke aloud. 'Perhaps Unwin caught some thieves trying to make off with the church silver.'

'What silver?' asked Michael, gesturing to the plain wooden cross and the rough table that served as an altar. 'There is nothing here worth stealing. Anyway, Wauncy does not strike me as the kind of priest to leave valuables lying around – especially if that feast were anything to go by.'

'I hope Unwin's death was not a deliberate attack on Michaelhouse,' said Alcote darkly. 'It might mean that we are not safe here, and that we will be picked off one by one until we are all dead.'

'Foolish monk!' snapped William. 'Why should anyone want to do that?'

'Unwin probably caught someone doing something he – or she – was not supposed to be doing,' said Bartholomew reasonably. 'The people are wild tonight, because it is the end of the Fair. Perhaps there were lovers here, enjoying the solitude, and he caught them.'

'In God's holy house?' bellowed William in horror. 'That is a disgusting suggestion, Matthew!'

'No more disgusting than murder in a church,' Bartholomew pointed out.

'Just like Thomas à Becket,' mused Alcote solemnly. 'He was slain by four swordsmen at his own altar. And he is a saint now.'

'Becket was a little more than a student-friar, and his murder was on the order of a king,' said Michael irritably. 'I do not think his death and Unwin's are in quite the same class. But we should tell Tuddenham about this, and ask him to send for the local Sheriff. The murder of a priest is a serious crime, and should be looked into immediately.'

'Whoever did this will burn in hell for eternity,' growled William. 'He will be consumed by fire and tormented by screaming demons—'

'Since Unwin was a member of Michaelhouse, I will conduct my own investigation,' said Michael, before William could start one of his colourful tirades about the terrors of hell. For a friar, William knew a great deal about hell. 'Meanwhile, I will also send word to the Bishop of Norwich, whose see we are in – because Unwin was a priest, this will come under the jurisdiction of canon, not secular law.'

'You might find Tuddenham does not agree,' warned Bartholomew. 'It might be prudent to make your enquiries discreetly, since there are no beadles to help you if the villagers resent your questions and become uncooperative or aggressive.'

'Do not fear, Matthew. I will be there to assist Michael,' announced William firmly. Michael looked uneasy. 'I will act as your Junior Proctor in this matter, Brother. It will be good practice for the future.'

'Oh, Lord!' breathed Michael to Bartholomew, as the Franciscan preened himself. 'What is about to be inflicted on me?'

While Bartholomew and Michael moved Unwin's body to one side of the chancel, Alcote went with Horsey to tell Tuddenham what had happened. Deynman was dispatched to borrow the parish coffin, and William offered to locate Cynric: one of the scholars would need to keep vigil over the body during the night, and whoever it was would be safer with Cynric and his long Welsh dagger nearby.

'It is extremely difficult to think clearly with William bawling his opinions at me all the time,' said Michael watching Bartholomew straighten Unwin's limbs and smooth down his clothes. 'I hope he is not going to dog my every move during these enquiries.'

'I think he will try,' said Bartholomew. 'Unless you want your tactful questions to become blatant interrogations, you will have to give him the slip. Discretion is an alien concept to William.'

Michael gave a laugh that was almost a sigh. 'He was a member of the Inquisition, Matt! He is not an easy man to escape from – as I am sure many of those poor so-called heretics in southern France will attest.'

'Then you will have to work with him. I suppose you could ask him to speak to some of the more hostile or uncommunicative villagers on your behalf.'

'Not a good idea, Matt. I do not think the Inquisition ever obtained confessions by the cleverness of their cross-examinations. I heard they used techniques during which even the most sainted of people would have admitted to any crimes the twisted minds of the inquisitors cared to dream up. And if William tries using those on the good people of Grundisburgh, we will lose the advowson for certain.'

'And we cannot risk losing the advowson, can we?' said Bartholomew, suddenly bitter. 'A Michaelhouse scholar lies murdered, but that is fine so long as we still have the advowson!'

'Matt,' admonished Michael gently. 'I am only being practical. There is no need to vent your distress over Unwin on me. We must ensure that William practises restraint, or we may never find the culprit of this terrible deed. So I shall need your help over the next few days.'

'How could we have been so foolish as to imagine that we had left murder and intrigue back in Cambridge,' groaned Bartholomew.

'Cambridge is not the only place where foul crimes are committed, you know,' said Michael. 'There is murder and intrigue wherever there are people. And the more people there are, the more crime there will be. Look at London and Paris and Rome! Murder is so commonplace in those places, that no one gives it a second thought.'

'But this is a village with two hundred inhabitants,' said Bartholomew. 'It is not a city with thousands. And we have had two peculiar deaths since Saturday. People may begin to think *we* have something to do with them, since that is when we arrived.'

'I think not,' said Michael confidently. 'First, no one believes there was a hanged man at the gibbet anyway; and second, why should we kill one of our own scholars – especially one who was about to leave us and take up a lucrative post?'

'They might suggest one of us wanted the position,' said Bartholomew, with a sigh. 'And with Unwin gone, one of us *will* have to take his place.'

'Not me,' said Michael firmly. 'I do not want to spend my days granting absolutions to sheep molesters and men who covet their neighbour's pigs.' He shuddered. 'Rural Suffolk is a place that seethes with unnatural vices, Matt, and I want nothing to do with it.'

'It cannot be me either – I am not a priest.'

'Then this might be an excellent opportunity to rid ourselves of Alcote or William,' said Michael, eyes gleaming thoughtfully. 'This is a benefit to the College I never looked for! Which would you rather lose – the bigoted William and his obsession with heresy, or the duplicitous Alcote with his secret wealth and unsavoury business connections?'

'Perhaps we could leave one here and persuade Deblunville to take the other at Burgh,' said Bartholomew, smiling. 'But we should not be talking like this – it is exactly what I meant when I said people might begin to look at who will benefit from Unwin's death.'

The latch to the door clattered, and agitated voices echoed in the dark church. Tuddenham strode up the nave and into the chancel, his metal spurs clanging on the tiles. Hamon was behind him, still wearing his best clothes and with a sword strapped incongruously to the decorative belt at his waist. In their wake scurried Alcote and the lovely Isilia, while Dame Eva followed more sedately, clinging to Horsey's arm for support. Tuddenham's steward kept curious villagers out, struggling against the press of bodies as they strained to see past him.

'What evil has been perpetrated here?' demanded Tuddenham, gazing down at the corpse. 'What has happened?'

'Unwin is dead,' said Michael.

Isilia's hands flew to her mouth and her eyes became round with horror. Dame Eva appeared to be more offended than shocked, while Hamon studied the body with the same dispassionate expression he had worn since he had discovered Janelle had married his arch-enemy Deblunville.

'How?' asked Tuddenham, when he had recovered from his surprise. 'There is blood on him. Did he have some kind of fatal seizure brought on by excessive choler?'

'He was stabbed,' said Bartholomew bluntly. 'In the stomach.'

'You mean he was killed by someone else?' asked Isilia in an appalled whisper. 'Murdered?'

'We believe so, madam,' said Michael. 'Doctor Bartholomew has some experience in these matters, and has helped me to investigate crimes of this nature in the past.'

'You mean you have been involved in murders before?' asked Tuddenham distastefully. 'I thought Michaelhouse men were scholars, devoted to matters of the intellect, not the kind of people to probe into the unsavoury affairs of killers.'

'Perhaps murder has followed you here, then,' said Hamon, looking at each of the Fellows in turn. 'I can assure you that unlawful slayings do not commonly occur in Grundisburgh.'

'I told you that is what they would say,' muttered Bartholomew to Michael.

'What about Alice Quy?' asked Isilia, startled. 'She was murdered last month.'

'She died of childbirth fever,' said Tuddenham dismissively. 'If you heard there was any foul play involved, then you have been listening to gossip that has no foundation in fact.'

'Well, what about James Freeman, then?' demanded Isilia. 'He was found with his throat cut only last week.'

'Suicide,' said Tuddenham brusquely. 'That is why he was buried in unconsecrated ground, if you recall.'

'None of this would have happened in my husband's time,' said Dame Eva sadly. 'Things were different when he was lord of the manor.'

'He did not have the after-effects of the Death to contend with,' snapped Tuddenham, rattled. 'He did not have vast tracts of land with no one to work them, or the constant clamouring of peasants for higher wages.'

'If he had, he would have known how to deal with them,' said Dame Eva defiantly. 'This was a prosperous manor in his time, and now it has murderers strutting unchallenged along its paths.' She regarded her son soberly. 'And Isilia is right about Alice Quy and James Freeman. Their deaths were not natural. We all know what they saw. And Deblunville saw it, too.'

'Saw what?' asked Alcote curiously. 'You mentioned Deblunville seeing "something" before.'

'Superstitious rubbish!' said Tuddenham in exasperation, ignoring Alcote's question. 'You will refrain from discussing such pagan matters in a church, madam, especially in front of our guests from Michaelhouse.'

'Deblunville may have seen it, but he is still alive, more is the pity,' said Hamon bitterly.

'Hamon!' barked Tuddenham angrily. 'I said that is enough. Now, we must arrange for a vigil to be kept over this poor friar. Master Wauncy, please see to it.'

'I will do it,' bellowed Father William, as he strode up the nave with Cynric gliding like a ghost through the shadows behind him. 'And Horsey will assist me.'

'No,' said Bartholomew, seeing that Horsey's face was still grey with shock. 'He needs to rest. Cynric will stay with you, and I will relieve you at midnight.'

There was a loud crash followed by muffled cursing, as Deynman, Michaelhouse's least able student, struggled into the church carrying the parish coffin. Whoever had built it had intended it to last, for it was made of solid oak, and was apparently very heavy. It comprised a rectangular box with a hinged lid, and a slat of wood inside on which to rest the head.

'I will have the midwife prepare the body,' said Tuddenham. 'She always performs that service for the village dead. It is too late to do much else tonight, but at first light tomorrow Hamon can go to Ipswich with a message for the Sheriff, and I will begin to make some enquiries of my own. I do not anticipate it will take long to uncover the monster who did this vile thing.'

'Do you have any idea why someone might want to kill Unwin?' asked Michael.

Tuddenham shook his head. 'Times are hard, Brother, and although we appear to be a wealthy village there are those among the bonded villeins who are resentful that some people are richer than they. I would imagine this to be a simple case of theft.'

'Theft of what?' asked Michael, unconvinced. 'Unwin had nothing to steal. His few possessions are in the saddle bags outside, and the cross he wears is fashioned of nothing more valuable than baked wood.'

'But he had a purse round his waist,' said Tuddenham. 'I saw it earlier, and it is not there now.'

Bartholomew looked down at Unwin's habit and saw that Tuddenham was right. He was angry at himself for not noticing it sooner. The leather thongs that had tied the purse to Unwin's belt had been severed – perhaps with the same knife that had been used to kill him.

'But Unwin's purse contained only a phial of chrism and a tiny relic – some hairs from St Botolph's beard in a twist of parchment,' said William. 'We friars do not permit ourselves to accumulate worldly goods.'

'A thief was not to know that the purse contained nothing of value,' Tuddenham pointed out. 'Especially in a dark, shadowy place, like this church.'

'So, you believe we should be on our guard?' asked Alcote, by far the wealthiest of the scholars. 'Anyone carrying a purse in Grundisburgh is asking to be murdered by jealous villeins? Should Matthew rid himself of his medicine bag, lest someone believes it to be stuffed full of treasures? Should I hire a bodyguard?'

'Of course not,' said Tuddenham testily. 'This is an isolated incident, not something that happens regularly – as Hamon said, murders do not occur in Grundisburgh. However, I imagine that the copious amounts of ale I supplied today had more than a little to do with it: a villager became drunk, saw Unwin enter the church with a purse swinging at his side, and killed him for it. I will begin a search for it at first light tomorrow, while you work on my advowson.'

He nodded curtly to the scholars and left the church, his family at his heels.

'If Unwin had no money, how did he come to have this relic?' asked Bartholomew. He was angry, mostly at whoever had dispatched Unwin so casually, but partly at Tuddenham for reasons he did not yet fully understand. When they had first arrived, the knight had seemed hospitable and charming, but Bartholomew had not liked his careless attitude towards the missing man from the gibbet, nor his pettiness over the border squabbles with Deblunville. He wondered afresh whether it was in Michaelhouse's best interests to accept gifts from such a man, and worried about what the knight might ask for in return – especially given his curious eagerness to have the advowson completed as soon as possible. Bartholomew knew Alcote would be unscrupulous in agreeing to whatever it took to secure the living of the church for the College, and was unsure whether he could trust Michael not to turn a blind eye to certain irregularities in order to place Michaelhouse third, rather than sixth, in the University's hierarchy of wealth.

'The relic was a gift from me,' said Horsey in a strained voice. 'I bought it for him while we were at St Edmundsbury Abbey. You see, St Botolph's body lay in Grundisburgh before it was taken to the Abbey, and I thought a relic from that saint would protect Unwin, and keep him safe in his new post . . .'

Bartholomew stood and rested his hand sympathetically on the student's shoulder. Horsey choked back a sob.

'And where did you find the money to pay for this relic?' asked William coolly. 'I did not know you were a wealthy man.'

'I had a silver cross that my sister gave me,' said Horsey. 'The only time I ever wore it, you lectured me about the immorality of worldly possessions, so when one of the monks at the Abbey offered me a few hairs of St Botolph's beard in exchange for the cross, I did not hesitate.'

'You mean one of the monks is removing parts of the saint's body and selling them off?' asked Michael, appalled.

William made an unpleasant noise at the back of his throat. 'What did you expect from a House of Benedictines? Every one of them has but a single ambition, and that is to amass fortune and power in this world with no thought for the one that comes after.'

Leaving William to begin his vigil for Unwin's soul, Bartholomew followed the others out of the dark church. The sky was a deep blue, and the branches of the trees that had shaded the graves from the sun were silhouetted black against it.

Bartholomew took a deep breath, trying to dispel the smell of mustiness and cheap incense that seemed to hang in the air around him.

'I will stay with Father William, boy,' said Cynric softly. 'And I will be here when you come to relieve him at midnight. I have my dagger at the ready.'

'Be careful,' said Bartholomew, not liking the way their visit to rural Suffolk had so suddenly degenerated to the state where Cynric felt he needed to have his weapon drawn while William kept vigil over a dead student. 'But do not forget that someone might enter the church with purely innocent intentions. We do not want another needless death today.'

Michael was watching Alcote and Horsey pick their way through the long grass of the graveyard toward the village green. 'When we first arrived here, I thought we had come to paradise, with all those children laughing and dancing around the pole, and those mountains of food waiting to be enjoyed. Now we discover from old Dame Eva that there have been other suspicious deaths in the village over the last month – the woman who died of childbirth fever and the man with the slit throat – not to mention the hanged man at the gibbet whose body has been stolen, and poor Unwin.'

'Women do die of childbirth fever, and people do commit suicide,' said Bartholomew. 'There is probably nothing in all this but the coincidence of four unexpected deaths occurring in a short period of time.'

Michael shook his head slowly. 'I am not so sure. I have the distinct feeling that there is something strange going on in this village.'

'If you start meddling in Tuddenham's affairs, you will lose your precious advowson for certain,' said Bartholomew, taking the monk's arm and leading him out of the churchyard. 'It would not be polite or prudent to start interfering with the way he runs his estates.'

'It might be very prudent considering that one of us is

already dead,' countered Michael. 'I do not like the notion of standing idly by while one of my colleagues is slaughtered – although I might be prepared to look the other way if Alcote is the next victim.'

'Michael!' admonished Bartholomew, more because Alcote might overhear than because he disagreed with the sentiment. 'But Tuddenham is probably right: someone killed Unwin in order to steal his purse. There is nothing to suggest that the rest of us are in any danger – although I would hide that jewelled cross you are wearing, if I were you.'

'Tuddenham claims the killer was probably drunk,' said Michael, tucking the cross down the inside of his habit. 'I can assure you that no one could have become drunk on the paltry amount of ale he provided. First, it was poor quality stuff with no flavour and no bite; second, most of it was spilled during the fight to get it; and third, no one could have managed more than a single cup of it at the very most – there was simply too much pushing and shoving.'

'And what is this "something" that Dame Eva keeps talking about?' asked Deynman, speaking softly behind them and making no secret of the fact that he had been listening. Bartholomew jumped, uncomfortably aware that he should be more cautious about people overhearing his conversations until he was certain Unwin's death was no more sinister than a case of random robbery. 'She says the two people who died saw "something". Does she mean that they witnessed a terrible act, and were killed so that they could not reveal it?'

'I doubt it, Rob,' said Bartholomew. 'Dame Eva seems to know what they saw, and she would not be telling everyone about it if she believed someone might kill her, too.'

'It is the same "something" that Deblunville is supposed to have seen,' said Michael. 'But he is alive and well, and doubtless enjoying himself tremendously with the woman of Hamon's dreams at this very moment. But it is late and we are all tired. We need to rest, not to start frightening each other with all these wild speculations.'

Alcote had met Walter Wauncy by the ford, and was waiting for them. The night had become chilly, and Alcote was shivering. The village priest, however, seemed more a creature of the night than of the day, and appeared almost lively. His cowl was pulled up against the cool night air and he carried a thick staff, so that Bartholomew thought he looked exactly like the depiction of Death on the wall paintings in St Michael's Church in Cambridge. He shuddered, unnerved by the similarity.

'I am on my way to help with the vigil,' said Wauncy with a graveyard grin. He raised a white, bony hand magnanimously. 'I will not, of course, be charging my usual fourpence for these services for Unwin – tonight anyway.'

'You are too kind,' said Michael expressionlessly. 'I am sure Unwin's soul will rest easier knowing he has a few free masses secured for this evening.'

'I was just explaining to Master Alcote that Sir Thomas has hired you rooms in the Half Moon for the rest of your stay,' said Wauncy, after regarding Michael uncertainly for a moment. 'Although the food is better at the Dog.'

'Sir Thomas had intended us to stay with him at Wergen Hall for the whole of our visit,' explained Alcote, 'but he thinks that we will be less cramped in the tavern. What he really means is that *he* will be less cramped at Wergen Hall without seven guests. I told you our party was too large.'

'That is kind of him,' said Michael, sounding relieved that he would not have to sleep under Tuddenham's roof again. 'Where is the Half Moon?'

Wauncy gestured across the green. 'Cross the ford here, and the Half Moon is near the edge of the village, overlooking the River Lark. Your servant has already deposited your bags there.'

It was almost completely dark by the time they found the tavern, a large building with an inexpertly thatched roof that looked like the head of an ancient brush, and thick, black supporting beams running at irregular intervals along its façade. It was dull pink, as a result of the local custom of adding pig's blood to the whitewash, and the horn windows gleamed a dull yellow from the flickering firelight within.

Alcote elbowed his way past Bartholomew and took the best seat nearest the fire. Immediately there were howls of laughter from a group of young people sitting at one of the tables, apparently directed at Alcote and one of their number – the flaxen-haired beauty who had asked Bartholomew to dance with her at the Fair. Alcote glowered at them, but that only seemed to add to their mirth.

As the others hovered uncertainly in the doorway, a taverner in a white apron came toward them. He was a man of indeterminate years with a neat cap of thick silver hair, a strangely swarthy face and restless dark eyes. Tied on a piece of twine around his neck was a smooth piece of glass, the kind Bartholomew had seen short-sighted scribes use to aid eyes worn out from years of deciphering illegible writing in bad light. The man saw him looking at it, and smiled.

'Please,' he said, gesturing with his hand to indicate that they were to enter. 'I have been expecting you. I am Tobias Eltisley, the taverner.' He held up his eye-glass like a trophy. 'At the risk of sounding presumptuous, I would like you to know that I am a man of some learning, and look forward to many intellectual discussions about science and the nature of the universe.'

'That sounds delightful,' said Michael, smiling politely. 'But not this evening, with our colleague dead in the village church.'

'Tomorrow, then,' said Eltisley. 'But it is chilly outside.

Come and sit near the fire while I finish preparing your rooms.'

As they took seats at one of the inn's tables, Bartholomew looked around him. The tavern had a large room on the ground floor, while a flight of narrow steps led to the upper chambers. The unsteady flames in the hearth made it difficult to see, but the walls seemed surprisingly clean for an inn, and the table tops had been scrubbed almost white. The room smelled of wood-smoke, cooking and the lavender that had been mixed with the rushes scattered on the floor. It was a pleasant aroma, and reminded Bartholomew of his sister's house outside Cambridge.

There were five tables with benches in the room, suggesting that Eltisley's trade was good. Two of them were already occupied, one by a group of sullen-looking men who hunched over their beakers in stony silence, and the other by the young people who had laughed at Alcote. Some of the girls wore flowers in their hair, while their beaus had coloured ribbons tied around their waists and wrists. A large, matronly woman sat to one side, sewing, although how she could see in the gloom, Bartholomew could not imagine. It seemed she was acting as a chaperon, for whenever one of the young men moved too close to the girls, she would give him a menacing glare and he would obediently, if reluctantly, back away.

'Can I fetch you anything?' asked Eltisley. 'Wine or ale? Something to eat?'

'Yes,' said Michael before anyone else could speak. 'I could eat a horse – although I would prefer you not to bring me one. A chicken will suffice, or perhaps some mutton. And plenty of bread to mop up the gravy. But no vegetables.'

'I will inform my wife,' said Eltisley, hurrying away through a door at the rear of the room.

'Wauncy said the food was better at the Dog,' complained

Alcote under his breath. 'What is wrong with you, Michael? Are you losing your taste for fine meals after all the rubbish we have eaten during the journey here?'

'I am ravenous,' replied Michael. 'And I am not prepared to go wandering around in the dark looking for another tavern, when this one is offering hospitality. What I need at the moment is quantity, not quality.'

'My wife said the food will be with you in a few moments,' said Eltisley, appearing breathlessly from the kitchens.

'Good,' said Michael. He rubbed his hands together and smiled pleasantly at the landlord. 'There is a chill in the air this evening, Master Eltisley, despite the warmth of the day. It is good to see a fire.'

The landlord beamed an ingratiating smile. 'In that case I will stoke it up for you, Brother.'

'That is not necessary,' said Bartholomew quickly, feeling the room was already too hot for the summer evening. 'Please do not trouble yourself.'

'It is no bother,' said Eltisley, seizing a pair of bellows that would have been more at home in a blacksmith's furnace than a tavern, and setting to work with considerable enthusiasm. Smoke billowed from the logs as the gigantic bellows did their work, and ashes began to fly everywhere. Michael coughed, flapping at the cinders that circled around his face, while Bartholomew's eyes began to smart and water.

The young people yelled at Eltisley to leave the fire alone, but the landlord stopped only when one of the handles, probably weakened from years of such abuse, broke with a sharp snap. There was a sigh of relief from all the patrons, and Deynman went to open the door to clear the room of the thick, swirling pall.

'There,' said Eltisley, standing back to regard the roaring fire with satisfaction. 'That should warm the place up. Who opened the door?'

'I did,' said Deynman. 'To let some of the smoke out.'

'No, no, no,' said Eltisley, closing it firmly. 'The flames will create a natural draught that will suck the smoke out of the room within moments. There is no need for doors.'

Coughing dramatically, Deynman went to open it again, but a silent, brooding man, who sat at the table nearest the window stood up threateningly, and Deynman hastily pretended to be inspecting the whitewashed walls instead. When the man took a step toward him, the student scuttled back to his companions, trying to hide behind Bartholomew.

'But we could be dead in a few moments,' gasped Michael to Eltisley. 'Did no one ever tell you that if you allow your patrons to breathe, you are more likely to keep their custom?'

'Then I will open a window for you,' said Eltisley reluctantly. 'That will create a cross-draught but will not allow any of the heat to escape.'

'This man is a lunatic,' said Bartholomew to Michael, watching the landlord in disbelief. 'Why does he imagine heat will escape through a door, but not a window? And flames do not suck smoke from a room!'

'Here is the food,' said Michael, reaching into Bartholomew's medicine bag for one of his surgical knives, smoke forgotten. 'What do we have here? Goose, I believe, and duck. And some mutton. What is this scarlet stuff, madam?'

'Red-currant sauce,' said Eltisley's wife, 'and this is a dish of buttered carrots, simmered in vinegar and honey and then flavoured with cinnamon.'

'Vegetables,' said Michael eyeing them in distaste. 'Never mind those. Where is the bread? And what have you smeared over that delicious meat?'

'That is hare, fried in white grease with raisins and onions, and garnished with dandelion leaves and cress.'

'Oh, well, I suppose the greenery can be scraped off,' sighed Michael in a long-suffering way. He glanced up, and smiled as a serving girl appeared with more dishes.

'Here comes the bread now. And what is this? Lombard slices! One of my favourites.'

'What are Lombard slices?' asked Bartholomew, unused to the rich food over which Michael was drooling.

'Almonds and breadcrumbs cooked with honey and pepper,' said the monk contentedly, 'and served with a syrup of wine, cinnamon and ginger. Delicious! Try some.'

He cut Bartholomew a small piece, and then ate it himself when the physician was slow to claim it, washing it down with a substantial swig of wine.

'This will be expensive,' said Alcote anxiously. 'I hope we will have enough money to pay. The Master's allowance for travelling was not overly generous.'

'Everything will be paid for by Sir Thomas,' said Eltisley graciously. 'You are Grundisburgh's guests, and it is our pleasure to ensure you have everything you need. Will there be anything else?'

'No, thank you,' said Bartholomew quickly, before Michael could ask for more. Eltisley had clearly been ordered to treat them well, and there would be no limits to Michael's greed unless his colleagues curtailed him.

'And you must each drink a measure of this before you start,' said Eltisley, waving a clear glass bottle in which something grainy-looking and black slopped ominously.

'What is it?' asked Bartholomew suspiciously.

'Just a little potion of my own that aids digestion,' said Eltisley proudly. 'I dabble in medicine occasionally – just like you, Doctor – and my remedies and tonics are in great demand in the village.'

'I see,' said Bartholomew, resenting the implication that he 'dabbled'. 'And what exactly is in this potion of yours?'

Eltisley tapped the side of his nose. 'That would be revealing a professional secret. I cannot have you stealing my ideas, can I?'

Bartholomew took the bottle from him and sniffed at its

contents dubiously. He jerked backward as the sharp odour stung his nose.

'You expect us to drink that?' he asked incredulously. 'It smells like urine and camphor, boiled together until burned.'

Eltisley looked disappointed. 'The urine of a she-goat,' he corrected pedantically. 'Simmered with white starch and camphor, and flavoured with cloves. It is a syrup that is hot and dry in the first degree – according to Galen – and is excellent for diseases of the stomach. I usually make it paler, but I forgot to bank the fire when I cooked it and it ended up a little blackened. But it will work all the same. Drink up!'

'Galen would never recommend drinking such a concoction,' objected Bartholomew. 'And neither will I.'

'Of course he would,' said Eltisley, pouring the charcoal sludge into some goblets. 'If you do not drink it, you will pay with dreadful indigestion during the night.'

'Why?' asked Bartholomew. 'Is your cooking so bad?'

'Matthew!' snapped Alcote sharply, as Eltisley looked offended. The fussy scholar snatched one of the goblets from the landlord, and had drained it before Bartholomew could stop him. 'There,' he said hoarsely, when he could speak again. 'Now perhaps we can eat in peace.'

'That was rash,' said Michael as Eltisley walked away, satisfied. 'I would not drink boiled goat urine flavoured with cloves – especially given that Matt advised against it.'

'You put far too much faith in his medicine,' said Alcote, regarding Bartholomew coldly. 'I do not trust his heretic methods at all. He could not save Unwin, and he could not save the criminal at the gibbet on Saturday.'

'Have some more of this sludge, Roger,' said Michael, pouring the Senior Fellow another cup of Eltisley's remedy. 'With any luck, he might not be able to save you, either.'

Alcote was about to reply with something equally unpleasant, when Deynman's elbow put an end to the discussion.

The bottle tipped to one side and knocked into the cups, spilling all their grisly contents into the rushes on the floor. Michael scuffed the mess into the beaten earth underneath with his foot, and gave the embarrassed student a conspiratorial wink.

'Best place for it,' he said. 'Other than in Alcote, that is.'

'There is rather a lot of this,' said Deynman, eyeing the piles of food with trepidation. 'Will we finish it all, do you think?'

'Of course we will,' said Michael, his cheeks bulging with fresh bread. 'It is a mere mouthful.'

'We should save some for William,' said Bartholomew, watching Michael scrape the greens from his portion of hare. Under the cress, the dish swam with grease, and Bartholomew felt queasy as Michael plunged his bread into it and sucked on the sodden crust.

'William claims not to like elaborate food,' said Alcote. 'He will not want any.'

'He will,' said Bartholomew, knowing that what William said, and what William did, were not always the same. 'But this is all very rich. We will be ill if we eat too much of it.'

'A contradiction in terms, Matt,' said Michael, spearing a duck's leg with Bartholomew's knife. '"Food" and "too much" are words that do not belong together, like "fun" and "physician" or "friar" and "intelligent conversation".'

'Or "monk" and "moderation",' added Bartholomew. 'Do not eat so fast, Brother. This is not the Pentecost Fair, you know. There is plenty here for all of us and there is no need to gobble.'

'I never gobble,' said Michael loftily. 'I merely enjoy the pleasures of this life while I can. And so should we all – after all, as Unwin has just shown, who knows how long we may have to do so?'

* * *

It was not long before Michael had reduced the fine meal to a mess of gnawed bones and empty platters. Alcote, always a fussy eater, consumed very little, and Bartholomew and the students had little appetite after seeing Unwin dead in the church. While Michael tried to lift the spirits of his subdued companions by telling some ribald tale about a Cambridge merchant's wife, Bartholomew stared at the fire and tried to recall whether he had seen any villager acting oddly after the feast, hoping he might remember a furtive look or a nervous manner that would provide some clue as to who killed the student friar.

After Eltisley's wife had cleared away the greasy dishes, a man from the lively group at one of the other tables came to join them.

'I am Warin de Stoate,' he said, bowing low. 'Grundisburgh's physician. I wanted to tell you that I was delighted to see you put that charlatan Eltisley in his place – he has been plaguing the village with his worthless cures and concoctions for years.'

Bartholomew rose to introduce himself, pleased to meet another medical man. Stoate was in his late twenties with thin hair, pale brown eyes and a face ravaged by ancient pockmarks, partially concealed by a large moustache. He wore hose and a matching cotte of a deep amber, and a fine white shirt. Bartholomew recalled him as the man who had been tossing – and dropping – the small child on the village green earlier that day. Like Bartholomew, Stoate carried a bag containing the tools of his trade, although his was smaller than Bartholomew's and of a much better quality.

'We were all shocked to hear about the death of your colleague,' said Stoate, gesturing to his friends at the next table. 'Do you have any idea as to why someone should do such a thing?'

'No,' said Michael. 'But he was almost certainly killed by someone who lives here. Can you think of a reason why anyone might want to murder a Franciscan as he prayed in the church?'

Stoate shook his head. 'But I saw someone leave the church not long before the alarm was raised by him.' He pointed at Horsey. 'I did not think much about it at the time, but now it seems as though it might be important.'

'It might,' said Michael, sitting upright. 'Who was it?'

'I did not see his face,' said Stoate, to Michael's disappointment. 'I was standing near the ford talking to Mistress Freeman, and I just glimpsed someone leave the building.'

'Why did you notice him at all?' asked Bartholomew curiously. 'I imagine people were in and out of the church all day.'

'They were, but he caught my eye because he was wearing a long cloak,' said Stoate. 'It was warm in the sun today, and I remember thinking how foolish he was to be wearing such a thick garment when he would overheat. We medical men notice that sort of thing.'

'Do you?' Michael demanded of Bartholomew.

The physician shrugged and then nodded. 'Yes, I suppose so. Do you recall anything else?' he asked Stoate.

'Not really. He did not look familiar, but there are so many people in this village that I might not immediately recognise someone – particularly swathed in a thick garment with the hood up.'

'Was this person acting furtively?' asked Michael. 'As though he had just done something he should not have done?'

'Oh, yes,' said Stoate with certainty. 'He kept looking about him, and then he disappeared off into the trees on the far side of the churchyard. At the time I just assumed it was a lad setting up a prank to play on his fellows – water in a bucket over the door, grease smeared on the doorstep, that kind of thing. But now I realise a practical joke was a long way from that man's mind.'

'And it was definitely a man?' asked Bartholomew. 'Could it have been a woman?'

'A woman? Why should a woman want to kill Unwin?' asked Alcote, looking up from where he was trying to read some of Tuddenham's accounts in the firelight.

'Why should a man want to kill him?' countered Bartholomew.

Stoate shook his head, trying to remember. 'It might have been a woman, I suppose. There was no way of assessing how big he was when there was no one else nearby. I am sorry, I know I have not been of much help. Had I known that this person was leaving the scene of such a terrible crime, I would have been a lot more observant.'

'Thank you for telling us,' said Michael. 'But we are forgetting our manners. Please, sit with us and take some wine. It is apparently the best that insane taverner has to offer.'

Stoate sat at the table next to Bartholomew, and began to enquire about the latest medical theories that were being expounded at Cambridge. Unfortunately, since the plague had killed so many physicians, and the few who were left could earn ten times the amount by practising their trade on the wealthy than they could teaching medical theory to students in a University, Cambridge was not overly endowed with them. Oxford fared little better, although Paris, Salerno and Montpellier were thriving. Stoate said he had studied medicine first in Paris, and later at the University of Bologna.

Sensing that the discussion would soon become unpleasantly spangled with references to grotesque diseases, Alcote slipped away. As he left, Stoate's companions began to laugh, and nudged and jostled the fair-haired woman in a gently teasing way. Alcote glowered furiously, and scuttled from the room as fast as his spindly legs would carry him.

'What are they laughing at?' asked Bartholomew, bemused by their reaction to the fussy scholar.

'Rosella found a pod with nine peas this morning,' said Stoate, as if that explained all.

'So?' asked Bartholomew.

'So, she takes the ninth pea, and places it on the lintel of the door,' said Stoate impatiently. 'The first man over the threshold will be her sweetheart.'

'And Alcote was the first of us to come in,' said Bartholomew, smiling. 'Poor Rosella! Alcote has a morbid dislike of women in any form, but young and pretty ones in particular.'

'Why?' asked Stoate curiously. 'They are among God's finest creations.'

'I have no idea. But if you have any regard for Rosella, you will advise her to shell a few more peas. And speaking of peas, have you tried them cooked in sugar to help those recovering from the sweating sickness?'

Deynman listened to the conversation for a while, but his concentration span was short, and he was soon kicking Horsey under the table to play dice with him. Michael closed his eyes and began to doze, pretending not to notice the illicit gaming in the darkest corner of the tavern and hoping it would keep Horsey from dwelling too much on the death of his friend.

It was not long before the plague became the topic of conversation, and Stoate told Bartholomew how he had cured people with a purge of pear juice mixed with red arsenic, lead powder and henbane. It was not a recipe with which Bartholomew was familiar, nor, after hearing the amounts of arsenic, lead and henbane Stoate used in his concoction, was it one he intended to try. If Stoate's patients had survived both the plague and the remedy, they were possessed of stronger constitutions than the citizens of Cambridge.

But it was good to be able to discuss medicine with someone who was interested. Stoate told him of country cures for chilblains, cramp and nosebleeds, and then went on to describe purges for all occasions.

'Is that what you do most?' asked Bartholomew. 'Prescribe purges?'

'That is what most people summon me for. It is my contention that it is cheaper for physicians to prevent diseases than to cure them. I recommend that everyone should be purged of evil humours once a week, and bled at least three times a year.'

'And you find this helps to keep people in good health?' asked Bartholomew, uncertainly.

Stoate gestured around him. 'Ask my patients. Most are in excellent health. Are yours?'

Michael gave a soft snort that might have been laughter or might have been an innocent noise made while asleep. His eyes remained closed.

'No,' said Bartholomew, looking back at Stoate. 'But then, living in a town is far less healthy than life in the country. There is often not enough to eat, and the water from the river is filthy.'

'What has the water to do with anything? Try some of my purges on these ailing patients of yours and you will notice a difference within a week. And there is nothing quite like bleeding to improve the health, of course.'

'Is there a surgeon in Grundisburgh, then?' asked Bartholomew, disappointed that Stoate was like all the other physicians he had met. Bleeding, to rid the body of the excessive humours that caused imbalances, was seen as the answer to everything – even the plague. In Bartholomew's experience, phlebotomy served to weaken the patient if he were ill, and was a waste of time if he were not.

'Our surgeon died during the pestilence,' said Stoate. 'Do you have a good remedy against lice? We had a spate of them last summer, and even Eltisley professed himself at a loss for a solution.'

'Not really,' said Bartholomew. 'But who bleeds your patients if there is no surgeon?'

'Master Stoate bleeds his patients himself,' said the formidable matron who had apparently been listening to their conversation from her fireside seat. Her eyes, however, were fixed on Deynman's dice. 'He is a most accomplished surgeon, and charges tuppence for a vein to be opened in the foot and threepence for the hand.'

'You practise surgery?' asked Bartholomew, startled.

Stoate looked uncomfortable. 'Well, blood-letting is not exactly surgery, and I only do it if I feel a patient should not make the journey to Ipswich.'

'That is excellent!' exclaimed Bartholomew, delighted. 'Well, not the bleeding, but to meet a physician who is prepared to use surgical means to help his patients. I have performed a number of operations including trepanation, cauterising and suturing wounds, amputations . . .'

'Have you?' asked Stoate doubtfully. 'That is strictly forbidden. The Lateran Council of 1215 says that priests are not allowed to practise cautery.'

'I am not a priest,' said Bartholomew impatiently. 'But what else do you do, besides phlebotomy? Have you tried pulling teeth? It requires more skill than most surgeons believe – if the tooth breaks in the jaw, it can cause infections and even death from poisons in the blood.'

'I have not,' said Stoate with a shudder. 'I have an infallible remedy for extracting teeth without the need for physical effort on my part: powder of earthworms. Just a pinch of this in the hollow of a tooth will make it drop out within days.'

Bartholomew winced. 'What about bone-setting? Do you do that?'

'No,' said Stoate. 'As I said, I do not practise surgery if I can avoid it, and I have not bled anyone for several weeks now. But I did once remove the blue skin that forms over the eyes of the old, so that the person could see again.'

'Really?' asked Bartholomew, fascinated. 'Tell me how you

did it. I have tried that procedure twice, but in both cases the blindness returned within three years.'

'My patient died of a bloody flux about a week later,' said Stoate. 'But I learned two things: the knife must be sharp, and the patient must lie still.'

'Well, that goes without saying,' said Bartholomew, regarding him doubtfully. 'But did you use witch-hazel as a salve afterwards? Or did you use groundsel as Dioscorides recommends?'

'I used sugar water,' came the unexpected reply. Stoate gazed at Bartholomew and suddenly slapped his hand hard on the table, waking Michael, who regarded him in alarm. 'That is it! I knew there was something else!'

'That is what?' asked Michael, irritably.

Stoate looked pleased with himself. 'Ever since I learned of your Franciscan's murder I have been thinking about the person I saw coming out of the church. I knew there was something I should have remembered, but it had slipped to the back of my mind. Talking about surgery to the eyes has suddenly jolted my memory, and I now know exactly what it was that has been bothering me: the person in the long cloak was rubbing his face.'

'You mean as though he had been crying?' asked Bartholomew, not sure that this had been worth waiting for.

'No, rubbing his eyes hard with both fists, as though there was something wrong with them,' said Stoate. 'So, you are probably looking for someone with an eye infection, Doctor Bartholomew. That should narrow down your list of killers!'

CHAPTER 5

B
Y THE TIME STOATE LEFT, BARTHOLOMEW WAS SLEEPY and excused himself to go to bed, knowing it would not be long before he would have to relieve Father William for Unwin's vigil. Eltisley led him to the upper floor, explaining that he and his wife used one room, while the other two were reserved for guests. The chambers were pleasant enough, with mullioned windows, polished wooden floors, and several straw mattresses that were piled with more blankets than even the most chilly of mortals could require during an early-summer night. Wearily, Bartholomew found a bowl of water and began to wash. After a moment he became aware that Eltisley was still in the room, fiddling with one of the windows.

'What are you doing?' Bartholomew asked, wiping his face with a piece of sacking.

'I am tying a piece of twine to the latch on the window so that you can open it without getting out of bed if you become too hot during the night.'

'Why should I need to open it without getting out of bed?' asked Bartholomew warily.

'Because then you would be too cold,' said Eltisley, still tinkering.

'But if I felt the need to open the window because I was hot, I would not be too cold the instant I stepped out of bed,' reasoned Bartholomew. 'Please do not worry. I am quite happy to open a window without the need for a piece of rope.'

'It will only take a moment,' said Eltisley persistently. He gave Bartholomew a superior look. 'I saw that the bottle containing my potion was empty when I came for the dirty dishes. You changed your mind and took it, I expect.'

'It was an interesting colour,' said Bartholomew evasively. 'I have never seen anything quite like it.'

Eltisley gave a happy grin, assuming an implicit compliment. 'I might be persuaded to part with the recipe when you leave, after all. I am not a man who believes in keeping effective remedies to himself. It is not ethical.'

Bartholomew nodded, and turned his attention back to washing.

'I was very sorry to hear about Unwin,' said the taverner, continuing to fiddle with the window. 'Did I tell you that?'

'Yes,' said Bartholomew. 'But thank you anyway.'

'It is a curious thing,' said Eltisley absently, engrossed with his piece of string, 'but I am sure I saw him talking to Sir Robert Grosnold – the bald lord of Otley manor – in the churchyard just after the feast started. Of course, that is not possible. I must be going mad.' He beamed at Bartholomew in a way that made the physician sure he was right.

'You must be mistaken,' said Bartholomew. 'Grosnold rode with us from Wergen Hall, and then set off immediately to return to Otley. He thundered across the village green like a maniac.'

'I saw him,' said Eltisley. 'Worse, he ran me over. Look at my leg.' Unceremoniously, he hauled down his hose to reveal a semicircular bruise that would doubtless match one of the shoes on Grosnold's destrier. 'I will take a purge for it tomorrow.'

'What good will a purge do a bruise?' asked Bartholomew, startled.

'It will take away the evil fluids from the wound and reduce the swelling. Bruises mean an increase of humours in the body, and so vomiting must be induced to balance them again.'

'I see,' said Bartholomew, understanding exactly why many physicians so fervently believed the adage that a little knowledge could be a dangerous thing.

Eltisley beamed at him absently. 'But this business with Grosnold is odd, is it not?'

'Very,' said Bartholomew. 'Are you sure he was not talking to Unwin *before* he trampled you with his horse?'

'Quite sure,' said Eltisley. 'I have been in considerable pain ever since. When I saw Grosnold talking surreptitiously to Unwin a few moments after he trampled me, I considered giving him a piece of my mind. Then I decided I did not want to hang for impudence, so I left it.'

'What do you mean by "talking surreptitiously"?' asked Bartholomew.

'"Surreptitious" means furtive or sly,' said Eltisley. 'I thought you would have known the meaning of that word, Doctor, you being from Cambridge. But we all learn, I suppose.'

'What I meant was what were they doing to make you think they were surreptitious?'

'Well,' said Eltisley, touching a finger to the bridge of his nose. 'Let me see. Grosnold – although it could not have been Grosnold since he had left the village – had Unwin by the arm and was whispering something in his ear.'

'Is there anyone else it could have been?' asked Bartholomew, beginning to feel a little irritated by the man's vagueness. Unwin had been murdered after all, and Eltisley might well have seen the man who had done it. 'Is there someone you might have mistaken for Grosnold?'

Eltisley stopped tampering and gazed out of the window, frowning. 'No,' he said eventually. 'There is only one man I know with a suit of black clothes and a pate that glistens like Grosnold's. But then, as I said, what I saw was not possible, because Grosnold had already gone home. I asked a few of my patrons whether any of them had seen Grosnold after he rode across our green so carelessly, but none of them had. So, I must have been mistaken.'

Bartholomew was perplexed. 'So did you see Grosnold with Unwin or not?'

Eltisley shrugged. 'My eyes told me yes, my mind tells me no.'

'Was he wearing a long cloak?' he asked, thinking of Stoate's observation. 'Or was there anything wrong with his eyes?'

'His eyes?' queried Eltisley, taken aback. 'No, not that I could see. They seemed normal enough – beady, just as usual. And he wore his black cotte and hose – he likes to think he looks like the Prince of Wales in them. Foolish man! The Prince is not bald, forty and pig-ugly! Have you ever seen him? The Prince?'

'Not recently,' said Bartholomew. 'But if the man you saw talking to Unwin was wearing these distinctive clothes, then it must have been Grosnold. There cannot be two people in the area with an outfit like that. Perhaps he came back for something.'

'I suppose he must have done,' said Eltisley, brightening. 'And it is certainly true that no one else that I know of possesses clothes like Grosnold's. Perhaps he forgot something, or realised that he needed to speak to Unwin before he returned to Otley. I am not mad, after all!'

That by no means followed, thought Bartholomew. Could he trust Eltisley's observation, or had the whole scene come from the jumble of nonsense that passed for his brain? He rubbed a hand through his hair, and flopped heavily on one of the straw mattresses. He was so tired, he did not know what to think.

'There,' said Eltisley triumphantly, standing back with his twine in his hand. 'This little invention of mine will work perfectly. Watch.'

He sat on the bed nearest the window, and gave the twine a

gentle tug. Nothing happened. Puzzled, he tried again. The third tug was more savage, and with a screech of ancient metal, the latch plopped out of its frame and dropped to the floor. The window remained closed.

'Mend it tomorrow,' pleaded Bartholomew, sensing the taverner was going to spend half the night with it.

It was not easy persuading Eltisley to leave, but at last Bartholomew was alone. He doused the candle, lay on the crackling mattress, and hauled one of the rough blankets over him. Somewhere, a mouse scurried across the floor-boards, its feet skittering on the shiny surface, and from the tavern below, the muted voices of his companions were raised in some kind of debate. Still thinking about why Grosnold might want to kill Unwin, he fell into a deep sleep, and knew nothing more until he was awoken by Michael shaking his shoulder some hours later. Candle wax splattered on his bed-covers as the monk leaned over him, his bulk casting monstrous shadows on the wall.

'I have no idea what the time is, Matt, but it is long past midnight,' he whispered, trying not to disturb Alcote. He was clutching his stomach, and in the candlelight Bartholomew could see that his face was contorted with pain.

'I suppose you feel ill,' he said unsympathetically.

Michael nodded. 'It must have been the green stuff that was all over the hare I ate. I scraped most of it off, but there must have been enough left to make me sick.'

Bartholomew reached out and touched the monk's face in the darkness. It was hot, but not feverish. 'I ate the vegetables, and I am all right.'

'But you have an unnatural constitution, Matt. I keep telling you that green things are bad for me, but you will not listen. Now I am proven correct. Again.'

'Take this,' said Bartholomew, groping in his bag for the remedy for over-indulgence and indigestion he frequently dispensed to Michael. 'And then go back to sleep.'

'Matthew,' came Alcote's tremulous voice in the darkness. 'I am ill. Help me!'

'Summon Master Eltisley, then,' said Bartholomew, unmoved. 'He can give you some of his goat urine and cloves to drink.'

Alcote retched suddenly, so Bartholomew went to his aid, holding his head while the goat's urine made its reappearance, along with the rest of Alcote's dinner.

'I feel dreadful,' he wept, clutching Bartholomew's hand. He raised fearful eyes to Michael. 'You will have to grant me absolution, for I shall not live to see the light of day. Help me, Matthew!'

'But you have no faith in my medicine,' said Bartholomew, feeling vindictive. 'You said so at dinner, while you were eating the hare that was swimming in grease.'

Alcote retched again, and when he had finished, Bartholomew helped him to lie back with a water-soaked bandage across his forehead.

'We have been poisoned by vegetables,' said Michael, still holding his stomach.

'You have been poisoned by greed, and Roger has been poisoned by Eltisley's foul concoction,' said Bartholomew. 'That will teach him to drink something prepared by a man who does not know what he is doing.'

But it was not a lesson Alcote would remember for long. It was not the first time Bartholomew had been summoned to tend Alcote in the dead of night because he had swallowed some potion that promised miraculous results, and it would probably not be the last. He mixed poppy juice and chalk in a little water, and handed it to the Senior Fellow to drink.

'Thank you,' said Alcote, pathetically grateful with tears glittering in his eyes. 'I shall never take medicines from anyone except you ever again.'

'Until next time,' muttered Bartholomew, who had heard

this before. 'Now rest, and you will feel better in the morning.'

'You should go,' said Michael. 'It feels later than midnight to me. William should know better than to trust you to wake up on time. You sleep the sleep of the dead, even when you are not tired.'

'Go to sleep,' Bartholomew whispered. He pushed Michael on to his back, sorted out the tangle of blankets, and pulled them up under the monk's chin.

He dressed in the darkness, crept out of the bedchamber, tiptoed down stairs that seemed to creak louder the more quietly he tried to walk, and let himself out of the front door. A breeze that smelled of the sea whispered in the trees, and somewhere a dog barked once and then was silent. He glanced up at the sky. The moon was a thin sliver, and the only other light was from the mass of stars that glittered above, dancing in and out of clouds that drifted westward.

He groped his way down the lane, past still, dark cottages. When he stumbled in a pothole, he realised how familiar he was with Cambridge's uneven streets. The raucous call of a nightjar close by made him jump, and he tripped again, wishing he had borrowed a candle to light his way.

Eventually, he arrived at the green and walked across the grass to one of the fords. He leapt across it, landing with a splash in the shallows on the far side, and aimed for the church. It was in darkness, and Bartholomew saw that someone, probably Cynric, had closed all the window shutters. He was raising his hand to the latch when a voice at his elbow almost made him leap out of his skin.

'Easy, boy!' said Cynric softly. 'I just wanted you to know that I am here.'

'I wish you would not do that,' said Bartholomew, clutching his chest. 'Is William inside?'

Cynric nodded. 'He is not pleased that you are late. He

wanted me to fetch you, but I told him you had instructed me not to leave him alone. I think he was rather touched.'

'Touched is a good word for him,' mumbled Bartholomew. 'Are you coming in, or do you want to stay here?'

'I think I will stay outside,' said Cynric. 'I like to see the stars. They remind me of home.'

'Wales?' asked Bartholomew, feeling sympathy for a man who was homesick.

'Cambridge,' said Cynric, sounding surprised. 'It is where I live, boy. And where that Rachel Atkin lives – your brother-in-law's seamstress. Do you think I should wed her?'

It was a question that caught Bartholomew off guard. 'If it will make you both happy,' he said carefully. 'Have you asked her yet?'

'She asked me,' said Cynric. 'I said I would let her know.'

'I hope you sounded a bit more enthusiastic than that. I am no expert with women, as you well know, but you should not regard an offer of marriage in the same way that you would consider some kind of business deal.'

'Why not?' asked Cynric. 'That is what marriage is, is it not? A business deal? Anyway, you should be going inside, or Father William will be after your blood.'

Father William, however, was sleeping. He sat with his back against one of the smooth white pillars, and snored loudly with his mouth open. Bartholomew did not blame him. It had been a long day, Bartholomew had been late in coming to relieve him, and it was always difficult to remain wakeful in a silent church. The physician knelt next to the parish coffin, bent his head and began to recite the offices for the dead.

It was not long before dawn began to break. The sky changed from black to dark blue, then grew steadily paler until the church was filled with a dim silvery light that flooded through the clear glass of the east window. Bartholomew stood stiffly, and went to open the shutters, waking William who looked around him blearily. He gave a sudden yell of terror that made Bartholomew spin round, and Cynric come rushing in from outside.

'I am swathed in a shroud!' the Franciscan howled, struggling to free himself from the sheet that was wrapped round him.

Bartholomew went to his aid. 'You were shivering and there was nothing else to use. I had already put my tabard under your head.'

'But a shroud, Matthew!' cried William aghast, flinging it from him in revulsion and scrambling to his feet. 'It was like waking up in a grave!'

'It is only a sheet,' said Bartholomew, surprised that the friar could be so easily unnerved. 'It will not be a shroud until it is wrapped around Unwin, later today.'

'A woman is due to come and do all that this morning,' said William with a shudder. 'Wash the corpse and put the shroud round it.'

'The woman is here,' came a voice from the back of the church. Bartholomew recognised her as the matronly figure who had been chaperoning the young people the night before.

'Mother Goodman?' asked Bartholomew politely, recalling that Tuddenham had said that the midwife usually took care of the village's dead. 'Can I fetch anything you might need?'

The woman shook her head. 'You are the physician,' she said, looking him up and down appraisingly, and making him feel like some piece of meat at the market. 'Although you do not look like a physician – you are too shabby.'

'That is because he likes to work among the poor,' said Father William. 'He, like me, does not care for fine clothes and possessions. Such things are nothing but vanity.'

'Well, I have no time for physicians, rich or poor,' said

Mother Goodman, pushing past them. 'Nor for pompous friars. So you two stay out of my way, and we will get along very well. Where is the corpse?'

'Unwin's earthly remains are in the coffin, madam,' said William coldly. 'I am going for some breakfast. I would stay to say prime, but I do not think I would be able to concentrate with all your chatter. I will see you later, Matthew.'

While Mother Goodman stripped the bloody habit from Unwin's body and washed him, Bartholomew knelt again and tried to say another requiem. But Father William had been right: it was difficult to concentrate through the sound of heavy breathing and splashing water, not to mention the pithy curses when Unwin's stiffening limbs proved difficult to handle. Finally, Bartholomew gave up, and sat on the chancel steps to watch her.

She was a large woman, whose powerful arms and competent red hands suggested she had performed such duties many times before. Her ample hips swayed as she worked, swinging her rough brown skirts this way and that. She wore a faded scarf around her head with her hair tucked inside it, although a wisp of grey had escaped on one side. Bartholomew supposed she was about fifty, although her skin was remarkably free of wrinkles and blemishes.

'You are the midwife, I understand,' he said. 'Janelle at Burgh mentioned you.'

'So?' she said, pausing in her scrubbing, and giving him a belligerent glower. 'What of it?'

'Nothing,' said Bartholomew, sorry he had spoken. He looked at Unwin's body as Mother Goodman began to wrap it in the shroud. It was pale from a life of studying indoors, and the stomach wound was dark and red. Impatiently, the midwife elbowed Bartholomew out of the way, and he went to sit on the chancel steps again, trying once more to recollect whether any of the celebrating villagers had paid Unwin and his purse particular attention. No matter how hard he thought, he could recall no one who had seemed to be acting suspiciously, even with hindsight.

And what about the people Stoate and Eltisley had seen? Had Grosnold returned unexpectedly to converse with Unwin? But why? With sudden clarity, Bartholomew remembered Unwin and Grosnold talking together at Otley the night before the scholars had arrived in Grundisburgh. Bartholomew had been surprised to see Unwin actually inside the bailey and even more surprised to see him talking to the lord of the manor. And then Unwin had declined to tell him about it.

Bartholomew rubbed a hand through his hair. Was that the answer? Had Grosnold been trying to lure Unwin into some future plot against his neighbour Tuddenham – or even Deblunville – and then killed him when he declined to become involved in a local squabble? Or did their acquaintance stretch back further than a few days? And what of Stoate's mysterious figure, with the heavy cloak and sore eyes? Was he the killer? Bartholomew put his hands over his face and scrubbed at his cheeks. It was some moments before he realised he was being watched.

'If I wanted a consultation with you, how much would you charge?' Mother Goodman demanded, hands on her hips.

'It depends on what was wrong with you,' said Bartholomew. He stood hastily as she marched towards him purposefully, feeling somewhat intimidated.

'I want to increase my milk,' she said unexpectedly. 'It is drying up.'

'You have had no child recently,' said Bartholomew, recovering from his surprise quickly and thinking that she would have had no children for a good number of years. 'Do you want to know a cure so that you can pass it on to one of your patients?'

She regarded him coldly. 'So, you will not tell me?'

'I did not say that,' he said. 'But you should not be dishonest with me, if you want me to help you. What I might recommend for a person of your years and . . . size, might be very different from what I would suggest for a younger, smaller woman.'

She glared at him angrily, her eyes glittering coals of hazel deep inside her puffy face, and he thought she was going to end the conversation there and then. If she did, it was none of his affair, and he was more concerned with thinking about who might have killed Unwin than with dispensing remedies to someone else's patients.

'Very well, then,' she said after a moment. 'She is sixteen summers, and this is her first infant.'

'Is it just a case of no milk?' he asked. 'Is there anything else wrong with her?'

She considered. 'She is always tired, but that is to be expected of a new mother.'

'You can try fennel boiled in barley water,' said Bartholomew. 'Use common fennel, because the wild variety will be too strong. If that does not work, you can give her a small amount of viper's bugloss steeped in milk. For the tiredness tell her to eat beans cooked in sugar, and eggs and cabbage, if she has them.'

'Do you suggest fennel because it is a herb of Saturn?'

'No,' said Bartholomew shortly. 'I suggest fennel because I have had considerable success with it for this complaint in women in the past. And anyway, it is a herb of Mercury, not Saturn.'

'Are you sure? Master Stoate told me it was Saturn.'

'I am quite sure. Master Stoate is mistaken.'

She gave him a sudden grin. 'I am glad to hear it. Master Stoate believes he is never mistaken. Now, how much will this consultation cost me? You have a choice: I will mend that rip in your shirt and sew a new patch on your tabard where it is beginning to fray; you can have a bottle of the wine I make from cabbage stems; or I can read your palm and tell your future.'

'None of that is necessary,' said Bartholomew, thinking the choices were at least an improvement on a ring made from a coffin, 'but if this woman's condition does not improve in two or three days, you should tell her to come to see me. She may require something stronger. Is there a wet-nurse for the child in the meantime?'

'Yes, but she is overly fond of garlic, and I do not consider that healthy for a baby.'

'Why not?' asked Bartholomew, interested. 'Do you think it causes colic?'

'I believe so,' she said. 'But a good cure for colic in babies is ground cumin with a little anise. Have you tried that?'

'No,' said Bartholomew. 'How is it prepared?'

'Equal parts soaked in wine for three days, then left on a board to dry for nine days, then ground into a powder over the fire.'

'I will remember that,' said Bartholomew thoughtfully. 'I have never used cumin for infants, but it is a gentle herb.'

'You are an odd sort of physician,' she said, regarding him curiously. 'Master Stoate never asks me for my cures.'

'Perhaps he has no need, if you can dispense them. But there is a shortage of good midwives in Cambridge. Master Stoate does not know how lucky he is to have one in his village.'

'That is certainly true! I have cured more people than he has, and killed a lot fewer! He practises surgery, you know. He bleeds people, and even stitches wounds on rare occasions.'

Bartholomew also stitched wounds, but, from the disapproving tone of her voice, he did not consider now an opportune time to mention it. He watched as she turned her attention back to Unwin's body, scattering fragrant herbs into the coffin so that their heady scent mingled with the all-pervasive odour of incense and the earthier smell of blood.

'The killer stole his purse, then,' said Mother Goodman,

picking up the stained habit from where she had thrown it. 'Much in it?'

'Nothing of any value to a thief,' said Bartholomew. 'A phial of chrism and a piece of parchment containing some of St Botolph's beard.'

She stared at him. 'A relic? Someone stole a relic?'

Bartholomew nodded. 'Why? Do you know someone who wants one?'

'Not one that has been stolen – it is more likely to bring a curse than a blessing. And anyway, I think poor St Botolph's remains have been treated badly enough in Grundisburgh already.'

'I read about that – some monks stole them from a chapel near here.'

She smiled suddenly. 'I would have expected you to say the monks "rescued" them, or "removed them to a safer place" – that fat Benedictine certainly would say so. But you are right. "Stole" is what those men did with our saint's relics. And now you say someone took his beard from this friar's purse? From here, inside the church?'

'It looks that way,' said Bartholomew. 'And killed poor Unwin to do so.'

She rubbed her chin. 'You might try having a word with Will Norys. He knows his relics like no other man, and is highly respected in the village. He might be able to help you – no one could sell a relic in this area without him knowing about it.'

'Will Norys?'

'He is a pardoner who lives with his uncle, the tanner. You cannot miss their cottage – you can smell that tannery from Burgh. Will Norys often works in Ipswich, because Walter Wauncy is not keen on him selling his pardons and relics in the village.'

'Thank you,' said Bartholomew. 'I will talk to him this morning.'

'Discreetly, though. I do not want him thinking I have been maligning him. You can use your medical training – there are few men who can lie as well as a physician.'

'Is that so? Well, I have met a few midwives, not to mention a good many priests and merchants, who could prove you wrong on that score,' retorted Bartholomew tartly.

She inclined her head to one side. 'I doubt it, but then I have never been to Cambridge. Is it as dangerous as everyone says? Will Norys went there last winter, and he said the students were rioting and setting the town alight every night. He said there were murders at every street corner, and that whores flaunted their wares openly in the Market Square.'

'It has its good points,' said Bartholomew. 'The Colleges have some splendid books. And anyway, it seems to me that Grundisburgh is not exactly a haven of peace: two men have died since we arrived – I *did* see a dead man on the gibbet no matter what Tuddenham says – and all the lords of the manors are at each others' throats.'

'It was very peaceful here until Roland Deblunville came two years ago. He married Pernel, the dowager of Burgh Manor, but he murdered her so that he could rule alone. Now he has married that harlot Janelle for her father's lands at Clopton, and will doubtless slay her in time, too.'

'What evidence is there that Deblunville murdered his first wife?' asked Bartholomew, sure that the merry Deblunville had done nothing of the kind and that the tale was a malicious rumour spread for the sole purpose of fanning the flames of hostility between Grundisburgh and Burgh.

'Evidence!' spat Mother Goodman in disgust. 'This is not a court of law, or one of your University debating chambers! Everyone knows Deblunville killed Pernel, and that is all the evidence we need. Deblunville is the Devil's familiar. He was dead on the gibbet only to appear alive at his castle the next day.'

'Deblunville was not the man on the gibbet. The hanged

man was wearing clothes stolen from him, so either it was a case of mistaken identity and someone thought he was dispatching the hated lord of Burgh Manor, or the fellow was killed for some completely unrelated reason.'

She looked relieved. 'A different man? Then Deblunville did not rise from the grave by diabolical means to torment us all for the rest of our lives?'

Bartholomew shook his head. 'Who told you he did? Tuddenham?'

'The rumour that Deblunville is now a living corpse is all around the village. But then, you see, we were expecting to hear about his death anyway, because he saw—'

'Saw what?' asked Bartholomew when she stopped, lips pursed. 'Dame Eva mentioned Deblunville seeing something, but Tuddenham said it was nonsense.'

'He is afraid to admit the truth,' said Mother Goodman. 'Dame Eva is not, but then her mother was a witch, and so she is familiar with such things.'

'I see,' said Bartholomew, feeling as though the conversation had suddenly left him behind. He knew many villages were steeped in superstitions and myths, but walking dead, witches, peas on lintels and rings made from coffin handles were far beyond anything he had expected to encounter.

'I am not sure if I should tell you any more about it,' she said, regarding him sombrely. 'You seem a pleasant sort of man for a physician, and I have no wish to frighten you.'

'I have been frightened before,' said Bartholomew dryly. 'And I would rather know about whatever it is than be taken unawares by it.'

'It is the white dog,' Mother Goodman announced in a ringing voice. She folded her arms across her substantial bosom, and regarded him expectantly.

'The white dog,' he repeated, looking blankly back at her. 'Does it belong to someone?'

'It is not a domestic animal,' she said, as though he was

stupid. 'It is Padfoot – a ghostly vision that appears to people when they are about to die.'

Bartholomew stared at her, suddenly recalling what the hanged man had whispered with his dying breath: 'Padfoot'. At the time he had not understood, and had even thought he might have misheard. But it made sense now – or at least, it explained what the man had said. He sighed, and wondered how to excuse himself so that he could return to his vigil. Chatting to the village midwife about spectral hounds and cures for colic would not be doing Unwin much good, and Father William would be outraged if he discovered how the physician had spent his time – although, Bartholomew thought wryly, he could always point out that at least *he* had not fallen asleep.

'You do not know the story,' she said, 'or you would not be so indifferent. Padfoot is a big white dog that appears to people before something dreadful happens. Deblunville saw it, and that is why none of us were surprised when we heard he had been hanged up at the gibbet. James Freeman the butcher saw it, too, and two days later he was dead of a cut throat.'

'Tuddenham said that was suicide.'

Mother Goodman shook her head. 'James Freeman had no reason to kill himself. He was newly wed, and he had just inherited his father's business. But Padfoot came to him, and two days later he was discovered in his own slaughterhouse with his neck slashed like one of the pigs he used to dispatch. Poor Dame Eva found him when she went to buy pork, and was lucky that Tobias Eltisley – the landlord of the Half Moon – heard her cries for help. Our priest, Walter Wauncy, said the great pools of blood and the stained knife were the vilest things he had ever seen.'

'Did you lay him out?'

She shook her head. 'His head was almost severed from his body, according to Master Eltisley. I saw his clothes, though, drenched right through with blood. It was a terrible business, and I am glad I did not have to tend his corpse.'

'I thought you would have been used to such sights.'

She looked surprised. 'This is a peaceful village, and we seldom have violent deaths. Because James Freeman's body was so mutilated, Master Eltisley kindly made a special coffin – he likes to make things – and closed it before Freeman's wife could see what had happened to her man. But for all his efforts, it dripped blood all the way from the slaughterhouse to the church.' She shuddered.

'So James Freeman was murdered,' said Bartholomew. 'Someone broke into his slaughterhouse and killed him.'

She gave him a mysterious look. 'It was no earthly hand that took his life: it was a demon's, directed by Padfoot. And we all knew James Freeman was a doomed man from the moment he set eyes on the white dog.'

'Are you sure it was not simple fear, and Freeman took his own life?' asked Bartholomew.

She took a deep breath, offended. 'I can see you place no faith in our stories. Well, that is your prerogative. But James Freeman ended up as dead as every other soul who sets eyes on Padfoot. Alice Quy was another. I did all I could for her, but she went to old Padfoot just the same.'

'She was the woman who died of childbirth fever?' asked Bartholomew.

'That is what Tuddenham told you, was it? Well, physician, how many women have you known to die of childbirth fever when the infant is six months old?'

'She was not bled, was she?' asked Bartholomew. 'That is not always good for people, and can cause them to die unexpectedly.'

'Stoate came nowhere near her, and I do not bleed people. All she took was a potion Master Eltisley made to ease her pain. She could not afford any of Stoate's remedies.'

'A potion of what?' asked Bartholomew suspiciously. 'Eltisley is not a physician or an apothecary. You should not dispense his cures to people, just because they cannot afford to buy real ones. They might do more harm than good.'

'They always work better than anything Stoate prescribes,' said Mother Goodman defensively. 'I take Eltisley's potions myself daily. He is very good – and his tonic made of she-goat urine for the stomach is marvellous. Most of the villagers take it. You must have noticed how healthy we are, compared to others around here.'

Bartholomew had indeed noticed that most people seemed fit and well.

'But we are digressing,' said Mother Goodman. 'Alice Quy died with Padfoot's name on her lips. She said he was in the doorway, waiting to drag her down to hell in his gaping jaws.'

'She must have been delirious,' said Bartholomew. 'People do ramble when they are in the grip of fatal fevers.'

'She died because she saw the white dog,' said Mother Goodman firmly. 'And any man, woman or child in the village will tell you the same.' She peered into his face as he took a sudden sharp breath. 'What is the matter? You have not seen a big white dog, have you?'

'Not me,' said Bartholomew, slightly unsteadily as he recalled with sudden clarity something else that had happened. 'But Unwin did. He said he saw it moving in the woods at the deserted village of Barchester, just before we arrived here.'

A handful of parishioners came to celebrate prime with the cadaverous Walter Wauncy, many of them shooting curious glances at the sheeted figure of Unwin, and at Bartholomew kneeling next to it. Not long after the last of them had left, the latch clanked again and Deynman arrived, bringing with him the white-faced Horsey. Bartholomew was reluctant to leave the grieving student with the body of his friend, but Horsey insisted that he be allowed to perform this final service for Unwin, and Deynman, unusually subdued and attentive to his fellow student, promised not to leave him alone.

Grateful to be away from the hushed atmosphere of death and bereavement, Bartholomew strode across the village green to the Half Moon, intending to join the rest of his colleagues for breakfast. The tavern was occupied only by the surly men, who ate a silent meal of thick oatmeal and watered ale while Eltisley bustled around his domain importantly. The landlord informed Bartholomew that Tuddenham had summoned the other scholars at daybreak to begin work on the advowson. When one of the men favoured Bartholomew with a hostile glower as he accidentally knocked a wooden plate from a table as he passed, causing it to clatter noisily to the floor, he decided to forgo breakfast in the unfriendly atmosphere of the Half Moon, and walk to Wergen Hall instead.

It was a glorious morning, and he enjoyed the stroll through the woods to Tuddenham's manor house, although the day was already warm and the exercise made him hot and sticky. When he arrived he found Alcote sitting at the table in the window, surrounded with deeds and writs, while Michael and William reclined near the hearth, devouring what was probably their second breakfast of the day. Alcote still seemed pale to Bartholomew, although breadcrumbs on his habit suggested that his stomach pains of the night before had not prevented him from enjoying someone's hospitality.

'I should begin an investigation into the murder of Unwin today,' said Michael, wiping his lips on his sleeve and reaching for another piece of bread.

'No,' said Tuddenham sharply. 'I will deal with that. You work on my advowson.'

'Let him investigate, Sir Thomas,' said Alcote. 'I am more

than capable of drafting an advowson by myself, and I would feel safer knowing that he and Bartholomew are hunting down this ruthless killer of poor Unwin.'

'And me,' said William eagerly. 'I will solve this case, too.'

'Lord help us!' muttered Michael. 'With Master Diplomacy dogging our every move, we will never catch the murderer.'

Alcote cleared his throat nervously. 'I would like you to remain with me, William – there are documents that need to be transcribed.' Michael and Bartholomew gazed at him in astonishment – no one willingly spent time in William's company, and his scribing skills were mediocre at best – and the Senior Fellow hastened to explain. 'The truth is that I would feel happier knowing that Michael is putting his skills and experience to good use without hindrance from William. I do not feel safe with a killer roaming unchecked in the village, and I want him caught.'

'Are you suggesting I am not up to the task?' demanded William huffily.

Alcote shook his head. 'Not at all, but you have the physique of a wrestler, and your robes are thick with the filth of poverty; I am more delicate, and my garments indicate that I am a man of some standing. The killer will be more likely to strike at me than you, so it is in my interests to have you here to protect me, while Michael and Matthew look into Unwin's death.'

'But there is no suggestion that Unwin's death was anything other than an isolated incident,' said Tuddenham, peeved. 'You make it sound as though someone plans to dispense with the whole lot of you.'

'I am not interested in the whole lot of us, only in me,' snapped Alcote, brutally honest. 'I am the wealthiest person here, and the one who will be doing most of the work on the advowson. Therefore, I am also the most vulnerable.'

'No one else will die,' said Tuddenham firmly. 'I plan to begin my own investigation this morning with my steward,

Siric. In fact, Siric is already in the village, asking questions and ferreting out information. He will send any promising witnesses to me here, at Wergen Hall, so that I can question them myself.'

'Good,' said Michael. 'But Unwin was a friar, and his death must also be explored by an agent of the Church, like me. You have no problem with me initiating my own enquiries?'

Tuddenham clicked his tongue in annoyance. 'I can assure you, Brother, that is wholly unnecessary. I will have whoever did this dreadful thing behind bars within a couple of days. That I can promise you.'

'I am sure you will,' said Michael in a placatory tone. 'But the chances of success will be greatly improved with two of us working on it.'

'Perhaps,' conceded Tuddenham reluctantly. 'But what about my advowson, not to mention the fact that there is also my will to be written.'

'All that is under control, Sir Thomas,' said Alcote. 'I will be able to work far more quickly on my own anyway, than with the others distracting me with their silly questions and careless mistakes.'

'I do not make mistakes,' said Michael indignantly.

'You do,' said Alcote. 'Writing an advowson is a complex business, and it cannot be rushed. Since this one will give Michaelhouse the living of Grundisburgh church "for ever", it needs to be drafted with care, and with considerable attention to detail. You are too impatient, Brother. Sir Thomas would do better to place me in charge of it, while you go away and do what you are best fitted for – chasing criminals.'

Tuddenham raised his hand to prevent Michael's outraged retort. 'Very well, then. But you will be wasting your time investigating this crime, Brother. I will have the culprit before you know it.'

Leaving Alcote and a resentful William to their deeds and documents, Bartholomew and Michael walked back through the woods toward the village. Bartholomew was concerned that Alcote was prepared to take all the responsibility for the advowson, afraid that he might not be fully recovered from his sickness of the night before.

'There is nothing wrong with him,' said Michael dismissively. 'He is relishing the opportunity to present himself as indispensable and important. You see how he has convinced Tuddenham that *he* is the only man competent to write this advowson.'

'That is fine with me,' said Bartholomew. 'I have no interest in spending days on end working on the thing. But that does not mean to say that I feel comfortable leaving Alcote to do all our work.'

They had not travelled far when they met Dame Eva and Isilia, who had been for a stroll in the sunshine. Dame Eva leaned heavily on Isilia's arm, and inched along at a stately pace that must have been frustrating to a young, healthy woman like Isilia. But Isilia was gently patient, and gave no indication that she would rather be doing something more invigorating. When she saw Bartholomew and Michael, her face broke into a beam of pleasure and the physician felt his heart melt.

'Any news?' asked Dame Eva, her faded blue eyes anxious. 'Has my son found the killer of that poor young friar yet?'

Isilia's smile dimmed when Bartholomew shook his head. 'Thomas has been up since before dawn, talking with Siric about how best to catch the murderer. Do not worry: the vile fiend will not escape him.'

'I am shocked that such wickedness should be perpetrated in the church, so near to where my husband lies buried,' said Dame Eva. 'But you two look tired. You doubtless slept badly last night after the shock of finding your friend dead. I know there is nothing I can say to lessen your distress, but if there is anything we can do to help, you must not hesitate to ask.'

'Thank you,' said Bartholomew, touched by her concern.

'How do you like the Half Moon?' asked Isilia. 'It was my idea you should move. I thought you would be more comfortable in a tavern, than fighting with the servants for places near the fire at Wergen Hall. I told Eltisley to spare no expense to make your stay a pleasant one. Poor Eltisley is rather eccentric, but he means well, and will take his obligations seriously.' She smiled again, and Bartholomew found he liked the way glints of laughter showed in the depths of her green eyes.

'And he has,' said Michael. 'He has been a most generous host.'

'Mother Goodman mentioned that you said Unwin saw a white dog near Barchester,' said Dame Eva, changing the subject. 'Is that true?'

Bartholomew nodded. 'No one else did, but Unwin spotted it moving in the trees.'

Dame Eva and Isilia exchanged a look. 'There,' said the old lady. 'What did I tell you? The poor boy saw Padfoot, and now he lies in his coffin. It was the same with James Freeman and Alice Quy – both saw Padfoot and both were dead within days.'

'But you also said that Deblunville spotted this ghostly hound, yet he is still hale and hearty,' Michael pointed out, determined not to let an inconsistency in their superstitions go unremarked.

'You wait and see,' said Isilia. 'It will not be long before Padfoot comes to claim what is his.'

Seeing he would not prevail against such firmly entrenched ideas, Michael nodded noncommittally, and took Bartholomew's arm to lead him away. He was obliged to tug fairly insistently when the physician indicated that he wanted to linger and speak a little longer to the lovely wife of their benefactor. Isilia declined Bartholomew's offer to escort her back to Wergen Hall, although she did so with some reluctance, clearly considering the prospect of spending some time in the company of intriguing strangers more appealing than walking with her mother-in-law. Eventually, they parted, the ladies to Wergen Hall, and the scholars to the Half Moon, so that Michael could exchange his heavy habit for a lighter one. At the same time, the monk took the opportunity to order some bread and cheese to fortify him for the questioning that lay ahead.

It was pleasantly cool in the Half Moon's upper chamber. The sky was an almost flawless blue, with only a line of pearl-grey clouds low on the horizon marring its perfection, and sunlight streamed into every corner of the room. Bartholomew flung the window – still latchless from the landlord's efforts of the previous night – open as far as it would go, and leaned out to inhale deeply a breeze rich with the scent of flowers and cut grass. Blackbirds sang loudly, one perched on the very highest twig of one of the mighty elms that stood in the churchyard. In the distance, cuckoos called, while on the hills the bleat of lambs was answered by the deeper grumble of ewes. It did not seem like the kind of day that should be spent investigating a murder.

'You believe the stories about these ghosts, don't you?' asked Michael, stuffing bread into his mouth as he waited for Bartholomew to finish mending his spare shirt – torn when the robbers on the Old Road had chased him through the undergrowth – so that he could look reasonably respectable when they went to question the villagers. 'You, a man of science and reason, accept that there is a spectral canine trotting around Suffolk driving people to their deaths?'

'It just seems a coincidence that Unwin saw a white dog that no one else did, and that the hanged man whispered the name "Padfoot" with his dying breath.'

'You have not mentioned this dying word before,' said Michael dubiously. 'Are you sure you heard it correctly?'

Bartholomew nodded. 'It was an odd word, and it stuck in

my mind. I did not mention it before, simply because I did not understand its significance.'

'And what is its significance?'

Bartholomew shrugged. 'That Unwin saw this dog, and that now he is dead.'

'You should not have eaten those vegetables last night, Matt – they are interfering with your powers of reason!'

Bartholomew sighed. 'Perhaps Tuddenham is right, and Unwin was killed just because a drunken reveller wanted to steal his purse. But what if theft were not the motive? What if it were something to do with this dog? We should keep an open mind about these folktales – there may be some grain of truth in them. And, therefore, I think we should talk to the families of the other two people who died after seeing this dog – the butcher and the woman who died of childbirth fever.'

'As you pointed out to me only yesterday, Matt, we have no authority to pry into village affairs. Unwin's death is a different matter – he was a friar, and as such his murder should be investigated by an agent of the Church. But these other deaths are none of our business.'

'But what if Tuddenham is involved in them?'

Michael gave a laugh of disbelief. 'Now you are allowing your imagination to gain the better of your common sense.'

'Then why is he so keen to give Michaelhouse the living of the church? You said yourself that such gifts are usually to atone for a sin. We should discover what this sin is before we accept it.'

'But there is nothing to suggest that this sin – if there is a sin – has anything to do with happenings in the village. Anyway, you heard Tuddenham suggest that the gift was to ensure the health of his unborn child.'

'How do we know he is not lying?'

Michael sighed. 'We do not. But even if he is, it is not for us to deny him an opportunity to make his peace with God by refusing his advowson. Besides, if we do not take it, he will only give it to someone else – he might even approach the Hall of Valence Marie or Corpus Christi, and then where would we be?'

'But it is one thing to accept a gift from a contrite sinner, and wholly different to accept one from a man who offers it while he continues his crimes.'

'Alcote will look into that while he is trawling Tuddenham's personal documents – and you know how meticulous *he* can be. If there is anything untoward written down, he will find it.'

'But things like this are never written down,' said Bartholomew. 'Alcote will find nothing.'

'Then there is no problem,' said Michael. 'But I am sure Unwin's death has nothing to do with Tuddenham's deed. You are trying to complicate a simple situation: Tuddenham is giving us the church because he lost three sons to the Death, and he wants to curry favour with the saints to protect his unborn child; meanwhile, Unwin was the victim of an opportunistic thief. The other two deaths, plus our hanged man, have nothing to do with any of it, and this ghostly dog of yours is rank superstition.'

Bartholomew leaned on the windowsill and rubbed a hand through his hair. Michael was almost certainly right, and he was giving the motive for Unwin's death a significance it did not have. Tuddenham's eagerness to have his advowson completed quickly was probably nothing more sinister than an attempt to secure allies in Michaelhouse before Deblunville took him to the courts over the disputed land near Peche Hall.

He broke the thread on the patch he had just sewn, and began to pull the shirt over his head. 'So, what do we have left? There is the black knight – Grosnold – seen talking "surreptitiously" to Unwin after Grosnold is supposed to have gone home; and we have the cloaked figure seen by

Stoate leaving the church just before Horsey found Unwin dead. Either one of those two might have killed him.'

'I cannot see why Grosnold would want to kill his neighbour's new priest,' said Michael doubtfully. 'He seems to be one of the few people Tuddenham likes.'

'Nevertheless, our landlord saw him with Unwin shortly before Unwin died,' said Bartholomew. 'If we can believe a word Eltisley says, that is.'

Michael agreed. 'We might be allowing Eltisley to mislead us with his story. Whilst I do not think he is lying, I also do not know that he is telling the truth. If you spend too much time in a different reality from everyone else, the distinction between truth and falsehood eventually blurs.'

'I suppose we should bear his story in mind, though,' said Bartholomew. 'Along with the fact that Unwin and Grosnold met in Otley, and Unwin refused to tell me what they had discussed together. We should also talk to Will Norys, the pardoner. Mother Goodman tells me that he deals with relics, and he may have heard something about the one that was stolen from Unwin.'

'A pardoner?' asked Michael, sitting upright, good humour gone. 'Pardoners are a loathsome breed of vipers who prey on the vulnerability and fears of the poor and foolish; rancid excuses for men who should not be allowed to taint the lives of honest folk. Evil, sinful agents of the Devil . . .'

'You do not like them, then?' remarked Bartholomew, who knew very well Michael did not.

The monk glared at him. 'They are carrion who ply their repulsive trade—'

'I take your point,' said Bartholomew, raising his hand to stem the flow of invective. 'Perhaps I should visit Norys alone, in view of your feelings. I would not like there to be another murder.'

'Do not worry,' said Michael disdainfully. 'I would not sully my innocent hands with the black blood of a pardoner.' He mused. 'So, we have the pardoner to question, and we need to find out whether Grosnold returned to the village after we all saw him leave.'

Bartholomew nodded. 'And then, in the interests of thoroughness, we will talk to the families of the two dead villagers, just to prove your contention that they are unrelated to Unwin's murder.'

Michael sighed gustily. 'You are in one of your stubborn moods, I see. Well, whoever killed Unwin – which was done with the sole intention of stealing the purse – is probably stupid enough to try to sell the relic it contained. We will catch him easily. And that will be the end of the matter.'

Bartholomew remained unconvinced. 'Why risk eternal damnation by killing a friar in a church, when anyone looking at Unwin would see he is not wealthy: his robe is threadbare, one of his sandals is broken, and he is a mendicant. Why not aim for Alcote, wearing that big golden cross? Or why not me, carrying a bag that could contain all sorts of valuables?'

'Probably because neither of you were alone yesterday. Or, as you have already suggested, perhaps Unwin caught the culprit doing something he should not have been doing, and was killed to ensure his silence. His purse was then stolen because it was there.' He stood and opened the door. 'Did I mention that Tuddenham has asked us to organise a debate for the entertainment and edification of the Grundisburgh villagers?'

'I am sure they will be thrilled by that prospect,' said Bartholomew dryly.

'Father William thinks it an excellent idea – far better than fairs and feasts.'

'He would,' muttered Bartholomew.

'I managed to persuade Tuddenham that Alcote taking part in the debate would interfere with the writing of the advowson,' said Michael, sounding pleased with himself. 'You know what a bore he can be at debates with his flawed logic, and his "anyone-who-does-not-agree-with-me-is-stupid" reasoning. The villagers will enjoy the occasion far more if Alcote does not take part. But we should not be standing here chatting: we have a murderer to catch.'

But it was not as easy to catch a murderer as Michael had predicted. While he asked the villagers they met about the person Stoate had seen leaving the church, Bartholomew enquired whether anyone had seen Grosnold after he had made his dramatic exit across the green on his destrier. Neither line of enquiry met with much positive response. Most of the villagers tried to be helpful, but none had anything to say that was of any import. A few seemed nervous or sullen, but Bartholomew could not blame them for being wary of any involvement in an enquiry regarding the death of a priest.

The investigation took another downward turn when William tracked them down and proudly placed his powers of detection at their disposal. It did not take a genius to deduce that Alcote had regretted keeping William near him for protection – even a murderer at large, apparently, was preferable to the friar's dour company.

Their spirits sank further still when William told them that Alcote had found some of Tuddenham's documents to be so old and faded that it was not possible to decipher them properly. Since the advowson needed to be based on accurate information if it were to last, Tuddenham had dispatched his priest, Wauncy, to Ipswich to acquire copies. Bartholomew groaned, anticipating that Alcote's exactitude would cost them days, and they would be later than ever in returning to Cambridge. William, however, assured them that any delay caused by Wauncy's trip was unlikely to be serious: Wauncy would not linger while there were pennies to be earned from saying masses for Grundisburgh's dead, and the facts to be checked against the newer texts were relatively minor.

'I suppose you can come with us when we question this

pardoner,' said Michael to William reluctantly. 'I do not mind you exercising your nasty inquisitional skills on him.'

'Will Norys?' asked the villager whom Michael had just finished questioning. 'He works in Ipswich on Tuesdays. You will have to catch him tomorrow.'

'Damn!' muttered Michael, who had evidently been looking forward to venting some of his frustration and spleen on a man whose trade he loathed.

And so, with William at their heels, they continued with their questions, each time gaining the same response: no one had seen anything amiss, and everyone was appalled by the brutal death of the man who was to have been their parish priest. Everyone, however, had heard that Unwin had set eyes on the spectre of Padfoot, and so few professed themselves surprised by the young friar's demise, horrified though they were by the manner of it.

The scholars returned to the Half Moon that evening tired and dispirited. As he undressed for bed, questions tumbled around in Bartholomew's exhausted mind. Who would want to kill Unwin? Was the culprit Grosnold, seen talking to him 'surreptitiously' by Eltisley after the feast and by Bartholomew in the castle bailey at Otley? Or was it the mysterious figure seen running from the church by Stoate the physician? What might the pardoner know about a relic that might have been offered for sale in the last day or so? And what of the white dog, which had so many of the villagers terrified out of their wits?

ChAPTER 6

BEFORE DAYBREAK THE FOLLOWING MORNING, BARTH-
olomew and Michael were waiting on the path
that led from the village to the fields, hoping to
speak to the people who were away from the village each
day from dawn to dusk working the land. As the sky began
to lighten, men, women and even children trudged wearily
towards them, hoes and spades over their shoulders, their
footsteps slow and unwilling. Although all seemed well-fed
and healthy enough, it was a hard and dull life, and most
were delighted to stop and talk to the Michaelhouse scholars, to break the monotony of toiling among Tuddenham's
ripening crops.

Many seemed to be exhausted before they even started,
and yawned and stretched as they answered Michael's patient
questions. Bartholomew wondered whether the celebrations
for the Pentecost Fair had extended longer than Tuddenham
knew.

No one had anything of value to add regarding Unwin's
death. Most had spotted him at the Fair – they had been
interested to see him because he was to have been their
priest – but none had noticed him enter the church, or
observed him speaking to anyone in particular before he
died. They seemed genuinely appalled that a friar had been
murdered in their village, but all declared that it was only to
be expected once Unwin had set eyes on Padfoot. Michael
tried in vain to convince them that Unwin had seen only a
stray dog, but, although they listened politely, it was obvious
they did not concur.

By noon, Michael and Bartholomew had spoken to dozens of people, but had learned nothing. Disgusted, Michael led the way back to Grundisburgh to interview the pardoner, leaving the neat strips of yellow and their dusty guardians behind. The village was peaceful. Those not in the fields were tending the sheep on the hills or minding the cows that grazed on the common land near the church. Two children laughed as they shepherded a flock of white geese along The Street, and somewhere a baby cried as a mother tried to sing it to sleep. Smoke seeped through the roofs of one or two huts where those too old or too ill to work had been left to do the cooking, but most homes were still and silent, and would be so until their owners returned after sunset that day.

As they passed the Dog tavern they saw Hamon inside, drinking deeply from a huge jug. He spotted them through the window and beckoned them over, wiping his lips on his sleeve as he set the empty vessel on the table.

'I spoke with the Sheriff's deputy this morning,' he said without preamble. 'He said he was happy that my uncle is doing all in his power to trace Unwin's killer, and has placed the matter officially in his hands.'

'You mean the deputy has been and gone?' asked Michael in horror. 'He did not even bother to pay his respects to me – the Bishop's agent and his representative in canon law?'

'You only represent the Bishop of Ely. This is the See of the Bishop of Norwich so, as far as the Sheriff is concerned, you have no authority here. We do not think that, of course,' Hamon added quickly, when he saw the monk's face darken.

Bartholomew was disgusted. 'So the Sheriff does not care that a priest has been murdered in his shire?'

Hamon shrugged. 'He is a busy man, and is more concerned with catching the outlaws who operate along the Old Road, than in wasting valuable time in duplicating the work my uncle is doing.'

'Investigating the murder of a priest is a waste of no one's time,' snapped Michael. He sat next to Hamon. 'This has made me quite weak at the knees. Landlord! Bring me some wine. And perhaps also a chicken, if you have one to hand.'

Hamon grinned, openly amused by Michael's transparent greed, and then stood. 'I must go. Since the Death, the village has been desperately short of labourers, and I have been forced to hire those sullen men who are staying at the Half Moon. If I do not supervise them constantly, they do not work.'

'They sound like my students,' muttered Michael. He nodded with approval as the food arrived, and Bartholomew sat next to him, tired after the long, fruitless morning.

'Damn that Sheriff!' said Michael, as he tore a leg from a chicken. 'Dick Tulyet would never delegate the murder of a friar to some local landowner. It is not right!'

'I do not like it,' said Bartholomew. 'Tuddenham is now under considerable obligation to solve Unwin's murder. I hope he does not manipulate the truth, and end up with a scapegoat rather than the real culprit.'

Michael sighed. 'You are far too suspicious and untrusting these days. You were not like this five years ago. Even I accept that people occasionally tell the truth and have motives that are honourable. But we should hurry. I want to catch that pardoner before he slinks off to ply his foul trade in Ipswich again.'

On their way to Norys's house, Bartholomew and Michael passed the latrine, where Eltisley the landlord was engaged in something that entailed a good deal of muttering and the frenzied use of heavy tools. The latrine was a splendid affair – as such structures went – and Eltisley had spent some time over dinner the previous evening explaining how he had built it, announcing proudly that it served most of the village. It comprised a low shed built over a trench that, as far as Bartholomew could tell, then drained straight through the soil into the river at precisely the point where most people collected their drinking water. It had three stalls, each with a separate door to ensure privacy – a feature seldom seen outside monasteries or palaces.

Eltisley had a hefty awl in his hand, and was busily hacking a hole the size of a plum in one of the doors, muttering to himself as he did so.

'What is he doing?' asked Michael curiously, pausing to look.

'Do not ask,' said Bartholomew, taking his arm and trying to walk past the landlord without becoming engaged in a lengthy conversation. 'As I have already told you, I do not think Eltisley is quite in control of his faculties. And that is my professional medical opinion.'

'He is probably going to sit there and look for that ghostly dog of yours through the hole he is making,' said Michael with an unpleasant snigger.

'What do you think of this?' called Eltisley, just as Bartholomew thought they had escaped. 'Come and see.'

'Oh, Lord!' groaned Bartholomew. 'Now we shall be here all day listening to some peculiar theory about latrine architecture.'

'You do not like him very much, do you?' said Michael, as they walked towards Eltisley.

'I do not like him at all,' said Bartholomew. 'He is dangerous. He told me last night he has a cure for palsies that involves drowning a patient, and then reviving him. He is planning to try it on some poor child in Otley. I told Stoate about it, and hope to God he manages to intervene in time.'

'No physician likes a patient who knows more medicine than he does,' observed Michael complacently, beaming at the landlord as they reached the latrines.

Bartholomew ignored him, and looked to where Eltisley was gesturing with barely concealed excitement. For some reason he had chopped holes in each of the three doors, and was waving some kind of device at them with evident pride.

'It is a latch I have designed myself,' he said enthusiastically. 'It will mean that the door can be locked from the inside and, as the bar drops, its weight will turn a mechanism so that the metal facing the outside will turn to this part that has been painted red.'

'Ingenious,' said Michael, bemused. 'But what is it for? If you are inside operating the lock, you will not be able to see whether the metal outside is red or not.'

'It is to warn people outside that the stall is temporarily unavailable,' said Eltisley primly. 'Then no one will be in the terrible position of being inside, while someone on the outside is frantically pulling on the handle to get in.'

'Well, that is a relief,' said Michael, struggling to keep a straight face. 'I shall rest easier in my bed knowing that.'

'The only problem is that I cannot get the device to stay in the doors without falling out,' said Eltisley, scratching his head. 'So, I suppose I will have to rethink the design.'

He began to walk away, taking his mechanism with him.

'All is not lost,' Bartholomew called to his retreating back. 'No one will need to rattle the handles now that you have placed these convenient holes in the doors – we can just look through them and immediately see whether someone is inside or not. No one will ever be embarrassed by unwanted rattling again.'

Michael roared with laughter, leaving Eltisley looking from his device to the doors in some confusion. Bartholomew shook his head in disgust.

'See what I mean? He has damaged three perfectly good doors in order to try out some unworkable mechanism, thus leaving everything in a worse state than it was in before. I am surprised that latrine is still standing, given that he built it.'

'Ah, but he did not,' said Michael. 'I admit I was impressed when I first saw it, and I mentioned it to Tuddenham. Apparently, Wauncy designed it, Hamon supervised the building of it, and all Eltisley did was to select the site.'

'So that explains why it drains into the river just where the people collect their drinking water,' said Bartholomew. 'The man is a liability.'

'It is unlike you to take such an irrational dislike to someone,' said Michael, laughing at the physician's vehemence. 'Poor Eltisley! He is not that bad.'

'Here he comes again!' hissed Bartholomew in alarm, gripping Michael's arm as the landlord stopped, turned and began to walk back towards them. 'Quick, Michael, run!'

He took the monk's arm and hauled him away before the eccentric landlord could catch them, Michael gasping and puffing as laughter made it difficult for him to move at the pace Bartholomew was forcing. Fortunately, it was not far to the small wattle-and-daub house with the reed roof that belonged to the tanner. He sat in his garden with a workbench between his knees, scraping at a hide with a piece of pumice stone.

The smell from his workshop was overpowering, just as Mother Goodman had warned – a combination of the urine and polish used to tan the leather, and a thick stench of rotting as newly prepared pelts were stretched to dry in the sun. He looked up as they approached, and gave a grin. Bartholomew was startled to see the Tuddenham teeth – long, yellow and not very functional. Some lord of the manor, perhaps even Sir Thomas himself, although he would have been very young, had evidently been active among the village maidens.

'New soles?' asked the tanner hopefully. 'Broken straps? Uncomfortable saddle that needs softening?'

'All saddles are uncomfortable,' said Bartholomew. 'But we came to speak to your nephew, Will Norys. Is he in?'

The tanner looked disappointed. 'He is preparing himself

for Ipswich market. Walter Wauncy has forbidden him to sell his pardons here, so he travels to the city to work most days.'

'He is leaving rather late, is he not?' asked Michael. 'The market will be almost over by the time he arrives.'

The tanner grinned. 'He came home very late last night.' He tapped the side of his nose and winked conspiratorially. 'He was enjoying the company of young Mistress Freeman.'

'Can we go in?' asked Michael, pushing open the garden gate and making his way to the door of the house. He was inside before the startled tanner had nodded his assent. Bartholomew followed quickly, afraid that Michael might lose his temper at the mere sight of a man who dealt in the trade that Michael despised with all his heart.

The tanner's cottage was dark, and smelled strongly of cats. The window shutters appeared to have been painted closed, so it was difficult to see. After a moment, Bartholomew's eyes grew used to the gloom and he made out a sturdy table standing on one side of the room, and two straw mattresses on the other. The beds were heaped with blankets, and both were alive with cats. There were also cats on the table and up in the rafters, while more rubbed themselves round his legs and tripped him as he followed Michael inside.

'Perhaps *this* is what your white dog wants,' the monk muttered. 'It is a hound's paradise in here.' He sneezed three times in quick succession.

'A sign of good luck, Brother,' came a sibilant voice from a dark corner.

'I beg your pardon?' demanded Michael nasally.

'To sneeze three times is a sign of good luck,' said the voice. 'It means someone will give you a present. Of course, a cat sneezing three times means that its owner will soon have an ague.'

'There is a new theory for your treatise on fevers, Matt,' said Michael, dabbing at his nose with a small piece of linen.

He peered into the room. 'Will Norys? Come out, where I can see you.'

'Have you come for a pardon?' A small figure emerged from what Bartholomew had assumed was just another pile of cats.

'We most certainly have not,' said Michael indignantly. 'I can do all the pardoning I need myself, thank you very much.'

'Of course, Brother,' hissed the pardoner. 'If it is new leather you want, my uncle is outside.'

Michael sneezed twice, but Norys said nothing – perhaps two sneezes was not a good omen.

'Perhaps we should stand outside,' said Bartholomew after Michael's sixth sneeze. Norys shrugged, and followed them into the garden. He had a round face and vivid green eyes. Unlike his uncle, he had tiny, rather pointed teeth, which he had a habit of running his tongue over in a furtive flicking movement. Bartholomew was sure he was not the first person to note the similarity between Norys and his feline friends.

'Do you sell relics, by any chance?' asked Michael, dabbing his nose fastidiously with his linen. 'Only we would like to purchase a souvenir from our visit to Suffolk for the Master of our College, and I thought something of St Botolph's might be suitable.'

'I do have some relics,' said Norys, moving towards the monk as he sensed a sale, 'but nothing from St Botolph. He is popular around here, given his history. I can do you a fingernail of St Cuthbert, and I have a piece of the bowl in which Pontius Pilate washed his hands.'

'Really?' asked Bartholomew, puzzled. 'Why would anyone want to buy something belonging to Pontius Pilate? He was scarcely on the side of the good and the just.'

'People will buy just about anything these days,' said Norys confidentially. 'I heard of a man in Norwich who paid ten marks for a rib-bone of the whale that ate Elijah.'

'But it was Job who was swallowed by a whale,' said Bartholomew.

'Precisely,' said Norys. 'But, to go back to your original question, it is not easy to come by relics of St Botolph. I have heard of none in these parts for many years. You might do better asking the monks at St Edmundsbury. The Benedictines there are not averse to raiding his hair and teeth on occasion. No offence, Brother.'

'You have not heard of a few hairs of his beard being available in Grundisburgh recently, then?' asked Michael casually.

Norys shook his head. 'But I can ask in Ipswich for you today, although I do not hold out much hope. And, if I am successful, it will be expensive.' Pointedly he eyed the wooden cross, which Michael prudently wore in the place of his silver one lest someone decided to kill him for it.

'Try anyway,' said Michael icily, offended that the pardoner should think he was impoverished. 'We are staying at the Half Moon.'

'Are you?' asked Norys, surprised. 'You would be better at the Dog. The food is nicer and the landlord is sane. A word of advice: keep your windows open at night, so you will be able to escape if Eltisley sets the place on fire with one of his experiments. It would not be the first time, and his patrons' luck is bound to run out sooner or later – although I might have a charm I could sell that would protect you against that sort of mishap.'

Bartholomew turned away to hide his amusement, while Michael looked suitably outraged that a man of God should be offered the opportunity to buy such an unashamedly pagan object.

'No, thank you,' said the monk stiffly. 'Were you at the festivities on the green recently?'

'Oh, yes,' said Norys. 'I would never miss the Pentecost Fair.'

'I do not suppose you own such a thing as a long dark cloak, do you?' asked Michael, while he shoved his piece of linen back in his scrip.

'Of course I do, Brother. All pardoners wear long dark cloaks. It is part of our traditional costume, so that people recognise us for what we are.'

'Unfortunately, most people do not,' said Michael. 'So, tell me, Master Norys, what it is about this Pentecost Fair that you enjoy, specifically. The food provided by Tuddenham? The drink? The people? Dressing in your finery? Sitting in the church when there is no one else there?'

Norys looked bemused. 'I am not robust enough to join Tuddenham's food fight, so I usually bring something from home. Most respectable villagers do, and only the rabble attempt to partake of Tuddenham's provisions. I saw you try, though, Brother. Very admirable. Were you successful?'

'Moderately,' said Michael. 'But what did you do at the Fair, other than eat your own food?'

'I spent time with Mistress Freeman. Her husband died recently – he had his throat slit a week ago – and she needs company. In the evening, we took a walk around the churchyard.'

'That is a curious place for a stroll,' pounced Michael. 'The church is scarcely a great distance from the Fair and it is an odd choice of location to inflict on a recent widow. What did you do: dance on Freeman's grave?'

Norys's face hardened. 'What are you implying? That I killed the priest in the church? I can assure you, I had nothing to do with that vile crime. Anyway, because James Freeman was deemed a suicide by Wauncy, he was not buried in the churchyard – we walked nowhere near his grave.'

'And what *do* you know about Unwin's death?' asked Michael with a predatory smile.

'There is not a man, woman or child in the village who does not know every detail about that, and has done since the crime was first discovered,' said Norys. 'This is the country, Brother; things do not stay secret for long.'

'Really,' hissed Michael. 'In that case, Master Norys, perhaps you will be so kind as to tell me who committed so foul a crime against a man of God? If your village is so terrible at keeping secrets, then who killed Unwin?'

'If I knew, I would tell you,' said Norys, his eyes glittering with anger, 'despite your offensive manner. The whole village was shocked by the murder, and we feel it as a personal loss – he was to have been our priest, you know. But I can tell you two things. First, I am sure you will find it was no common villager who killed the priest – you should look elsewhere for your culprit.'

'I suppose you are thinking of Roland Deblunville?' said Michael sarcastically. 'Well, he is newly wed, and I am sure he had other things on his mind that night than killing priests.'

'Then you do not know him,' snapped Norys. 'Ask him where he was when Unwin died. I wager you St Botolph's teeth it was not in his wedding bed. And you might do well also to look to the other manors near here. Tuddenham may give you the impression he is on good terms with his neighbours, Bardolf and Grosnold, but they might well tell you a different story. Either one of them might dispatch the priest provided by his powerful new Oxford friends—'

'Cambridge friends,' interposed Michael. 'We do not mention that other place.'

'. . . just to prove to him that he is not untouchable. And the second thing I can tell you is that while I was in the graveyard I saw someone leave the church in a great hurry. Mistress Freeman and I thought nothing of it at the time, but with hindsight, I see it might have been the killer.'

'It might,' said Bartholomew, glancing at Michael to warn him to silence. Norys was trying to be co-operative, but Bartholomew sensed he would not tolerate much more of Michael's rudeness. The fact that Michael did not like pardoners was no reason to lose what might prove to be a valuable witness to the murder of their colleague. 'What did he look like? Did you recognise him?'

'We just saw him run, zigzagging through the graves and jumping over the wall behind the church, to the fields beyond.'

'Was it a man or a woman?' asked Bartholomew. 'You keep saying "him".'

Norys frowned. 'I assumed the killer would be a man. There is nothing to say it was not a woman, though: it could have been either. The only other thing I can remember is that he was wearing new leather shoes with silver buckles, and a leather belt with silver bosses.'

'How can you remember a belt and shoes when you do not even know what sex the person was?' demanded Michael, exasperated. 'This is ridiculous! How can you expect us to believe all this?'

'I do not care whether you do or not,' said Norys coldly. 'But before I became a pardoner, my uncle was training me to be a tanner, like him. I happen to know a great deal about leather, and I nearly always notice shoes and belts and suchlike. For example, I only had a glance, but I could tell you exactly what your saddles were like from when you first rode into Grundisburgh.'

'This belt,' said Bartholomew, feeling in his bag for the stud he had found after the body of the hanged man had disappeared from Bond's Corner. 'Were the silver decorations like this?'

He handed Norys the boss, and the pardoner inspected it minutely, spitting on it and scrubbing it on his sleeve to see it better. In the end, he handed it back with a shrug. 'It might be. It would be about the right size, but I cannot be certain because he – or she – was too far away. The same goes for the buckles on the shoes, although they were clearly too small for him – his feet did not fit in them, and they slopped.'

'I do not suppose you noticed whether this person was wearing a blue doublet sewn with silver thread, and whether he carried an ornate dagger, did you?' asked Michael heavily, watching Bartholomew put the stud back inside his bag.

Norys shook his head. 'Whoever it was wore a short cloak that hid his upper clothes – and before you ask, I saw the belt because the cloak caught on one of the trees, and I saw the studs sparkle in the sun as this person tried to free it.' He rubbed his chin. 'I almost went to help, but he wrenched free when he saw me watching. It was just as well I did not offer to assist him, or I might have gone the same way as the priest.'

'Yes, that was lucky,' said Michael nastily. 'So, it looks as if the person you saw could well have been the killer – running in such haste from the church that he became entangled on a branch. Very convenient!'

'What are you insinuating?' demanded Norys.

'He means no offence . . .' began Bartholomew.

'Yes, I do,' interrupted Michael. He pushed his face close to that of the pardoner. 'I do not like men who prey on the weaknesses of others, and I find your occupation odious in the extreme. Someone killed my colleague and, as far as I am concerned, a man like you might well be the culprit.'

Norys's eyes widened, but he did not flinch at Michael's menacing hiss. 'You have no evidence to connect me to that. I was with Mistress Freeman when Unwin was killed. Ask her!'

'Oh?' asked Michael smoothly. 'And when was Unwin killed precisely?'

'Just after the feast,' replied Norys. 'The whole village knows that, so do not think my knowing it proves anything.'

'Thank you for your help, Master Norys,' said Bartholomew,

tugging at Michael's habit to try to make him leave before he irreparably damaged the chances of prising further information from the pardoner in the future. 'We appreciate your help.'

'We most certainly do,' said Michael, finally allowing Bartholomew to pull him away from his confrontation.

'I was with Mistress Freeman all afternoon,' Norys repeated firmly. 'Just ask her.'

'Oh, we will,' said Michael threateningly.

'Come on,' said Bartholomew, dragging the monk out of the garden past the tanner, who watched in confusion. 'That is enough, Brother!'

'We will be back to see you again, Master Pardoner,' Michael yelled as Bartholomew opened the gate. 'Besides being a trusted ally of the Bishop of Ely, I am an agent of the Bishop of Norwich in whose see you live, so do not even think of angering him by absconding to Ipswich.'

'You are not an agent of the Bishop of Norwich,' said Bartholomew under his breath. He shot the monk an uncertain look. 'Are you?'

'So, just watch your step!' Michael howled as Bartholomew bundled him out of the gate. The physician shoved the monk away with both hands, then glanced back at the pardoner, concerned that Michael's outburst might have given an innocent man cause to complain to Tuddenham. He did not want Michaelhouse's grand deputation sent back to Cambridge in disgrace because Michael was unable to keep his temper under control while in the presence of pardoners. It was not the first time Bartholomew had been forced to rescue one of them from the monk's irrational fury.

'Thank you,' he shouted politely to Norys. 'You have been very helpful.'

'My pleasure,' called Norys with a pleasant smile, apparently oblivious to Michael's spitting hatred. 'And I will see what I can do about a relic of St Botolph for you by next week.'

'We must consider this debate tonight,' said Father William the following morning as he, Michael and Bartholomew sat in the Half Moon. 'We must put on our best performance.'

Bartholomew sighed heavily, reluctant to indulge Tuddenham in his whim when he knew the villagers would not be in the slightest bit interested in listening to an academic debate of the kind held daily in the Universities. Alcote had been keen to take part, but Tuddenham had taken very seriously Michael's suggestion that this might delay the completion of the advowson, and the fussy scholar was virtually a prisoner in Wergen Hall, only allowed out when it was so late that everyone else had gone to bed.

Wauncy had returned from Ipswich the day before with copies of the documents Alcote had said he needed, but it had not taken Bartholomew long to sort through them and see that they were mostly irrelevant. Alcote did not seem overly surprised, leaving Bartholomew to wonder whether he had dispatched Wauncy to Ipswich and suggested that Bartholomew and Michael investigate Unwin's death purely so that he could work on the advowson alone. If that were true, then Bartholomew suspected Alcote's motives had nothing to do with finding Unwin's killer, and a good deal to do with what he could gain personally from rummaging unsupervised through Tuddenham's business transactions.

The previous evening, Alcote had become even more smug and self-important than usual – a remarkable feat in itself – and Bartholomew had felt his suspicions were justified. In the darkness of the bedchamber, the Senior Fellow had talked deep into the night about how only a man of his intellectual calibre could unravel the confused chaos of Tuddenham's personal affairs, and the physician had been relieved to escape to take his turn at the vigil for Unwin in the church.

'Right then,' said Michael rubbing his hands enthusiastically and beaming at Bartholomew and William. 'I shall preside over the debate, and you two can present the opposing arguments. The question we shall consider will be "Let us enquire whether the Earth rotates".'

Bartholomew groaned. 'Not again! We have debated that at least six times this year already. What about something more interesting, such as whether the cosmos is created of concentric spheres as Aristotle suggests in his *Physica* and *De Caelo*, or eccentric and epicyclic ones such as are described in Ptolemy's *Almagest*?'

Michael and William exchanged weary looks. 'This is supposed to be an entertaining and edifying experience for all concerned, Matt, not something to be endured,' said Michael. 'Hearing you tie everyone else up in logical knots over issues of geometry that the rest of us never knew existed is not most people's idea of fun.'

'And especially not mine,' growled William. 'We should use this occasion to enlighten the audience, and should therefore consider a religious question. What about "Let us enquire whether God created the heavens or the Earth first"?'

'How about "Let us enquire whether God is able to create more than one world"?' asked Bartholomew innocently, knowing it would send the Franciscan into a frenzy of moral outrage. He was not mistaken.

'That is a heretical notion, Matthew! Article 35 of the Condemnation of 1277 sought to eradicate discussion of such vile notions as the limitations of God's power.'

'You mean Article 34, and it was nullified thirty years ago,' corrected Bartholomew. 'It is no longer considered heresy. Article 35, of course, says that God cannot have created man from nothing. We could debate that if you prefer, Father? Either would make for a lively discussion.'

'It might be a little too lively,' said Michael hastily, intervening before the affronted friar put to use on his friend some of the skills he had learned with the Inquisition. 'We do not want the good people of Grundisburgh thinking University scholars are a crowd of belligerent fanatics.'

'Why not?' muttered Bartholomew. 'It is not so far from the truth.'

'I am the presiding master, and I will decide what we will discuss,' said Michael haughtily. 'And I have decided we will debate the issue of whether the Earth rotates.'

'I should be the presiding master,' said William, turning on him. 'I am more senior than you.'

'You are better at arguing a case than at mediating and summing up,' said Michael soothingly. 'We should use our skills to their best advantage, so that we can impress the audience with our dazzling logic and verbal acrobatics.'

'Are you sure this is a good idea?' asked Bartholomew uncertainly. 'I think the villagers would rather spend the night in a tavern, or watch Cynric give a display of archery.'

'What people want is not always what is best for their souls,' said William in a superior manner. 'They will learn a great deal from hearing our intellectual sparring.'

'All they will learn is that they would have enjoyed themselves better elsewhere,' said Bartholomew. 'They will be bored to tears.'

'Father William can argue that the Earth does not rotate, and you can argue that it does,' said Michael, ignoring the physician's grumbling.

'Why do I always have to argue the absurd positions?' protested Bartholomew. 'Of course the Earth does not rotate!'

'Consider the story of Joshua,' said Michael. 'God made the sun and the moon stand still at the battle of Gibeon, so that the Amorites could be defeated. But it would have been a lot easier to halt the Earth than to halt every other celestial body in the sky, and so it must be concluded that it was the rotating Earth God stopped in order to lengthen the day of the battle, not the heavens.'

'It is easier to jump off the church tower than to walk down the stairs,' said Bartholomew. 'But easier does not mean better. And anyway, it says God ordered the sun and the moon to stand still, not the Earth. If He had ordered the Earth to stop rotating, the story would have said so.'

'Are you questioning the veracity of our Holy Scriptures?' demanded William looking from one to the other, sensing heresy, but not quite sure where, or how, or from whom.

'Of course not,' said Michael. 'But it must have been the Earth God halted at the battle of Gibeon. Can you imagine how fast the sun and the moon would be moving if they are revolving around us? It defies imagination, and they would be very difficult to stop.'

'I do not think economy of effort is something the Creator of the Universe needs to take into consideration when He is intervening in human affairs, Brother,' said Bartholomew, making Michael smile with his imitation of William's dour voice. 'And so that is not a valid argument.'

'It is odd that Matthew is presenting a traditional viewpoint, while you are extolling the virtues of a subversive one, Brother,' said William, oblivious to the fact that he had been parodied. 'It is normally the other way around, and it is he who favours the absurd and the heretical.'

'That is untrue,' objected Bartholomew. 'Many of my beliefs are very traditional – especially in relation to geometry.'

'That is because there is very little that is controversial concerning geometry,' said William disdainfully. 'And if there were, only men who favour the sciences like you would understand it. I am talking about your beliefs in medicine and theology, which have caused people to question whether you are in league with the Devil.'

'Like using all the knowledge and skills at my disposal to try to save a patient's life, you mean?' asked Bartholomew archly.

'That among other things,' said William, unaware of the irony in Bartholomew's voice. 'It is not always God's will that a person should be saved, Matthew. Sometimes, God – or the Devil – has called a person to his side, and you should not attempt to prevent that person from going.'

'So, if my patients are being called by the Devil, are you suggesting I bend to his will and let him take them?'

'No,' said William stiffly. 'If they are being called by the Devil you should attempt to snatch them back.'

'And how am I supposed to know whether they are being called by God or snatched by the Devil?' asked Bartholomew. 'It is not usually possible to tell.'

'You could ask,' said William coldly.

'Ask the Devil?' queried Bartholomew, raising his eyebrows in mock horror. 'Are you instructing me to commune with the Devil, Father?'

'Of course not!' temporised William. 'But there are ways to deal with such situations.'

'Such as what?' persisted Bartholomew.

'Enough, Matt,' said Michael, trying to hide his amusement. 'We can save all this for the debate tonight. But now, we should at least offer to help Alcote.'

Alcote, however, did not want their help. He was seated at the large table in Wergen Hall, surrounded by Tuddenham's scrolls and writs. A large dish of raisins stood near his elbow, and, judging from the frequency with which his fingers reached for them, Bartholomew saw he might well be in need of another cure for stomach ache that night.

Tuddenham, taking a respite from the villagers he had been questioning about the death of Unwin, stood behind him and peered over his shoulder until, exasperated, Alcote dismissed them all from his presence, promising to recall them should the impossible happen and he should need their advice. Relieved, Bartholomew and Michael left, quickly slipping away while William's attention was elsewhere lest the Franciscan should decide to spend the rest of the day trying to impress Michael with his interrogatory skills.

To one side of Wergen Hall was a pleasant bower and Isilia, who was sitting there with Dame Eva, beckoned them over. It was a pretty place, surrounded by a tall hazel-weave fence to keep animals out. Inside was a tiny herb garden and an orchard of gnarled apple and pear trees. In the shade of one tree, a long turf bench had been built, and here the ladies sat, sewing and chatting in air that was rich with the aroma of basil, sage, thyme, rosemary and lavender.

'How is my husband's advowson proceeding?' asked Isilia, as they approached. She gestured that they were to sit next to her.

'Well enough, I think,' said Michael, leaning back on the bench and stretching his long, fat legs in front of him. 'Master Alcote is working on it, while Matt and I are trying to discover who killed Unwin. You should ask Alcote if you want to know exactly how the deed is progressing.'

'I did,' said Isilia, with a grimace. 'But he could not bring himself even to look at me, let alone answer my question. He does not like me, although I cannot think what I have done to offend him.'

'It is nothing personal,' said Michael. 'Roger is uncomfortable in the presence of women, and avoids them whenever he can.'

'Why?' asked Dame Eva curiously.

Michael shrugged. 'He is just a peculiar man. Take no notice of him.'

'But you do not object to the company of women, do you?' asked Isilia of Bartholomew, eyes glinting with merriment as she saw him blush. 'I hear you and that young Deynman are the only men in Michaelhouse's deputation who have not sworn vows of chastity.'

'Well,' began Bartholomew, uncertain how to form a reply – although Isilia was clearly expecting one.

'He is quite free to enjoy a woman's charms,' said Michael. 'And enjoy them he certainly does. Why, in Cambridge—'

'Here comes Siric,' said Bartholomew quickly, pointing out Tuddenham's steward walking toward them. 'Perhaps he has news of Unwin's killer.'

But the steward shook his head as he leaned wearily against one of the apple trees. 'It is almost as if the friar never existed,' he said despondently. 'No one knows anything. No one saw anything. No one heard anything. All we have is Eltisley saying he spotted Sir Robert Grosnold talking to Unwin before he died – but it is never wise to believe anything that lunatic claims – and Master Stoate's observation of a cloaked figure running from the church. It is almost certain the man Stoate saw was the killer, but he is the only one with the courage to admit to what he saw. Everyone else is too afraid.'

'Afraid of what?' asked Bartholomew.

'Padfoot,' said Siric. 'There is a belief among the villagers that Padfoot will claim them if they help us uncover the person he used as his instrument to take Unwin.'

'So, they are afraid of ghosts,' said Michael in disgust.

'Who is not?' asked Dame Eva. 'They are not things people can defend themselves against.'

'True,' agreed Siric. 'But Sir Thomas will have this killer, whether the villagers help us or not. You will see.'

'Good,' said Isilia. 'I will suggest that Wauncy gives a sermon on the subject saying that failing to pass you information that will catch a priest-slayer will mean damnation for certain.'

Siric nodded, although his expression implied he did

not believe a sermon by Wauncy would do much good. 'Eltisley is looking for you,' he said to Bartholomew. 'He has brewed a substance that he says will cure warts, and he wants you to taste it. He is coming this way, carrying it in a bucket.'

Isilia smiled mischievously. 'I will tell you the back way to the village so that you can avoid him. Eltisley's cures for warts are infamous, and many villagers use them as weed-killers and to clear blocked drains. They also cure warts, but I would not recommend that you taste them.'

Bartholomew and Michael left immediately. Following her directions they walked along a pathway that led through pleasant groves of birch and elder, where birds sang sweetly and bees buzzed loudly in the still, warm air.

Michael chuckled. 'By going this way we have managed to lose William, too. I do not like him breathing down my neck while I am asking people questions. So, when we reach Grundisburgh, I shall visit the Dog – named, would you believe, after your spectral hound – and conduct my enquiries from there. That wretched Franciscan is unlikely to look for me in a tavern.'

'Never underestimate the Inquisition, Brother,' said Bartholomew. 'And anyway, you might be better off having him where you can see him.'

Later, when the fields were bathed in bright gold light, Warin de Stoate came to invite Bartholomew to ride with him to a nearby leper hospital. Bartholomew accepted readily, and spent a happy afternoon discussing medicine with a man who, even if he did not understand or agree with all that was said, was at least interested. Rashly believing that such an opportunity might be beneficial to Deynman's medical studies, Stoate extended the invitation to the student, dismissing Bartholomew's words of caution with a magnanimity he was later to regret.

While Stoate and Bartholomew reviewed the lepers' symptoms with the friar who ran the hospital, Deynman slipped away and decided to experiment with a theory of his own: namely that leprosy could be cured with a poultice made from garlic, nettles and the hair of a stallion. By the time the unpleasant aroma had drifted to where Stoate and Bartholomew sat talking with Father Peter, Stoate's horse had been relieved of its tail (Bartholomew's and Deynman's mounts were exempted on the grounds that they were mares). Fortunately, none of the lepers had been foolish enough to allow Deynman to try his stew on their skin, and Father Peter managed to knot a bunch of grass around what remained of the stallion's tail, thus enabling the bereft animal to flick away the flies that plagued it. Stoate, however, was not amused, and did not appreciate his horse being the object of mirth from the people they passed on the road.

By the time Bartholomew had placated Stoate by listening with rapt attention to his odd theories on the bloody flux, he was hot, tired and irritable, and certainly not in the mood to participate in a debate that evening. Sensing that a quick disappearance might be prudent, Deynman slunk off to seek out Horsey as soon as they arrived in Grundisburgh, while Stoate went to visit Eltisley, to see if a replacement tail for the stallion could be devised that would look less like the handful of grass that had been fastened to it. Bartholomew went to find Michael.

The monk was still in the Dog. Feeling magnanimous after several cups of strong claret, he had invited William to accompany him to speak again to the people who lived opposite the church about Unwin's death, hoping that one of them might have remembered something new. It was not long before Michael appreciated more than ever Bartholomew's easy and intelligent companionship, and he had almost came to blows with William regarding the degree of coercion that could and could not be applied when questioning innocent bystanders. After half a dozen such encounters, he threw up his hands in despair and left William to his own devices. The rest of his day was spent in the peaceful garden of the Dog enjoying the far more congenial company of the landlord, who had won the monk's heart by requesting his expert opinion on various pastries.

'The apple is superior to the raisin,' he announced authoritatively, wiping greasy fingers on his small piece of linen. The linen had evidently seen a good deal of use that day, and was looking grubby and rumpled. Almost as if he sensed Bartholomew's observation, the landlord presented Michael with a new piece, embroidered around the edges and made of finest quality white cloth. It was also much larger than the old one, and therefore a more suitable size for a glutton like Michael.

'A gift to show my gratitude for your advice on my recipes,' said the landlord solemnly.

Michael inclined his head graciously, and accepted it, dabbing delicately at his sticky lips.

'Norys predicted that someone would give you a present,' said Bartholomew, sitting next to him and taking a slice of something containing dates, which Michael had somehow missed.

Michael's face creased in annoyance. 'I was perfectly happy until you mentioned that vile name. Can we not talk of more pleasant things? Like boiled cream custard – a delicious combination of thick cream, egg yolks and butter, flavoured with sugar and saffron, presented to me by my good friend the innkeeper here. Try some. Oh! There seems to be none left.'

'We have not really discussed the man Norys saw running from the church the afternoon Unwin died,' said Bartholomew, taking a long draught from Michael's pot of ale. He was grateful to sit in the shade for a while, before the debate started. Obligingly, the landlord brought more food –

chicken in almonds, and some buttered cabbage that Michael regarded as though it were poisonous.

'I have been thinking about nothing else,' said Michael untruthfully, regarding the number of empty platters that surrounded him. 'Norys did it. That weasely pardoner killed poor Unwin just as surely as you are sitting there.'

'I do not think so, Brother,' said Bartholomew, leaning back against the wall and closing his eyes. 'What evidence do you have, other than the fact that you do not like pardoners?'

'He has gone to Ipswich and will not be returning,' said Michael. 'That is a sign of his guilt.'

Bartholomew opened his eyes quickly. 'Really? How do you know he will not come back?'

Michael sniffed. 'No one can find him. He is not in the village.'

Bartholomew sighed and closed his eyes again. 'That does not mean he has gone permanently. His uncle said he often stays in Ipswich for several days at a time.'

'But I told him not to go. I believe his sudden absence is too coincidental, given that I hinted I thought he might be involved in Unwin's murder. The man has fled, I tell you.'

'He would have fled a lot earlier if he had been guilty. You are on thin ice with this, Brother.'

'He knew I suspected him of the murder, and so what did he do but invent a fictitious figure running out of the church in great haste. No one else saw this person – I have been tramping all over the village with William this afternoon, and no one saw a thing.'

'But Stoate also saw someone leaving the church.'

Michael glared at him for interrupting. 'And Norys expects me to believe that he noticed this person's belt and shoes, but not his face, or even whether it was a man or a woman!'

'But that happens,' objected Bartholomew. 'And to prove it, I did a similar thing with the lepers I visited this afternoon.'

Michael edged away from him. 'I could tell you in great detail what stages the disease was at, and what symptoms the leper was suffering, but I am not sure I could tell you how many men and how many women I saw.'

'But that is completely different,' said Michael. 'It is not easy to tell a man from a woman when the face is swathed in bandages.'

'But women wear dresses and men wear hose, just as they do anywhere else,' said Bartholomew. 'I did not pay attention to that while there were more interesting things to see.'

'You enjoyed yourself, then?' asked Michael dryly. 'Did Deynman?'

Bartholomew laughed. 'I should say. He had the tail off Stoate's horse, and cooked it with garlic as a cure for leprosy. But Norys is right – we often *only* notice the things that interest us. I saw a fascinating case of leprosy of the mouth today, but I could not tell you what that person wore, or what was the colour of his – or her – hair.'

'Do you know, Matt, if someone had told me ten years ago that my closest friend would be a man whose chief sources of pleasure in life are poking about with leprous sores and telling people about sewage in drinking water, I would never have accepted the Fellowship at Michaelhouse.'

'Really?' asked Bartholomew, intrigued. 'What would you have done instead? I should have thought nothing could suit you as well as all the subterfuge and intrigue at the University, not to mention the enjoyment you get from working as the Bishop of Ely's spy.'

'True,' admitted Michael. 'Politics and affairs of state pale by comparison.'

They sat in comfortable silence, listening to the agitated twitter of a wren as a cat slunk past its territory, and the hypnotic coo of a dove in the churchyard elms. As the sun sank lower in the sky, people began to return from the fields, their tools carried over their shoulders, and their clothes caked in dust. They looked bone weary, all of them with sweat-stained faces and skin that was burned a deep red-brown. A few stopped at the Dog for ale to wash away the grit that stuck in their throats, but most went home to where smoke issued from the roofs of their houses, indicating that something was cooking on the hearth. Why they would then want to walk a mile to Wergen Hall to hear a debate about the rotation of the Earth was beyond Bartholomew.

'Father Peter, who cares for the lepers, keeps a diary of his observations,' he said conversationally, turning his mind from the tired labourers to his visit to the hospital.

'A diary of leprosy! That must make fascinating reading,' said Michael caustically. 'In fact, it probably equals the preliminary draft of the advowson Alcote wrote today.'

'These long-term observations have made a number of things clear to me about the progress of the disease,' began Bartholomew. 'First, when the lesions appear initially—'

'Perhaps you can tell me about leprous sores when I have finished eating,' said Michael, quickly snatching up a piece of chicken. Once the physician started to discuss some aspect of medicine that interested him, he was difficult to stop, and Michael was not in the mood to be regaled with lurid descriptions of nasty diseases.

'Hurry up, then,' said Bartholomew, looking at the mountain of food that still waited to be packed away inside the monk's ample girth. 'Or we will be late for the debate.'

'As I was saying, before you so cunningly changed the subject, that pardoner is as guilty as sin. Did you see his face when I pointed out how he would be unable to see a person's belt if he wore a cloak? That trapped the little weasel!'

'Actually, I think he raised that point himself,' said Bartholomew. 'You have no reason to accuse him of anything.'

'Your midwife thinks he is guilty. She suggested we interrogate him.'

'She suggested we ask him whether anyone had tried to sell the stolen relic,' said Bartholomew patiently. 'She was not presenting him as a suspect, but as someone who might be able to help us solve the crime. And Norys did not have to tell us what he saw; he did so because he wants the killer caught as much as we do.'

'Rubbish!' snapped Michael. 'He made all that up. What better way to divert suspicion from himself – and he only admitted he was in the churchyard because he knows someone probably saw him there, and he does not want to be caught out in a lie – than to invent some mysterious character running from the church at the precise time that the murder was committed? It is brilliant! It is like something I would have thought up myself.'

'But Stoate also saw a person running from the church,' Bartholomew pointed out again. 'Or is he lying, too?'

'Of course not, but Norys and Stoate have not given us the same description. The man Stoate saw wore a long dark cloak, which led him to think that a prank was being played and made him concerned that the wearer would faint from overheating. Of course, our esteemed pardoner owns a long cloak, as do all vermin of his trade, so the cloak Norys's man wore is short, and conveniently caught on a tree to reveal his studded belt. Stoate mentions no studded belt or over-small shoes . . .'

'But Norys explained why he noticed those: because he was trained as a tanner, and so tends to observe leather. Similarly, Stoate noticed the person rubbed his eyes, because he is a physician.'

'But Norys did not mention the rubbed eyes, did he? Something as obvious as that, and he did not mention it. Did you look at *his* eyes, Matt? Did they look as though they had been rubbed?'

'Something as obvious as that, and you did not notice it?' asked Bartholomew in a very plausible imitation of Michael. The monk narrowed his eyes, not amused. 'But you see my point, Brother? You do not recall whether Norys's eyes were sore, and neither, necessarily, would anyone else, unless they happened to have a special reason for doing so.'

'So were his eyes red or not?' snapped Michael irritably.

'They were not. Mind you, that is not to say that they were not red when Unwin died.'

'Aha!' pounced Michael. 'You think he is guilty, too.'

'God's teeth, Brother!' cried Bartholomew in exasperation. 'You are like the Inquisition, twisting words in a way that Father William could only dream of! What is the matter with you? Will you allow a mere pardoner to ruffle your immaculate composure in a way that crooked merchants, cunning murderers and deceitful academics can never do?'

Michael leaned back against the wall and eyed him narrowly, breathing heavily as he fought to bring his temper under control. Eventually, he gave a wan smile.

'Forgive me, Matt. You are right. I will never prove this pardoner's guilt if I allow him to make me too angry to see reason.'

'And you will not see reason if you are too fixed on this man's guilt,' said Bartholomew.

Michael gnawed on his lip. 'I do not know why I listen to you telling me how unreasonable I am in my dislikes, when you have developed an irrational hatred of our poor landlord, Eltisley.' He took a gulp of wine and sighed. 'And you can say what you like, but there are inconsistencies in the tale Norys told us, and the one Stoate did. Mistress Freeman, for a start.'

'Yes,' said Bartholomew, considering. 'Norys maintains he was with her all afternoon, until after Unwin was killed, while Stoate says he was talking to her when this mysterious person came running from the church.'

'We will ask her about it first thing tomorrow,' said Michael, picking listlessly at his chicken. He flung down his knife in disgust. 'That odious pardoner has made me lose my appetite!'

'You are not hungry because you have not stopped eating all day,' said Bartholomew, laughing.

'I do not suppose Master Stoate furnished you with any more details about the man *he* saw running from the church?' asked Michael, ignoring the comment.

'No,' said Bartholomew, 'although we twice went over what he saw as we rode to the leper hospital. I thought if he told the story more than once he might add a detail that he had previously forgotten, but he had nothing new to say.'

'And the cloak he saw this person wearing was definitely a long one?' asked Michael.

'Yes, down to the ankles. I asked whether it might have concealed a suit of black clothes, but he said no. He thinks the person he saw was not big enough to be Grosnold.'

'Well, that is something,' said Michael. 'Can we eliminate the bald lord from Otley, then?'

'Not yet,' said Bartholomew. 'He has plenty of retainers. He may have had this odd conversation with Unwin that Eltisley saw in the churchyard, then dispatched someone else to kill him in the church later.'

'He would have to act quickly, though,' said Michael, frowning. 'Think about the chain of events: just before the feast, Grosnold thunders out of the village, trampling half the residents, and then doubles back to waylay Unwin in the churchyard. Immediately after the feast – and we saw how little time that took – Norys takes Mistress Freeman for a stroll around her late husband's grave (or Mistress Freeman stands talking with Master Stoate by the ford, depending on who you believe), and out comes this mysterious figure in the cloak.'

Bartholomew took up the tale. 'Within moments, Horsey goes in search of his friend, and finds his body. We know Unwin had not been dead long, because he was still warm and I thought I might be able to bring him back to life.'

'So, three people saw this figure running from the church: Norys, Stoate and Mistress Freeman. Siric, Tuddenham's steward, said he spoke to Mistress Freeman, and she confirmed she saw someone run from the church just after the feast, but she was unable to provide a description of him.'

'Did Siric ask whether she was with Norys or Stoate when this took place?'

Michael shook his head. 'He had only been instructed to ask her what she had seen, not who she was with. But we can ask her ourselves tomorrow. And I will catch her out if she lies to me.'

'Why should she lie to you?'

'It seems to me Norys is more fond of this widow-of-a-few-days than is entirely appropriate. She may have claimed to have seen this person running from the church because Norys told her to.'

Bartholomew sighed, and thought about Norys's story. 'What about the shoes and silver-studded belt that Norys described? They sound remarkably similar to the garments worn by the man we found hanging at Bond's Corner. I do not see how Norys could have known about that, and so I am inclined to believe him.'

'He would have known about them if he were also the man who did the hanging in the first place,' pounced Michael. 'It is simple. Norys kills some poor peasant, who happened to have stolen Deblunville's clothes, and hid the body after we almost caught him at it. He then pretends to have seen someone wearing these same clothes running from the scene of Unwin's murder – or perhaps he even wore them himself. In order to confuse us further, he suggests Deblunville, or another of Suffolk's quarrelling knights, is responsible, and not one of the villagers. He is muddying the waters, but he cannot stir up the filth enough to fool me.'

'Then why, when I showed him the stud I recovered, did he not use it to his own advantage?' asked Bartholomew. 'He could have assured us that it definitely belonged to the belt worn by the hanged man. Instead, he said he was uncertain.'

'He *might* have been uncertain. For all he knew, you might have just pulled it off your own belt, and then he would have been caught out in an untruth.'

'For someone you consider dull-witted, you are accrediting Norys with a good deal of intelligence,' said Bartholomew doubtfully.

'Not intelligence, Matt. Raw cunning. Like one of those damned cats he has creeping about the house. Did you notice how much he looked like one?'

'Of course,' said Bartholomew, standing and stretching. 'But we cannot do anything more tonight because of this debate. After we bury Unwin tomorrow morning, you and I will visit Mistress Freeman, and then we will know who is lying and who is telling the truth.'

'Where is William?' hissed Michael anxiously to Bartholomew as the light faded from the sky behind Wergen Hall.

Bartholomew shrugged, wondering whether he should go to look for the absent friar. The debate was due to start at any moment, and it would be a very short one if only one side of the argument were presented. Michael fretted, pacing up and down in the dusty courtyard outside Tuddenham's manorial home, as the villagers filed past him to take their seats in the main chamber. Bartholomew felt almost guilty when he saw the keen anticipation on their weary faces, certain that they were in for a tedious evening.

He was on the verge of leaving to hunt William down, when the friar appeared, hurrying along the path from the village. His grey robe flapped round his ankles, and his face was red with effort and agitation.

'Where have you been?' demanded Michael. 'We are almost ready to begin, and I wanted to go through a couple of your arguments with you beforehand, to . . .' He hesitated.

'To make sure Matthew does not savage me too brutally in the debating chamber?' finished William. Unaccustomed to such self-effacement from the friar, Michael was, for once, at a loss for words. 'Well, you need not concern yourself, Brother. I have had more than enough time since you left me to hone and refine my own contentions.' He scowled unpleasantly.

'Why, what have you been doing?' asked Bartholomew, puzzled.

'I have been locked inside that damned latrine for the best part of the afternoon,' snapped William angrily. 'Some lunatic put a device on the door that can only be operated from the outside. Once you are in and the door is closed, the only way to get out is if someone opens it for you.'

'Eltisley!' said Bartholomew, trying not to laugh. 'He was meddling with the doors yesterday, trying to fit some mechanism that would prevent desperate people from rattling the handles of occupied stalls. It was probably that which caused you problems.'

'It was a red metal thing,' said William. 'In the end, I had to unscrew the hinge and remove the whole door, or I would still be there now, since no one answered my calls for help. Eltisley intended that lock to mean business!'

'Come on,' said Michael, taking his arm and leading him inside the manor house. 'Or the people of Grundisburgh will be thinking we are afraid to show them our talents.'

'Or perhaps they do not want to see them – hence William's imprisonment,' said Bartholomew. 'I cannot imagine that no one walked past the latrines all afternoon. Perhaps it is their way of telling us they would rather be elsewhere.'

'Nonsense,' said William grimly. 'These peasants will have an excellent time this evening.'

'Will you tell them that, or shall I?' asked Michael, grinning behind the friar's back.

He walked up the stairs, entered the main hall and sat in a large wooden chair that had been placed in the middle of the room, while Bartholomew and William stood on either side of him. The hall was full and overly warm, with some people leaning up against the walls at the back and others sitting on the floor near the front, as well as those perched on benches in the middle. Somewhere a goat bleated, and there was an atmosphere of tense expectation. The window shutters stood open, but the air was too still to admit a breeze, and the room smelled of sweat, stale rushes and cut grass. Michael cleared his throat and an instant silence fell over the crowd.

'We are here to discuss a question,' the monk began grandly. 'And the answer to that question lies at the very heart of our understanding of the universe. The ideas and theories you will hear expounded today come from some of the greatest minds the world has ever known – ancient philosophers, such as Aristotle and Ptolemy, and respected authorities from our own time, such as John Buridan.'

He paused for dramatic effect, and Bartholomew saw that one or two people were already beginning to shift restlessly, while a group of small children at his feet was far more interested in racing some insects through the rushes than in anything Michael had to say.

'The only way to learn and to understand complex philosophical, theological and scientific issues is through disputation,' continued Michael pompously. 'If any one of you wishes to state a theory or to ask a question, you are welcome to do so at any time.'

'How long is this going to last?' called a burly man from the back, who held a piglet in his arms. 'Only I need to get back to the sow.'

'I will bear that in mind,' said Michael. 'But I prefer that any questions asked relate to the issue we are debating, namely: "Let us consider whether the Earth rotates".'

'Rotates? You mean spins round?' asked the man with the pig.

'Precisely,' said Michael. 'On the one hand, we can consider that the Earth is at the centre of the universe and is immobile; on the other, we can assume that it rotates on a daily basis, which accounts for the rising and setting of the celestial bodies. Father William will argue that the Earth is motionless; Doctor Bartholomew will argue that it is not.'

'He is wrong, then,' said Dame Eva with conviction. 'I have never heard such rubbish.'

'Which is wrong, madam?' asked Michael. 'That the Earth rotates or that it is motionless?'

'She means that it rotates,' said Tuddenham. 'Of course it does not rotate. It is not a maypole!'

'I am quite capable of answering for myself,' said Dame Eva. She turned a bright, somewhat hostile, eye on Bartholomew. 'Well, go on, then. Explain yourself. Explain how you have dreamt up such a gross flight of fancy.'

'Not so gross,' said Eltisley thoughtfully. 'A rotation of the Earth would explain why we have winter and summer.'

'It would?' asked Bartholomew uncertainly.

Eltisley nodded, scratching his chin. 'The Earth rotates toward the sun in summer, making the weather warm, but rotates away from it in the winter, bringing snow and cold winds.'

'The notion is that the Earth rotates on a daily basis,' said Bartholomew, 'not on a yearly one. A daily rotation explains why the sun rises and sets, and why the stars move, but not why the seasons change.'

'Well, what does explain the advent of winter and summer, then?' demanded Eltisley. 'I defy you to come up with a better explanation than the one I have suggested.'

Expectant eyes turned towards Bartholomew.

'And then you can tell us how to control it,' said the man with the pig, looking around him for the support of his friends. 'Summer was too late in coming this year. And it would be better if we could miss winter altogether, and just go from autumn to spring each year.'

There was not a person in the room who was not nodding

enthusiastically. Bartholomew glanced at Michael, struggling to keep a straight face.

'It is outside the topic of our discussion today,' said Michael quickly, before William could start accusing people of heresy because they wanted to take control of the seasons out of the hands of God. 'Perhaps we could debate that question on another occasion. But Father William, perhaps you would begin, and state the arguments against the rotation of the Earth?'

William opened his mouth to speak, but Isilia was there before him, shaking her head admonishingly. 'Of course it does not spin. We would all feel dizzy if it did.'

'And sick,' added Mother Goodman. 'And there would be no end to the potions I would need to make for queasy stomachs.' She shook her scarfed head firmly. 'No. The Earth does not spin. The Franciscan is right.'

'One point to you,' said Michael, glancing up at William and trying not to smile. 'Do you have anything else to add, before you rest your case?'

'Aristotle, Ptolemy and the Bible all state that the Earth lies immobile at the centre of the universe,' said William drawing himself up to his full height, and looking around at the assembled audience. 'I cannot see the need to cite any more potent authorities to prove my argument.'

Michael sighed under his breath. 'Come on, Father. These people want more than flat assertions. This will be a very short debate, or a very tedious one, unless you make more effort.'

'Aristarchus of Samos said the Earth rotates on its axis,' said Bartholomew, trying to enter the spirit of the occasion, 'and it is this daily rotation that makes it seem as though the celestial bodies move, when they are actually still.'

'No one believes *him* any more,' said William dismissively. He folded his arms, and exchanged a victorious smile with the man who held the pig.

'But Buridan, in his commentary on Aristotle's *De Caelo*,

states that the problem with understanding the rotation of the Earth lies in relative motion,' said Bartholomew. 'So, if you are at sea in a ship, and you see another ship passing you, it is not possible to determine from observation alone whether it is the other ship moving or your own.'

'Only if you are drunk,' shouted Hamon, drawing a murmur of agreement and vigorously nodded heads from his friends. 'I always know whether I am moving or not when I sail down the river to Woodbridge.'

'I said on the sea,' said Bartholomew, trying to be patient. It was like having a debate with a room full of Deynmans. 'On a river you would have points of reference to tell you whether you are moving or still. On the sea there is no point of reference, except the other boat – hence you cannot tell whether it is your vessel or the other that is moving.'

'I need none of these "points of reference" to tell me whether I am still or not,' said Hamon firmly. 'I just know.'

A chorus of cheers rose around the room, drowning out Bartholomew's attempt to explain further what he had meant.

'Two points to William,' muttered Michael, amused. 'This is far more entertaining than a debate at the University.'

Bartholomew sighed, wishing he had never agreed to comply with Tuddenham's request in the first place. William, in the rare position of winning a debate against Bartholomew, was beginning to enjoy himself. His booming voice cut through the hum of conversation that had erupted.

'Buridan says that if the Earth rotates, and if I threw a stone straight up into the sky, it would not land at the place from where I had thrown it – the Earth would have moved, and it would land somewhere else.' He looked around at the audience, and spread his hands in an expansive shrug. 'And we all know that is not the case. A stone thrown directly upwards, lands directly underneath where it was thrown from.'

'Like this?' asked Eltisley, grabbing a heavy pewter goblet

from one of his surly customers and hurling it, contents and all, up at the ceiling. Ale splattered over the audience, and the cup clanged deafeningly against a rafter before clattering down at Michael's feet.

'It did not come down under the place from which it was thrown,' said Hamon, regarding it in awe. 'It came down to one side. Perhaps the Earth does rotate after all.' There was a rumble of agreement, and some sagely exchanged nods. Hamon looked at Bartholomew for confirmation.

'That was not a straight throw,' said Bartholomew. 'It did not come down on Master Eltisley's head because he hurled it at an angle.'

'You have just scored a point in favour of rotation, Matt,' said Michael, his green eyes glittering with mischief. 'Do not dismiss it so lightly. You are unlikely to win another if you persist with all this theoretical nonsense.'

'No, no, no,' said Tuddenham, shaking his head. 'The Earth cannot be rotating: if it were, we would feel the wind of it on our faces.'

'But we do,' said Hamon fervently. 'There is nearly always a wind at Peche Hall, whispering in the trees and rippling the water on the moat.'

'But the wind does not always comes from the same direction,' Bartholomew pointed out. 'If the Earth was moving from west to east, then the wind would always come from the east – and we all know it does not.'

'Perhaps that is because the Earth does not always rotate in the same direction,' reasoned Hamon. Several of his friends voiced their agreement.

'But it must always rotate in the same direction,' said Bartholomew, regarding him askance. 'Otherwise the moon would not always rise after the sun sets.'

'But it does not,' said Eltisley. 'We have all seen the moon in the sky while the sun is still up, and sometimes we cannot see whether it has risen at all because of clouds.'

'But it is still there,' said Bartholomew, startled. 'Even if we cannot see it.'

'Prove it,' challenged Eltisley. Several villagers began to shout encouragement, some to Bartholomew, others to Eltisley. 'You do not know what is above the clouds.'

'Only God knows that,' put in William loudly.

'But this rotation of the Earth would explain the wind,' said Hamon thoughtfully, once the racket had died down. 'And when it is very windy, it means the Earth is rotating faster than usual.'

'No, it does not,' said Bartholomew, feeling as though the points raised were becoming steadily more outrageous. 'The wind is independent of rotation. As the Earth moves, everything – the earth, the air and all sublunar matter – moves with it in a circular motion, the wind included.'

'Rubbish!' said Dame Eva in a surprisingly strong voice for a woman of her years. 'And, despite Eltisley's experiment, I have tossed things in the air that have returned directly to me, not landed half a league down the road.'

'There are two types of motion associated with an object thrown into the air,' said Bartholomew, remembering a lecture he had heard by the young scholar Nicole Oresme. 'The first is an upward motion, and the second is west to east, following the circular motion of the Earth. Therefore, an object thrown into the air that returns to the place where it originated, does not prove or disprove that the Earth rotates.'

'But we can only see one motion,' argued William. 'The vertical one.'

'That is because we are part of the Earth's circular motion, too,' said Bartholomew.

'We cannot see the circular motion because we are part of it?' asked Tuddenham, eyeing Bartholomew doubtfully. 'I cannot imagine where you scholars find the time to concoct all these peculiar ideas.'

'Let us conclude,' said Michael, sensing the whole affair might become acrimonious if allowed to drag on. He rubbed at a flabby chin. 'It has been argued that the Earth does *not* rotate, because we would feel dizzy and we would all be after Mother Goodman for remedies for sick stomachs. It has also been argued that we do not need points of reference to know whether we are moving or not, because we just know.'

'Right.' Hamon nodded vigorously. 'That makes sound sense. We just know.'

'On the other hand, Master Eltisley demonstrated that an object thrown in the air does not fall to the Earth at the point from which it originated, thus proving that the Earth *is* spinning in a west-to-east direction.'

'And it explains the seasons,' added Eltisley, reluctant to let that one pass.

'And the wind we feel is because the Earth is spinning,' added Hamon. 'Any changes in wind direction means that the Earth is spinning a different way.'

Bartholomew sighed in exasperation.

'Quite,' said Michael. 'Argued most intelligently, Sir Hamon.' Hamon exchanged a smile of pride with his uncle, and Michael continued. 'And so, weighing up both sides of the argument, as is my duty as presiding master, I can only conclude that the evidence is insufficient on either side to answer the question satisfactorily.'

There was silence in the room, and a number of mystified looks exchanged.

'Now, just a minute,' said Tuddenham indignantly. 'There was plenty of evidence presented here for you to make up your mind. You are just trying to please everyone by calling it a draw.'

'The point of a debate, Sir Thomas,' said Michael, 'is not to discover the definitive answer to a question, but to present the evidence, such as it is, and examine it logically, demonstrating the human ability to think and process information.'

'You what?' demanded the man with the pig. 'Does the Earth spin or not? That is what we all want to know, not whether you can examine evidence loquaciously.'

There was a cheer from the audience at his eloquence, and he enjoyed the adulation of the people who stood around him.

'Did I say "loquaciously" instead of "logically"?' asked Michael of Bartholomew, as the audience clapped and banged their feet on the floor. 'I may have done, you know. I have seldom been less in control at a disputation than at this one. At least scholars generally keep to the rules.'

When the racket showed no sign of abating, he stood and raised his hands to quieten the excited villagers. 'We will decide this democratically, by asking the audience which theory it thinks is correct,' he yelled.

'No!' said Hamon, leaping to his feet and looking around at the assembled villagers. 'We will not decide democratically. We will have a vote!'

'I should have let you be presiding master, after all,' muttered Michael to William, his words barely audible over the thunder of applause that met Hamon's suggestion, while Bartholomew sat in Michael's chair and laughed. 'This is all quite beyond me.'

'All those who think the Earth rotates, raise one hand,' bellowed William, the only one with a voice that could be projected over the babble. Immediately, nearly all the hands in the room were waved at him. 'I said raise *one* hand!' thundered William. He made a sound of exasperation as most of them went back down again. 'I meant one hand each, not one hand between all of you!'

'Come on!' cried Hamon, prowling around the room and grabbing the arms of those who were not voting. 'What is wrong with you? All of you have felt the wind on your faces as the Earth moves. Think about that storm we had last autumn – that was the Earth speeding up.'

'Now, all those who believe that the Earth is motionless, raise one hand,' said William, once he had made a quick count. Bartholomew started to laugh again when he saw an equal number of hands raised, most of them from the people who had already voted the other way. Hamon leapt around the room slapping them down until he was certain his side had the majority, and grinned at Dame Eva triumphantly.

'The Earth *does* spin,' he announced. 'You are wrong in thinking that it does not.'

She gave him a weary look, and hobbled from the room. Hamon led his supporters in a chorus of loud cheers, which quickly petered out when Tuddenham fixed them with an admonishing glare. As people began to disperse, Tuddenham sought out Michael.

'So, that is how debates are held at the universities,' he said. 'Most intriguing, although I am a little surprised at its brutality of reason. I expected something a little more probing and subtle, not all this yelling and hurling of objects up to the ceiling.'

'They vary,' said Michael vaguely. 'It really depends on the participants. Come to visit us in Michaelhouse, and I will take you to a real one.'

'Perhaps I will,' said Tuddenham, a little wistfully. 'But thank you, Brother. I have not enjoyed an event as much since last year's muck-spreading competition.'

'I am glad to hear it,' said Michael.

Bartholomew awoke the following morning to a dawn that gleamed dully with a silver mist that lay in uneven strips across the fields and along the river. Gradually, as the sun rose above the tree-ridged hill, it bathed the mist in red and then gold, before burning it away altogether. He stood with his arms resting on the windowsill, listening to Eltisley's cockerel crowing in the yard below, and watching two of the surly men heave barrels of ale from a cart into the cellar. Eltisley saw him, and waved cheerfully. Absently, Bartholomew waved back, thinking of the colleague whose funeral was that day.

He walked down the stairs, and found Eltisley laying out bread and ale for breakfast. The innkeeper smiled at Bartholomew and indicated that he should sit, but Bartholomew was not hungry and did not feel much like eating when he was about to bury Unwin. Alcote was already there, pale faced and heavy eyed from a night rendered restless by too many raisins.

'That potion you gave me did not work,' he complained to Bartholomew. 'I still feel dreadful.'

Bartholomew felt Alcote's forehead. It was cold and clammy, but Alcote was a cold and clammy person, and Bartholomew was not overly concerned. He imagined that the chief cause of Alcote's continued ill health was because he was anxious about the advowson, and was working too hard to ingratiate himself with Tuddenham.

'We have had more than our share of funerals this month,' said Eltisley conversationally, as they waited for the others to arrive. The physician did not feel the landlord's jovial tone was appropriate for such a discussion, particularly bearing in mind they were about to attend another.

'So I understand,' he said shortly, wishing Eltisley would go away.

'First there was poor Alice Quy and then there was James Freeman,' Eltisley continued happily, clattering about with his pewter plates. 'I had to invent a special box for him, because otherwise all that blood would have damaged the parish coffin, and leaked over the church.'

'Mother Goodman said yours leaked, too,' said Bartholomew unkindly.

Eltisley looked crestfallen. 'Well, I did my best. I was sent inferior wood, and even though I sealed all the joints, the blood simply seeped out. It took me a whole day to make that box – even with some of my customers helping me.' He nodded at the surly men who were labouring with the barrels in the yard. 'They are casual labourers, hired by Hamon to help with the crop weeding.'

'What happened to Alice Quy?' asked Bartholomew. 'Mother Goodman says you gave her a potion for her childbirth fever. What was in it?'

'Ah,' said Eltisley, regarding Bartholomew with a hurt expression. 'You think my potion hastened her end. I can assure you, Doctor, I gave her nothing that would cause her harm. It was a mild mixture of feverfew mixed with honeyed wine. Surely there can be nothing noxious in that?'

'I suppose not,' said Bartholomew.

'And what was in that one you gave me on Monday night?' demanded Alcote, holding his stomach for dramatic effect. 'I am still suffering.'

'I have already told you,' said Eltisley, offended. 'It was not my potion that made you ill – Tuddenham's cook told me that you ate raisins all day, and too many of those are very bad for you. Anyway, my wife and I take a dose of my black potion nightly, and we are both well.'

Bartholomew could not imagine how.

'James Freeman's death was a shock to us all so soon after Alice Quy,' continued Eltisley, shaking his head. 'Poor Dame Eva found him when she went to collect Wergen Hall's pork, and I heard her cries of shock. She is a sensible lady, but even she was shaken by what she saw – the butcher's neck hacked with one of those great knives he used for chopping up animal carcasses. It was her suggestion that I build a special coffin because of all the blood. Next time, I will line the thing with pitch. Pitch is used to render boats watertight, you know.'

'Yes,' said Bartholomew. 'I do know, although I hope there will not be a next time.'

Most of the villagers were waiting at the church to pay their last respects to Unwin. Bartholomew wondered whether they were there on Tuddenham's orders, or whether they were as genuinely shocked by the murder as they claimed. Father William rattled through the requiem mass at a speed that had most of the villagers nodding appreciatively and Walter Wauncy's eyes hard with envy. William was renowned for his fast masses in Cambridge, although he usually made up for them with excessively long sermons, during which he railed about heresy, making frequent reference to the lurid wall paintings in St Michael's Church. There were no Judgement Day paintings in Grundisburgh, and William found little inspiration in the restful mural depicting St Margaret, whose timeless gaze watched over the assembly with a curiously sad smile.

As the requiem proceeded, Bartholomew, standing with his Michaelhouse colleagues in a line next to the coffin, looked at the villagers in the body of the church. Warin de Stoate was with some of his young friends at the back, gazing down at the floor and poking the earth with the toe of his boot. Eltisley was regarding the roof speculatively, and Bartholomew saw him raise an arm and measure something by squinting at his thumb with one eye. Wauncy would need to be on his guard if Eltisley had designs on improving what was already a perfectly functional ceiling.

Tuddenham and his family had wooden benches in the chancel. Dame Eva sat with her back against one of the walls, gazing at the painted rood loft, a small gallery that ran across the church between the nave and the choir. Isilia sat next to her, shifting uncomfortably on the hard wood, one hand resting on her stomach, where her unborn child kicked. She caught Bartholomew's eye and gave him a small smile of sympathy. Next to her was Tuddenham himself, his eyes fixed on the shrouded figure in the coffin, his expression unreadable. Hamon stood behind him, kicking the wall with a spurred heel, hands pushed deep inside his leather jerkin.

Opposite the Tuddenhams were some specially invited guests. Grosnold sat in the best chair, his jet armour exchanged for a black cotte, hose and cloak. Next to him was a small man with a crooked spine and shabby clothes, who fidgeted throughout the mass as though sitting still was painful for him. Wauncy, his robes swinging about his skeletal form and his white face more than usually gaunt, looked like the Angel of Death in the gloom. He joined in the singing of a psalm with a voice so deep and resonant that it sent an unpleasant chill down Bartholomew's spine. The physician sang louder so that he would not have to hear it, drawing curious glances from Michael and Alcote.

By the time the mass was over, the sky had clouded to a menacing grey. Bartholomew and Cynric lifted Unwin's shrouded body from the parish coffin and lowered it gently into the gaping rectangular hole under the yew tree that had been prepared the day before. By the time they had finished, rain was beginning to fall in a misty pall. Drops pattered lightly on the now-empty coffin, making a dismal accompaniment to the drone of William's prayers.

Eventually, it was over and the villagers began to drift away. There was work to be done in the fields and woods, and there were animals to be fed and turned out to graze. Stoate touched Bartholomew lightly on the elbow and offered his condolences again, following up with a shy invitation to visit an infirmary at Ipswich, which had something of a reputation for dealing with diseases of the lungs. Bartholomew thanked him, but even the prospect of learning new medicine could not rouse him from his sadness at the futility of Unwin's death.

He stood with Michael while Cynric shovelled dirt on top of the white bundle that lay in its sandy grave. Alcote and

William accepted the sympathies of the departing parishioners, while Deynman had his arm around Horsey, who was sobbing uncontrollably.

The man with the crooked spine, whom Bartholomew had noticed in the church, was talking to Tuddenham and Grosnold. The rain was now coming down hard, making Grosnold's pate gleam even more than usual, and people were scurrying for cover.

'John Bardolf,' said Tuddenham briskly, introducing the small man to Bartholomew. 'My neighbour from Clopton, whose daughter disobeyed me and married that scoundrel Deblunville.'

Bardolf came to stand next to Bartholomew, who was still watching Cynric methodically shovelling, neither hurried nor impeded by the sheeting rain.

'I was sorry to hear about this,' said Bardolf, nodding down at the grave. 'I had hoped that young man might heal the rifts that are widening between our manors.'

'Between yours and Tuddenham's?' asked Bartholomew.

'Yes. And between Deblunville's and Hamon's, and Deblunville's and Grosnold's, and Grosnold's and mine. And so on.'

'I had the impression that everyone was united against Deblunville,' said Bartholomew.

'At the moment,' said Bardolf, 'although that will change if Grosnold dams his stream again this summer, or sparks from my wheat stubble ignite Tuddenham's ripening crops. And the parish priests are just as bad: they fight with just as much viciousness as we do.'

'The marriage of your daughter to Roland Deblunville should reduce some of the conflict,' said Bartholomew.

Bardolf shrugged. 'Between Clopton and Burgh, certainly. But it seems to have aggravated matters between me, and Grundisburgh and Otley. Tuddenham is talking about applying for an annulment of the marriage, would you believe!

But Unwin could have made peace among the priests – they could then have worked for unity among the lords.'

'Do you think that is why he was killed?' asked Bartholomew uneasily. 'To prevent him from acting as peacemaker?' He thought about what Eltisley had claimed to see. Had Grosnold returned after his spectacular and very obvious exit to see where Unwin stood on the notion of harmony between the manors? Unwin would almost certainly have told him he would strive for an armistice, and thus provided Grosnold with the motive to kill him.

But then what about the cloaked figure? Was that one of Grosnold's henchmen fleeing from killing Unwin as he prayed at the altar? Or did Grosnold stab Unwin himself, so that there would be no other witness to the crime? He gazed down at the half-filled grave, wishing yet again that he had been able to do something to save the student-friar.

Bardolf squinted up at him. 'Yes, I would say that Grosnold would kill a priest, if he thought that priest might negotiate for an end to the fighting that would leave him the poorer – he would have to give up the toll he has imposed on Clopton and Burgh folk to use the road through his manor for a start. But then both Tuddenham and Hamon would kill if they thought they might lose the land on which Peche Hall stands; Deblunville might kill if peace meant an annulment of his marriage to Janelle; I might kill if Tuddenham tried to claim Gull Farm – my father stole it from his, but I have grown fond of it over the last thirty years.'

Bartholomew regarded him in amazement. 'How can you live with all this uncertainty?'

'It keeps us on our toes, and adds a spice to our lives that has been missing since Crécy. But I am growing too old for such things, and my bones throb from the cold and the damp. If I am attacked while I am stricken with this damned backache, I will lose everything anyway.'

'So, you want a truce because you think your neighbours might wait until you are ill, and then pounce?' asked
Bartholomew.

Bardolf moved his head from side to side in a curious
motion. 'Essentially. If I do not press for conciliation while
I am still strong, I will lose everything when I am weak. I
suppose you do not have a cure for me, do you? Stoate is
worse than useless. I take his damned purges every Sunday,
and all they do is make me feel like death for an hour.'

'There are poultices you can try,' said Bartholomew, not
wanting to poach what was probably one of Stoate's most
lucrative sources of income. 'Ask Stoate about them.'

'He does not prescribe poultices. He bleeds, and he purges,
and he gives astrological consultations,' said Bardolf. 'I have
tried all those things and my back still pains me. I want
a cure.'

'Did you find anything in all that earth?' asked Tuddenham
casually, coming up behind them and addressing Cynric. He
gazed speculatively at the pile of soil the book-bearer was
shovelling.

'Such as what?' asked Cynric, puzzled by the question.

'Objects?' said Tuddenham vaguely. 'Bits and pieces.
Things.' He became aggressive. 'This is my land. Anything dug up here belongs to me, and no one had better
forget it.'

'Cynric is not a thief,' said Bartholomew coldly, immediately
understanding the reason behind Tuddenham's enquiry. 'If
he had found Grundisburgh's lost golden calf, he would
return it to you.'

Bardolf gave a sharp laugh. 'These scholars are too quick
for you, Thomas! You should keep an eye on them, or
they will be going back to Cambridge with more than your
golden calf!'

Sir John Bardolf turned his back on Bartholomew, and began

to hobble to where a servant held the reins of his horse. Tuddenham poked Unwin's grave with his toe, but apparently decided the pile was too small to hide a golden calf and went to join Hamon and Siric in the shelter of one of the churchyard yews. It was now raining hard, and Bartholomew was soaked through. He waited until Cynric was patting down the soil in a muddy mound, and then started to return to the Half Moon with him.

A shout of alarm from Deynman made him turn back. Horsey was sitting in the grass, his face as white as snow. Kneeling, Bartholomew rested his hand on the student's head. He was shivering, but Bartholomew thought his illness no more serious than the chill of the rain and a sudden spell of dizziness induced by grief. He instructed Deynman to take him back to the tavern and put him to bed, making it clear that he should ensure that Horsey changed into a dry robe first. It was something that would have been obvious to most people, but Bartholomew had learned from bitter experience that nothing should be left to Deynman's common sense.

'I want my astrological consultation today,' said Grosnold to Bartholomew, as the physician prepared to accompany the students to the Half Moon.

'Ask Stoate,' said Bartholomew, none too politely. There was something about the belligerence and insensitivity of the Suffolk lords that he found unusually provoking.

'I want you,' said Grosnold uncompromisingly. 'Now. I take it you have no objection?' The last question was directed towards Tuddenham, not Bartholomew.

'Master Alcote is drafting my advowson, so you will not be inconveniencing me by taking him,' replied Tuddenham, with an indifferent shrug.

'Right, come on, then,' said Grosnold, snapping his fingers at Bartholomew.

'Sir Thomas is not my master to say where I can and

cannot go,' said Bartholomew stiffly. 'And I do not conduct astrological consultations.'

'I do,' offered Deynman, who had been listening. 'And I am much less expensive than him.'

'You are also unqualified,' said Alcote in alarm, hurrying over from where he had been talking to Walter Wauncy. It did not take a genius to know that letting Deynman loose on Grosnold would prove disastrous for all concerned, but especially for Grosnold. 'Doctor Bartholomew will be delighted to do your consultation,' he added, smiling ingratiatingly at the black knight.

Bartholomew rounded on him angrily. 'You are not my master, either. I am not doing it. Horsey is ill, and I want to stay with him.'

'Horsey has only fainted like some fragile maiden,' hissed Alcote unsympathetically. 'You will do as Master Tuddenham desires, so long as we are his guests. Everyone in Grundisburgh has been good to us, and we will not offend them by behaving churlishly.'

'Someone in Grundisburgh murdered Unwin,' retorted Bartholomew, goaded to imprudence by Alcote's bossiness.

Tuddenham pursed his lips, angry at the implied criticism. 'I can assure you that I am doing all I can to locate Unwin's killer.'

'Of course he is,' gushed Alcote, glowering furiously at Bartholomew. He took the physician by the arm, and hauled him out of earshot. 'For God's sake, show some grace, man! I worked hard to persuade Tuddenham to give us this advowson. I do not want it all ruined because you are an unmannerly lout!'

'And how did you "persuade" Tuddenham to give it to us?' demanded Bartholomew furiously, pulling his arm away. He was almost angry enough to accuse anyone of compliance in Unwin's murder, even Alcote, whose negotiations with Tuddenham had resulted in Unwin being appointed as

Grundisburgh's parish priest. 'Do you know some dreadful secret about him, which you threatened to tell unless he gave Michaelhouse the deeds to the church?'

Alcote glared at him. 'That is a foul thing to say. What do you think I am? And, for your information, I arranged the transaction with Tuddenham through one of my business connections in Ipswich. Tuddenham was going to donate the church living to one of the merchant guilds there, but I was able to convince him that a Cambridge college would be a better option for him. I mentioned that we have lawyers who will act as his executors when he dies, and who will ensure his will is carried out exactly as he wants it to be – not to mention the fact that his heirs will save a good deal on legal fees when the time comes.'

'So, why is Tuddenham so desperate to have it completed quickly?' asked Bartholomew, strongly suspecting that Alcote was being less than honest with him. 'He has not stopped pestering you about finishing it since you arrived. There is something odd going on, and I think you know what it is.'

Alcote looked smug. 'I know a great many things that you do not, my boy. But you should not vex your little mind with them. Just trust me. I know what I am doing.'

'I would sooner trust a viper,' snorted Bartholomew, disgusted. 'And if I find out that you know some dreadful secret about the Tuddenhams, and you accept this advowson and bring Michaelhouse into disrepute, I will see you never interfere in College affairs again.'

Alcote gave a sneer. 'And how will you do that? You are only interested in chopping off people's legs and inspecting their urine. Tuddenham is insisting that the advowson is written quickly because he is an impatient man. He knows that I am the only one who can do it, and that the rest of you are next to useless. He wants you all gone, so that he does not have to pay Eltisley to keep you.'

'Thomas has always been impatient,' said Dame Eva, the

closeness of her voice making them jump. 'It is just his way. But do not let him bully you into working quicker than you should, Master Alcote. He would have you labouring all night if you let him.'

Alcote eyed her with some hostility, before hurrying off to placate Grosnold. The old lady watched him depart with her sharp eyes, while Bartholomew fervently wished he would trip over his flagrantly expensive robe and break his scrawny neck. Considering that he had just been berating Bartholomew for his rudeness to Grosnold, Alcote's behaviour towards Dame Eva was inexcusable. Predictably, however, the old lady was slow to take offence. She smiled at Bartholomew and took his arm, patting it sympathetically when she sensed the tension and anger in him.

'Isilia was right – that man fears women more than he fears the Devil himself.'

Bartholomew looked down at her. She was wearing her yellowed wimple and an over-large cloak that looked as if it might belong to her son. But, unfashionable and inelegant though she might appear, she was the only member of Tuddenham's household who was not wet and shivering. Once again, Bartholomew admired her for putting her personal comfort before appearances.

'Poor Rosella,' said Isilia, coming to join them, and following their eyes to Alcote, who scurried fawningly at Grosnold's heels. 'She had high hopes that a handsome young student would step past her pea on the lintel, but instead it was Alcote – a man who prefers men to women.'

'He does not particularly like men, either,' said Bartholomew, trying to force his irritation with Alcote to the back of his mind. 'He just sees them as a lesser evil.'

Isilia laughed, and he noticed, yet again, how lovely she was with her pale pink cheeks and fine green eyes. 'I have tried hard to make him feel welcome at Wergen Hall – my husband expects too much of him sometimes, with all those piles of writs – but I think I only succeed in making him more nervous than ever. He would rather starve than have me bring him his food.'

'I see young Horsey is unwell,' said Dame Eva, pointing to where Deynman was helping the student-friar to the tavern. 'Poor boy – it must be the shock. I will send some eggs for him from Wergen Hall, and some beans. I do not like to see him so wan.'

'That would be kind,' said Bartholomew, touched that someone as grand as the lord of the manor's mother should notice a mere student, and consider his needs.

'We are so sorry about this,' said Isilia, gesturing towards Unwin's grave. 'We would do anything to bring him back.'

'Isilia and I have already given Walter Wauncy ten shillings, so that a mass for Unwin's soul can be said each morning for the next thirty days,' said Dame Eva. 'If he thinks more masses are needed after that, we will pay him to continue.'

'Thank you,' said Bartholomew.

The old lady gazed across at the far corner of the churchyard for a moment, and then took Bartholomew's arm and led him toward a group of ancient yews that stood over a jumble of coffin-shaped tombs.

'This is my husband's,' she said, stopping at the only one that was well tended and that had fresh flowers on the top. 'He was a good and honourable man, and would be so saddened to see the day when a poor young priest was slain in the church he loved.'

'How long since he died?' asked Bartholomew gently, seeing tears gather at the corners of her wrinkled eyes and trickle down her cheeks.

'Twenty years,' said Isilia, when the old lady could not answer. She looked sympathetically at Dame Eva, and took a frail hand in her young, smooth ones. 'Come, mother. We should not stand here in the rain for you to take a chill. I will sing to you this afternoon – one of the songs your husband wrote, if it would please you.'

Dame Eva nodded gratefully, and clung to Bartholomew's arm as he escorted her back to Tuddenham, who was waiting for her with a litter. She stopped suddenly, and gripped Bartholomew so fiercely that he winced.

'You are a kind young man, and I would not like to see you come to harm. You must promise me you will go nowhere near Barchester. It is one of the gateways to hell, and no place for the god-fearing. If Unwin had not gone to Barchester, he would not have seen Padfoot and we would not be attending his requiem mass today.'

Bartholomew nodded, feeling sure he would have no cause to visit the deserted village anyway. 'I will avoid Barchester, if I can.'

'You must never set foot in the place,' declared Isilia with huge eyes. 'It seethes with evil and is Padfoot's domain!'

'Padfoot!' spat Hamon in disgust, coming to help them into the litter. 'What nonsense have you been spouting, Isilia?'

'It is not nonsense,' said the old lady, a spark of anger flashing in her eyes. 'It is simple truth, and only a fool would choose to ignore it.'

'Hamon *is* a fool,' said Isilia, eyeing him coldly. 'He is an insensitive oaf, who is only interested in hunting and dogs and smelly horses.'

Hamon gave an unpleasant laugh. 'Better that than wasting my time on frightening gullible physicians with tales of ghostly dogs.'

He gave Dame Eva a hefty shove that accelerated her into the cart faster than was necessary. Bartholomew stepped forward in alarm, afraid that the rough push might have damaged the old woman's brittle bones, but she waved him back with a resigned flap of her hand. Eyes flashing furiously, Isilia thrust Hamon away and climbed in unaided.

Then Dame Eva saw the ugly nag that had been coupled to the litter that would bear her home, and she and Hamon began a spirited argument about that, while Bartholomew looked around desperately for Michael, seeking a way to escape before he was dragged into it.

'Are you ready for this consultation with Grosnold?' asked the monk, bowing politely to the ladies before seizing Bartholomew's arm and bearing him off.

'I am not doing it,' said Bartholomew firmly.

Michael shook him gently by the arm. 'Alcote is right. You cannot refuse your services to one of our prospective benefactor's friends, just because you feel like it. That kind of behaviour might lose us the advowson in itself.'

'I do not care about the advowson. I have had enough of this place. It has killed Unwin, and now we are ordered about like servants. As soon as Horsey is well, I am leaving.'

'Fine, Matt. You can go tomorrow, if you like. I may even come with you, if I have tracked down Unwin's killer. We can leave Alcote here to complete this business, and we can wait for him at St Edmundsbury. But you should go with Grosnold now.'

'No,' said Bartholomew.

'Think, Matt,' said Michael urgently. 'This is an opportunity for you to discover whether Grosnold doubled back on himself and returned to Grundisburgh to speak to Unwin as Eltisley claims. We might not have another chance like this. Go, and take Cynric with you.'

Bartholomew sighed and rubbed a hand through his wet hair, reluctant to capitulate, but knowing that Michael was right – it might well prove to be the only opportunity to wheedle information from the black knight of Otley. 'Very well. But please make sure Deynman looks after Horsey. We do not want him catching a fever that will keep us here for days.'

Michael nodded. 'I will see him to the tavern myself. Then

I will locate Mistress Freeman to ask her about this cloaked figure she saw. She has been out every time I have called at her house so far, but, if she is away today, I will wait there until she returns.'

He leaned back against the church wall, where rain slicked down his fine brown locks to make his head seem pear-shaped. Suddenly, his sandalled foot shot out from underneath him, toppling him to the ground. His first reaction was shock, his second amused embarrassment.

'Wet grass,' he explained as Bartholomew and Cynric helped him up. 'Leather-soled sandals are useless in the rain, and this is not the first time this has happened to me. I only hope it does not occur when I am in the midst of some solemn proctorial ceremony. What is the matter, Matt?'

Bartholomew was staring at the ground where Michael had slipped. It was stained a reddish brown.

'Is it blood?' asked Cynric, peering over his shoulder. 'There is masses of it!'

Bartholomew nodded, pointing to where more of it turned the white heads of daisies dark. He looked at Michael.

'I think you have just found the place where Unwin was killed.'

chapter 7

IT WAS NOT A PLEASANT JOURNEY THROUGH THE DRIP-
ping woods from Grundisburgh to Otley. Bartholomew
had assumed that Grosnold would have his astrological
consultation at Wergen Hall, but the knight had insisted
that all the information Bartholomew would need was at
his own manor, and so Bartholomew was obliged to travel
home with him. Since Bartholomew had been loath to read
Grosnold's stars in the first place, he bitterly resented riding
miles through the rain to do it, especially since what had
started as a shower seemed to have settled in for the day,
and fine, but drenching, drops pattered on his shoulders
and head and trickled down the back of his neck.

Otley was several miles to the north-west, along the valley of
the River Lark and across the Old Road where Bartholomew
and Cynric had encountered the outlaws the previous week. As
they passed the Grundisburgh–Otley boundary, Tuddenham's
scrubby pastureland gave way to Grosnold's strips of corn
and barley, waving brilliant green in the rain. Off to the
left were the ruined roofs of the abandoned village of
Barchester, and Bartholomew noticed that Grosnold and
his steward, Ned, did not follow the path that ran through
the centre of it as the scholars had done, but took a newer,
well-used one that skirted the settlement at a safe distance.
Cynric, riding behind Bartholomew, crossed himself and
looked in the opposite direction.

'Barchester is inhabited by plague dead,' Grosnold stated
matter-of-factly when Bartholomew asked him about it, more
to take his mind off his sodden clothes and wet feet than for

information. 'And a great white dog often roams there – any who set eyes on that will be dead within the week.'

'Unwin saw a white dog,' said Bartholomew. 'When we left Otley last week, we took the path that runs through the middle of Barchester by mistake, and Unwin said he spotted a white dog in the trees. No one else saw it.'

'Well, there you are then,' said Grosnold, exchanging a knowing glance with his redheaded steward. 'That explains why he met his end so suddenly.'

'But you do not believe these tales of haunted villages and spectral hounds,' said Bartholomew, certain that a proud soldier like Grosnold would not be unnerved by such stories. He saw the intense expression on the black knight's face. 'Do you?' he added uncertainly.

'Of course I do,' said Grosnold, with such conviction that Bartholomew wished he had never broached the subject. 'Barchester has been infested with demons since the pestilence. It drove poor Mad Megin to her death in the river last winter, although how she lived among those tortured souls all those years is beyond me.'

'She was mad,' said Ned, the steward, by way of explanation, adding mysteriously, 'and she did not keep her Good Friday loaf.'

'Her what?' asked Bartholomew, nonplussed.

Ned shook his head at this monumental ignorance. 'Her Good Friday loaf – the loaf of bread cooked on a Good Friday that hangs on a string in the homes of all good Christians.'

'It prevents the bloody flux,' explained Grosnold. 'I thought you would have known that, being a medical man. Megin ate hers, instead of keeping it safe, and look at the terrible end she met.'

Ned jerked his head toward the woods. 'Padfoot was out and about last night,' he remarked conversationally. 'Siric, Sir Thomas's man, heard it snuffling about near the moat.'

'Did he see it?' asked Bartholomew, aware that a good many things snuffled about in the night.

Ned regarded him as though he were insane. 'Well, of course he did not. If he had set eyes on it, he would die, wouldn't he?'

'But if he did not see it, how did he know it was the white dog, and not some other animal?'

'He knew,' said Ned. 'And so would you if you heard it. There is no mistaking Padfoot.'

'Aye, that is true,' agreed Grosnold. He changed the subject slightly. 'I heard Will Norys, the pardoner, is wanted for questioning in relation to Unwin's murder.'

'Apparently Brother Michael questioned him, and by the next day he had fled the village,' said Ned. 'Such flight is a sure sign of his guilt.'

'True, true,' said Grosnold. 'Poor Norys! He will swing for the murder of the student-priest, even though he was only a tool in the hands of Padfoot. As far as I am concerned, Unwin set eyes on Padfoot, and his fate was sealed. Norys was just in the wrong place at the wrong time, and Padfoot used him.'

Or was he? Bartholomew was still not certain that Norys was the culprit. He frowned, wondering how to broach the subject of Grosnold's own mysterious meetings with Unwin – one in the castle bailey at Otley, and the other in the churchyard shortly before Unwin's death. Grosnold glanced at him, and misunderstood his thoughtful expression.

'Have no fear, physician. Norys will not get far. Tuddenham will have him under lock and key before you know it.'

And if that happened, Bartholomew was sure the pardoner would be given a token trial with a foregone conclusion, and would end up on the gibbet at Bond's Corner like the mysterious hanged man. The whole thing would be swift and decisive and, whether Norys was guilty or not, Bartholomew was certain there would be questions that would remain unanswered after his execution.

'Do you think the evidence is sufficient to convict Norys of Unwin's murder?' he asked.

Grosnold seemed surprised. 'Evidence? What are you talking about? Norys killed the priest for his purse. What other evidence do you need?'

'That is not evidence, that is conjecture,' said Bartholomew. 'Supposing Norys is not guilty? You might be condemning the wrong man.'

'You think he is innocent?' asked Grosnold, astonished. 'But he is a pardoner and an occasional pedlar of relics. He had every reason to kill your friend.'

His logic, if that was what it could be called, would have appealed to Michael. Bartholomew sighed, deciding he would not proceed very far with that line of enquiry. Poor Norys was already perceived as guilty by men like Grosnold, and basically, it was all because Michael did not like pardoners. But, Bartholomew recalled, Norys had suggested that a lord of the manor might be responsible for Unwin's death. Was that significant? Or was Norys simply trying to cast doubts on the impartiality of the men who might ultimately have the power to hang him? Bartholomew wiped the rain from his eyes, not sure what to think.

He considered Bardolf's claim that one of the warring noblemen might have killed Unwin, because he might have effected a peace agreement, and tried to see how it might fit with Norys's accusation – if Norys were telling the truth. Still, by the time Bartholomew had finished Grosnold's consultation and returned to Grundisburgh, Michael would have spoken to Mistress Freeman, and at least they would know whether Norys had been honest about that part of his story. Mistress Freeman had already told Tuddenham's steward she had seen the figure running from the church, and so all that remained was to ascertain whether she was with Norys or Stoate.

They rode in silence. The rain had turned the path into

a quagmire, and the horses stumbled and skidded in slick mud. But once they had crossed the Old Road it was not long before they reached Grosnold's manor of Nether Hall, dark and squat inside its wooden palisades. The bailey seemed to be inhabited by nothing but men, all wearing dull brown homespun tunics, so that it appeared a dreary place. Alcote would have approved, thought Bartholomew, looking in vain for some female presence, although the atmosphere was more debauched than monastic.

Grosnold led the way into a hall-house that was gloomy, and stank of kitchen slops and garderobe shafts that had long been due for a rinse. The reeds on the floor crawled with vermin, and a pig rooted happily among them for scraps. Ned herded it to the other end of the room, while Grosnold flung himself into the only chair and yelled for refreshments.

A dirty-faced squire brought greasy goblets and a jug of wine so sour that Bartholomew wondered that Grosnold still had any teeth if he drank it regularly. The physician set it down on the windowsill after a single sip, for some desperate servant to find and drink later.

'Now,' he said, keen to start – and therefore to leave – as quickly as possible. He drew a bundle of astronomical tables from his bag – tables that were frayed and battered not from frequent use, but because they were always dropping out when he was searching for something else. 'Where is this information that you wanted me to have?'

Grosnold nodded to Ned, who rummaged around in a large chest near the fireplace until he emerged with a sheaf of parchments. He set them on a small table near the window, and provided Bartholomew with a pen and a small bottle of ink. While Bartholomew tried to resurrect the viscous pigment into something serviceable using dribbles of the wine, Grosnold bellowed at his squire to light the fire and bring him something to eat.

What came were bread trenchers that had been used before, and some cold lamb that had fused into a solid mass from the grease that had been cooked into it. There were also some small, sharp apples, a handful of nuts and a rind of sweaty cheese. Bartholomew left the meat and cheese to Grosnold, while he took the nuts and fruit. They ate in silence, punctuated by occasional grunts from the black knight – once when the pig made a nuisance of itself near his feet, and once when he dropped a piece of food in the rushes and could not find it again. Bartholomew silently cursed Michael for suggesting he comply with Grosnold's demand. He even began to think Alcote's self-important prattle would be better than the brooding company of the bald soldier.

After the meal, Grosnold picked his teeth with a long knife and Bartholomew sat on the windowsill to look at the documents he had been given. Several were old manorial rolls, giving information regarding who lived where and who owned what cattle. Another was a list of the cost of spices from the Ipswich market in June of 1347. Bartholomew was interested to see how much prices had risen since the plague, but it did not help him to construct Grosnold's horoscope. Finally, there were two documents proclaiming that Grosnold had paid fourteen shillings for six sheep and a cow, and a crumpled parchment proving his ownership of Nether Hall.

'I should keep this safe, if I were you,' said Bartholomew, showing it to him. 'You might need to produce it in a court of law if your neighbours persist in their squabbles over manor boundaries.'

'What is it?' demanded Grosnold, holding it upside down.

'Proof of purchase of Nether Hall by Hugh Grosnold in 1292,' said Bartholomew. 'He was your grandfather?'

'That is none of your business,' snapped Grosnold, crumpling up the deed angrily. 'And it is false. Everyone knows that I was given Nether Hall by the King for my bravery at Crécy.'

Bartholomew did not want to meet the knight's eyes. He was no authority on deeds to manors, but this one seemed genuine enough to him. Grosnold's claim that it had been granted by the King was a blatant falsehood. He had probably inherited it from a grandfather who had never bothered to visit it, as was often the case when a man owned several manors, and so Grosnold had found he had been able to invent his own story about how he came by it. So, thought Bartholomew, as he walked back to the window, Grosnold was a liar. What other untruths had he told? And what had been his business with Unwin?

Grosnold continued to glare at Bartholomew. 'Just get on with the horoscope. That is what I am paying you for, not to pry into my personal affairs.'

'I need more than this,' said Bartholomew, gesturing at Grosnold's household papers.

'Why?' demanded Grosnold. 'They are all Stoate ever uses. If they are good enough for him, they should be good enough for you.'

No wonder Stoate did not mind performing consultations, thought Bartholomew. If he based them on the cost of pepper six years before, and on the breeding records of sheep, then there would be very little arithmetic involved, and Stoate basically could predict what he pleased. Or what he thought might please Grosnold. For a fleeting moment, Bartholomew considered doing the same: Grosnold was an arrogant lout, who could not tell the difference between a shopping list and an incriminating deed of sale and who would not know whether anything Bartholomew calculated was accurate or not. But when he had become a physician Bartholomew had taken an oath he considered sacred, and he was not prepared to break it by cheating Grosnold, tempting though that might be.

'I will be able to predict your horoscope far more accurately if you can remember certain dates,' he said. 'We can start with when you were born.'

'Winter,' said Grosnold helpfully. 'Quite a few years back now.'

It was slow going, and Bartholomew's head began to ache. In order to relate the celestial calendar to the kind of information Grosnold was giving him, he needed to invent formulae to cope with the degree of error, and it was far more complex than anything he had done before. Cynric was asleep by the hearth, and Grosnold was already thinking about his next meal by the time Bartholomew put down the pen and showed Grosnold his conclusions.

The knight was impressed. He took the scraps of parchment with the tiny figures and equations scribbled all over them, and peered at them from every angle.

'All these are mine?' he asked, awed. 'For my stars?'

Bartholomew nodded and began to tell him what it meant, although he could not imagine that predicting the knight would be vulnerable to rheums in the head when Venus was dominant in three days' time, or that he should avoid herbs of Saturn while the moon was waxing lest they inflame the liver, could be of remote interest to a hardened warrior like Grosnold. He was wrong. The knight listened intently and then repeated it faithfully to Ned, to be passed on to the cooks in the kitchens, with every intention, apparently, of following it to the letter. When Bartholomew had finished, Grosnold leaned back and smiled.

'Good,' he said, clearly relieved. 'Now I know that I should go to Ipswich next Tuesday, not Wednesday, and that I should decline the invitation from Bardolf to dine with him on Monday. I shall inform him that I will come on Thursday instead. But you took your time with all this, man; Stoate is far quicker at his calculations. Still, I expect you will get better with practice.'

'I am sure I will,' said Bartholomew, amused. He stood and stretched. 'I should leave. It will be dark soon.'

'You have your servant with you,' said Grosnold, gesturing to Cynric. 'He looks like a fellow who knows how to look after himself. Anyway, outlaws will not bother themselves with a physician who is slow with his horoscopes, especially one who is as impoverished as you appear to be.'

Bartholomew was almost out of the door before he realised that he had not attempted to discover what Grosnold had been discussing with Unwin in the bailey, or whether Eltisley really had seen them together in the churchyard before Unwin's death.

'I must tell you how much I admire your armour,' he said as they stood together in the doorway, hoping to appeal to the man's vanity and start a conversation. 'It is very splendid.'

'Modelled after that of the Prince of Wales,' said Grosnold proudly. 'He always wears black. I can give you the name of the smith who made it, if you are interested.'

'I am no fighting man,' said Bartholomew, wondering what his colleagues would say if he arrived at high table in Michaelhouse wearing a suit of metal. 'Your destrier is a handsome animal, too.' Bartholomew actually had no idea whether the stocky beast was a handsome animal or not: he was an abysmal judge of what did or what did not constitute a good horse.

'He is,' agreed Grosnold, pleased. 'He served me well at Crécy. I fought at the side of the young Prince of Wales, you know. Now, there is a fine soldier!'

'Really?' said Bartholomew. He began to run out of things to say, since military chit-chat had never been a particular strength of his – especially considering that, in view of his lie about how he had come to own his manor, most of Grosnold's was probably more wishful thinking than reality. 'It must take a long time to train a horse like that.'

'It takes time and patience to train any horse,' said Grosnold. 'But you are right: I did take extra care with old Satan.'

'When you galloped it across Grundisburgh's green the other day,' said Bartholomew, choosing his words carefully, 'were you not afraid that someone might do something to damage it – like lie in its way? I understand those things are expensive.'

'Good destriers are very expensive. Satan cost me more than you will earn in your lifetime, by the look of you. But I like to give him his head now and then. I raced him right down the banks of the Lark until I reached the Old Road.'

'Did you go back to Grundisburgh after that?' asked Bartholomew, knowing it was unsubtle, but not knowing how else to ask.

'No,' said Grosnold suspiciously. 'I did not go back. Why do you ask? Do you imagine you saw me talking to that priest, Unwin, or something?'

'Of course not,' said Bartholomew, wholly confused. He could not decide whether Grosnold was a complete buffoon and had just confessed that he had indeed returned to Grundisburgh and spoken to Unwin, or whether his words were a simple, truthful denial, and that he had mentioned Unwin because he knew Unwin's death was the reason why Bartholomew was asking.

He smiled at the knight in what he hoped was a reassuring manner. 'I just asked because I thought a fine animal like yours might need more exercise than a mere trot to the Old Road.'

'Did you?' asked Grosnold, harshly. 'Well, after I left Grundisburgh I came home. I sat by the hearth all night with Ned, cleaning my nails. Look.'

His nails were reasonably clean, although thin red crescents under most of them suggested that he should not have used such a sharp knife. There was nothing more to be learned: Grosnold was now on his guard, and had said all he was going to. The physician bowed his farewell and walked over to Cynric who was holding his horse in the rain. He was almost out of the bailey when Grosnold stopped him with a tremendous yell.

Because of the drizzle and the lateness of the day, most of the men Bartholomew had seen earlier were in the outbuildings, with the doors and shutters closed against the evening chill. White smoke from cooking fires seeped from thatched roofs and through windows that had been poorly blocked Bartholomew could glimpse men inside sitting in the flickering yellow of flames. A range of smells drifted out – stews of peas and beans, baked bread and boiling meat, all mingled with the acrid, comforting aroma of burning wood. At Grosnold's shout, shutters and doors were eased open as the curious inhabitants came to see what was happening.

'I did not pay you,' Grosnold hollered, waving his purse in the air. 'Here is gold for your troubles. I am pleased with that horoscope. I might have you come back and do me another.'

Not, thought Bartholomew, if it could be avoided. Ned ran across the muddy yard, brandishing the coin aloft like a talisman until he reached Bartholomew and handed it over.

'I never met a physician who forgot his money before,' he said with a disbelieving grin. 'Master Stoate would not.'

Bartholomew thanked him, and turned towards Grundisburgh. The rain had brought an early dusk, and the daylight was fading fast. It was cold, too, and Bartholomew's cloak, dried in front of the fire at Grosnold's manor, was soon drenched again. The thick scent of wetness pervaded everything, and the downpour hissed gently among the trees. By the time they reached the Old Road it was gloomy, and Bartholomew would have taken the wrong path had Cynric not been with him. They rode in silence, travelling faster than Bartholomew felt was safe. He kept expecting his horse to stumble and deposit him in the thick, sucking mud through which they squelched.

'It will be dark before we are back,' said Cynric, glancing up at the sky. 'I did not realise it was so late, or I would have hurried you.'

'We must have taken the wrong turning at that sheep pen, Cynric,' said Bartholomew, peering ahead through the trees. 'There is Barchester in front of us. We are on the road that runs through it, rather than the one that passes around the outside.'

'I suppose it does not matter,' said Cynric, eyeing the hamlet nervously. 'They both lead to Grundisburgh, after all.'

'Is that a light?' asked Bartholomew, straining his eyes in the gloom. 'It looks as if someone has lit a lamp in one of the houses.'

'Let's find the other path,' said Cynric abruptly, hauling his horse's head round. 'I want to see no ghostly gatherings in haunted hovels, thank you very much.'

He had spurred his pony back the way they had come before Bartholomew could suggest that the light probably belonged to a traveller, using one of the houses as shelter for the night. With a sigh, realising that the detour would mean they would be out in the foul weather for longer than ever, he was about to follow Cynric when something launched itself at him with a tremendous screech that hurt his ears and turned the blood in his veins to ice.

Bartholomew caught the merest glimpse of a shadowy figure coming at him from the trees before it thumped into his horse so hard that the animal reared and screamed in terror. He fought to control it, but something was clawing at the medicine bag that was looped around his shoulder, snatching at it to try to pull him from his saddle. Bartholomew kicked out blindly, hearing a grunt of pain as his leg made contact with something soft. His horse continued to prance, and

Bartholomew felt his foot seized and hauled on. Immediately, he began to lose his balance. The horse bucked violently, and Bartholomew fell, landing in an undignified tangle in the wet grass.

For a moment all he could hear was the sound of his horse's hooves thundering back toward Otley. He looked around him wildly, trying to see his attacker in the darkness. The next assault came from behind. With another deathly howl, he was knocked forward so that he fell on his face. Mud splattered into his eyes, nose and mouth, so that he could not see or breathe. He struggled furiously, trying to free himself from the suffocating weight that pressed him into a soupy puddle.

He succeeded in raising his head, and took a great gasp of air before it was forced down again. Hot breath gusted on to the back of his neck, and his ears were full of roars and grunts. He reached backward, trying to pull whatever it was off him. His fingers encountered something soggy and covered in wiry hair. Another howl split the air, and he twisted sideways, partly dislodging the thing from his back.

The air around him was rank with the stench of animal. He could smell wet fur and warm, carnivorous breath. He squirmed and kicked with all his might, clawing at the ground in his desperation to escape. There was a rumbling growl that seemed to vibrate the very ground on which he lay, ending in a series of guttural grunts. He struggled more frantically when another snarl ended with the drip of hot saliva on his cheek. Revolted, he turned his face away.

And then, suddenly, it was gone. He rolled on to his back and sat up, coughing and wiping the mud from his eyes with his sleeve. The village was deserted. The light in the house had been doused, and the squat black shapes of the huts stood immovable, like stones in the darkness. Rain pattered gently in the trees, all but drowned out by the sound of his rasping breathing and the thump of his heart.

'Did you see it?' came Cynric's terrified voice at his ear. Bartholomew started backward at the sound of something so close, and tried to scramble to his feet. Cynric helped him.

'No,' said Bartholomew shakily. 'Whatever it was attacked me from behind. I saw nothing other than a shadow. What was it? A wolf?'

But Cynric was not of a mind to stand chatting in the forlorn village. 'Come on, boy,' he said, his voice uncharacteristically unsteady as he hauled on Bartholomew's arm. 'It might come back at any minute. The horses have fled, so we will have to run. Can you manage?'

The notion of a second encounter with the smelly beast was enough to spur Bartholomew into action, and even his trembling legs could not prevent him from racing away from Barchester as fast as he could. Without waiting to see if Cynric followed, he took to his heels, tearing blindly past trees and scrub, through the river and across fields, and only stopping when he failed to see a ditch and went flying head over heels into someone's lovingly tended barley. Cynric was right behind him.

'That should be far enough,' the Welshman panted, doubling over to rest his hands on his knees as he fought to catch his breath. 'Did the beast bite you?'

Bartholomew shook his head, looking around him wildly in anticipation of another attack. 'It just sat on me and drooled. Did you see it? It felt like a bull with a wolf's breath!'

'It was the white dog,' said Cynric, swallowing hard. 'I saw it. It was a big white dog.'

'It was certainly big,' gasped Bartholomew, drawing his knees up to his chest to ease the burning stitch in his side. 'Can you see it now? Has it followed us?'

Cynric shook his head, scanning the dark fields. 'Maybe it does not stray far from the haunted village. Maybe it lives there, feeding on the souls of the people who died in the plague.'

'Maybe someone set it on us,' said Bartholomew more practically. 'Someone who knew we would be travelling that way.'

'Spirits have a way of knowing such things,' muttered Cynric, crossing himself vigorously. He hesitated, continuing in a low whisper. 'Will I die now that I have set eyes on it? Unwin did, and so did those two villagers – the suicide and the woman who died of childbirth fever.'

'That was no ghost, Cynric,' said Bartholomew with a shudder. 'It slathered all over me. Spirits do not slather. Nor do they stink.'

'They do so!' said Cynric, with absolute conviction. 'My mother always smelled almonds before my grandfather's spirit appeared to her, and the next morning the floor was always wet where he had stood.'

There was little Bartholomew could think of to say in answer to that. 'Where are we?' he asked eventually. 'I am completely lost.'

'So am I,' admitted Cynric, something Bartholomew had never before known to happen, suggesting that their encounter with the white dog had unnerved Cynric more than the physician had appreciated. 'It does not matter anyway,' the book-bearer added gloomily, 'since I am soon to lie in my grave next to Unwin.'

'You are not going to die,' said Bartholomew firmly. He grabbed the Welshman by the arm, and looked him in the eye. 'That was not a ghost, Cynric, it was real. You saw all those men looking out of their houses as Ned ran across the bailey waving that gold coin in the air. One of them followed us with his dog, intending to steal it. Or perhaps it was Grosnold himself, because of my clumsy questioning of him about Unwin – or even because I know that he inherited his manor from his grandfather, and that the

King and the Prince of Wales have probably never set eyes on the man.'

'But it was horrible, lad,' said Cynric, his dark eyes wide with fear. 'It was huge – bigger than any earthly dog I have ever seen; more like a pony, with a thick white coat to protect it from the fires of hell. When I saw it crouching over you and making all those dreadful noises, I thought it was trying to suck the soul from your body!'

'Did you see anyone with it? I am sure it was human hands that pulled me from my saddle – the dog came later.'

Again Cynric crossed himself vigorously in the darkness. 'No, thank the good Lord! All I saw was the beast. I fired an arrow at it, and it fled back to its lair in that ghostly village.'

'Well, there you are, then,' said Bartholomew reasonably. 'A spectre would not run away from an arrow. It was a real dog and someone owns it.'

'Then why did you run away?' demanded Cynric. 'It was a fiend from hell and you know it.'

With hindsight, Bartholomew was rather ashamed of the blind panic that had prompted him to rush away from the village as fast as his legs could carry him, but the fact was that an earthly hound drooling in his ears was just as frightening as a spectral one would have been.

'We can walk back to Otley and see which of those villagers has a white dog,' he said, deftly side-stepping Cynric's question.

'No!' exclaimed Cynric with a look of abject horror. 'I never want to set eyes on the likes of that thing again. Although I will not have long to see anything now. I can feel it in my bones.'

'It was just an ordinary dog,' said Bartholomew, becoming exasperated in his battle against Cynric's superstition. 'Nothing is going to happen to you.'

'No?' said Cynric warily. 'Then perhaps you should explain that to *them*.'

Bartholomew spun round to see where Cynric was pointing. From the fields around them, men had materialised, some of them carrying bows with arrows already nocked, and others with swords that glittered dully in the darkness.

'Who are you?' one of them called. 'Why are you trespassing here?'

'They are the dead souls of Barchester, protecting their fields,' groaned Cynric, clutching at Bartholomew's arm. 'They have come for us!'

'For God's sake, Cynric!' snapped Bartholomew, the shock of his experience with the dog making him unusually irritable with his book-bearer. 'Pull yourself together! We are probably on Bardolf's or Deblunville's land, and these are their men wondering why we were racing across their crops in the middle of the night all covered in mud.'

An arrow thumped into the ground nearby. Cynric closed his eyes and began to mutter incantations against the Devil.

'I asked who you were!' shouted the voice.

'We are from Cambridge,' Bartholomew called back. 'We were returning to Grundisburgh from Grosnold's manor, but we are lost.'

'You *are* lost,' agreed the man. 'This is not the way from Otley to Grundisburgh. I suppose you were sent here to spy. Who paid you? Grosnold or Tuddenham? Or has that weakling Hamon finally become a man, and come out from behind his uncle's skirts?'

'Someone tried to rob us,' said Bartholomew, lowering his voice as the man with the bow came closer. 'Our horses ran away.'

The archer gave a sneering laugh. 'Is that so? Next you will be trying to tell us that these robbers had a big white dog.'

'They did, actually,' said Bartholomew, puzzled. 'How did you know?'

'Everyone claims to have seen Padfoot these days,' said

the archer with affected weariness. 'They think fleeing from him is a good excuse to come sneaking on to our land. Come on. Master Deblunville will be wanting a word with you.'

The archer refused to listen to anything more. He nodded to his friends, and Cynric and Bartholomew were searched roughly: Bartholomew lost his medicine bag, and Cynric was relieved of enough metal to start his own forge. Bartholomew was astonished: he knew the Welshman never went unarmed, but the number of knives, blades and even sharp nails that were removed from every available place in Cynric's clothing was staggering.

The archer jabbed Bartholomew with one of Cynric's weapons, to indicate that they were to start walking. It was a miserable journey. Bartholomew's body ached from his encounter with the dog, and he was wet and cold. Cynric seemed to have given up altogether, and trailed listlessly at Bartholomew's side, more morose and apathetic than the physician had ever seen him. It seemed that, as far as Cynric was concerned, he was already a dead man.

At last the bumps and ridges of Deblunville's enclosure could be seen against the night sky, and Bartholomew and Cynric were prodded inside. They were directed through both sets of embankments and led into the inner bailey, where they were ordered to wait while someone went to fetch Deblunville. The wooden keep was in darkness, suggesting that Deblunville and his household had already retired to bed. It was some time before the door opened and Deblunville appeared; his wife, Janelle, and her father, John Bardolf, were behind him. Janelle walked slowly and her eyes were red-rimmed and sad, a far cry from the confident defiance she had displayed a few days before, when she had announced her marriage to Tuddenham and his cronies.

'You disappoint me, physician,' said Deblunville, walking towards him, holding a flaring torch. He was wearing baggy hose and a shirt that dangled almost to his knees. 'You seemed above all this subterfuge and trickery when we met the other day. I even gave you one of my cramp rings as an act of good faith.'

'I am sorry we trespassed on your land,' said Bartholomew. 'We were attacked as we were riding through Barchester from Otley, and we ran the wrong way when we escaped.'

'That is *my* land,' interposed Bardolf coldly. 'Barchester lies on my land – despite what Grosnold and Tuddenham might claim.'

'Attacked?' asked Deblunville, ignoring his father-in-law. He looked Bartholomew up and down. 'What was stolen? Not my cramp ring, I hope.'

'Nothing was stolen,' said Bartholomew, although he would not have been dismayed to lose the funeral jewellery Deblunville had given him. 'Cynric drove the robbers away with an arrow.'

'He claims Padfoot ambushed him,' said the archer with a grin. 'It is strange how Padfoot always seems to chase people from Grundisburgh on to *our* land.'

Deblunville nodded thoughtfully and addressed Bartholomew. 'Two people claim to have been chased on to my land by Padfoot within the last month: both are now dead, although I assure you that it had nothing to do with me. I personally believe that they were spies in the employ of one of my neighbours, who then executed them for getting caught – a cut throat and a childbirth fever were the official causes of death, I understand.'

'We are telling you the truth,' insisted Bartholomew. 'Why should I want to spy on you?'

'Look.' The archer held up the gold coin Grosnold had given Bartholomew, discovered when he had searched Bartholomew's bag. 'If they were robbed, why did the outlaws leave them this?'

'Who paid you to spy?' demanded Bardolf of Bartholomew, pushing forward to stand next to his son-in-law.

'Grosnold paid me for—'

'There!' exclaimed Bardolf triumphantly, interrupting Bartholomew and turning to Deblunville. 'A confession! I knew these scholars would soon start to meddle in our affairs. Tuddenham summoned them from Cambridge, so that he could set their cunning minds to undermining our rightful claims to this land. You know how lawyers are with words, twisting and turning them, so that they can be made to mean the opposite of what was intended.'

Janelle stepped forward and laid a hand on his arm. 'All these accusations will get us nowhere, father,' she said in a low voice. 'The scholars are not unreasonable men, and if we explain to them why we do not want spies on our manors they will understand.'

'You are ill,' said Bartholomew, noting the tremble in her voice and the unhealthy pallor of her skin. 'Is it the child?'

She nodded, and then shook her head. Tears sprouted from her eyes, and Deblunville thrust the torch into Bardolf's hands, so that he could put his arm around her.

'There is no child,' he said bitterly. 'Not any more. Master Stoate has killed it.'

Bartholomew was bewildered. 'Killed it how?'

Deblunville sighed. 'I sent a man to Ipswich for the cumin you said Janelle should have, but he has not yet returned. When Janelle was sick again this morning, we used Stoate's old remedy, since there was nothing else. Then she had griping pains and a flux of bleeding. The child has gone.'

'I am sorry,' said Bartholomew gently. 'But she should not be out here; she should be resting.'

'Will you give her something to help her sleep?' asked Deblunville. 'I do not want to ask Stoate to come. I might feel obliged to wring his neck.'

'Just a moment!' cried Bardolf, grabbing Deblunville's arm and swinging him round. 'These scholars have been caught red-handed spying on your land. Will you now let them give potions to Janelle, potions that might kill her? Physicians are not to be trusted at any time, but especially not ones who are in the pay of Tuddenham, and who have already lied to you.'

'What would he gain from hurting Janelle?' said Deblunville, pulling away angrily. 'And anyway, I believe him when he says he was attacked by Padfoot.'

'What?' Bardolf was almost screaming in disbelief. 'Padfoot is a story invented by Tuddenham to allow his spies to come and go at will.'

'But Tuddenham does not believe in Padfoot,' protested Bartholomew. 'He told us it was superstitious nonsense.'

Deblunville ignored him, but snatched the torch to thrust it so close that the physician winced, certain that he would have caught fire had his clothes not been so wet. 'Look at his cloak, Bardolf. It is covered in white hairs!'

Bartholomew sat on the edge of the bed in Janelle's chamber, and replaced the covers carefully. She smiled up at him, her face so lovely in the candlelight that it made him feel suddenly lonely. He wondered what Matilde was doing back in Cambridge, and whether he, like Michael, was destined to spend the rest of his life without the joy of a female companion.

'Are you really sure?' she asked yet again.

Bartholomew nodded. 'I am certain. There was no child in the flux of blood, and everything suggests to me that you are still carrying it. The potions I have given you will help, but you must rest for the next few days – weeks, even – and no more betony and pennyroyal, no matter what Stoate tells you.'

'You have been kind to me, despite the fact that we have been less than hospitable to you twice now.' She looked at the flames in the hearth, her tiny fingers fiddling restlessly with the bed-covers. 'In return, there is something I know that you might be interested to hear.'

'About the murder of Unwin?' he asked hopefully.

She shook her head. 'I am sorry, but no one seems to know anything about that. Usually, if a crime is committed, someone knows the culprit, and it does not take long for the truth to come out. But whoever killed Unwin has been very clever in hiding his tracks. I think you should not look to the common villagers for your killer; you should look higher.'

'That has been suggested before,' said Bartholomew, thinking about what Norys had told him. And then there was Eltisley's claim to have seen Grosnold with Unwin in the churchyard shortly before the friar's death, plus her father's belief that Unwin might have been killed because of the strife among the lords of the manor and their priests, 'Is that what you wanted to tell me?'

'No, something else. About my husband's clothes – the ones that you saw on the hanged man at Bond's Corner.' She paused again, and looked at the fire, its lights flickering in her eyes.

'You know who took them?' asked Bartholomew, gently prompting.

'Yes.' She looked up at him, and there was some of the grim determination in her face that he had seen when they first met. 'But you must not reveal that I told you this, or use the information against my father.'

'Your father?' said Bartholomew, puzzled. 'How is he involved?'

'I gave him those clothes,' said Janelle reluctantly. She shrugged at him. 'I am the thief. I stole from the man who was going to be my husband.'

'I see,' said Bartholomew, not seeing at all.

'Roland never wore those clothes; they sat in a chest all year round, gathering dust and slowly being eaten by moths. They were too big for him, and he did not like them. My father is not as wealthy as he would have you believe – his manor is small, and any spare money he has is spent on winter fodder for the cattle and extra grain for the village, not on clothes. He would be furious if I told you this, but he is so poor he does not even pay taxes.'

That meant he was poor indeed, for there were few who escaped the greedy hands of the King and his tax collectors. Before an exemption was granted, all accounts were inspected rigorously by men who were neither generous nor sympathetic to hardship. Janelle continued.

'So, a week or so ago, I took the clothes and the dagger, and I left them for him in a bundle near the Clopton–Grundisburgh parish boundary. Roland would not have been keen for me to give them to my father had I asked, but he would not have demanded them back once they had gone. I wanted my father to wear them at our wedding, you see, so that he would not look shabby and old.'

'And did your father ever receive these clothes?' asked Bartholomew.

She shook her head. 'I had instructed one of his men to meet me there, but he was late. I did not want to waste the whole day waiting for a servant, so I left the bundle under a tree and went about my own business. By the time the servant arrived, the clothes had gone.'

'So, someone else found them?'

She nodded. 'It could not have been a villager from Clopton, because the finder would have announced his luck, and then someone would have told him that the bundle was intended for my father. It must have been someone from Grundisburgh.'

'So, someone from Grundisburgh found a bundle containing some clothes and a dagger, donned them and ended up hanged,' said Bartholomew, trying to make sense of it.

She nodded again. 'So you see, whoever hanged the man you found probably did not believe he was hanging Roland, as you seem to think. The man you found must have been hanged because he found the bundle and was dishonest enough to keep it.'

'But that makes no sense, either,' said Bartholomew. 'The man to judge that sort of crime would be Tuddenham, and he seemed to know nothing about anyone being hanged for theft.'

'Perhaps he did not want to cast a pall of gloom over the Pentecost Fair, and so kept it quiet,' she said with a shrug. 'You should not believe everything he tells you.'

'I will bear it in mind,' he said with a smile. He was not surprised that she had kept the business of the stolen clothes to herself; the most obvious people who would avenge an act of finders-keepers would be either her father – an impecunious man who needed his daughter to steal him new clothes for her wedding – or her husband, perhaps startled to meet a man parading around in the finery he thought was safely packed away in a chest at home. Bartholomew frowned. Or was the real killer Tuddenham, the man whom Deblunville and Bardolf thought had been spreading tales of the mysterious white dog? 'Padfoot' was, after all, the word uttered by the dying man.

He left Janelle in the care of her maidservant. Deblunville was waiting for him in the lower chamber, huddled near the fire, while Bardolf paced back and forth angrily. Cynric was folded into a corner with an untouched cup of ale at his side, staring morosely into the rushes.

'Thank you,' said Deblunville, standing to greet him. 'This child means a great deal to her. She was afraid she might be too old to have children.'

'You should find her a midwife in Ipswich,' said Bartholomew. 'Or better still, try to persuade Mother Goodman to come. She seems a competent woman.'

'She is,' said Deblunville. 'But she is also loyal to Tuddenham. She will never attend Janelle.'

'What are you going to do with him?' demanded Bardolf of his son-in-law. 'All this talk of midwives and infants is becoming tedious.'

Deblunville turned on him angrily. 'I will talk about midwives and infants from dawn until dusk in my own home if it so suits me.'

He offered Bartholomew a stool near the fire. The physician sat gratefully, weary from his efforts to save Janelle's child, which had lasted through most of the night. Despite his tiredness, he felt more cheerful than he had done since they had arrived at Grundisburgh. He might have lost two battles with death – the hanged man and Unwin – but he was fairly sure he had won the third, and that Janelle would bear a healthy child if she followed his advice.

'So,' said Deblunville, passing him a goblet of wine. 'A dog from Barchester attacked you, your servant drove it off, and you ran away as fast as you could to end up on our land.'

Bartholomew nodded. 'I felt a person's hand grabbing my foot, although I did not see him. Cynric saw only the dog.'

'And you think the motive was theft?' pressed Deblunville.

Bartholomew shrugged, sipping the wine. 'Half the men in Otley saw Grosnold give me that gold coin, and any one of them could have slipped out and followed us.'

However, since no attempt had been made to search him for it, Bartholomew was far from certain that the purpose of the ambush had been to steal. He thought it far more likely that Grosnold or Ned had followed them, seeking to silence him over the matter of the knight's meeting with Unwin just before his murder, or perhaps to ensure he did not expose Grosnold's lies about the acquisition of his manor. But he kept his suspicions to himself. The last thing he wanted was to be drawn deeper into the murky affairs of the squabbling Suffolk manors.

'But no Otley villager owns a big white dog,' said Deblunville, reaching out to pluck one of the pale hairs from Bartholomew's cloak, set to dry by the fire. 'All theirs are small, yellow mongrels with bad eyesight. Grosnold is bitterly envious of my fine hunting hounds, and would do anything to acquire one of the pups that has just been born.'

'Perhaps it was a stray,' said Bartholomew. 'Unwin claimed to have seen a big white dog in Barchester, two days before he died.'

'So I understand.' Deblunville smiled at Bartholomew's surprise. 'This is the country. Rumours and stories spread faster here than rats through a granary.'

'Then you should know there is also a rumour that you set eyes on the thing.'

Deblunville shook his head, amused. 'I saw a wolf that scurried off when I tried to shoot it. I expect one of my archers mentioned the episode to some kinsmen in Grundisburgh – for all our bickering and fighting, nearly all Burgh folk have relatives there – and the story was put out that I had encountered Padfoot.'

'So, you do not believe Padfoot exists?' asked Bartholomew.

'I believe someone has resurrected a silly tale that dates back to pagan times, and that Tuddenham and Grosnold have capitalised on it to provide an excuse for their spies being found on my land. I also believe that the two Grundisburgh villagers, who died after supposedly seeing Padfoot, were killed by Tuddenham as a punishment, because they were caught red-handed by me trespassing on my manor. And I believe that someone in his cups heard I saw a wolf, and started the rumour that what I really saw was Padfoot.'

'Do you honestly think that James Freeman and Alice Quy were sent to spy on you?' asked Bartholomew. 'A butcher and a woman with a new baby?'

'I know they were,' said Deblunville firmly.

'Well, at least you have not completely taken leave of your senses,' grumbled Bardolf, flopping down next to them. Bartholomew inspected the older man's clothes covertly, and saw that they were almost as shabby and old as were his own. 'I thought maybe you would accept that these scholars were on your land to pick wild flowers, or to watch the stars, or some other such nonsense.'

'You are irritable today,' said Deblunville mildly. 'Take some wine to soothe your temper.'

'Take some laudanum to soothe your back,' said Bartholomew.

'Do you have some?' asked Bardolf eagerly. 'Give it to me!'

Bartholomew mixed some of the powder with the wine in his goblet and handed it to Bardolf, who almost snatched it in his desperation.

'If this kills me, I will kill you,' he warned.

'Drink it slowly,' instructed Bartholomew, ignoring the odd logic. 'Or it will make you dizzy.'

'Dizziness would be a blessing,' muttered Bardolf. 'I have no relief from this pain. My father was the same and his father before him. Stoate bleeds me each full moon, but it makes no difference.'

Bartholomew could well believe it. 'So, why are you so sure that Tuddenham wants to spy on you?' he asked, still not certain that he understood all the twisted facts and reasoning behind the Padfoot legend.

'Well, I suppose it is not really spying,' said Deblunville, watching Bardolf sip Bartholomew's potion with exaggerated care. 'It is really searching.'

'Searching for what?' asked Bartholomew. He sat back, and gave a sudden laugh of disbelief, recalling Tuddenham's unpleasant questioning of Cynric at Unwin's graveside. 'The golden calf! He is looking for the golden calf! Is that what Janelle said you should tell us earlier tonight, so that we would understand why you do not want spies on your land?'

It was Deblunville's turn to look surprised. 'Tuddenham told you about the calf?'

'Of course he did,' spat Bardolf. 'That is what they were doing on our land – looking for it.'

'I read about it at St Edmundsbury,' said Bartholomew, ignoring the old man. 'But it is a myth, a legend that is entertaining but that has no base in fact.'

'That is not what Tuddenham believes,' said Deblunville. 'The lords of Grundisburgh have been hunting for the golden calf for as long as anyone can remember. They think it was hidden when the monks stole the bones of St Botolph, and that all they need to do is to dig until it is found.'

'But no one knows where this chapel was supposed to be,' said Bartholomew. 'How can Tuddenham hope to find it by random digging?'

'You are a scholar; your mind is too logical,' said Deblunville. 'Each time a tree is felled, Tuddenham or Hamon goes to pore over the roots; when a grave is dug, they sift through the soil; when foundations for a new building are laid, they pay men to dig a little deeper.'

'But Tuddenham has decided that the chapel might not have been on his land after all,' said Bardolf, drowsy from the laudanum. 'So he is widening his search to Burgh, Clopton and Otley.'

'Virtually every night, people from Grundisburgh slip out to poke around on their neighbours' land to see what they can find,' said Deblunville. 'Grosnold does not object – he knows Tuddenham will share the profits with him if it is found on his manor – but Bardolf and I do not want our precious crops damaged by futile treasure-hunting.'

'Sheep, man, sheep,' said Bardolf. 'You have crops, but I have sheep. I do not want my poor animals terrified in the middle of the night because some greed-crazed lunatics are digging in my pens. Nor do I want my beasts worried by the mongrels that always accompany them.'

'His people are edging ever nearer my manor house,' said

Deblunville. 'He invented the tale of Padfoot so that any of his villagers who are caught on our land will have an excuse for being there – they can say they were being chased by this ghostly hound.'

'Perhaps Tuddenham owns a white dog,' said Bardolf, yawning. 'Perhaps he lets it loose at night to frighten people, so that they will not go out. And then no one will see his diggers at work.'

'That is possible,' said Deblunville, nodding. 'The animal is definitely real. Ghosts do not leave hairs behind them, and there are enough hairs on the doctor's cloak to stuff a mattress.'

'So, all this is about a mythical golden idol,' mused Bartholomew, almost to himself. 'I suppose poor Unwin was killed because of it, too.'

'How?' asked Deblunville. 'He was stabbed in the church, not on someone else's land, and anyway, he had not been in the village long enough to have been recruited for gold-digging.'

Bartholomew did not care to speculate, although the obvious answer was that Grosnold had told Unwin about it, and then killed him when he declined to have anything to do with it. And Unwin was not killed in the church, but outside it, where his blood still stained the grass and grey stones of the buttress. He stood, and prepared to take his leave.

'All I know is that I would like this wretched deed signed and sealed as soon as possible, so that we can leave this treasure-hunting and intrigue for those that enjoy it. I will come back tomorrow to see your wife, if you like, although I am certain she will recover, if you let her rest.'

'You can come back to see me, too,' said Bardolf comfortably. 'That laudanum is powerful stuff. I can feel my aches draining away.'

'Good,' said Deblunville. 'Perhaps it will improve your temper.'

'Cheeky whelp!' muttered Bardolf, shooting his son-in-law a genuinely venomous glower. He turned to Bartholomew. 'I am only here to ensure he does not do away with Janelle in the first two weeks of his marriage, as he did the poor old widow, Pernel.'

Deblunville laughed carelessly, although Bartholomew was not entirely certain that Bardolf had been jesting. The physician went to help Cynric to his feet, alarmed by the lack-lustre look in his book-bearer's eyes, and took his leave of Deblunville and Bardolf. As they walked the short distance to Grundisburgh in the pale light that lit the land before dawn, Bartholomew did all he could to convince Cynric that the dog was as mortal as any other animal, but Cynric refused to accept that Padfoot was anything other than a hound from hell, sent to snatch him away in the prime of his life.

'I should have married before I left Cambridge,' he mumbled. 'Then I would have died happy.'

'So, you have decided then?' asked Bartholomew encouragingly, to try to take Cynric's mind off his impending doom. 'You sounded uncertain whether the married life was for you when we last spoke about this, and now you say it will make you happy?'

Cynric did not answer but pointed down the road. 'Someone is there,' he said flatly. 'Waiting for us in the bushes.'

'You mean lying in ambush?' asked Bartholomew, alarmed. 'Again?'

'We do not seem to be particularly welcome around here,' said Cynric morosely.

'Is your bow ready?' asked Bartholomew, peering down the still-dark lane to where Cynric had pointed. He could see nothing, but his book-bearer's intuition in such matters was infallible. 'We might frighten him off.'

Lethargically, Cynric took his bow from his shoulder and stood with it held loosely in his hands.

'An arrow might help,' suggested Bartholomew nervously.

'Waving an empty bow is not very menacing. Come on, Cynric! You do not need me to be telling you all this. Do you want us attacked and killed?'

'You will survive it well enough,' said Cynric gloomily. '*You* did not see the white dog.'

Bartholomew sighed. 'Stay here, then, and keep watch. I will cut round behind him and see if I can flush him out.'

Cynric nodded careless acquiescence, and Bartholomew ducked off the path and began to make his way to the back of a thicket, where he assumed the ambusher was hiding. He was concerned, aware that the Welshman would never have allowed him to undertake such a task had he been himself. Wincing as he trod on sticks that cracked loudly, and rustling through leaves like a rampaging boar, he crept steadily forward, wishing he had paid more attention to Cynric's past advice on stealth.

The would-be attacker knelt behind a bush, peering up the path. In the half-light of early dawn, Bartholomew could see nothing more than a shadow muffled in a cloak. As far as he could tell, the man was alone; no accomplices lurked in the undergrowth. With a yell that made the figure leap to his feet in shock, Bartholomew dashed toward the bush and hurled himself at him. There was a brief struggle, during which Bartholomew shouted to Cynric not to fire, and fists and feet flew wildly on both sides, but neither with any precision. It was not long before Bartholomew, taller and stronger, had the man pinned down on the ground by both wrists.

'Stoate!'

Bartholomew gazed at Grundisburgh's physician in confusion, while Warin de Stoate stared back, his eyes huge in the gloom.

'Bartholomew! What in God's name are you doing? Let me up!'

Bartholomew hesitated, but then released him, watching

as Stoate stood and brushed himself down. Cynric remained where Bartholomew had left him, his bow dangling from his hands. He showed no reaction at all when he saw it had been Stoate waiting in the bushes, and trailed miserably toward them with his feet scuffing the litter on the woodland path.

'What were you doing?' Bartholomew demanded of Stoate. 'Men with nothing to hide do not skulk around in the bushes first thing in the morning.'

'I did not want to be seen,' said Stoate enigmatically, still picking leaves and grass from his cloak. 'I was going to wait until you passed, and then be on my way.'

'Why?' asked Bartholomew. 'Cynric thought you were going to ambush us.'

'Why should I do that?' asked Stoate, genuinely puzzled. 'You have nothing I want – no offence intended. And I am not the kind of man to commit robbery on the roads – I am a respected member of the community, and people look up to me.'

'I wanted a word with you, anyway,' said Bartholomew, still not certain that he believed him. 'I have just come from Janelle Deblunville. She became ill after drinking a potion you prescribed her, containing betony and pennyroyal.'

Stoate's jaw dropped. 'She *drank* it? She *drank* my potion?'

'Yes,' said Bartholomew coldly. 'That is what you instructed her to do, is it not?'

Stoate drew himself up to his full height. 'I can assure you it was not! She is with child – betony and pennyroyal are abortive agents. The potion I gave her was to be added to vinegar and inhaled as a cure for dizziness – as the great Pliny suggests. She was most certainly not supposed to drink it. Is she all right?'

Bartholomew nodded slowly. Pliny's *Historia Naturalis* did indeed recommend the inhalation of pennyroyal and mint infused in vinegar as a remedy for fainting. His anger towards

Stoate dissipated to a certain extent; he had prescribed ointments and salves himself, and patients had later complained that they tasted unpleasant or had made them sick. However, he had learned from his experiences, and never left people with potentially dangerous medicines until he was certain they understood what they were to do with them. And Stoate, Bartholomew thought, should have done the same with Janelle. But Stoate's casual attitude towards dangerous herbs did not explain why he was skulking in the woods so early in the morning.

'What were you doing here anyway?' he asked. 'A man of your station should not be grubbing around in trees in the dark.'

'Unlike you, you mean?' retorted Stoate. He relented suddenly, and smiled. 'I suppose it does look odd, but I can assure you I was doing nothing untoward. I am just going to visit Tuddenham.'

'At this time of day? And why the secrecy?'

'He does not want anyone to know,' said Stoate mysteriously.

'Know what?' Bartholomew was tired from his eventful night, and his patience was beginning to wear thin.

'Come with me, and I will show you.'

Bartholomew hesitated, not wanting to be party to any more secrets – particularly ones that necessitated hiding in bushes before sunrise – but Stoate was insistent, piquing Bartholomew's interest by hinting it was a medical matter. With Cynric trailing behind like a mourner at a funeral, Stoate led the way along a little-used path that ran behind the village, and up the hill to Wergen Hall. It was in darkness, but Stoate tapped three times, very softly, on one of the window shutters, and within moments the door was opened. Siric, Tuddenham's faithful steward, stood there.

'You are late,' he mumbled to Stoate. His eyes narrowed

when he saw Bartholomew and Cynric. 'What are they doing here?'

'I brought them,' whispered Stoate. 'It would be good to have Doctor Bartholomew's opinion.'

'Are you mad?' hissed Siric furiously. 'Sir Thomas will never allow it!'

'He would be a fool to refuse,' Stoate snapped back.

He elbowed his way past Siric, and beckoned for Bartholomew to follow, while Cynric waited by the embers of the fire in the hall. Stoate made his way stealthily up the spiral stairs and headed for the upper chambers. He listened carefully, before opening a door and slipping inside, pulling Bartholomew after him. Siric remained outside, evidently keeping watch. Their movements were so practised that Bartholomew could only suppose that they had been going through the same routine for weeks, if not longer.

'What is he doing here?' demanded Tuddenham hoarsely from the large bed that almost filled the room. 'For God's sake, Stoate! What are you thinking of?'

Stoate raised an imperious hand. 'I met Bartholomew on my way here, and it occurred to me that it might be wise for you to draw on his expertise as well as my own.'

'But if news of this seeps out . . .'

'Physicians are known for their discretion,' interrupted Stoate smoothly. 'You can trust Bartholomew, as you can trust me.'

'But I cannot trust you, it seems! You promised me you would never tell a living soul about this, and now you bring one of the Michaelhouse scholars to see me. It could ruin everything!'

Bartholomew looked from one to the other in confusion. 'Master Stoate has told me nothing,' he said. 'And if you do not want me to be here, I will leave.'

'Stay,' said Tuddenham, leaning back against the pillows wearily. 'Speculation about what you have seen will do far more damage than hearing the truth. Well, come on then, man, examine me. I imagine that Stoate brought you here so that you can tell me what he dares not utter himself. You are a damned coward, Stoate, with your false cheer.'

Thus admonished, Stoate busied himself by inspecting the flask of urine that Tuddenham had provided, studiously avoiding the knight's eyes. Bewildered, Bartholomew went to sit on the bed, taking Tuddenham's hands in his to feel their temperature. He was surprised he had not noticed before, but there seemed to be a tautness about the skin of the face and a dullness about the hair that did not signify good health. Hoping his own hands were not too cold, he began his examination. There was a hard lump the size of an apple under the skin of Tuddenham's stomach.

'How long have you had this?' he asked, pulling the night-shirt down and sitting back.

'I noticed it at Christmas. It has been growing steadily larger and more painful ever since. Stoate tells me I will live to be an old man yet. What do you say, Bartholomew?'

Bartholomew glanced at Stoate, who was still holding the urine up to the light and refusing to look at anyone. Tuddenham gave a sharp laugh.

'Are you afraid to contradict the opinion of a colleague? Or are you afraid to tell the truth?'

'Neither,' said Bartholomew. 'Despite Master Stoate's attempts to cheer you, you seem to know the truth anyway.'

'I did not want him to give up,' said Stoate, lowering the flask and looking at Bartholomew defiantly. 'In my experience, telling a patient he will die simply hastens his end – he loses the will to live and gives up on life.'

There was more than a grain of truth in Stoate's reasoning. Bartholomew had seen many patients give up the ghost when they might have lived longer: it was certainly true of Cynric, sitting shrouded in gloom in the hall downstairs. But it made no sense to use such tactics on Tuddenham, who had already guessed the seriousness of his condition. He looked back to the knight, who was still waiting for his answer.

'A few months,' he said. 'No longer.'

'Will I live to be a father? The child should be born in November.'

'No,' said Bartholomew.

Tuddenham stared at him for a moment, and then took a deep breath. After a moment he smiled sadly. 'What a pair you two make! One too frightened to tell me I am ill; the other so brutal in his honesty. Somewhere in between might have been more pleasant.'

'I am sorry,' said Bartholomew. 'But you are lucky to be expecting a child, Sir Thomas. This disease often brings infertility.'

'Oh, yes,' said Tuddenham bitterly. 'I am lucky indeed! I would have been luckier still if I could have had my first sons with me now, but the Death took them. I survived that, only to die of this insidious disease that is rotting my flesh, even as I live and breathe.'

Bartholomew turned to Stoate. 'What are you doing for him?'

'A potion of three grains of foxglove, mixed with wine and honey. I bring it each morning, so that Sir Thomas can pass the day without too much pain, and without anyone knowing of his condition.' He shrugged. 'I was considering sending him to Ipswich for surgery.'

'It is too late for surgery,' said Bartholomew. 'There is very little you can do now. I would recommend you use poppy seeds, rather than foxglove, but you will need to increase the dose as time passes.' He looked at Tuddenham. 'And your family do not know?'

'No one knows,' said Tuddenham. 'Just Stoate, Siric and now you. Even Wauncy does not know.' He gave a soft laugh, a rustle at the back of his throat. 'It is ironic –

Wauncy looks like a walking corpse, yet it is I who am mortally sick.'

'They will find out,' said Bartholomew. 'You will not be able to hide it from them for much longer.'

'I will keep it from them as long as I can,' said Tuddenham. 'I do not want to worry Isilia yet, and it will only give Hamon and Dame Eva something else to argue about. You will not tell them, will you?' He gripped Bartholomew's hand hard.

'Of course not.'

Tuddenham relaxed. 'Good. You see, Bartholomew, one of the things I am bargaining for with that crafty Alcote is the provision of a mass priest to pray for my soul when I am dead. His stipend will be paid for out of the money Michaelhouse will make from the living of the church. Alcote may not agree to that condition if he thinks Michaelhouse will have to start paying at the end of the summer, and not in twenty years' time.'

Bartholomew smiled. 'He will not discover any of this from me. And anyway, our rates for masses are not quite so high as those of Master Wauncy.'

Tuddenham smiled faintly. 'Thank you. Now, give me my medicine, Stoate. And tomorrow I will have poppy, not foxglove.'

Bartholomew collected Cynric from the hall, and headed for the Half Moon, relieved to be away from a consultation for once. There were aspects of his trade that he did not enjoy, and breaking that kind of news to a patient was one of them. With Cynric trailing listlessly behind him, he walked down the path to the village.

'Matt!' cried Michael, running down The Street as fast as his plump legs would carry him. 'Where have you been? You are covered in mud! And what is wrong with Cynric? He looks as though he has seen a ghost.'

Cynric groaned and put his hands over his face, while

Bartholomew told the monk what had happened. Michael took a deep, unsteady breath.

'I am sorry, Matt. This is all my fault! I urged you to go with Grosnold when I should have seen it was not safe, even with Cynric. And things are not much better here. Tuddenham has arrested Eltisley for the killing of Unwin, and has him locked in the cellar at Wergen Hall. And I went to see Mistress Freeman yesterday, as I told you I would, only someone had been to see her first, and she lies dead in the church with her throat cut, just like her husband!'

CHAPTER 8

THE BODY OF MISTRESS FREEMAN LAY IN THE SAME parish coffin that had been used for Unwin. Mother Goodman was fussing over the corpse, cursing under her breath when the cloth she had tied around the woman's throat did not succeed in hiding the gaping gash from view. Bartholomew had inspected the wound while the midwife washed the rest of the body. It was an ugly cut that sliced through the muscles of the neck, exposing the yellow-white of the pipes underneath. Judging from the marks on her arms and hands, and the chaos that Michael had reported in her house, Mistress Freeman had put up something of a fight.

'Do you think her neighbours might have seen or heard something?' asked Bartholomew of Michael, as they stood together in the nave watching Mother Goodman work.

Michael shook his head. 'Very conveniently for her killer, the butcher's property stands alone on the outskirts of Grundisburgh – on the river, so that the blood and offal can be washed downstream and away from the village.'

'That is unusually courteous,' said Bartholomew. 'Butchers do not often concern themselves about such matters. Of course, the river then flows on through Hasketon, so I suppose Freeman could rest contented that he was probably poisoning someone. So, the neighbours did not report anything untoward, then?'

'No,' said Michael. 'Although I would not expect him to say so if he had heard anything. Her nearest neighbour is none other than our good friend, the pardoner.'

'Norys?' asked Bartholomew. He frowned. 'I suppose you consider that evidence of his guilt?'

'Of course,' said Michael. 'Particularly since he still has not returned from Ipswich. I knew we should not have let him remain at large. He has absconded, just as I guessed he would if we did not tell Tuddenham to arrest him immediately.'

'But if he has been in Ipswich since we spoke to him, then he could not have killed Mistress Freeman,' Bartholomew pointed out. 'He would not have been here.'

'She was last seen by her friends early Wednesday morning,' said Michael immediately, clearly having worked it all out. 'That was *before* we went to speak to Will Norys. She was supposed to change the church flowers after nones that same day, but failed to arrive. Wauncy – who remembers the time because he had just delivered the documents he had collected from Ipswich to Alcote at Wergen Hall – assumed she had forgotten, and asked someone else to do it instead.'

'He should have known something was wrong right then,' announced Mother Goodman, who had been listening. 'Mistress Freeman loved to arrange the church flowers and never missed her turn. That she did not come should have warned Wauncy that something was amiss.'

'Well, it did not,' said Michael, none too pleased at being interrupted by the forceful midwife. 'And no one thought to look for her until I found her yesterday – Friday – at about noon. I am no medical man, but even I could see she had been dead for at least a couple of days, and not just a few hours. I am getting better at this kind of thing, Matt; I will have no need of your services soon.'

'Good,' said Bartholomew with feeling. 'My business is with the living, not the dead, and I would be delighted if you did not call on me to pore over corpses.'

'Corpses demand every bit as much respect as the living,'

put in Mother Goodman haughtily from the coffin. 'More so, since they are already gone the way we will soon go.'

'She is a cheery soul,' muttered Michael, regarding the midwife coolly. 'But, as I was saying, Mistress Freeman was probably killed on Wednesday. She was last seen a short time before we spoke to Norys, and then no one saw her until I found her yesterday. Meanwhile, Norys has been missing since just after we questioned him. He must have paid a visit to Mistress Freeman as soon as we had gone, killed her, and then absconded.'

'But Norys wanted us to talk to Mistress Freeman,' said Bartholomew. 'He believed she would prove his innocence. Why should he kill her?'

'Because she refused to lie for him,' said Michael promptly. 'I imagine he went to see her the moment we left, and told her what she had to say to us. Then, when she refused to back him in his falsehood, he slashed her throat.'

The speed with which Michael's answers came suggested to Bartholomew that he must have spent the better part of the previous night mulling over the evidence and thinking of ways to convince himself of the pardoner's guilt. Michael claimed to have spent the time with William and Deynman, fretting over Bartholomew's failure to return. They had been saddling up to search for him when he and Cynric had arrived back again.

'So, you think Will Norys killed Unwin *and* Mistress Freeman?' asked Mother Goodman, looking up from her work and addressing Michael. 'Master Norys is a popular man in the village, and has never been involved in anything like this before.'

'He is a pardoner,' said Michael, as if that explained all. 'Anyway, we have evidence: Norys was seen running from the church at about the time Unwin was murdered.'

'Stoate saw someone wearing a long cloak,' said Bartholomew. 'He did not say it was Norys.'

'And Norys, very conveniently, also claims to have seen someone running from the church,' said Michael, not to be outdone. 'Only his someone was wearing a *short* cloak. And the rascal said he was talking with Mistress Freeman at about the time that Stoate said he was doing the same.'

'I saw them,' said Mother Goodman unexpectedly. 'Both of them.'

'You mean figures with long and short cloaks running from the church?' asked Michael, bewildered. 'You might have mentioned this earlier.'

'No, not them,' said Mother Goodman impatiently. 'Stoate and Norys. I saw Norys walking Mistress Freeman around the churchyard – he is fond of her – and then I saw her speaking to Stoate by the ford just after the feast started.'

'She cannot have been in two places at the same time,' said Michael, unconvinced.

'She need not have been,' said Bartholomew, thinking quickly. 'Perhaps she walked around the churchyard with Norys, and then stopped to talk to Stoate after Norys had left her.'

'Yes,' said Michael, eyes narrowing. 'So, Norys escorts Mistress Freeman around the churchyard, sees Unwin go inside alone, and decides to rob him.'

'But the blood we found by the buttress, and the fact that Unwin was moved after he died, suggests he was killed *outside* the church,' Bartholomew pointed out.

Michael pursed his lips impatiently. 'Then he must have seduced Unwin out of the church, and carried him back inside again after he was dead.'

'Without anyone seeing?' asked Bartholomew incredulously.

'Unwin was not heavy. His killer could have moved him by draping one of Unwin's arms over his shoulder and carrying him – from a distance they would look like a pair of revellers the worse for drink. But, as I was saying, after Norys sees

Unwin alone in the church and decides to murder him for his purse, he leaves Mistress Freeman by the ford, dons his long cloak to hide his clothes, and stabs Unwin. He then hauls the body back inside the church to keep it hidden long enough to make good his escape. Mistress Freeman and Stoate spot him running from the church in his long cloak, and Norys kills her when she will not lie and tell us he was with her all day.'

'It is possible, I suppose,' said Bartholomew reluctantly.

'It is more than possible,' said Michael keenly. 'It makes perfect sense. And Norys has now fled the scene of his crime, and is in hiding somewhere.'

'He would not leave his cats for long,' said Mother Goodman. 'He adores cats. If it were not for them, I think he would have offered to marry Mistress Freeman when her mourning was over.'

'Why should cats prevent him from making a lonely widow happy?' asked Michael, puzzled.

'Mistress Freeman did not like cats,' said Mother Goodman. 'Some people do not, although they provide good protection against Padfoot. He will not come where there are cats, because they hiss at him, and Padfoot does not like to be hissed at.'

'Who does?' said Michael.

'Norys loves animals, especially cats. He gives me their urine for treating warts.'

'Most generous of him,' said Michael, taking Bartholomew's arm and leading him outside so that he could expound his theories without the midwife offering her opinions. 'You must excuse us, madam. We have business to attend.'

A low wall surrounded the churchyard, mainly to act as a barrier to keep out the pigs, cows and sheep that wandered freely through the village. Bartholomew sat on it, and looked out across the green. The scene was peaceful, with a robin singing sweetly from the top of one of the willow trees and a duck waddling toward the ford with a clutch of fluffy yellow chicks strewn out behind her. The gentle bubble of the stream, slightly swollen from the rains of the previous day, was almost drowned out by the raucous caw of rooks from the elms behind the church.

Michael sat next to him, stretching his fat legs to display a pair of pallid ankles. Bartholomew rubbed a hand through his hair, still wet from where he had washed the mud from it. He had donned his spare tabard and Cynric was supposed to be cleaning the one he usually wore, although the physician was not sure that his book-bearer would do a particularly good job given his preoccupation with his impending death. He dragged his thoughts away from Cynric's predicament, and considered Michael's unseemly determination to have the pardoner convicted of murder.

'Maybe Stoate did it,' he said, trying to consider all possibilities, and not just the one Michael had adopted with unnatural passion. 'He might have killed Unwin, run from the church, and then stopped to talk to Mistress Freeman at the ford.'

'Oh, that sounds very likely,' said Michael caustically. 'He would have been drenched in blood, and you are suggesting that he paused in his bid for escape to exchange pleasantries with the butcher's widow? "Good evening, Mistress Freeman. And how are you today? Do not mind the fact that I am covered in blood; it has nothing to do with the dead priest in the church, you understand, and you will be used to a little gore, being the wife of a butcher." I do not think so, Matt!'

Bartholomew tipped his head back and looked up at the leaves of the elms shivering in the morning breeze. 'You are too fixed on Norys's guilt.'

'Because he is the most obvious suspect?' asked Michael.

'Well, your suggestion is ludicrous! Stoate is a wealthy man, and does not need to kill impoverished friars for their purses. Anyway, Stoate is not under suspicion: he told us what he saw because he was trying to be helpful.'

'He is a dismal physician,' said Bartholomew. 'He should have made certain that Janelle knew not to drink the potion he prescribed; he gives purges that people do not need; and he treated inflamed eyes with sugar water!'

'How disgraceful,' said Michael dryly. 'But it does not matter whether Stoate is a charlatan or the best physician in Suffolk: he could not have killed Unwin, because whoever did it would have been covered in blood – we know that because we saw it splattered outside the church.'

'True,' said Bartholomew. 'And Stoate wore the same clothes when we met him at the tavern the evening Unwin died that he had worn all day – dark amber cotte and hose. I remember, because at the feast I saw him tossing a baby in the air and catching it again – well, actually he dropped it, which is why the incident stuck in my mind. I recall him in his yellow clothes quite clearly.'

'And Norys had changed by the time we went to see him!' Michael pounced triumphantly.

'Yes, but we saw him two days later,' said Bartholomew. 'He was probably wearing his best clothes for the Fair, and is hardly likely to wear them to Ipswich market, too. And there is still the issue of Grosnold. Did Eltisley see him talking to Unwin in the churchyard or not?'

'Grosnold's reaction when you questioned him about it seemed odd,' said Michael, scratching one of his chins. 'Thus, I am inclined to believe it was he – or his men – who attacked you at Barchester to ensure you kept quiet about it. I cannot believe you were so rash as to tell Grosnold what Eltisley said he saw – especially given that we are talking about a murder here.'

'I was running low on ideas,' said Bartholomew tiredly.

'To be honest, I expected there to be an innocent explanation of what Eltisley saw, and did not anticipate Grosnold denying it.'

'Perhaps it was Grosnold who hired Norys to kill Unwin,' said Michael thoughtfully. 'So, our black knight slips back to Grundisburgh after his dramatic exit, for a secret meeting with Unwin. He found Unwin would not do what he wanted – whether it was working for peace as Bardolf believes, or becoming involved in the hunt for the golden calf – and paid Norys to dispatch him.'

'Was there enough time for all this to have happened?' asked Bartholomew. 'Eltisley said he saw Grosnold with Unwin moments after the end of the feast, and it was not too long after that when Horsey went in search of him. I would have thought it would take longer than that to hire a killer.'

'We will go to Norys's house and have a good look for bloodstained attire this morning,' said Michael, ignoring the inconvenient question. 'If Norys wore his best clothes to the Fair, he would not throw them away because they are spoiled – he would keep them and try to wash the stuff out. Pardoners are a mean breed, and do not waste fine garments just because they are bloodstained.'

'There was probably a lot of blood when Mistress Freeman was killed, too,' said Bartholomew, too tired to contest Michael's gross generalisations. 'Slit throats are invariably messy.'

'This was,' said Michael with a shudder. 'I have seldom seen such a grisly sight. Blood was splashed up the walls, and there was not a piece of furniture that was not covered in it.'

'It was not windy last night,' said Bartholomew, gazing out across the green. 'Sounds carry on quiet nights, and even though Mistress Freeman's house is a fair distance from the nearest neighbour, I am surprised nothing was heard.'

'But her nearest neighbour is Norys, and Norys killed her,' said Michael. 'And he killed her because she would not give him the alibi he needs to cover his murder of Unwin.'

'But Mother Goodman saw Norys talking to Mistress Freeman outside the church, just as he claimed,' Bartholomew pointed out.

'True. But not many moments after, she saw Stoate chatting to her by the ford, and no Norys in sight. I told you Norys was our killer, and I was right. A little solid evidence might prove useful, though, because Tuddenham is convinced Tobias Eltisley killed Unwin.'

'On what grounds?' asked Bartholomew. He had quite forgotten the landlord's predicament. 'That Eltisley is a dangerous lunatic?'

'Because Tuddenham's man, Siric, found a bloody knife in Eltisley's garden. Eltisley, not surprisingly, says it is not his, and that anyone might have thrown it there.'

'And this is all the evidence Tuddenham has against Eltisley?'

Michael nodded. 'You said you thought Tuddenham might start casting about for a scapegoat, if he could not deliver his promise and produce Unwin's killer quickly: Eltisley is it. So, now we need to prove that Norys is our murderer, or Eltisley will pay for it, and I am certain he is innocent.'

'At least Eltisley cannot endanger people's lives with his inventions, if he is safely behind bars,' said Bartholomew unsympathetically. 'Tuddenham's cellar is the best place for him.'

'That is an uncharitable position to take, Matt. You will feel terrible about saying that if he hangs for Norys's crime.'

'Then you can grant me absolution,' said Bartholomew. He was not seriously concerned about Eltisley, certain that even Tuddenham would not execute a man solely on the discovery of a bloody knife in his garden. 'We can let William prove Eltisley's innocence, since he so desperately wants to practise his investigative skills.'

Michael sighed. 'He is already doing that, quite independently of me. He questioned everyone who lives on The Street yesterday, in a manner that can only be described as single-minded. I only hope we catch Norys before William decides to use more physical techniques.'

'We should go to Mistress Freeman's house,' said Bartholomew, standing and stretching. 'There might be some clue there regarding the identity of her killer.'

'I have already checked,' objected Michael. 'We would do better to go to Norys's cottage, and look for blood-drenched garments and something really incriminating – like Unwin's relic.'

He stood and walked purposely towards the ford. Ducklings scattered in his path as he splashed across the stream and made his way to the pardoner's home. Norys's uncle was in his garden, hammering on a piece of leather. He glanced up as Michael loomed imperiously over the gate.

'Have you found him?' the tanner asked anxiously. 'He has never left me for more than two nights in a row before.'

Michael pushed open the gate, and walked in. 'We will find him soon. Meanwhile, perhaps I might look in your house, to see if I can find any evidence of where he might be.'

'Such as what?' asked the tanner, alarmed, and standing to block his way. 'I cannot read, so he would not have left me a note, if that is what you mean.'

'I have traced many missing people in Cambridge,' said Michael, insinuating himself past the tanner and into the house. 'I will just ensure there is not some vital clue you might have overlooked.'

'But I am too busy to help you,' squeaked the tanner desperately. 'I must have this leather ready for Walter Wauncy's new shoes by mid-morning, or there will be hell to pay.'

Michael looked backward and gave him a cunning smile. 'No matter, Master Tanner. I will find what I am looking for much faster if you are not with me.'

Bartholomew felt sorry for the tanner, who was bewildered by Michael's blustering presence. He gave what he hoped was a reassuring smile, and followed the monk into the cottage.

'There is no need to terrify the poor man,' he said in a low voice, so that the tanner would not hear. 'He is clearly worried about his nephew, and you have no right to intimidate him like that.'

'Do I not?' demanded Michael, trying to disentangle himself from an over-friendly cat. 'Eltisley's life is at risk, and you are concerned about the feelings of a pardoner's uncle? Damn these wretched animals! They are everywhere. God's blood, Matt – that one bit me!'

A large tabby cat shot from under Michael's foot and scampered out of the door. Another hissed, arching its back and revealing sharp, white teeth. Michael backed away and sneezed.

'You look around,' he said to Bartholomew. 'These beasts do not seem to like me.'

'I wonder why,' muttered Bartholomew, picking his way into the room. It was difficult to search for anything under the furry bodies. Two cats wound their way round his legs while he shook the blankets on the bed and rifled through the room's only chest.

'Look at this,' whispered Michael in sudden revulsion, looking into a strongbox that stood on one of the wall shelves. He pulled his new piece of linen from his scrip, and dabbed his nose on it while he rummaged through the box with his other hand. 'These are his pardons!'

'Leave them, Brother,' warned Bartholomew, peering into the cooking pans one by one.

'I would not soil my hands,' said Michael loftily, lifting one out, and reading it with distaste. 'Here is a pardon for having lusty thoughts over another man's wife. You should ask him if you can buy it, given the way you have been ogling Isilia. And here is one for the sin of greed.'

'One for you, then,' said Bartholomew. 'There is nothing here, Brother. We should leave that poor tanner in peace.'

Michael made as if to demur, but there were few places in the single-roomed cottage where anything could be hidden, and even he had to admit they had searched it as well as they could. He sneezed once more, took a final look round and stalked out, closely followed by three yellow cats.

'Have you finished?' asked the tanner, hammering furiously and looking up as they passed. 'Did you find anything that might help him? I wish he would come back; he knows I worry about him when he stays away more than a night or two, and this time he has been gone since Wednesday.'

'Where does he sleep when he is in Ipswich?' asked Michael. 'A tavern?' He managed to give the word an insalubrious feel, as though it were somehow sinful to be staying in such a place, regardless of the fact that he was thoroughly enjoying his own sojourn at the Half Moon.

'He always stays at the Saracen's Head,' said the tanner nervously. 'Are you thinking you might go there to see if he is all right? You must be concerned if you are considering that – you must think something dreadful has happened to him.'

'No,' said Bartholomew, to soothe him. 'We have no intention of going to Ipswich. I am sure your nephew will arrive home safely soon.'

'What is that?' asked Michael suddenly, pointing at something. The tanner's cottage was untidily thatched with reeds, and had a chimney in the middle to allow smoke from the cooking fire to seep out. Near the chimney was a bundle, almost hidden by the nettles that had sprouted all over the roof. The tanner peered at it, too, surprised by its presence.

'I do not know what that is,' he said, squinting at it with the narrowed eyes of a man whose long-distance vision is poor. 'Perhaps my nephew put it there.'

'Did he now?' said Michael, snatching up a stick and trying to hook the bundle down. 'Damn! I cannot reach. Matt, you will have to climb up and grab it.'

'I will not,' said Bartholomew, laughing at Michael's audacity. 'You do it.'

'Would you have this poor tanner homeless because my weight has collapsed his roof?' asked Michael with arched eyebrows. 'You are lighter than me, and I will help you. Here.'

Michael formed a stirrup of his hands and, reluctantly, Bartholomew placed one foot in it, scrabbling at the roof as he was propelled upward faster than he had anticipated. He gained a handhold on one of the bands that held the thatch in place, and hauled himself up. The object of the precarious exercise was just out of his reach, and he began to ease himself toward it, almost losing his grip as a cat leapt on to the roof next to him. Eventually, the very tips of his fingers touched the bundle, and he leaned to the side as far as he could to try to dislodge it. It came loose at about the same time that the thatch band broke, precipitating Bartholomew, bundle and cat downward in a tangle of hands, legs, claws, dirty cloth and tail. The cat gave a tremendous yowl and shot back into the house. Bartholomew sat up, rubbing his elbow.

Michael's attention was on the bundle, which had burst open when it hit the ground. Scattered under his triumphant gaze were a bloodstained shirt and hose, and Unwin's purse, all wrapped in a long, dark cloak.

'But my nephew does not own hose that colour,' protested the tanner, as he sat on a low stool in the middle of the main chamber at Wergen Hall. He was watched by Tuddenham's household, who sat in chairs near the hearth, or leaned against the walls with folded arms. If Tuddenham had meant the circumstances to be intimidating, he had been successful. He and Hamon were cold and menacing; Wauncy fixed the tanner with a sepulchral gaze, as if reminding him of the terrors of hell to come; Dame Eva was angry, and Isilia was simply repelled.

Alcote sat at the table near the window with his scrolls and deeds, while Bartholomew and Horsey were employed in sorting through a large box of household accounts that Dame Eva had discovered in her chamber the previous day. None were relevant to the advowson – which was why Alcote was prepared to accept their help. Meanwhile, Michael stood over the tanner with Tuddenham; Deynman, not trusted with documents – even unimportant ones – was looking after the morose Cynric; and William was out questioning the remaining villagers.

When Siric had returned from Ipswich a second time without tracing Norys, Michael had decided that the only way forward was to question the tanner again, and had asked Tuddenham to arrest him, hoping that a night in Tuddenham's cellars might frighten him into revealing his nephew's whereabouts. Since William had declared such an interrogation could not take place on a Sunday – none too subtly implying that anyone who disagreed with him was in league with the Devil – the tanner had been left in peace until dragged from his bed at dawn on the Monday, interrupted in the very act of downing a cup of Eltisley's black tonic to fortify him for a day with his leathers.

Bartholomew had gone with Hamon to fetch him to Wergen Hall, because he felt sorry for the little man and was sure he knew nothing of Norys's disappearance or Unwin's murder. He wanted to make sure that Hamon did not use more force than was necessary, although he need not have been concerned: Hamon had been hostile and angry, but not rough.

'Anyone could have thrown that bundle on to our roof,' the frightened tanner protested bleatingly, as Tuddenham paced in front of him.

'Brother Michael tells me that it was cunningly concealed next to the chimney,' said Tuddenham coldly. 'I ask you again, Master Tanner, where is your nephew?'

The tanner was almost in tears. 'Please believe me! I do not know where he is – he has been away since Wednesday, and no one in the village has seen him since.'

'But you admit these bloody clothes and the murdered priest's purse were on your roof?'

'Of course I do!' cried the tanner. 'I was there when they were found. But they do not belong to me or my nephew. I have never seen them before. The cloak is not his – he is not very tall, and it would be too long for him.'

'And what about Unwin's purse?' asked Michael, in a kinder tone than the one used by Tuddenham. 'In it, he had some chrism and a few hairs from St Botolph's beard wrapped in parchment. The chrism has been left – holy oil does not fetch much of a price unless you happen to know any witches or warlocks – but the relic is missing.'

'I do not know where it is,' whispered the tanner, swivelling to look at Michael. 'Really, I do not. And my nephew would never steal a relic – it would earn him eternal damnation.'

'He was prepared to ask around Ipswich market for a relic of St Botolph for me to take home as a souvenir,' said Michael. 'He was most obliging on that front.'

'But obtaining a relic to sell to you is not the same as stealing one,' said the tanner. 'My nephew knows lots of merchants in Ipswich, and he is very good at finding people things they want. But he does not steal.'

'You really should consider being more co-operative,' said Tuddenham sternly. 'Or I might begin to suspect that you have something to do with all this, as well as your nephew.'

'No!' The tanner was on the verge of dropping to his knees in front of Tuddenham to plead with him. 'I know nothing about any of this. And my nephew is not a violent man. He would never harm anyone, let alone a priest.'

'And you have no idea where he might be?' pressed Tuddenham. 'You do not have him hidden away somewhere, waiting until all the fuss has died down so that you can enjoy the spoils of your wicked crimes at your leisure?'

'I do not!' cried the tanner, tears trickling down his leathery face. 'My nephew has not been seen since he went to Ipswich. In fact, the last people to see him were these Cambridge men. Perhaps they killed him, and threw that bundle on to our roof so that Eltisley will be freed and they will not have to stay in the Dog instead of the Half Moon.'

Bartholomew wondered whether he and Michael really appeared to be the kind of men who would kill in order to reside in the tavern of their choice.

'So, we had better release Eltisley, then,' said Hamon, from where he leaned against the wall watching the scene in some disgust. 'It is clear that this bloody knife Siric found in the landlord's garden was tossed there by Norys as he ran from the scene of his crime.'

'That is not clear at all,' said Bartholomew. 'There is no evidence to support such a conclusion.'

Hamon spat into the rushes. 'Evidence! You scholars are not interested in justice, only in finding ways to weave and twist your way around the law.'

'Accusing Norys of throwing the knife into Eltisley's garden is not justice,' said Bartholomew.

'Matt,' warned Michael. He turned to Tuddenham and Hamon, both of whom were looking angry at Bartholomew's interruptions. 'He is still shocked from being attacked in Barchester . . .'

'And I suppose that was Norys, too?' said Bartholomew caustically. 'All the evidence you have against Norys is circumstantial: no one actually *saw* him enter or leave the church, or *saw* him with this bloody knife, or *saw* him put the bundle of clothes and Unwin's purse on the tanner's roof.'

'And what about the cloak?' asked Michael. 'Who, but a pardoner, would own a long cloak?'

'Many people, I expect,' said Bartholomew. 'This is not a poor village, and a number of people might be able to afford such a garment. In any case, perhaps the person who was seen running from the church was not the killer at all. It might have been some innocent who stumbled on the body and was too frightened to raise the alarm lest he be accused of the crime. It does not prove that Norys is Unwin's murderer.'

'Perhaps not, but it all adds up to a pretty good indication that Norys is involved in something untoward,' said Michael. 'And now he is missing. But we should let Sir Thomas go about his business, so that Eltisley can be released.'

'Eltisley was freed as soon as I heard about this bundle,' said Dame Eva from her wicker chair near the hearth. Tuddenham looked startled, and she shrugged. 'I told you yesterday that I did not think Eltisley killed Unwin, Thomas. He was in his tavern all that day, serving ale to the villagers. There was no way he could have slipped out and murdered someone, without there being a riot by villagers demanding their drink. The Fair was in full swing when Unwin was murdered, remember?'

'That sullen troop who are here for crop-weeding would have mutinied had Eltisley slipped away, even for a few moments,' agreed Isilia. She cast Hamon a disgusted look. 'I do not like them. They huddle over their ale in the Half Moon like a band of cut-throats, and have no place in a village like ours. They should not have been hired.'

'They were the only men available for work,' said Hamon defensively. 'It is not easy to find labourers these days.'

'So you hired a band of ale-swilling louts,' said Dame Eva disdainfully. 'Typical of you!'

'What do you mean by that?' demanded Hamon, looking belligerent.

Dame Eva shook a pitying head at him. 'Only that Thomas is wrong to believe that you will make a good heir for his estates. My husband would never have agreed to leave them to you.'

'Your husband is long dead, and has nothing to do with who inherits here,' snapped Hamon. 'And I do not know why you believe him to be such a fine man. He was a bully and a scoundrel!'

'Hamon!' exclaimed Tuddenham, shocked.

'It is true!' shouted Hamon, too angry to be silenced by his uncle's displeasure. 'We think our claim on Peche Hall is legitimate, but Wauncy tells me he is not certain of the authenticity of the deeds that prove it is ours. In his cups one night, he told me he thought they were forged by her noble husband.' He glared unpleasantly at Dame Eva, while Wauncy, horrified at this indiscretion, turned even whiter than usual.

'And is this how you think you can run our manors?' asked the old lady in disgust. 'By losing them on the word of a drunken priest? You are not fit to mention my husband's name!'

'He will not inherit, anyway,' said Isilia, to soothe her. She patted her stomach, bulging under her dark green dress. 'There will soon be children with a greater claim than his.'

Bartholomew thought she looked particularly beautiful that day, with her glossy hair tied in two thick plaits that hung down her back, and a delicate gold cross around her neck. Unlike poor Janelle, whose child made her sick and pale, Isilia bloomed with health and vitality.

'Your husband was unfaithful to you!' howled Hamon, now incensed beyond reason. The colour drained from

Dame Eva's face, making her seem suddenly older and more frail. She gazed at Hamon with such an expression of anguish that even he could not meet her eyes.

'Will you send a man to Ipswich to look for Norys again?' Bartholomew asked Tuddenham, acutely embarrassed by the exchange, and keen to change the subject before Hamon revealed any more family skeletons.

'He never was,' whispered Dame Eva, gazing at Hamon in shock. 'You are a liar!'

'Siric has been twice already,' said Tuddenham, relieved to be discussing something else. 'But there was no trace of Norys. He must have left the country.'

'Look at him,' spat Hamon spitefully, pointing at the tanner. 'Just look at his face, his eyes, his teeth, and tell me he is not your husband's offspring.'

The tanner ducked his head down quickly, in a way that suggested that the identity of his natural father was already known to him. It was not known to Dame Eva, however, who stared at the tanner in mute disbelief.

'Hamon,' warned Tuddenham softly. 'Your anger is making you rash. It is not only my mother you are offending with these accusations, but me, too. I have always treated you like a son, so please show me some respect. It is not respectful to accuse me of being a tanner's brother.'

Finally ashamed, Hamon hung his head. Isilia went to kneel next to the old lady, whose wrinkled face glistened with silent tears, and put an arm around her thin shoulders. Dame Eva had been right, Bartholomew thought, as he watched them: Hamon was an ignorant lout.

'Now, perhaps we can work on my advowson?' asked Tuddenham, although his voice lacked its usual enthusiasm for the subject. He turned to smile wanly at Alcote.

Alcote had listened to Hamon's accusations with a malicious amusement that Bartholomew found distasteful. Despite the fact that he had complained of stomach pains since

his arrival in Grundisburgh, Bartholomew saw Alcote finish one bowl of raisins, and flick his fingers at Siric to
be brought another, pointedly disregarding Bartholomew's
advice to abstain from them to allow his digestion to recover.
Bartholomew, who did not like raisins, thought it was not
surprising that the fussy little scholar suffered cramps and
loose bowels.

'I need to read and summarise these,' Alcote said, gesturing at a pile of deeds and dipping thin fingers into the
new dish of raisins. 'I will work better and faster alone,
without people looking over my shoulder and delaying me
with stupid questions.'

This was a none too subtle dig at Wauncy, whose own
interest in Tuddenham's material possessions was driving
Alcote to distraction.

'All this is all taking a damnably long time,' complained
Tuddenham. 'You arrived ten days ago, and the thing is still
not written.'

'It takes time to do properly,' said Alcote pettishly. 'You
would not want me to rush it, and then discover in three
years' time that there is something we have overlooked
that invalidates the whole transaction. This advowson is
to last for ever, so we must ensure it is done correctly,
no matter how keen we all are to have it finished in a
hurry.'

As much as Bartholomew disliked Alcote, he knew the
man was right: an important deed needed to be written
with care if it were not to be overturned in a court of law
at some later date. However, at the back of his mind was the
nagging suspicion that Alcote's care was not wholly altruistic,
and that scraps of information were being carefully stored to
be brought out later, when they could benefit him in some
way – particularly financially.

'But rest assured,' Alcote continued, 'I am working as fast
as I can. In fact, I can predict with some confidence that I

will have completed all the groundwork this evening, and should have a working draft for you late tomorrow.'

'I am going hunting,' said Hamon, unfolding his arms and looking out of the window at the sun. 'The last of the venison is finished and we should not slaughter any more of my pigs.' He spoke bitterly, although Bartholomew could not imagine why. 'Will you come, uncle?'

Tuddenham caught Bartholomew's eye and hesitated. It was clear he was tempted, but it was also clear he knew it was not advisable, given his worsening physical condition.

'I will remain here, and spend a little time with my wife,' he said.

Isilia's lovely face broke into a happy smile, and she took his hand in hers.

'We can walk by the river,' she said brightly. 'Or pick elderflowers in the orchard.' Her delight faded when she remembered the old lady sitting dejectedly by the fire. 'No. We will stay here and work on Dame Eva's tapestry. The light is good for needlework today.'

Tuddenham smiled gratefully, and they went to sit on either side of the old lady, bantering with each other to try to take her mind off Hamon's thoughtless words. Bartholomew felt sorry for her, knowing that the elderly often looked back on days more golden in their thoughts than in reality. It had been cruel of Hamon to disillusion her.

'Will you come hunting with me, Master Alcote?' asked Hamon politely, apparently feeling remorse, and deciding that some relief from his guilty conscience might be gained by extending an invitation to the man who was working so hard for his uncle. 'If we are lucky, we may catch a wild boar.'

'No,' said Alcote with a shudder at the notion of the physical effort that would be needed. 'I will stay here and work. Bartholomew would be no kind of companion for you, either – the only lancing he enjoys is that of boils. But

Michael rides well, and may relish a little blood sport. He *is* a Benedictine, after all.'

'I would,' said Michael keenly. 'But not today with Norys at large and insufficient evidence to prove his guilt. I should spend the day talking with your villagers, if you have no objection.'

Hamon shrugged indifferently, and went into the yard to prepare for the hunt. Horses wheeled and whinnied as they were brought from the stables, their shod feet clattering on the hard ground. Each man carried a bow and a long lance, as well as a quiver full of arrows. Hamon looked happier than he had been since Bartholomew had first met him. His hair shone in the sun, and his long teeth flashed white as he grinned at his uncle. Servants dashed this way and that, carrying cloaks, knives and saddles, while hounds bayed and circled, adding to the general mayhem.

Eventually, they were ready, and the horses streamed out of the courtyard with the servants running behind them. The last two hauled a cart on which the prey would be stacked if the hunt were successful. When they had gone, Isilia and Tuddenham walked slowly towards the bower near the house with Dame Eva between them. Isilia looked back and gave Bartholomew a cheerful wave and the smile of an angel.

'You should not encourage her to do that,' said Michael critically. 'It is bad enough having Tuddenham thinking we are dragging our feet over this wretched deed, without you exchanging lecherous looks with his wife. Still, at least William is out of trouble.'

'Why? What have you done with him?'

'Here he comes now,' said Michael. 'You can ask him yourself.'

William strode briskly toward them, rubbing his hands together in a businesslike fashion. 'Right. I have now questioned everybody who lives on The Street and the Otley road. I will make a start on the houses on the hill this afternoon.'

'Good,' said Michael, pleased by his diligence. 'And what have you discovered?'

William's self-satisfaction reached new heights. 'I have found another six people who saw the cloaked figure running from the church after the feast.'

'Excellent,' said Michael, impressed. 'But how did you manage to find them, when I asked these same people and was told they had seen nothing?'

'It is amazing how lies dissolve into truth when people are threatened with eternal damnation,' said William proudly. 'I merely informed them that they would burn in hell for lying, just as they would for stealing and murdering.'

'But why should they lie at all?' asked Bartholomew. 'Everyone keeps telling me how the entire village will do anything to help us catch Unwin's murderer.'

'Apparently, they feel sorry for Norys,' said William in some disdain. 'They all know he is the one accused of killing Unwin, and they are reluctant to provide us with information that may harm him. He is a popular man in the village, because he grants them pardons.'

'He does not,' said Michael immediately. 'Wauncy does not allow him to practise his vile trade in the village – he goes to Ipswich.'

'He goes to Ipswich a good deal less now than he did before the plague,' said William, delighted to answer Michael's questions and show off his prowess at interrogation. 'Wauncy is so busy saying masses for the dead that he has little time for his living parishioners. They feel it is better to buy a pardon from Norys than to wait all day for Wauncy to find a spare moment to grant them absolution.'

'No wonder Wauncy was keen to have Unwin as his apprentice,' said Michael thoughtfully. 'Unwin could have taken on all the dealings with the living, while Wauncy himself could continue to amass a fortune from the dead.'

'And Wauncy is not even a real parish priest,' said William with relish. 'He was only an acolyte before the Death, and simply took on priestly duties when Tuddenham could find no one else.'

It was a tale repeated in villages all over the country – after the plague, priests had tended to select the more lucrative posts, leaving small parish churches struggling to find replacements. Bishops had been reduced to employing men from the laity, who had no proper training, but who were better than nothing at all.

'I see,' said Michael. 'And did anyone recognise this person who rushed from the church?'

William looked crestfallen. 'Unfortunately not. And three of them said he wore a short cloak, and three said a long one.'

'Damn!' said Michael softly. 'That gets us nowhere at all. We still cannot prove that Norys is lying when he said he saw a short cloak.'

'So, we have Stoate and three others saying the fellow wore a long cloak, and Norys and three others saying it was a short cloak,' summarised Bartholomew. 'Were there two of them, then?'

'How could there be?' asked Michael wearily. 'Unwin was only killed once.'

'Then perhaps one was an innocent party – either coming from the church before Unwin was placed there, or fleeing afterwards because he did not want to become involved with the unlawful slaying of a priest. Who can blame him? Both Norys and Eltisley have been accused, and the evidence to implicate either is thin.'

'So,' said Michael dispiritedly, 'all we can say with certainty is that six people plus Norys, Stoate and Mistress Freeman saw a figure in a cloak running from the church at about the time Unwin was slain. We do not know whether one or both of them had anything to do with Unwin's death. Did you learn anything else, William?'

'That no one has seen Norys since Wednesday, and that no one saw him throw a bloody knife into the garden of the Half Moon, although I realise of course that does not mean he did not do it.'

'Well done,' said Michael, appreciative of William's reasoning – especially since it fitted with his own. 'You will make a splendid Junior Proctor one day. Is that all?'

'Only that the village thatcher claims the bundle you discovered on Saturday was not on Norys's roof on Friday morning,' said William. 'It is one of the roofs he thinks need replacing, apparently, and he always looks at it as he passes, hoping to see signs of leakage. He said the bundle must have been put on the roof after midday on Friday.'

'That is odd,' said Michael, puzzled.

'That means either Norys did not put it there, or he is not in Ipswich,' said Bartholomew.

'He must have returned,' said Michael, refusing to accept the alternative.

'But why would he hurl such an incriminating package on his own roof?' asked Bartholomew. 'It would have been better to throw it on someone else's, to implicate them. He is not stupid.'

'Perhaps he is just trying to confound us,' said William. 'There is no understanding the criminal mind, Matthew. It is not made of the same physical material as yours and mine.'

'Really?' asked Bartholomew. 'And how would it be different, exactly?'

'I am going to the Half Moon to see if Eltisley has recovered sufficiently from his ordeal in Tuddenham's cellar to make me something to eat,' interrupted Michael before they could start a debate. 'You two can do what you like.'

'We will join you,' said William. 'I have not eaten anything today and questioning people always gives me an appetite.' He stretched expansively and then looked at Bartholomew. 'Have you fully recovered from your encounter with the white dog, Matthew? Cynric has not. He is convinced he is going to die, and is refusing to leave the tavern.'

'I know,' said Bartholomew. 'I have tried to reason with him, but he will not listen to me. Deynman is supposed to be looking after him.'

'Cynric will be seeking his death a lot sooner if you impose that ignoramus on him for long,' said William, following them along the woodland path to the village. Bartholomew was perfectly aware of that, hoping that too much of Deynman's company might jolt the Welshman from his gloom. While Michael and William discussed the relative merits of the cuisine at the Half Moon and the Dog, Bartholomew fretted about his book-bearer, racking his brain for a way to break the black mood that had turned Cynric into someone he barely recognised.

'There is Eltisley,' said Michael, as they reached the Half Moon. 'I wonder where he is going.'

Eltisley, looking around him so furtively that it was comical, was tiptoeing across the yard of his tavern to one of the sheds that stood as a lean-to against the rear wall. Curious, Bartholomew followed him, wondering what he was up to. With Michael and William watching in amusement, he walked stealthily to the shack into which Eltisley had disappeared.

'Sir Thomas released you, then,' he said, in a deliberately loud voice to the landlord's back. Eltisley spun round in alarm, pots flying from the table in front of him to smash on the floor. Bartholomew looked around the room with interest. It was a workshop, with herbs and plants hanging in bunches from the rafters, pots and bottles ranged along shelves, and a bench that ran the full length of one wall. It smelled of burning, and of mint vying for dominance over rosemary, but it was not unpleasant.

'What are you doing here?' demanded Eltisley, placing a firm hand on Bartholomew's chest, and shoving him outside. He slammed the door behind him, and glared at the physician. 'This is private property, not part of the tavern. It is not open to customers.'

'Is this where you make your remedies?' asked Bartholomew. 'You need a licence to be an apothecary, you know. You cannot just produce concoctions, and then test them on people.'

'I can if I do not sell them,' said Eltisley. 'I never ask for more than they cost to make, because I want to see my fellow villagers in good health.'

'It is illegal,' said Bartholomew. 'You might kill someone, whether you mean to or not.'

'What I do with my free time is none of your business,' said Eltisley unpleasantly. 'I am not some scholar, bound by rules and regulations. I am an explorer of science, and my task in life is to understand the meaning of things and how they work.'

'Tell Father William that and he will have you burned for heresy,' said Bartholomew. He pointed to the shed. 'What is in this room that you are so keen to hide away?'

'Nothing to interest a man with a closed mind,' said Eltisley, turning away from him and securing the door with one of the largest locks Bartholomew had ever seen. He wondered whether Cynric would be able to pick it. 'Just an experiment.'

'What kind of experiment?' pressed Bartholomew. 'Is it dangerous?'

Eltisley smiled his vague smile. 'Not in the slightest.' He sighed heavily. 'All right. I will tell you, since you are interested in my work, but you must promise to keep it to yourself.'

Bartholomew said nothing, but Eltisley, already forgetting his hostility now that he had captured an audience, did not seem to notice that the physician had promised nothing.

'I am inventing a way to make cows produce more milk. It involves feeding them with water infused with chalk. You see, I reason that if you put a lot of something white into them, you will get a lot of something white out.'

'I think you will find that cows' digestions do not operate like that,' said Bartholomew, now convinced more than ever that the man was not fit to be out of Tuddenham's cellar. 'All you will do is block their innards and give them colic.'

'What would you know of cows?' asked Eltisley dismissively. 'You are a mere physician. I, on the other hand, am a man of vision.'

'But why the secrecy? Is it because you are afraid of someone stealing your ideas?'

'It is because I do not want to raise the hopes of the villagers,' said Eltisley. 'Not all my experiments work immediately, and I do not like to see them disappointed.'

'So, you think you will fail?'

Eltisley glared at him. 'I will succeed eventually. These things take time. But I would not expect you to understand: you have no scientific imagination. How do you know my experiment will not work until it has been tried?'

'Common sense,' said Bartholomew. 'I also know that you will not fly if you jump off the church tower, but I would not recommend you to try it just to prove my point.'

Eltisley looked up at the tower and frowned thoughtfully, and Bartholomew could see his peculiar mind mulling over the probabilities. It would not take much to convince him to attempt something so stupid, and Bartholomew wondered whether someone, for the sake of the rest of the perfectly normal, law-abiding members of the village, should undertake the responsibility.

Leaving Eltisley gazing at the church, he went to the

garden, where Michael and William were sitting, enjoying the sun. Michael took a deep breath through his nose, and smiled.

'This unpleasantness is almost over. As soon as Alcote has our deed finished – and he says he will have a version tomorrow – we can be away from this place, hopefully never to return.'

'One of us will have to stay,' said William grimly. 'With Unwin dead, one of us will need to take over his duties as vicar.'

'No,' said Michael. 'We will go back to Michaelhouse, and the Master will appoint another student. Jakobus de Krek would do well here: he is devious and mean-spirited.'

William agreed. 'I will recommend him to the Master. That is an excellent idea, Brother: he would suit Tuddenham very well. I never did think Unwin was a good choice – far too tolerant.'

'But we cannot leave until we have brought Unwin's murderer to justice,' said Bartholomew.

Michael sighed irritably. 'We have Unwin's killer, Matt. Norys will soon be under lock and key. He cannot remain in hiding for ever.' He chuckled nastily. 'Anyway, if he is like the rest of the villagers, he will be afraid to be out at night in case he claps eyes on the spectral hound.'

'Speaking of Padfoot, have you spoken to Alice Quy's husband?' asked Bartholomew of William, thinking of the woman who had died of childbirth fever. 'Did he mention anything about her death?'

'He tried, but I told him that to acknowledge the existence of such beings was opposing the omnipotent will of God,' said William grandly. 'And I said that if he persisted in such beliefs, he would burn in the fires of hell for eternity and so would all his children. He did not mention it again.'

'But what did he say before you terrified the life out of him?' asked Bartholomew.

William scratched his nose. 'He said she was out near Barchester one evening, just after sunset, and she saw the white dog sniffing around in the trees. She ran so blindly with fear that she ended up on Deblunville's land. He sent her home, and within two days she was dead of child-birth fever.'

Bartholomew sipped the cool ale Eltisley's wife brought them, and considered. Was Alice Quy out digging for the golden calf as Deblunville had believed? Was her death coincidence, or had some mysterious force been at work to kill her, as so many villagers thought? As he pondered, he heard someone call his name, and looked up to see Stoate approaching. The Grundisburgh physician smiled at the scholars, and sat down on the bench opposite, wiping his face with the sleeve of his shirt.

'It is hot today. We will have a good harvest if this keeps up.'

'Eltisley,' called Michael to the taverner, who still gazed up at the church tower. 'Bring wine for our guest. And none of that sour stuff you gave us last time, either; I want that sweet red claret that tastes of honey. You might bring a morsel to eat, too, such as a bit of pheasant or a slice of bacon. But nothing green. My stomach is still unsettled from when you poisoned me with those weeds last week.'

'You have not taken any of Eltisley's black tonic, have you?' asked Stoate anxiously, after the landlord had gone. 'Only it is said to contain goat urine. I wish he would not dispense that particular remedy to the villagers.'

'The man is a menace,' said Bartholomew. 'He claims to be a man of science, but he no more understands the basic rules of physics than does his cockerel.'

Stoate smiled. 'You are a little harsh. He is a good-hearted man who invests most of his energy and a good deal of his income in developing cures for the villagers. He is working on a method to increase the yield of cows' milk at the moment, because poor Master Quy's animal is drying up. With his wife dead of the childbirth fever, he needs that milk to feed his children.'

'Eltisley seemed to consider that experiment a secret,' said Bartholomew.

Stoate laughed. 'This is the country. Secrets do not remain secrets for long, and everyone is hoping Eltisley will be successful. But just because Eltisley is kind-hearted does not mean to say that you should drink his black tonic.'

Michael chuckled. 'It made Alcote as sick as a dog, but it was his vegetables that made *me* ill.'

'Eltisley's wife is an excellent cook and the fare is rich and plentiful,' said Bartholomew. 'Not all of us know when to stop.'

'Typical of a monk,' muttered William, reaching for a large helping of pheasant. 'Greedy!'

Stoate regarded Michael thoughtfully. 'A cup of water before a meal helps to fill the innards and reduces unnecessary overloading. Have you tried that?'

'I most certainly have not,' said Michael frostily. 'I only take water as a last resort – and never before food.'

'Does water help?' asked Bartholomew of Stoate, interested.

'No medicine while we are eating, if you please,' said William firmly. 'You can do that when you are alone together.'

'Did you tend Alice Quy?' asked Bartholomew, ignoring him.

Stoate shook his head. 'Of course not. Physicians do not deal with women's problems, particularly when there is a midwife like Mother Goodman to call on. I was summoned eventually, but she was dead before I arrived. Had I been contacted earlier, I might have been able to counteract the infection, although I do not really think so.'

'Mother Goodman said this fever came six months after

the birth of her last child,' said Bartholomew. 'That seems unusual.'

Stoate sighed. 'It was six months after the birth of one child, but it is my belief that she became pregnant again almost immediately, and it was the loss of that baby which killed her. She claimed she saw a ghostly white dog, and came tearing home in such a panic that I am not surprised the unborn child was lost.'

'Do you think she convinced herself that she was going to die because she saw the white dog?' asked Bartholomew. 'You said only the other night that people often give up all hope of recovery if they believe themselves to be seriously ill.'

'Yes,' said Stoate nodding keenly. 'I have seen that many times. It is very possible that Alice Quy simply gave up. It explains why she died so quickly, too, when other women with that fever tend to linger.'

'Then do you think that James Freeman slit his throat because he believed he was going to die?'

'Possibly,' said Stoate. 'The poor man was beside himself with terror. You need to make sure the same thing does not happen to your servant. There is a rumour that he saw Padfoot, too.'

'I cannot imagine why Cynric is so disturbed by it,' said Bartholomew. 'It was not a pleasant experience, but it did us no real harm.' For Stoate's benefit, he described the attack.

'But you did not *see* the thing,' Stoate pointed out. 'It sat on you and breathed on you, but you did not actually set eyes on it. Cynric did, and that is why he is so afraid. Padfoot is supposed to herald the death of anyone who *sees* it, not anyone it sits on.'

'But it was a real dog, not some spectre,' protested Bartholomew. 'It was flesh and blood.'

'That is not the point,' said Stoate. 'The legend says

nothing about how it feels, sounds or smells, or even tastes. It says that anyone who sets eyes on it will die within a few days.'

'You speak almost as if you believe it,' said Bartholomew.

Stoate finished his wine and stood. 'I do. I learned years ago not to mock local customs and stories. There is nearly always some grain of sense behind them that should not be dismissed too lightly.' He tapped Bartholomew on the shoulder as he left. 'Do not close your mind without fully investigating the issue, my friend.'

Having devoured another monumental meal at Tuddenham's expense, Michael was in no state to accompany Bartholomew to the Freemans' house, and was forced to retire to the bedchamber to lie down. Bartholomew took William with him instead. He left the friar at the tanner's home – against Bartholomew's pleas for clemency, the petrified tanner had replaced Eltisley in Tuddenham's cellar – while he walked along the river until he reached the butcher's property. It was deserted and silent, almost like the wooden hovels at Barchester. He pushed open the door and stepped inside.

Seldom had he seen so much blood in one place. It had splattered the walls, splashed on to the ceiling, and pooled on the floor. In fact, there was enough of it to make Bartholomew wonder whether Alice Freeman was the only person to have had her throat cut there. The blotches of dark red, now turning to black, were obscene in the little house. The Freemans had not been wealthy but they had evidently taken some pride in their home. The wooden stools and table were lovingly crafted, while the coarse woollen blankets, now strewn carelessly about the room, were edged with yellow ribbons in a spirited attempt to make them more attractive.

On the windowsill was a small vase containing flowers, now drooping and brown, while the shelves held pewter dishes and two clay goblets. The table had been over-turned, and smashed pottery crunched under Bartholo-mew's feet as he walked. Something else cracked, too, and Bartholomew saw that one of the bowls that lay up-ended on the ground had contained shellfish. Poor Alice Freeman had apparently dined on mussels before she had died, and the empty shells were now scattered all over the room.

To test Michael's claim that Alice Freeman's screams for help could not be heard from the tanner's cottage, he took a deep breath and called William's name. After several moments, when William did not appear, he shouted again, a little louder. Finally, he yelled at the top of his lungs. When William still did not come, he went outside and waved to him.

'I heard nothing,' said William, walking down the lane. 'If she screamed, then it could not have been heard from the tanner's cottage. How many times did you shout?'

'Three,' said Bartholomew. 'Is Norys's the only house near here?'

William nodded, and peered through the Freemans' door to the room beyond. 'Good God! It is like a slaughterhouse in there.'

Bartholomew frowned thoughtfully. 'A slaughterhouse. Freeman was a butcher.'

'Norys will swing for this, and that is certain,' said William. 'Look, there is even blood on the doorstep and along the path. The poor woman must have dragged herself out, looking for help as she died.'

Bartholomew looked to where William pointed. The stains were not mere drips, but huge splatters that coloured the grass a reddish brown. Something else caught his eye. To one side of the path, partly concealed under a rosemary bush, was the body of a cat. Bartholomew touched it, but it was cold and motionless.

He walked back into the house, and crouched to inspect the dry pools of blood that were scattered around the room, noting thick, black clots in most of them. Finally, he went to the butcher's workshop further down the garden. The door was ajar, so he pushed it open.

The stinking body of a pig lay on a bench, waiting in vain to be dismembered and returned to its owner in manageable portions. It had the veins in its neck slit, and its intestines removed. The buzz of flies and the stench of decay made Bartholomew feel sick, but he forced himself to complete his inspection. To one side of the pig there was a large vat in which blood was collected, before being made into puddings or used to thicken soups. The vat was almost empty, and a dark dribble on the floor showed that some of its contents had been spilled.

'We cannot blame this on Norys,' said William, sounding almost resentful as he watched Bartholomew stare at a bowl that was stained almost black with blood. 'I know from my questioning of the villagers that Hamon ordered a pig killed two Saturdays ago – apparently he wanted to make blood pudding as a gift for the harlot Janelle, now Deblunville's wife.'

'But he did not know she was Deblunville's wife until last Sunday.'

'Quite,' said William. 'That is why the pig lies unclaimed. The pudding was to be a token of his devotion, but even the insensitive Hamon balked at the notion of sending a fine blood pudding to another man's wife.'

'I would not send one to anybody,' said Bartholomew, who found the notion of blood puddings repellent. Still, he thought, at least he now understood Hamon's odd comment about not wanting to slaughter any more of his pigs. Perhaps the young knight would have been more successful in his courtship of the lovely Janelle had he plied her with more appealing gifts – such as a ring made of his first wife's coffin handle.

William looked around him. 'When Freeman died, his wife took over his business. It must have been she who slaughtered the pig.'

'But Norys did not slaughter her,' said Bartholomew, meeting his eyes. 'In fact, I think we will find that no one did.'

CHAPTER 9

FATHER WILLIAM STOOD AT THE DOOR OF THE CHURCH to keep watch, while Michael stamped furiously down the nave after Bartholomew toward Mistress Freeman's corpse in the chancel. The two thick candles that burned at the head of the coffin were almost invisible in the brilliance of the setting sun, and the skeletal Walter Wauncy knelt in prayer at her feet, his words whispering around the shadowy building like a voice from the grave. A butterfly flicked through a window in a flash of red, and was gone again, while outside a robin sang piercingly from one of the elms.

'Master Alcote asks if you would join him at Wergen Hall,' said Michael, as the priest glanced up. 'He is having difficulties with one document. I will continue the vigil for Mistress Freeman.'

Wauncy looked puzzled. 'Alcote professes himself very proficient with these affairs; I cannot see why he should request my help. And anyway, I have been paid for this mass. Would you have me share the fee with you?'

'I would not dream of taking it,' said Michael, offended that Wauncy should regard him as the kind of man to haggle over a dead woman's fourpence.

'Well, in that case,' said Wauncy, climbing to his feet with an ease that suggested he had not been on his knees for long, 'I shall go. He asked for me particularly, you say?'

'He did,' Michael confirmed, and the flattered Wauncy made his way towards the door, nodding genially to William as he left. Michael watched him leave, then turned to Bartholomew, his green eyes sceptical.

'So, your latest theory is that Alice Freeman was not murdered, but that someone doused her house with pig's blood to make it look as though she had been?'

'It is a theory based on fact,' said Bartholomew. 'The slaughterhouse vat should have been filled with blood from the dead pig, but it was virtually empty. There was a bowl hidden behind it, suggesting to me that someone had scooped the blood out of the vat and taken it to the Freemans' cottage. And basically, there is far too much of it in the house to have come from one person.'

'But we have both seen what a mess even a little blood can make,' protested Michael. 'A goblet of it spread around can look as though an entire herd of cows has been massacred.'

'Look,' said Bartholomew, easing aside the piece of linen that hid the wound in the dead woman's throat. 'This is a vicious slash that would have caused massive bleeding instantly.'

'So?' asked Michael. 'Massive bleeding is what we have.'

'With this wound, she would not have had the strength to spread blood all over her home and garden. I think she would have taken one or two steps, and then collapsed and died where she fell.'

'She did,' said Michael. 'I found her lying in the middle of the floor with all the furniture overturned and smashed.'

'Then how did the blood get into the garden?'

'Perhaps it fell from Norys as he rushed away from the scene of the crime. The clothes we found on his roof tell us that he was drenched in the stuff.'

'There was far too much of it to have merely dripped from a man's clothes – these are large splashes, Brother, not a few drops. I think they spilled from the bowl as someone carried the pig's blood from the slaughterhouse to throw around the house.'

'No,' said Michael firmly. 'Mistress Freeman probably left these splatters as she staggered around, reeling from her injury.'

'Someone with a wound like this does not wander all over the place,' persisted Bartholomew. 'And anyway, I told you, there was too much blood to have come from one person.'

Michael frowned. 'I do not really understand what you are concluding from all this. Do you think someone else died there with her? That Norys claimed not one victim, but two?'

'No,' said Bartholomew. 'I am suggesting that no one was killed.'

Michael folded his arms and regarded his friend with wary eyes. 'Well, come on. Explain.'

'I saw lots of mussel shells in Mistress Freeman's house. I think bad shellfish killed her.'

'Mussels?' asked Michael, confused. 'Where would she find mussels?'

'Ipswich has a fish market, and so does Woodbridge, both of which are only a few miles away. Many people die from eating shellfish, particularly mussels, and especially between May and October, so it is not improbable to suppose she ate some bad ones. And her cat.'

'Cat?' queried Michael, startled. 'How does her cat fit into all this?'

'There was a dead cat in her garden. I think she fed it some of the mussels and it died, too.'

Michael raised one finger in triumph. 'Your theory has a fatal flaw. Mother Goodman told us that Mistress Freeman did not like cats – which was why Will Norys did not offer her the honour of his hand in marriage. So Mistress Freeman would not have fed a cat mussels – good ones or bad.'

Bartholomew ran a hand through his hair, and stared at the woman in the coffin. After a moment he leaned down toward her mouth and sniffed. Michael looked away, revolted.

'Well, she vomited before she died, which I doubt she would have done had her throat been cut. So, there are three possibilities: she may have eaten bad shellfish and died accidentally; she may have been given bad shellfish by someone who knew they would kill her, and she was therefore murdered; or she may have kept them until she was certain eating them would make her fatally ill.'

'So what you are saying is that you have no idea whether her death was an accident, suicide or murder?' asked Michael. 'Well, that is helpful!'

'Those are the possibilities,' said Bartholomew. 'She ate the bad mussels and died – whether deliberately or accidentally we may never know – and then someone slit her throat after she was dead. Her hands and arms were slashed, too, to make it appear as though there was a struggle.'

'But what for?' cried Michael exasperated, his voice ringing around the church and making William start from his position at the door. 'What could anyone gain from such an obscene act?'

'It means Norys no longer has an alibi for the time of Unwin's murder.'

Michael rubbed a flabby cheek with a pallid forefinger. 'You think someone desecrated her corpse, so that Norys would be found guilty of Unwin's murder?'

'It worked. It is exactly what you told Tuddenham – that Norys needed a false alibi from her, she refused, and so he killed her.'

'I told Tuddenham that, because that is what I am sure happened,' said Michael. 'And we have Norys's bloodstained clothes hidden on his roof to prove that he did it.'

'Norys's uncle says those clothes are not his.'

'Well, he would,' snapped Michael. 'People lie to us all the time, Matt, and you should know better than to believe them – particularly when they have very good cause to be dishonest.'

'So, are you saying Norys used these same clothes to kill Unwin, too?' demanded Bartholomew, becoming angry in his turn. 'Do you think he keeps them on his roof so that he can use them again and again, and not spoil more than one set with bloodstains?'

'He might,' said Michael harshly. 'Perhaps that is why Mistress Freeman put up such a fight – she opened the door, anticipating a neighbourly visit, and saw Norys standing there in his murdering gear.'

'That would mean he knew in advance she would not lie for him about the alibi,' said Bartholomew. 'Or your theory would have him arriving at her house dressed in blood-drenched clothes, holding a sharp knife at the ready, and calmly asking her if she would mind telling everyone she had enjoyed a pleasant stroll with him around the church while he was killing Unwin.'

'So what is your explanation?' demanded Michael irritably.

Bartholomew considered. 'I think Norys may have been with Mistress Freeman when she died. Since, as you pointed out, Mistress Freeman is unlikely to have shared her dinner with a cat, Norys probably did so. He loved cats, and I do not think he would have poisoned one with bad shellfish deliberately. So, I think he is probably dead, too.'

Michael made an exasperated noise at the back of his throat. 'This nonsense is getting us nowhere. Put the poor woman back as you found her, and leave her in peace. This is a case of simple murder: Norys killed Unwin for his purse, killed Mistress Freeman for not lying for him, and threw the bloody clothes on to his roof where he hoped they would never be found.'

'But Norys is not a foolish man,' persisted Bartholomew. 'Why did he choose to hide them on his own roof when their discovery would be so incriminating?'

'Perhaps because he intends to use them again,' said

Michael. 'And he put them somewhere where he would be able to get at them.'

'And what about all the other things that have happened?' asked Bartholomew. 'What about the attack on Cynric and me in Barchester? What about Grosnold being seen talking to Unwin shortly before his death? What about the fact that Unwin, Mistress Freeman's husband and Alice Quy saw this white dog, and all three are now dead? What about Deblunville's suspicion that Tuddenham has his villagers out looking for this lost golden calf in the depths of the night? Finding a thing of such value might well make people resort to evil deeds. And what about this poor man we found hanged wearing Deblunville's clothes that no one has bothered about?'

'Irrelevant,' said Michael promptly. 'Our only interest in – and our only jurisdiction over – this affair is to find Unwin's killer. That is Norys, and Tuddenham will soon have him under lock and key. The rest is not our concern.'

'It is our concern if something sinister is going on that might affect the advowson.'

'Wrong. The relevance to the advowson is not that there is something untoward going on, but that someone at the University might discover what it is. Alcote has been very meticulous on that score: he has uncovered nothing.'

'So, you are saying that it is perfectly all right for the advowson to be steeped in filth and treachery as long as none of the other Colleges find out?'

Michael smiled. 'Basically. And it will be well worth the trouble: there will be a post for a Michaelhouse man at Grundisburgh in perpetuity, and most of the tithes will come the way of the College. You might even be offered the post yourself one day, when you are too old and drooling to teach medicine, or if you continue to disgrace yourself by lusting after prostitutes.'

'So, Michaelhouse is to provide Grundisburgh men who

are either too old to be of any use, or who have embarrassed the College in some way? That is a fine way to treat Tuddenham's generosity!'

'I have already told you that this has nothing to do with generosity, Matt. Tuddenham will have a reason for relinquishing some of his personal fortune to a distant College to which he has no affiliation. Alcote has been bribing the servants to gossip about their master, and I have been developing friendships with his cooks. However, neither of us has discovered his motive yet.'

Bartholomew shook his head in disgust. 'That is horrible, Brother. What will Tuddenham say if he finds out you are encouraging his people to betray him?'

'Probably the same thing I said when Horsey told me he had been offered a new pair of sandals for information about us, or when I discovered Deynman's handsome ivory dice were a gift from Hamon in exchange for a cosy chat.'

Bartholomew was aghast. 'You mean Deynman was bribed to tell tales about us?'

'Of course,' said Michael, smiling at the physician's shock. 'There was no harm done – that lad thinks very highly of you for some reason, and seems to have informed Hamon that you are only a little short of sainthood. But we should let William say mass for this poor woman's soul. Hopefully, Alcote will complete the advowson in the next couple of days, and we can be on our way. Then you can go back to your diseases and wounds and contagions, and be happy again.'

Bartholomew was disappointed at Michael's reaction to his discoveries and suppositions, but not entirely surprised. The monk had taken a hostile dislike to the vanished pardoner purely because he hated the profession with all his heart. Hearing that pardoners were selling their wares in Cambridge was one of the few things that could disturb the usually self-composed monk's equanimity and reduce him to a state of quivering rage. There was little that would please him more than being able to indict one for the crime of murder.

Bartholomew wandered outside the church feeling exhausted. Cynric had slept badly the previous night, crying out in his dreams several times, and waking everyone, including Eltisley and his wife. After the third time, Bartholomew had caught Eltisley trying to persuade Cynric to drink some potion that he insisted would bring dreamless sleep. Bartholomew had snatched it away even as Cynric was lifting it to his lips, horrified to detect the odour of dog mercury in it, a powerful and wholly inappropriate herb for sleeplessness. He had given Cynric a sleeping draught of his own, and placed a mattress against the door to prevent Eltisley entering uninvited again.

While Michael returned to the tavern, Bartholomew sat on the village green under a willow that shaded him from the fading evening sun. Its graceful branches swept down to trail in the stream, and the duck, her cluster of young in tow, approached him, nervous, but hopeful for scraps. The sandy bottom of the stream showed crystal clear through the swiftly running water, occasionally marred by swirls of silt as a cart or an animal plodded across one of the fords upstream. It was peaceful, with little to disturb him but the squabbling rooks in the churchyard elms, and the gentle tapping at his leg by the hungry duck. Her young chirruped and pipped, falling over each other as they poked about in the grass for seeds.

If he listened very hard, he could hear Father William's stentorian voice booming from the church as he rattled through the requiem mass for Mistress Freeman, making up in volume and speed what he lacked in concentration.

As he gazed across the green to the haphazard line of houses opposite the church, Bartholomew saw that he had two choices. He could ignore the whole business and let

Norys hang for the murders of Unwin and Mistress Freeman, and return to Cambridge never to think about the miserable affair again. Or he could make some enquiries of his own.

There were too many unanswered questions for him to accept that Norys was guilty: for example, why had Mistress Freeman's throat been cut after she had died, and the pig's blood scattered over her house to make her death appear a murder? Had Norys really been stupid enough to hide his bloody bundle in such an obvious place? Where was Unwin's relic? What had Grosnold been talking about to Unwin before the friar died? Why had Bartholomew been attacked in Barchester as he had ridden back from Otley with Cynric? There had been a slathering white dog, but there had been people, too, and earthly, not ghostly, hands had toppled him from his horse. Were they thieves after the gold coin Grosnold had given him, or did Grosnold want him silenced for some reason? Had Tuddenham resurrected the legend of Padfoot so that his villagers would have a valid excuse when they were found on Deblunville's land looking for the golden calf? And finally, who was the man who had been hanged in Deblunville's stolen clothes, and what had happened to his body?

He sighed. The more he thought about it, the more queries rattled about in his head. He was tired and he was worried about Cynric, afraid that Eltisley might try to 'cure' him of his gloom with some potion of his own making. He walked slowly across the village green in the dying light, and headed for the Half Moon. Michael was in the main chamber, eating again, and accompanied by Horsey and Deynman. The sullen men were, as usual, hunched over their ale at the table nearest the door, while Stoate joked with some of his young companions near the fire. It was a contented scene that signalled cosiness and normality. Michael beckoned him over for supper, but Bartholomew had no appetite for the rich food over which the monk was drooling, and said he was going to bed.

In the chamber upstairs, Cynric sat at the window and watched the dusk with unseeing eyes. He was pale, and his usually neat clothes were dishevelled and dirty. He did not even look up as Bartholomew entered, and jumped nervously when the physician spoke, claiming he had not heard him. Such inattention was unprecedented in the wary Welshman, and Bartholomew appreciated, yet again, quite how seriously his book-bearer took Padfoot's threat to his life.

'How do you feel?' he asked kindly, sitting next to him on the windowsill.

'How do I look?' asked Cynric anxiously. 'Do I seem to have a contagion? You must think so, or you would not have asked after my health.'

'You look like a man who needs a good sleep and a decent meal,' said Bartholomew practically. He made a decision: Cynric's well-being was more important than trying to prove the innocence of a man who had sensibly fled Grundisburgh, and who probably had no intention of returning. 'I am taking you back to Cambridge tomorrow – whether the advowson is completed or not.'

Cynric smiled sadly. 'That will not prevent the inevitable, boy. I am doomed, and there is nothing you can do about it.'

'This is insane,' said Bartholomew, standing and pacing in agitation. 'You are willing yourself to die, because of some silly fairy tale.'

Cynric turned his morose gaze to the dusk again, and declined to reply. Through the window, Bartholomew could see that the door to Eltisley's workshop was open, and a series of smashing sounds indicated that the landlord was in it. As he watched, a huge tongue of flame shot out of the entrance with a dull roar. Almost as quickly, it had gone.

Alarmed for Eltisley's safety, Bartholomew was about to run down the stairs when the landlord staggered out, soot covering his face and his clothes smoking. Hacking and wheezing, he brushed himself down, and regarded his workshop with a puzzled expression, as though he considered it, and not himself, responsible for the mishap.

'You are in far more danger from that maniac than from your spectral hound,' said Bartholomew, sitting down again. 'He will have his tavern in flames if he is not careful.'

Cynric gave a wan smile. 'You do not think much of Eltisley and his inventions, do you?'

'No,' said Bartholomew shortly. 'He believes he has an intellect superior to everyone else's, and that this gives him the right to test his theories on the unsuspecting. He might have killed you with that dog mercury he tried to give you last night.'

'He told me it would make me sleep.'

'It would have done, although whether you would have woken again is another matter. Apparently, he gave Tuddenham a poultice made from death-cap mushrooms for his bunions last winter. Thank God Tuddenham had the sense not to use it.'

'Medicine is not the only profession he likes to dabble in,' said Cynric, casting a mournful glance out of the window to Eltisley, still standing outside his workshop. 'He took my bow and said he was going to treat it with a special oil that would make the string more taut, so that my arrows would fly faster.'

'Did you let him? I would have thought that the string is already at its optimum tautness for the strength of the bow. If he tampered with it, you might find it does not draw properly.'

'I told him to leave it alone, but he took it anyway while I was out. I tried to use it when we were attacked in Barchester, but the balance was all wrong – that is why I missed Padfoot.'

'Damn the man,' said Bartholomew crossly. 'Did he take anything else of ours to "improve"? I am only grateful I never leave my medicine bag behind, or I might find half my salves had been replaced with something toxic.'

'I have no idea,' sighed Cynric. 'Can I close this window? I do not want to die of a chill from the night air.'

'I thought you liked sleeping under the stars,' said Bartholomew, reluctant to shut the window when the room was so stuffy and hot.

'That was before,' said Cynric, pulling it closed firmly.

After a while, as the room grew steadily darker, Deynman entered, bringing apples and a piece of cheese for Cynric, who stared at them as though they might choke him. Bartholomew was reading by candlelight, scanning a list of remedies for gout that Stoate had lent him. The candle was one of Eltisley's creations – a shapeless lump of tallow studded with cloves, which he assured his guests would give off a pleasant scent as it burned. The cloves either dropped into the pool of melted tallow long before the flame came anywhere near them, or they popped and crackled nastily before emitting a foul odour of scorching.

'I know how to break this curse of Padfoot,' said Deynman, flopping nonchalantly on to Bartholomew's mattress. 'Mother Goodman told me.'

'And how is that?' asked Bartholomew absently, more interested in Stoate's cures.

'You steal a piece of beef at midnight, and bury it under an ash tree in a piece of white cloth. Then, at sunrise the following day, someone must stand on the exact spot where you saw Padfoot, and recite the *Paternoster* in Latin as fast as he can. And then you will be free of the curse.'

'There you are then, Cynric,' said Bartholomew, smiling at the ludicrous nature of the charm. 'You are saved.'

'And this will work?' asked Cynric. Bartholomew looked up sharply when he heard the note of hope in the book-bearer's voice.

'Oh, yes,' said Deynman confidently. 'Mother Goodman was positive. I wrote it all down and then read it back to her to make sure I had it right. You know how I can get muddled sometimes.' This understatement almost made Bartholomew laugh. 'She said the charm had to be done exactly right or it would not work. That is why it failed to save those two villagers.'

'Alice Quy and James Freeman?' asked Cynric. 'The two who died after seeing Padfoot?'

Deynman nodded. 'One used pork instead of beef, and the other recited Psalm Twenty-Three instead of the *Paternoster*. So, when will you do it, Cynric? Tonight?'

The book-bearer's face changed abruptly from hope to resignation. 'I can never do it, boy. I cannot recite the *Paternoster* in Latin. I can barely recite it in Welsh.'

'But Doctor Bartholomew can,' said Deynman, beaming at his teacher. 'He knows everything like that. He will do it for you.'

'Thank you, lad,' said Cynric, clutching Bartholomew's hand in a grip that was painfully tight. 'I will never forget this.'

'Just a moment,' said Bartholomew in alarm. 'We cannot go stealing beef in the middle of the night, and creep off to a plague village to perform all sorts of bizarre rituals in the dark.'

A look of intense hurt crossed Cynric's face, while Deynman frowned in confusion. 'You mean you will not do it?' the student asked, bewilderment giving way to disbelief. 'You will let Padfoot have him instead?'

'Padfoot is not real,' said Bartholomew, unnerved by Cynric's distress. 'It is just a folktale – one embellished by Tuddenham to allow his villagers to hunt for the golden calf on other people's land, according to his neighbours. This ritual will make no difference to Cynric's well-being.'

But he could see it would. The flicker of optimism that had sparked in Cynric's eyes had gone, to be replaced by a pained dismay. Bartholomew thought about Stoate, and how he had advised Bartholomew not to dismiss people's beliefs and ideas too quickly in favour of rational, scientific explanations. He rubbed his face tiredly. Stoate prescribed dangerous herbs to pregnant women, and his choice of foxglove to treat Tuddenham's illness was a poor one, but for all that he was a better physician than Bartholomew. Stoate understood his patients, and he gave them what *they* felt they needed to make them well – purges and tonics and bleeding. Stoate, Bartholomew was sure, would not have hesitated to recite a prayer at Barchester, if he felt it would effect a cure.

'I will do it, Cynric,' said Deynman, with a defiant look at Bartholomew. 'I will ask Father William to teach me the Latin tonight, and I will go to Barchester and recite it for you at dawn.'

Cynric nodded gratefully, but Bartholomew could see the Welshman did not trust Deynman to learn it sufficiently accurately for the charm to work – and with good reason, given Deynman's reputation for intellectual pursuits.

'Very well, then,' said Bartholomew reluctantly. 'I will help you. But this *must* remain a secret between us. No one – not even Michael – can know about it.'

Cynric grinned at him in relief, and took an apple from the plate, eating with more enthusiasm than he had done for days. Bartholomew took the paper with the charm written on it, and read.

'An oak tree, Rob,' he said. 'It says the beef should be buried under an oak tree.'

'That is what I said,' protested Deynman.

'You said ash,' said Cynric, worried. 'Which is right?'

'Whatever is written down,' said Deynman. He blew out his lips in a gusty sigh. 'You can see why I wrote it out; my memory is dreadful. If it says elm there, then elm it is.'

'Right,' said Bartholomew, putting it in his bag. 'We need a bit of beef and a white cloth.'

'Here is the white cloth,' said Deynman, holding up the piece of fine linen that the landlord of the Dog had presented to Michael to dab his lips with after his monstrous meals.

'That will do very well, boy,' said Cynric, sounding pleased. 'And there will be plenty of beef in the village. That should not be difficult to find at midnight.'

'When do we start this shady mission, and how do we leave here without anyone asking us where we are going?' asked Bartholomew, his misgivings growing the more he thought about what they were going to do.

'We will say we are going to pray for the murdered woman in the church,' said Cynric promptly. 'No one will question that.'

'We had better go now, then,' said Bartholomew. 'But not you, Rob. You stay here.'

'But you will need me,' protested Deynman, appalled at the prospect of being excluded from the nocturnal adventure. 'Cynric might be attacked while he is waiting for you to finish reciting the prayer, and I will be able to save him.'

Bartholomew regarded him doubtfully, but supposed there would be no harm in allowing the lad to join them, although he suspected he would later regret it. It seemed Deynman had given Cynric a new lease of life, and Bartholomew felt he owed him something. Feeling like a schoolboy embarking on some mischievous prank, he followed Cynric and Deynman down the stairs and through the tavern.

'Where are you going?' asked Michael immediately. 'It is almost dark.'

'Nowhere,' said Bartholomew guiltily, a response that promptly earned the monk's full attention.

'To pray for Mistress Freeman's soul,' said Deynman, for once showing more presence of mind than his teacher.

'Then I shall join you,' said Michael, levering his bulk up from his chair.

'No!' said Bartholomew in horror. 'We do not want you.'

'I see,' said Michael, easing himself down again, and now entirely convinced that there was something illicit in progress. He shrugged, pretending to be uninterested, and sketched a cross at them in the air. 'Go, then, with God's blessing.'

With relief, Bartholomew escaped into the cool night air, certain that the fat monk now knew exactly what they were doing.

'You handled that skilfully,' remarked Cynric facetiously, becoming more his old self with each passing moment, now that there was something practical he could do against the curse of Padfoot. 'Now he will be certain to follow us.'

'Let him,' said Bartholomew. 'We will spend several hours in the church anyway. He will tire of watching us long before midnight. If not, I will distract him while you steal the meat.' He turned to Deynman. 'Are you sure it needs to be stolen? Can we not just ask for a piece?'

'Mother Goodman was most insistent about that. A lump obtained honestly will not work.'

'Eltisley will have some,' said Cynric. 'It is a good thing we are not at Michaelhouse. Stealing food from the kitchens with Agatha the laundress on the prowl would be dangerous work indeed.'

'Especially given what happened to her teeth,' said Bartholomew, giving Deynman a sidelong glance. The student flushed deep red and looked sheepish. It would be a long time before that unfortunate incident would be forgotten at Michaelhouse.

They arrived at the church. To Bartholomew's alarm, Wauncy was there, kneeling at the altar. At first Bartholomew thought he was praying, but the clink of metal soon told him that the priest was toting up his earnings from his masses for the dead. In the half-light of the flickering candles Wauncy looked even more deathlike than usual, and his face gleamed white like a skull in the depths of his cowl.

The priest was resentful when Bartholomew informed him that he had come to say another requiem for Mistress Freeman, and it was evident that he strongly suspected that his trade was being poached. It was not easy to persuade him otherwise, and it was some time before he finally left. While Cynric prowled the churchyard, watching Michael skulk in the shadows, and Deynman wandered restlessly up and down the aisle, Bartholomew sat at the base of one of the pillars and recited two complete masses, before his eyes became heavy and he dozed off.

When Cynric tapped him on the shoulder to inform him it was time to mount the assault on the beef, Michael had long since tired of waiting for something to happen, and had returned to the Half Moon. With Deynman shaking with excitement next to them, Cynric and Bartholomew made their way to Eltisley's darkened kitchens. Bartholomew began to have serious second thoughts.

'I do not like this at all,' he said, looking about him nervously. 'What if a dog barks, or there is a servant sleeping in the kitchen? How will we explain ourselves?'

'Eltisley will understand if we tell him the truth,' said Deynman.

'Eltisley might, but our colleagues will not,' said Bartholomew. He groaned. 'There is a light coming from Eltisley's workshop. He is awake – we will have to do this tomorrow.'

'That might be too late,' whispered Cynric. He patted Bartholomew on the shoulder in an attempt to steady his nerves. 'You keep an eye on the workshop, young Deynman can watch the tavern, and I will get the meat.' He gave Bartholomew an encouraging grin. 'This is the easy part. Have you never burgled a house before?'

'Of course not,' said Bartholomew, genuinely shocked. 'It is not something physicians are often called upon to do.'

Heart thumping, he crept across to Eltisley's workshop, and peered around a door that had been left slightly ajar. The landlord was there, his back to the entrance as he leaned over something that filled the room with a thick, pungent smoke. He was humming to himself, a contented sound that stopped abruptly when something exploded with a sharp pop. Shaking his head in disgust, Eltisley turned his attention to a pot that simmered on a brazier in one corner. He stirred it, lifted a spoonful to his nostrils and jerked back violently as the fumes were apparently stronger than he had anticipated. He began to hum again, and then turned toward the door.

Bartholomew backed away in alarm, certain that the landlord must have seen his shadow. He glanced around desperately for a place to hide. There was nowhere: the yard was remarkably free from clutter, and Eltisley would see him long before he made it to the kitchen. He looked inside the workshop again. Eltisley was almost at the door, his hand reaching out to push it open. The only thing Bartholomew's panic-stricken mind could think of was to slam it and lock Eltisley inside.

Eltisley had reached the door, but Bartholomew found he was unable to move, or even shout. He fought to pull himself together, and jerked an unsteady hand forward to grab the handle. At the very last moment, the landlord changed his mind about leaving, and instead leaned down to retrieve something from the floor, almost at Bartholomew's feet. It was a small dead dog. Eltisley picked it up by the tail and carried it to one of his benches, arranging it so it lay on its side. Bartholomew felt sick, partly from relief that he had not been discovered, but partly because he was certain the eccentric taverner was about to perform some ghastly experiment on the animal's corpse. Fortunately, Eltisley had his back to the door, so all Bartholomew could see of the grisly operation was vigorously pumping elbows and a good deal of rising smoke.

He almost yelled out when Cynric touched his arm, and he had to lean against the workshop wall for several moments until he was sure his legs had stopped shaking sufficiently to allow him to walk. He wondered what state he would be in by dawn, if he could not even help Cynric steal a sliver of beef without trembling and starting like a frightened fawn.

It was no sliver Cynric had stolen, however. Hoisted over his shoulder was a lump the size of a small barrel. Bartholomew was appalled, nervousness giving way to shock.

'Cut a piece off,' he whispered hoarsely. 'We do not need all that, and there will be hell to pay tomorrow when Eltisley finds it is missing.'

'I need to make sure this works,' Cynric whispered back. 'Padfoot is a powerful beast, and needs a strong charm to beat him. A bigger piece is better than a small one.'

'If you say so,' said Bartholomew wearily, surrendering in the face of such rank superstition. 'Let's find an oak tree before someone sees us with it.'

Anxious that they should not be seen, Bartholomew chose a tree well away from the village, near Barchester. He did not want the sounds of digging carrying on the still night air. While Cynric burrowed, Bartholomew sat to one side, wondering how he had allowed himself to be inveigled into skulking in the bushes in the dead of night burying a piece of stolen beef in Michael's newly acquired piece of linen. Eventually, Cynric completed his task, wiping sweat from his face and announcing with satisfaction that the first part of the charm had been successfully completed. A bird flapped suddenly in a nearby tree, and all three jumped.

Dawn was still some way off, and Bartholomew did not want to return to the village and risk being seen by one of his colleagues. Instead, he led the way closer to Barchester, since they would need to be there at dawn anyway, and found a group of dense bushes near its overgrown path. In them, they settled down to wait, Bartholomew hoping that Deblunville's archer was not out and about, because he was sure that carrying out Mother Goodman's charm would not be considered a good enough reason for trespassing yet again on land that was probably not Tuddenham's.

Cynric was nervous now there was nothing immediate for him to do, and jumped at each rustle or squeak from the woods around them. Deynman was patient and kind, exhorting him to courage, and assuring him that the curse would soon be broken. Seeing his clumsy words of comfort went some way to calming the agitated Welshman, Bartholomew was glad the student had insisted on coming after all.

The night was cool, but not cold, and Bartholomew was very tired. The litter of dead leaves was soft underneath him, and the silence of the woods was soporific. It was not long before he fell into a restless doze. He was woken abruptly when Deynman grabbed his arm in a painful pinch. People were walking along the path toward them. Cynric pulled Bartholomew and Deynman farther back into the bushes, and they watched a strange procession file past in the gloom.

Six cloaked figures walked in a silent line that was led by a man whose height, build and swagger showed him to be none other than Hamon. Each person carried a spade. Bartholomew shook his head in amused disbelief. Deblunville had been right: the Tuddenhams did venture out at night to dig for the mythical golden calf! He thought back to earlier in the week, when he and Michael had questioned some of the labourers who toiled in the fields. No wonder the villagers were tired, if they worked all day and then spent their nights digging for gold. There was an anxious moment when Hamon paused and peered into their bushes, as if he knew someone was there, but he moved on when one of his diggers made an impatient sound.

Once they had gone, Bartholomew dozed again, while Deynman played dice with Cynric to take the anxious Welshman's mind off the agonisingly long wait. It was not long before more voices drifted along the path, and Bartholomew was woken a second time when Cynric clapped a hand over his mouth to ensure silence. As they waited to see who else was out in the woods in the dead of night, Bartholomew wondered whether there was anyone in Suffolk asleep in his own bed that evening, or whether the entire population was abroad with a spade or a piece of stolen beef.

It was Deblunville and his archers. They were less furtive than Hamon's band, and laughed and joked with each other as they walked. As they reached the thicket where Bartholomew, Cynric and Deynman hid, Deblunville stopped and wiped sweat from his face with his sleeve, while his archer poked around on the path with a stick. With horror, Bartholomew saw one of Deynman's dice lying on the path inches from Deblunville's foot. Now they would be discovered for certain! Cynric had seen it, too, and Bartholomew could feel him as taut as a bowstring.

'Someone passed this way tonight,' said the archer knowledgeably. 'The track is all rucked up from milling feet. It was Hamon's crew, probably. It would be good to catch them red-handed!'

'We will get them,' said another, a small man with no incisors and a ring of long, greasy hair straggling from a balding pate. He turned to Deblunville. 'You go home to your wife.'

'I do not care to go home,' said Deblunville coldly. 'When Janelle is not puking over the bed-covers, she is nagging me to end this feud with the Tuddenhams.'

'She thinks we should sue for peace,' explained the archer to the toothless man. 'She is of the same mind as her father: he is always telling us to make a truce – although it does not stop him from spreading gossip about the Tuddenhams and Grosnold.'

'She does not approve of me going out each night trying to catch Hamon digging on my land for the golden calf,' said Deblunville. 'She says I should leave that to you, while I enjoy the pleasures of the wedding bed. She does not understand that I want to catch Hamon personally.'

'Perhaps she has a point,' said the toothless man with a lecherous grin. 'It has only been a few days since Walter Wauncy married you, and I do not think you can have tired of her this soon.'

'When you wed, you should hire Wauncy,' said Deblunville. 'He is cheaper than our own priest by three pennies. That was Janelle's doing – she is always on the alert for a bargain.'

'It would be like being wed by a corpse,' said the archer with a dramatic shudder. 'I would not want his skull-like features presiding over the happiest day of my life, three pennies cheaper or not.'

They moved on, leaving Cynric reeling with relief that they had not been spotted and Bartholomew laughing softly to himself. So, Tuddenham's priest had slipped away from his own flock to poach a little trade from his neighbour. Bardolf had said that the priests of the manors fought as much as their masters – and now it seemed as though they even stole each other's business by offering competitive rates for weddings. No wonder the skeletal priest had stressed to Tuddenham that the union was a good thing, and had been so keen to know from Bartholomew what Deblunville and Janelle had said about their wedding – he probably feared

Tuddenham's displeasure if the knight discovered what he had done.

The woods grew silent again, although Cynric claimed he could hear sounds of digging in the distance. So that he could see to gamble with Deynman, Cynric lit a candle, and Bartholomew spotted a patch of sea wormwood, a plant that did not usually grow so far from the coast. Delighted, he gave Deynman, who was far more interested in his game, an impromptu lecture on the benefits of the herb to rid small children of worms. Afterwards, lulled by the click of ivory and the occasional victorious snigger from Deynman, Bartholomew dozed again, waking damp and chilled later, when Cynric stood and stretched.

'It is almost dawn, boy. You need to be in place to start reciting when the sun comes up.'

Bartholomew glanced at the sky. Large thunderclouds had gathered, a deep, menacing grey in the faint glow of early morning. 'Sunrise will be difficult to gauge. It is going to pour soon.'

They left their hiding place and started to walk along the path that led to the deserted village. They had not gone far when Cynric stopped and put a finger to his lips, listening intently. Before Bartholomew could recommend that they use another route to Barchester, Deblunville's archer came hurtling along the track and almost bowled into them. He recognised the physician and grabbed the front of his shirt, not seeming to care that it was an unusual place to meet.

'It is Master Deblunville!' he gasped, his eyes wide with terror. 'There has been an accident!'

Without waiting for a response, he hauled Bartholomew along the path. Disengaging himself so that they could move more quickly, Bartholomew followed, while Cynric muttered nervously about the passing time. They did not have far to go. After a few moments, they entered a glade in the woods, a pleasant place fringed with trees and with a moss-banked brook trickling through the centre. Deblunville's archers stood in an uncertain circle with their hats in their hands, all looking at a figure that lay unmoving in the grass.

'We just found him like this,' said the toothless man, turning a white, shocked face to Bartholomew. 'He died because he saw Padfoot!'

Bartholomew glanced at Cynric, who was gazing at the figure in horror.

'He said he saw a white wolf, but all the Grundisburgh folk said it was Padfoot,' the archer added fearfully. 'None of us believed them – we thought it was a story Tuddenham made up so that Hamon could dig for the golden calf on our land, but now it is clear that the story of Padfoot is true.'

Bartholomew knelt in the dew-laden grass, and leaned down to inspect the figure on the ground. Deblunville's eyes were closed as though he were sleeping. At first Bartholomew thought he might have had a seizure, but then he felt behind his head and his hand came away dark with blood. He turned the body over. The back of the skull was smashed, so that it was soft and soggy under his fingers. Deblunville would have died instantly, and was far beyond anything Bartholomew could do for him.

Under Deblunville's head was a stone, which had contours and edges that seemed to match the wound. When Bartholomew tugged at it, it came loose, but the deep, sharp impression in the earth suggested that it had been there for some time. So, unless someone had selected the stone, hit Deblunville with it, and then returned it to exactly the same place, it seemed the lord of Burgh had simply slipped on the wet grass, and had had the misfortune to crack his skull on an unfortunately positioned rock.

'I will never doubt again,' wailed the archer, watching the proceedings with a fear so intense that it was beginning to unnerve Bartholomew. 'It was said Padfoot would come for him, and he has!'

'Time is running on,' muttered Cynric anxiously, glancing up at the sky. 'We will miss sunrise if we do not hurry, and then this will be me!'

'What happened?' asked Bartholomew of Deblunville's men. 'Did any of you see?'

'He went off alone into the trees,' said the toothless man. 'Too much ale at dinner. When he did not come back, we went looking for him, and found him like this.'

'Did you see anyone else?' asked Bartholomew, thinking uncomfortably that Hamon and his cronies were probably not far away.

'No,' said the toothless man. He gave a grim, gummy smile. 'Believe me, nothing would give us greater pleasure than to blame Master Deblunville's death on Hamon, but it is obvious it was an accident: he fell and hit his head. There are the torn weeds where his foot slipped, and you can see that stone is buried in the ground, and has been for years. If someone had killed him, it would be lying on top of the grass, not half hidden in the soil.'

'It was Padfoot,' said the archer in a whisper. 'Why did we not listen? Why did we ever come out here? Maybe Padfoot is the calf's guardian, and he does not want the thing dug up.'

All the men and Cynric crossed themselves hastily, looking about them as though the white dog might appear at any moment and drag them off to hell. Bartholomew stood up. There was nothing more he could do, and Cynric was becoming increasingly agitated about the time. Everything pointed to the fact that Deblunville's death was simply a tragic accident, although coming so soon after the others, there was a nagging doubt at the back of Bartholomew's mind.

'Take him home,' he instructed the waiting men. He thought about Janelle and her unborn child. 'And you will have to inform his wife that she is now a widow. Be sure to do it gently – shocks like this will not be good for her.'

'She will not be overly distressed,' said one of the men, a skinny fellow with strangely pale eyes. He shrugged at his friends' reaction to his indiscretion. 'Well, it is true! I would say it took them about two nights to realise what a dreadful mistake they had made, and after ten days they are already at the point where they loathe each other.'

'It was because of that Walter Wauncy,' said the archer sagely. 'I said it was not good luck to be married by a walking corpse, but Janelle insisted because of the saving of three pennies.'

'She said last night that she was afraid she might go the same way as his first wife, Pernel,' said the pale-eyed man, his expression knowing. The others nodded agreement, and looked expectantly at Bartholomew, who wondered what they wanted him to say.

'I see,' he replied noncommittally, aware of Cynric's impatience to be away.

'Master Bardolf has gone home now, you see,' said the pale-eyed man. 'Without her father to protect her, Mistress Janelle felt her husband was already making plans to dispatch her.'

'That is why he died like this,' said the archer, gazing at the corpse as if it explained everything. 'It is God's judgement on a black soul.'

'I thought you said his death was Padfoot's fault,' said Bartholomew.

The assembly crossed themselves again, and peered nervously into the trees.

'He pushed Pernel, you see,' said the pale-eyed man. 'He pushed her hard, and she hit her head on the stone windowsill and died. And now he has died in the same way – his brains dashed out on a stone. It is God's judgement and Padfoot's revenge.'

'I suggested a convent for Pernel,' said the archer, still gazing down at Deblunville. 'It seemed a better way to deal with an unwanted wife than murder, but he said it was not necessary.'

So Deblunville *had* killed his first wife, just as the Grundisburgh villagers had speculated, thought Bartholomew, surprised to learn that there was truth in what he had assumed was a piece of nasty gossip put about by Tuddenham. He supposed it was possible that Deblunville had not intended Pernel to die, but by all accounts she was a good deal older than him, and a man in his prime had no right to be pushing old ladies around, no matter what the provocation. He watched the men gather up their dead lord and bear him away through the dark forest. He turned to Cynric, fretting at his side.

'Now for the prayer at sunrise,' he said, wishing he was anywhere but at Barchester.

Dawn that morning was just a case of the sky growing steadily lighter, and it was almost impossible to tell at what point the sun rose, since it was concealed behind a thick bank of clouds. In the distance thunder growled, and the air was thick and still, as it always was before a storm. Lightning zigzagged towards a faraway hill, and there was a red blaze as it struck a tree. Bartholomew did not relish the prospect of being caught in a cloudburst but he followed Cynric's rapid pace through the trees without complaint.

As they drew parallel to it, with the River Lark between them, Bartholomew could see the top of the church tower poking above the trees, and noticed that Cynric had drawn his sword.

'I am having second thoughts,' said the book-bearer fearfully. 'I cannot go through with this.'

'Cynric,' said Bartholomew gently. 'This is unlike the brave warrior from Gwynedd, who has fought more battles than he can remember and is afraid of no man.'

'I am still afraid of no man,' said Cynric unsteadily. 'It is this spectre that terrifies me, boy. And if you had any sense, you would be terrified too.'

'Stay here, then,' said Bartholomew. 'I will go alone.'

'No!' said Cynric, gripping his hand. 'I will not let you throw away your life. Padfoot has killed once already tonight, and his fangs will be hot for more blood.'

'Or perhaps he is sated,' reasoned Bartholomew. 'Come on, Cynric. It will be sunrise soon, and I am not going through all this beef-stealing again tomorrow because we missed it.'

'But you do not know where I saw Padfoot,' said Cynric weakly. 'You will not be able to stand in the right place.'

'Of course I will. The thing was sitting on me – I know exactly where it was. So hurry.'

'I am not going,' said Cynric, with sudden firmness. 'And neither are you. There will be a storm soon, and we do not want to get wet.'

'We have been wet before,' said Bartholomew. He laid his hand on Cynric's arm. 'Stay here with Deynman.' He pointed to a small, sod-roofed shepherds' hut that, judging from its unkempt appearance, had long been disused. Its roof was cloaked in ivy, and weeds choked the single window. 'You can shelter there if it starts to rain.'

'I will protect you from demons and devils, Cynric,' said Deynman earnestly. 'We have almost done all the charm, and we cannot give up now.'

Tucking his bag under one arm, Bartholomew began to trot down the slope toward the stream, splashing across where it was shallowest, and up the other side. Cynric's fear seemed to have rubbed off on him, and he could not help but notice that it was very quiet as he neared Barchester. The birds that had been singing as dawn approached had suddenly stopped, and even the breeze had died in the trees. All he could hear was his own laboured breathing, and the clink of phials in his bag.

As he drew closer to the village, he slowed, pausing to look and to listen, as he had seen Cynric do so many times. It seemed that the rain had been waiting for him to reach Barchester, because as he inched toward it, drops began to fall, becoming steadily harder as he neared the hamlet, almost as if it were warning him to stay away, Impatiently he forced such fanciful thoughts from his mind, and concentrated on what he was doing.

Carefully, he picked his way through the tangle of elm and birch, and emerged in the main street. It was as still and unwelcoming as the grave. The spot where he had been attacked was easy to find. It was puddled and pitted with hoof marks, and one of Cynric's arrows still protruded from the ground nearby. Bartholomew stood in the pool of muddy water and, assuming the sun was rising somewhere behind the glowering grey clouds, he began to chant.

'*Pater noster, qui es in coelis, sanctificetur Nomen tuum.*'

Recalling that he was supposed to say it as fast as he could, he started again, glancing around uneasily, partly concerned that some tatty and vicious dog would attack him, but more worried that he would be caught in the act of doing something very odd by some perfectly sane traveller.

'*Adveniat regnum tuum. Fiat voluntas tua, sicut in coelo, et in terra.*'

As he spoke, the heavens finally opened. The rain hissed and pattered, increasing in volume until it was a steady drone against the roofs of the hovels.

'*Panem nostrum quotidianum da nobis hodie, et dimitte nobis debita nostra . . .*'

It fell in a solid sheet, obscuring the distant trees completely, and veiling the closer ones with a sheet of downward-moving haze. Raindrops hammered into the mud, making the puddles dance and shudder, while leaves shivered and long blades of grass twisted this way and that.

'*Sicut et nos dimittimus debitoribus nostris.*'

Just when Bartholomew thought it could grow no heavier, a floodgate opened and the drone became a roar. He began to shout, the words barely audible over the thunder.

'*Et ne nos inducas in tentationem. Sed libera nos a malo.*'

He found it was not difficult to gabble, since all his instincts told him to run for cover in one of the huts.

'*Per omnia saecula saeculorum. Amen.*'

With relief he finished and looked around him, blinking water out of his eyes. The rain began to ease, not that it made much difference to him now that he was completely sodden.

Since he was there, and since there were no disapproving colleagues looking over his shoulder, he decided to conduct a quick search, wondering if he might find Norys hiding, or some clue as to the nature of the white dog that held the entire area in terror. Or even the golden calf, unearthed by one of the diggers and secreted there until it could be spirited away and sold without Tuddenham's knowledge. Cautiously, he slunk along the side of the first house, and looked in through a window that had shutters dangling uselessly on broken hinges.

There was nothing to see. The roof had collapsed, and any furniture or belongings that had been left were buried under a heap of rotting reeds. The second house was little different, although the roof was not quite so decayed. The third had only two walls standing, while the fourth cottage had been badly damaged by fire. A sudden gust of wind made dried leaves rustle across the charred floor, and a precarious timber groaned ominously. Outside there was a skeleton of what seemed to be a dog, still wearing a leather collar and tethered to the doorpost, stark white bones gleaming in the litter of dead leaves.

And so it went on. The dozen or so shacks that had once held families and their livestock were gradually being reclaimed by the woodland. Many had weeds growing through the beaten earth of their floors, and all had green shoots poking through the roofs. Bartholomew kept a careful lookout for any signs that a dog had been there, but could see no evidence. Finally, he came to the house where he had seen the discarded clothes on his first visit to the village. Rain dripped into his eyes from his sodden hood, and drops tapped from the thatch on to the spreading dock leaves below. The skirt and the shoe were gone.

Curiously, he pushed aside the strip of leather that had served as a door, and looked inside. The wizened carrots that had been on the table were still there, along with a turnip that he did not recall seeing before. He dropped the leather back into place and looked up the street. There was only one more place left to search: the church.

For some reason, the church seemed to exude the feeling that it did not want its secrets disturbed, far more than did any of the houses. He almost gave up, reasoning that there was nothing to be gained from forcing himself to look inside it when he did not want to, but the thought of Unwin spurred him on.

The church's graveyard was the domain of the forest, and tombs were rendered invisible under long grass and nettles. The building itself was a low, long structure with a squat tower at the west end, both larger than he would have expected for such a small village, suggesting that at some point in the past a lord of the manor had considered the village worth spending money on.

The main entrance had been through a porch in the south wall, but this was thick with ivy, and Bartholomew could see it would not easily be breached. He walked around the church, looking up at its wet, forbidding walls as he wiped the rain from his eyes with his sleeve. There was not a window that did not have something growing from it, while the tiled roof was sadly decayed: it would not be very much longer before the entire thing collapsed.

A priest's door led into the chancel, and Bartholomew saw that it hung askew, one of its leather hinges having decayed away. His hand was reaching out to push it inward, when a flicker of movement caught his eye.

He spun around, stomach churning, but there was nothing to see but drops falling silver from the trees and a faint stirring of the undergrowth in the wind. Taking a deep breath to control himself, he turned and lifted his hand to the door once more. It was just swinging open when a blood-curdling screech froze his blood, and made his heart pound in panic.

He swung around just in time to see something hurtling out of the undergrowth to throw itself at him. Raising his arms to protect himself, he was knocked backward against the wall, losing his footing in the slippery grass. Glancing up, he saw the glint of a weapon, and dodged to one side as it flashed toward him. He heard it screech against the stone, and then saw it rise for a second strike. He twisted away again, feeling it thump into his medicine bag, and struggled to his feet. There was another unearthly howl, and clawed hands raked at his face. He grabbed at one of them and caught it, flinching back as the other flailed wildly, aiming for his eyes.

But it was an unequal battle in the end, and it was not long before Bartholomew found he held an old woman, spitting and fighting in his grip. Her grey hair was long, filthy and matted, and she had no teeth at all that he could see. She wore an odd combination of clothes, including the skirt he had seen ten days before, all of them sticky with dirt. It was her eyes that caught his attention, however: the whites were rubbed to a startling pink rawness, and the lids were inflamed and swollen. Tears ran unheeded down her wrinkled skin, mingling with the rain that rolled smoothly from her greasy hair. Was this the cloaked figure whom Stoate had seen run from the church in Grundisburgh at the time when Unwin had been murdered, rubbing its eyes? Surely not, he thought. What could an old woman have against Unwin?

'Easy, mother,' he said softly, trying to quell his own fright. 'I will not hurt you.'

She struggled even more frantically, and he began to worry that she might hurt herself. He released one hand, but she tried to claw him with her long nails, and he was forced to grab her again, pushing her against the church wall to stop her fighting him. Just when he thought he had succeeded, and her futile attempts to attack him were beginning to subside, he heard a low growl from the bushes. He glanced around, but could see nothing. When he looked back at the old woman she was smiling, her inflamed eyes bright with malice. The growl came again, louder, and she began to croon softly to herself, rocking back and forth in Bartholomew's arms.

There was an explosion of movement from the undergrowth as something pale smashed through it. Swallowing hard, Bartholomew released the old woman and took several steps backward. He had the merest glimpse of a white form tearing toward him before he turned and fled. He could hear its rasping breath at his heels and was certain it was gaining on him. He ran harder, oblivious to the branches that slashed and slapped at his face. He reached the main street and raced across it toward the shrubs on the other side, ducking and weaving through the trees, and aware that the dog was right behind him.

Then his foot caught on the root of a tree and he tripped, tumbling head over heels down the hillside, his world spinning as he crashed through the bushes. He thought he saw the dog tracking him as he rolled, and he knew it would be on him the moment he stopped moving. He was helpless; he did not even know which way was up and which was down. Then he collided with a sturdy oak tree that stopped him dead. Aware that the thing would tear him to pieces if he lay still, he scrambled to his feet, but staggered as the woods tipped and swirled in front of him. He closed his eyes and waited for the worst to happen.

The woods were totally silent except for his ragged panting. Rain dripped on him from the trees that arched overhead, and he could hear the crackle of twigs under his feet. When he opened his eyes, there was nothing to see and nothing to hear. The white dog had gone, just as if it had vanished into thin air. Shakily, he peered through the undergrowth to see if he could see flashes of white as the animal moved through it. But the forest was as still and soundless as the grave.

With unsteady hands, he brushed himself down and began to make his way back to Cynric and Deynman. Casting nervous glances over his shoulder, and expecting to hear the guttural growls that would herald another attack, he crossed the stream and jogged up the slope on the other side. As if by magic, the rain eased to a light drizzle. By the time he reached the shepherd's hut it had stopped completely, and his heart was no longer thudding deafeningly in his ears.

A wisp of smoke eased through the door, and he assumed Cynric had made a fire to keep himself warm. He rubbed a shaking hand through his hair and strode into the shelter, craving normal human company. It took a moment for his eyes to adjust to the gloom and the smoke inside the hut. What he saw made him cry out in horror.

Cynric lay face down on the ground. Or what was left of Cynric. Smoke rose in thready tendrils from his body, of which little remained but two charred arms, a torso and a head.

'Did you say it?' came Cynric's eager voice behind him. 'Is

it done? Am I safe?' Bartholomew spun round, and grabbed at the door frame for support.

The Welshman nodded at the corpse on the floor. 'We did not feel much inclined to share with him while you were off on your mission, so we sheltered round the back. You have been a long time. Are you sure you recited the prayer as fast as you could?'

Bartholomew nodded unsteadily. He looked from Cynric, to the corpse, and then back again. 'I thought that was you. Did you not hear me coming?'

Cynric nodded. 'Of course. Do you think I have lost my touch?'

'Then you might have warned me. You must have known I would see that thing and think it was you. I thought my Latin was too late!'

'But this body has been here for days,' said Cynric, puzzled by his reaction. 'Come on, boy, what is the matter with you? You are supposed to be the one skilled in this kind of thing, not me.'

Bartholomew looked closer, and saw that Cynric was right. The body had been smouldering for some time, and molten fat had seeped across the floor in a sticky mass. An animal, probably a fox, had attacked it, so that parts of the intestines had been eaten away. The smell was sickening, and Bartholomew pushed past Cynric to sit on the grass outside. Resting his head on his arms, he tried to control the churning in his stomach. Cynric knelt next to him, and put a hand on his shoulder.

'What happened?' Deynman's voice was fearful. 'Did you see Padfoot, too? Will we need to do all this again tonight for you?'

Bartholomew shook his head, not looking up. 'I saw a white blur before it chased me out of the village. But I met its owner.'

Cynric drew in his breath sharply. 'The Devil?'

'An old hag with no teeth and filthy clothes. She attacked me and the dog came to help.'

'Oh, Lord, boy!' groaned Cynric. 'Why did I let you go? That vile place is the Devil's home!'

'It is the home of some crone and her dog,' said Bartholomew tiredly. 'Do you think I could best the Devil in a hand-to-hand tussle? I know some people believe my medicine borders on the heretical, but I am not Satan's equal!'

Cynric smiled, and held out his hand to Bartholomew to help him to his feet. 'Rob and I have not been totally useless while we waited. We found these.'

He led Bartholomew round to the back of the hut, and pointed at something on the ground. There were two legs, presumably belonging to the person in the hut. They, too, were charred, and someone had been trying very hard to chop them into small pieces, bits of which had probably been spirited away by animals.

Bartholomew went to look at the torso again, taking a deep breath so he would not have to inhale the heavy, sweet odour of burned flesh. Against the wall leaned a long knife with a curved, stained handle, and a hefty mallet lay next to it. The body was warm to the touch where it still smouldered.

'Why not burn it completely?' asked Deynman in revulsion. 'It would be much less repellent than all this chopping.'

'Bodies do not burn very easily,' said Bartholomew. 'There is too much liquid and grease in them. It seems to me that whoever did this thought he could rid himself of the body by burning it, and then found himself with a half-charred corpse to dismember instead.'

'Then why not bury it?' persisted Deynman. 'No one would find a shallow grave out here.'

Bartholomew shrugged. 'I have no idea. All I can say is that whoever did this must be desperate. Chopping up a body must be a vile task to undertake.'

Distastefully, he turned it over to look at its face, but it was too charred to be recognisable. The head flopped limply at an awkward angle, but the body seemed to have undergone such rough treatment since its demise that Bartholomew had no way of telling how it died. He laid it back and looked at the clothes, trying to see if there was anything he could take to effect some kind of identification. They were either burned away or fused to the body, and there was nothing that would help any bereaved next of kin to recognise it.

He was about to give up and suggest that they leave the grisly business to Tuddenham, when he saw he had missed something. Glittering dully under one shoulder was a dagger. Bartholomew tugged it out. It had once been covered with gilt, but most of that had come off, and all that remained was a rather shoddy-looking iron knife with a hilt decorated with coloured glass. The dagger Janelle had stolen from Deblunville to give to her father had been gilt, not gold, and Bartholomew recognised its shape and size immediately. So did Cynric.

'Well, boy,' said the Welshman, taking it from him and carrying it out into the light. 'It looks as though we have found our hanged man at last.'

CHAPTER 10

THERE WAS NOTHING MORE TO BE DONE WITH THE dead man in the shepherd's hut, so Bartholomew walked with Cynric and Deynman back to Grundisburgh. It was a cold, wet morning that seemed more like March than May, and heaped grey clouds threatened another storm. Bartholomew wanted to find Michael, and tell him about Deblunville's death and the body in the hut, so that they could reason some sort of sense into the jumble of facts and circumstances that had accumulated, before passing the information to anyone else. But as he headed up The Street he was hailed by Tuddenham, who was just leaving the church.

The knight looked tired and ill, and leaned heavily on Hamon's shoulder. Bartholomew saw it would not be long before his family would realise that there was more to his pale face and unsteady gait than just a case of too much wine the night before. By contrast, Hamon looked fit and vital, and had about him the air of a man for whom things were going well. Did he already know about Deblunville, because he had had a hand in his death? Or was he always cheerful and hearty after funerals – the Tuddenhams, apparently, had just attended the mass for Mistress Freeman.

Dame Eva and Isilia walked behind, looking suitably solemn. Isilia wore a dark blue dress under a matching cloak, a colour that suited her black hair and turned her green eyes to turquoise. As she turned to help the old lady down the step, Bartholomew was struck yet again by her grace and elegance. Dame Eva gave her a grateful smile that faded when she saw Bartholomew.

'You have the look of a man who is about to impart bad news,' she said astutely, regarding him with her sharp, bright eyes. 'Has the shock Master Alcote had last night made him sick?'

'What shock?' asked Bartholomew, suddenly nervous. 'Has something happened to Roger?'

'Alcote was attacked by two men last night,' said Tuddenham. 'He worked on my advowson until well after midnight at Wergen Hall, and someone tried to ambush him as he returned to his bed in the Half Moon. How is it you do not know of this? Where have you been?'

'Attacked?' asked Bartholomew in horror. 'Is he hurt?'

'No,' said Hamon, with an inappropriate grin. 'He is made of sterner stuff than he admits, and suffered no ill effects from the experience, except the indignity of falling in some cow dung.'

'This is no laughing matter,' admonished Tuddenham sternly. 'What will these Michaelhouse men think if they cannot walk from my house to the village in safety?'

'But who would attack Alcote?' asked Bartholomew, aghast.

'It was Will Norys,' said Hamon confidently.

'Unfortunately, last night was dark because it was cloudy, and Master Alcote did not see who attacked him,' corrected Tuddenham. 'But he said that there were two of them, and that one might have been Norys.'

'Of course it was Norys,' said Dame Eva. 'Who else could it have been? He escaped justice for the murder of Unwin, and decided to chance his luck again. After all, everyone here knows that Alcote is the most wealthy Michaelhouse scholar, and would be the best one to rob.'

'You think the motive was theft?' asked Bartholomew.

'Why else would a scholar be ambushed in the middle of the night?' asked the old lady. 'Norys must have lain in wait on the path that leads between Wergen Hall and the village, knowing that no one would hear Alcote's cries for help there.'

'It is a terrible business,' said Tuddenham worriedly. 'Alcote told me yesterday that the advowson was almost complete, and that he would have a working draft today. I had hoped to have the thing all signed and sealed by tomorrow, but I can see that this attack will delay matters.'

'Was anything stolen from him?' asked Bartholomew. 'Documents or writs?'

'Alcote says not,' said Tuddenham. He frowned anxiously. 'I told him to ask Hamon to accompany him to the Half Moon, if he planned to work after dark – especially given what happened to Unwin – but he slipped out while Hamon was asleep.'

'I awoke to find him gone,' said Hamon. 'There was no need for him to return to the tavern anyway, when he could have had a blanket next to the fire in Wergen Hall.'

Recalling that a good many servants vied for the coveted position near the hearth in Wergen Hall's main chamber, Bartholomew understood exactly why that proposition was not an appealing one to the fastidious Alcote.

Dame Eva eyed Hamon critically. 'You knew it was not safe for the poor man to leave the hall with Norys at large, and yet you selfishly slept while he did battle with ruthless killers. You are a self-centred lout, Hamon!'

'Deblunville died last night,' said Bartholomew, before a full-blown row could begin. 'He hit his head on a rock.'

There was a startled silence. Dame Eva and Isilia exchanged a glance of stupefaction, while Tuddenham and Hamon regarded each other rather uncertainly, as though each were wondering whether the other had anything to do with it.

Tuddenham swallowed hard. 'Are you saying my neighbour was murdered? Again? Or is this another mistake – like the fellow you claim was hanged at Bond's Corner?'

Bartholomew bit back a flash of irritation. 'I saw Deblunville's body. His men do not think he was murdered – they believe he slipped on wet grass and brained himself.'

'Just like his first wife, Pernel,' said Hamon in awe. 'She died of a cracked head.'

'We all know Deblunville killed his first wife,' said Dame Eva to Bartholomew. 'No one ever believed that was an accident – even his own people. But I heard rumours that Janelle's marriage was not as happy as a union of a few days should have been. She has had a lucky escape from that monster.'

'Poor Janelle,' said Isilia softly. 'I think she was genuinely fond of Deblunville when she beguiled him into taking her to the altar.'

'But this is good news,' said Hamon, pleased. 'It means Janelle is a widow.'

Dame Eva regarded him coldly. 'Foolish boy! Do you think she will fall into your arms now Deblunville is dead? Had she wanted you, she would have accepted you when you offered yourself at Yuletide. And you should curb your unseemly delight at Deblunville's death, or there will be rumours that you did it.'

'But I did not!' cried Hamon, alarmed. 'I did not even see him last night.'

'That is a curious thing to say,' pounced Dame Eva, fixing him with a wary look. 'Why should you see him last night? What were you doing while Christian folk slept?'

'Nothing,' said Hamon guiltily, realising too late the implication of his words.

Tuddenham stepped between his mother and his nephew. 'We will not discuss this matter here. However Deblunville met his death, there will be no celebration in Grundisburgh. I will not have the Sheriff told that there are people here who delight in my neighbour's demise.'

'So, Padfoot had Deblunville after all,' said Dame Eva,

more in awe than malice. 'I told you no one escapes a vile fate after setting eyes on Padfoot, and I was right. Deblunville may not have been the corpse on the gibbet, but Padfoot had him in the end, regardless.'

'We found that corpse, too,' said Bartholomew. 'It is in the shepherd's hut near Barchester, where someone has been trying to incinerate it.'

'How do you know all this?' asked Tuddenham, suddenly suspicious. 'You say you saw Deblunville dead, and now you announce that you have found the body of the hanged man. Brother Michael told me you were praying for Mistress Freeman last night, but now I discover you were roaming half the county under cover of darkness. What were you doing?'

It was a question Bartholomew had hoped would not be asked, and it was one he did not know how to answer. He hesitated.

'He was looking for sea urchins,' said Deynman defensively, fiercely protective of his tutor. He fingered the small dagger in his belt, and Bartholomew saw that Cynric was doing the same.

'Sea urchins?' echoed Tuddenham, bewildered. 'Just how far *did* you roam last night?'

'Sea wormwood,' corrected Bartholomew, relieved that at least someone had his wits about him. He opened his bag, and showed Tuddenham the bunch he had picked. 'It is good for worms and diseases of the liver.'

'There is no truth in these tales about the golden calf, you know,' said Tuddenham abruptly. 'So there is no point in you digging up my fields to look for it, while pretending to pick flowers.'

For a man who had been keen to know whether Cynric had discovered anything when he had dug Unwin's grave, Tuddenham's denial of the possibility that the golden calf existed was revealing. Was it he who had killed Deblunville, Bartholomew wondered, as, like Hamon, he supervised his villagers in their nightly searches of his neighbours' lands? Was a sleepless night the real reason why he looked so weary that morning and not his encroaching illness at all?

'I can assure you that the golden calf could not have been further from my mind,' said Bartholomew, resenting the implication that he was a thief. 'These leaves are far more valuable to me than some idolatrous ornament!'

'It is not wise to wander from the safety of our parish in the dead of night,' said Isilia reprovingly. 'And you promised us at Unwin's funeral that you would stay away from Barchester. It is no place for honest folk.'

Dame Eva agreed. 'Not as long as Padfoot sees fit to haunt our paths and woodlands.'

'But why not collect your herb during the day, anyway?' pressed Hamon suspiciously. 'Why steal about during the night looking for it, like a criminal?'

'Collecting it on a moonless night increases its efficacy,' said Bartholomew, feeling the colour mount in his cheeks as it always did when he told brazen lies.

'Hamon,' admonished Tuddenham mildly, assuming Bartholomew's sudden redness was because he had been insulted. 'You are not my heir yet, and you have no right to assail my guests with unpleasant accusations.'

'He will never be your heir,' said Isilia, clutching at Dame Eva's arm for moral support. Her chin jutted defiantly. 'My child will inherit before him.'

'Yes, I know,' said Tuddenham wearily. 'But not until I am dead and gone. So, Bartholomew, you say you have your hanged man back at last. Who is he, do you know?'

Bartholomew shook his head. 'But the fact that someone is so intent on disposing of his remains suggests that he was murdered.'

'Deblunville said the clothes worn by the hanged man were stolen from him,' said Tuddenham thoughtfully, 'and so it seems to me that Deblunville took the law into his own hands, and had the man executed for theft. Now Deblunville is dead, there is nothing more to be done. Later today I will send Siric to bring the remains here, to be buried decently in the churchyard.'

'Is that it?' asked Bartholomew, startled. 'The affair is closed without any further questions?'

'Yes,' said Tuddenham. 'Deblunville killed your hanged man, and Deblunville is dead. There is an end to the matter.'

His determined look suggested that Bartholomew would be wise to drop the subject. Confused and angered by Tuddenham's callous dismissal of the hanged man's fate, Bartholomew trailed along The Street in search of Michael.

He was surprised to find the Half Moon in chaos. Eltisley's sullen customers ran this way and that, while Eltisley himself stood in the middle of his courtyard looking like a lost child. There were dark patches on his clothes and his hair appeared to be singed. Bartholomew supposed that his appearance had something to do with the flames that had spurted from his workshop the previous evening.

'There you are,' said Michael, emerging from the tavern and wiping the remains of breakfast from his mouth. He looked Bartholomew up and down, taking in his sodden, mud-splattered clothes. 'What have you been doing?'

'Collecting sea wormwood,' said Bartholomew, brandishing his bunch at Michael. 'Tuddenham told me Alcote was attacked last night. Is that what all this fuss is about?'

Michael dabbed at his lips with his sleeve. 'Have you seen that fine piece of linen, which that nice landlord of the Dog gave me? It seems to have disappeared – along with a sizeable piece of beef from Master Eltisley's kitchen. That is what all this commotion is for – Eltisley is looking for it.'

'I see,' said Bartholomew.

'I am sure you do,' said Michael, regarding him expression-lessly. 'This could not be anything to do with Mother Good-man's charm against Padfoot, could it? Stealing a piece of beef and wrapping it in a white cloth at midnight?' Bartholomew shot him a guilty look and Michael sighed. 'If you had told me, Matt, I might have been able to help.'

'Would you?' asked Bartholomew. 'I assumed you would dismiss it as witchcraft.'

'Well, so it is, but that is not to say that I would not have gone along with it to see Cynric restored to his usual self. You could have trusted me!'

'I am sorry. But how did you guess what we were doing?' asked Bartholomew curiously.

'Deynman interrogated Mother Goodman about it merci-lessly last night, and it did not take a genius to guess what had transformed Cynric from a man doomed to a man with a purpose. I assume it worked, then? My piece of linen was sacrificed for a good cause.'

'Cynric believes he is free of the curse, and that is what matters. But aside from stealing from my friends and dab-bling in pagan rituals, I have had a busy night.'

He took Michael's arm and led him to stand under the eaves of the tavern, out of the drizzle, while he told the monk about Deblunville and the hanged man, and of the reaction of Tuddenham's family to the news. Michael listened care-fully, without interruption, until he had finished.

'Perhaps Tuddenham is right,' he said. 'If Janelle stole Deblunville's clothes as a gift for her father, and someone else found them by chance, it is entirely possible that Deblunville hanged the poor fellow for theft. Then, real-ising perhaps that the man was innocent, he suddenly found himself with a corpse to dispose of, if he wanted his mistake to remain hidden.'

'Deblunville's dagger was with the corpse in the shepherd's hut,' said Bartholomew. 'So, it seems as though the charred remains and the hanged man are one and the same. But there was no sign of Deblunville's other clothes. Since Norys saw someone running from the church *after* we found the hanged man wearing what sounded to be the same belt and shoes, we are still left with a mystery.'

'Not if we accept that Norys is lying because he killed Unwin,' said Michael. 'We can even take this further – Norys might have been the one who found the bundle of clothes, and sold them to some poor unfortunate, who then was hanged for theft while he was wearing them.'

'Poor Norys,' said Bartholomew. 'It seems he is to blame for everything. It is probably his fault that it is raining this morning, too.'

'There is no need for heretical thoughts, Matthew,' said Michael primly. 'But what of Deblunville? You say you could not tell whether his death was accident or murder?'

'There are so many people who want him dead that an accident seems rather opportune. I cannot help wondering whether Deblunville caught some of Tuddenham's villagers digging for the golden calf, and one of them killed him.'

'You mean you think they might have found the calf, and murdered Deblunville to keep the discovery a secret?' asked Michael, green eyes glittering at the thought.

'Of course not, Brother,' said Bartholomew. 'Deblunville was probably killed – if he was killed deliberately – because he caught some of the Grundisburgh villagers trespassing on what he thinks is his land. God knows, there were enough of them out there last night.'

He looked up as Alcote, leaning heavily on Father William's arm, walked slowly from the direction of the church. He was limping, and he held one hand to his chest as though in pain.

'He has been saying a mass to thank God for his safety,' said Michael contemptuously. 'While Mistress Freeman was committed to the ground, Alcote knelt at the altar and prayed for himself.'

Alcote was almost at the Half Moon when he saw Eltisley's wife walking toward him. Immediately, the limp disappeared, and he scurried on what seemed to Bartholomew to be two healthy legs into the tavern, slamming the door behind him. William exchanged a grin with Michael, and came to join them.

'What was that about?' asked Bartholomew, bewildered, as Mistress Eltisley tried to open the door, only to find it had been locked from the inside. She rattled the door impatiently, but the sole response was the sound of a heavy bar falling into place.

'She brought some water to wash the mud from Alcote's face after he was attacked last night,' Michael explained. 'Rather rashly, but only to be kind, she attempted to perform the service herself. Feeling a woman's hand on his person terrified him a good deal more than the ambush, I think!'

'That is not surprising,' said Father William mysteriously. 'Given his history.'

'You mean the reason he is hostile to women?' asked Michael with interest. 'You know it?'

'Of course,' said William haughtily. 'There is nothing a man like me cannot discover, if he puts his mind to it. That is why I would make such an outstanding Junior Proctor.'

'Quite so,' said Michael impatiently. 'But what do you know about Alcote?'

William paused for effect, looking around him to ensure he could not be overheard. 'I asked a few questions when he first arrived in Cambridge. He comes from Winchester, where I have several very good friends from my days in the Inquisition. I primed them to make enquiries on my behalf.'

'And?' prompted Michael, when the friar paused again. He snapped his fingers in sudden enlightenment. 'Ha! Do not tell me, I can guess. Alcote had a wife – he escaped from a marriage that had turned sour.'

'He escaped from two,' said William, smiling in satisfaction when he saw the expressions on his colleagues' faces. 'Roger Alcote is a bigamist.'

Bartholomew and Michael stood outside the Half Moon and gazed at William in astonishment. Then Bartholomew started to laugh.

'I do not believe you, Father! Alcote hates women, and would never allow himself to be put into that sort of position. Your friends were playing a joke on you.'

'They were not,' said William firmly. 'It so happened that I had business in Winchester myself a year or so later. I met both his wives – and I am sure it will not surprise you to learn that they were women of some wealth. They told me they had been wed to Alcote for several months before one discovered the presence of the other. They joined forces, and I had the impression they planned some dire revenge on his manhood, but were thwarted when he escaped.'

'Then why did he become a scholar?' asked Bartholomew, far from certain that William's story was not a product of his vivid imagination. 'Bigamists, who by definition like their women, do not suddenly become misogynists like Alcote.'

Michael grinned. 'I think you probably already have your answer to that. William has just told us that it was not for love that Alcote took these two beauties, but for their money.'

'I still do not believe it,' said Bartholomew.

'You might if you heard his views on the plague,' said Michael thoughtfully. 'He thinks it will come again, unless men give up all relations with women. He told me only yesterday that the Devil would claim as his own anyone who was not celibate.'

'And why should he mention that to *you*, Brother?' asked Bartholomew, raising his eyebrows.

'What in God's name is *he* doing?' said William, watching as Eltisley took a large saw to the leather hinges on the door, still firmly barred and with Alcote safe from Mistress Eltisley on the other side of it. The saw slipped, leaving a long, pale scar across the lovingly polished wood. Eltisley raised it again, hacking vigorously at the hinges, while his sullen customers stood around him, and watched in disbelief as the landlord inflicted as much damage on the saw as he did on the door in his bungling attempts to enter.

'Master Eltisley,' called Bartholomew, watching his efforts with amusement. 'Would it not be easier to go through the entrance at the back of the tavern, and then unlock the front door from the inside?'

Eltisley regarded him uncertainly, but his wife gave an exasperated sigh before disappearing round the side of the house. Moments later, she emerged through the door Eltisley had savaged, and stood to one side to let her husband in, giving him a clout on the ear as he did so.

Alcote had locked the door to the upper chamber, too, and it took some smooth talking on Michael's part to persuade him to open it. Casting anxious looks this way and that, Alcote hauled his colleagues inside and barred the door again.

'I do not want *her* near me,' he announced, returning to a small table piled high with parchments, pens, and sand-shakers for drying wet ink. 'Women are agents of the Devil. I became a scholar at Michaelhouse to escape their evil clutches, and all I want to do is return there. Not only does one of them attempt to seduce me, but I am attacked by a band of ruffians, armed with ferocious scimitars, in the middle of the night.'

'A band?' asked Bartholomew. 'Tuddenham told me there were only two of them.'

'So there were last night,' said Michael. 'Their number, like their weapons, seem to have grown in the telling.'

Alcote regarded him coldly. 'Are you accusing me of lying?'

'I am merely curious to know how an unarmed cleric bested a band of determined, sword-wielding villains,' said Michael, unruffled by Alcote's indignation.

'I was protected by God. He knows I am doing His work with this advowson.' Alcote rubbed his stomach. 'This place disagrees with me. I have not felt well since we arrived.'

'That is because you are eating enough raisins to feed half of Suffolk,' said Bartholomew. 'They are not good for the digestion in such vast quantities.'

'How is the advowson going?' asked Michael, as Alcote glowered at the physician. 'Tuddenham is afraid that the attack on you may delay matters.'

'Fortunately, it will not,' said Alcote, 'although I must stress that writing this deed has been extremely difficult, because of the complexities of the arrangements made by Sir Thomas's grandfather. It has taken me a long time to ensure that the advowson is his to give.'

'I checked all that in the abbey at St Edmundsbury,' said Michael. 'It is his.'

'But I had to ensure *he* had the documents to prove it.' Alcote leaned forward and lowered his voice conspiratorially. 'However, there were one or two items that muddied the waters, which therefore needed to be consigned to the fire.'

'You burned Tuddenham's writs because you did not like their contents?' asked Bartholomew, aghast.

'You make it sound so underhand,' grumbled Alcote, flinging down his pen, and scrubbing tiredly at his thin hair.

'Well, so it is,' said Bartholomew. 'Tuddenham trusts you with these documents, and what you have done is worse than underhand: it is dishonest and illegal!'

'Believe me, I am only doing what is best for the College.

You would not want Michaelhouse associated with some of the shady dealings I have uncovered since we arrived here.'

'What kind of shady dealings?' asked Bartholomew nervously. 'If you suspect this advowson is tainted, then we must not accept it at all.'

'Do not be so finicky, Matthew. I have destroyed what I do not want people to see, and so it is all perfectly above board. Anyway, a few more hours should see the whole thing completed, and we can be on our way.'

'Then we can leave tomorrow?' asked Bartholomew with relief. 'Thank God!'

'For once we are in complete agreement,' sniffed Alcote. 'I do not like this place, and I want to be away from it before we all follow Unwin to his grave. I will have this thing written today.'

Bartholomew had wondered whether Alcote had been dragging his heels over the advowson, making the whole thing seem more complex than it was. His sudden announcement that he was in a position to complete the document within hours made Bartholomew realise his suspicions had been well founded, and that it had taken a physical attack on Alcote to frighten him into finishing it.

'Why were you ambushed, do you think?' asked Bartholomew. 'For your gold cross?'

'Or because you consigned Tuddenham's documents to the fire?' asked Michael, amused.

'Or because the villagers resent our presence here?' asked William. He glanced around him and shuddered. 'Hanged men wearing stolen clothes, who disappear only to be found half burned in some shepherd's hovel; ghostly dogs that terrify people in the night; friars murdered by pardoners for their paltry possessions; women with their throats slit in their own homes; and scholars attacked viciously and without provocation. You are right, Roger! The sooner we are away from this place, the better.'

'Will you join me for something to eat?' enquired Michael of no one in particular.

'I will not leave this chamber until I am on my way home,' announced Alcote firmly. 'Arrange for my meals to be served here, Michael – and not by that woman, if you please. Eltisley can do it.'

'I will pray for Unwin's soul,' said William, his voice holding a note of censure that they should be considering food when there was praying to be done. 'I shall forgo the pleasures of the flesh in order to shorten his time in Purgatory with a mass.'

'I heard that Eltisley was cooking fish-giblet stew today,' said Michael wickedly. 'Shall I tell him you do not want any?'

There was little the Franciscan enjoyed more than the rank flavour of fish-giblet stew, and he hesitated, deeply tempted.

'Tell him to keep some for me,' he said after a brief internal struggle between duty and greed, from which greed emerged the victor. 'I will have it later to fortify my frail body for more prayers.'

'My sentiments exactly,' said Michael, looking down at his own ample girth.

Downstairs again, Michael shouted for Eltisley to bring them food. He regarded Bartholomew's muddy clothes disapprovingly, and complained that he smelled of burning. Bartholomew was not the only one: there was a strong odour of burning when Eltisley brought the meal.

'Problem with one of your theories?' Bartholomew asked, noting the blisters on Eltisley's hands and his singed clothes. 'I saw you almost destroy your workshop last night.'

'None of your business,' snapped the landlord shiftily. 'When one works on things no other man can comprehend, one must anticipate a degree of error and miscalculation.'

He slapped a dish down with such vigour that it broke in two, sending gravy dribbling through the cracks in the table into Michael's lap. The monk gave him a withering look, and began to dab it off.

'I will fetch you another dish,' said Eltisley, not sounding particularly repentant. 'Although it will take me a while to prepare. You can change while I cook it.'

'Perhaps we will dine at the Dog,' said Michael, peering resentfully at the stain in his lap as Eltisley left. 'I prefer my food to make its way to my stomach by going through my mouth first, not my habit, and I have had enough of Eltisley's peculiarities for one day. I am always afraid he will bring me fried earwigs, or a plate of grass, just to see what would happen if I ate them.'

He left before Eltisley could return, beckoning Bartholomew to follow. The monk set an uncharacteristically rapid pace up The Street, a clear indication that Eltisley's clumsiness had needled him. Since it was raining, they found a table inside the Dog near the roaring fire, where Michael continued to swab at the gravy stains on his habit. The landlord brought them a spiced leek and onion tart, and a stew of pigeon cooked in garlic, with hunks of coarse-grained bread to soak up the sauce. Contemptuously, Michael thrust the tart at Bartholomew, and took the stew for himself, using the bread to scrape off a few offending carrots that had the audacity to adhere to the meat.

'Eltisley should not be permitted to run a tavern,' he muttered. 'I would order him to clean my habit, but I am afraid it might come back grey, because he has used some stain-removing concoction of his own invention. And then I might be mistaken for a Franciscan.' He shuddered dramatically.

Bartholomew smiled. 'I do not think so, Brother. You are far too fat to be anything but a Benedictine.'

Michael thrust a large piece of bread into his mouth,

gagging slightly on the crumbs. 'Do not witter, Matt. Tell me again about your foray to Barchester last night.'

'It seems to me that some old madwoman has taken it for her home, and she and her dog do not like visitors,' said Bartholomew, rubbing his eyes.

'Tuddenham will drive her out.'

'I hope not,' said Bartholomew. 'Where would she go? The village is deserted anyway, so why not let her live there if she likes.'

'Because she ambushes travellers,' said Michael promptly. 'She has attacked you twice now, and her dog has people from miles around too terrified to go anywhere near the place.'

'Not from what I saw last night,' said Bartholomew. 'I am sure there were more Grundisburgh folk out in the woods than there were at home.'

'Looking for the golden calf,' said the landlord of the Dog in a soft voice behind them, making them jump. 'The reward for finding it and giving it to Sir Thomas is ten marks – two years' pay for most people. But ten marks would not induce me to go out at night to hunt for the thing.'

'And why is that?' asked Michael.

The landlord crossed himself. 'Because of Padfoot. Ten marks is no good to a dead man, and that is what anyone who sees the beast will be. I heard Deblunville died last night. I always said it was only a matter of time before he was laid in his grave after seeing Padfoot.'

Having made his point, he left them to their meal, talking in a low voice about the inevitability of Deblunville's demise to the man with the pig who had been so vociferous at the debate.

'The Barchester woman had badly infected eyes,' said Bartholomew. 'Stoate said the person he saw running from the church was rubbing his eyes.'

'I see,' said Michael, taking a large gulp of wine. 'It was this crone who donned a cloak and killed Unwin in the church last week, was it? How silly of me not to have thought of that before!'

'It might have been her,' said Bartholomew, unruffled by Michael's sarcasm. 'Stoate and Norys both said they were unsure whether it was a man or a woman. Although she was very small and somewhat crooked – you would think one of them would have noticed that.'

'And can you see this woman having the guile to wear a cloak – long, according to Stoate, but short according to Norys – to hide her wretched rags? She does not sound to me as though she has enough of her sanity left to take care of herself, let alone effect a crafty murder that has confounded the University of Cambridge's Senior Proctor.'

'Well, that proves it was not her, then,' said Bartholomew dryly. 'Far be it for old women to get the better of the University of Cambridge's Senior Proctor. But at least we now know who owns the abandoned skirt and shoe we found there.'

He was eating a slice of tart when there was a deafening roar that shook the building to its foundations. Fragments of plaster drifted down from the ceiling, and the cat that had been stalking mice in the rushes flattened its ears with a yowl and tore from the room. Bartholomew and Michael looked at each other in confusion.

'What was that?' asked Michael, picking a flake of wood out of his stew and flicking it on to the floor. 'It sounded as though one of the bells has fallen out of the church tower.'

Wiping his hands on his apron, the landlord went to find out, accompanied by the man with the pig. Excited shouts and running footsteps suggested that others were curious, too, but Bartholomew could see nothing through the window to warrant abandoning his meal. He had barely sat down again when Cynric burst into the room.

'The Half Moon!' he cried, reaching out to haul Bartholomew from his seat. 'It has gone!'

'Gone where?' asked Michael, not pleased at being interrupted while he was feeding.

'Gone!' yelled Cynric frantically. 'Gone completely!'

With trepidation, Bartholomew followed him out of the tavern and down The Street. Cynric was right. The Half Moon was nothing but a vast pile of burning rubble and teetering walls. A thick pall of black smoke poured from the twisted beams, and timbers and pieces of glass crunched under the feet of the milling spectators. The thatch was ablaze with flames that licked this way and that, sending showers of sparks high into the sky and, even as Bartholomew watched, one precarious wall collapsed with a tearing scream in a cloud of dust.

The villagers gasped in horror and started back as sharp snaps heralded pieces of plaster and burning timber being catapulted across the ground toward them. One man shrieked as his cotte began to smoulder. With great presence of mind, Stoate bundled him to the stream and pushed him in before the flames could take hold. But Bartholomew saw only the burning building.

'Alcote!' he whispered in shock. 'Roger Alcote was in there.'

Eltisley was surrounded by sympathetic customers, his face as white as snow as he gazed at the inferno that had been his tavern. Tuddenham leaned heavily on Hamon's arm as he surveyed the mess with a stunned expression, while Hamon's glazed eyes showed that he had not even begun to comprehend what had happened to Grundisburgh's largest and most prestigious tavern. Isilia stood next to them, as numbed by the spectacle as were her menfolk, while Dame Eva had both frail arms wrapped around the weeping Mistress Eltisley. As Bartholomew shouldered his way through the crowd, the landlord gaped at him and his eyes filled with tears.

'Thank God!' he said shakily. 'I thought you were inside changing your clothes.'

'Where is Alcote?' asked Bartholomew urgently.

'I do not know,' said Eltisley in a whisper. 'I was in the kitchen cooking your meal when this happened. I only escaped because the force of the blast blew me outside.'

'You mean the tavern exploded?' asked Hamon in bewilderment. He came toward them, dragging his shocked uncle with him. 'How can that have happened?'

'Gasses,' announced Walter Wauncy, in his sepulchral voice. 'I have heard of this happening in other places. Malignant gasses build up and then give vent to their fury – like volcanoes.'

'It was him,' said William, pointing an accusing finger at Eltisley. 'This is the result of one of his vile experiments, not any gasses!'

'I do not experiment with exploding compounds,' protested Eltisley in a high squeak. 'My mission in life is to repair and heal things, not destroy them. I have no need to explore the nature of such diabolical powders. But maybe it was him,' he said, turning suddenly on Bartholomew. 'He went out last night picking strange plants in the dark. Perhaps they did this.'

'Do not be ridiculous,' said Michael coldly. 'But we should discuss this later. Now, I am more concerned about Alcote. Has anyone seen him?'

'Alcote was in there?' whispered Tuddenham in horror. 'With my advowson?'

'Damn the advowson!' shouted Bartholomew furiously. 'What about my colleague?' He appealed to the crowd, desperation cracking his voice. 'Have any of you seen him?'

There were shaken heads, and fearful glances toward the fire.

Eltisley followed their gazes, and rubbed a hand over his face. 'My tavern! My home! My workshop! All gone!' he groaned.

'But Alcote!' yelled Bartholomew, grabbing the shocked landlord by the front of his shirt. 'He must still be in there. We have to put out the fire.'

'If he was in there when it went up, he will be beyond any medicine we can give him,' said Stoate gently, prising him away from Eltisley.

'No!' shouted Bartholomew, refusing to believe that the fussy little scholar should die in such a horrific manner. 'He might be buried and still alive. We have to help him.'

'We should douse the fire anyway,' said Hamon practically, 'or we might lose the entire village to it.'

Tuddenham dragged himself out of his state of shock, sensing the need for quick and effective action if the fire were not to spread to the thatched roofs of the neighbouring houses. 'Fetch water holders,' he ordered the gaping bystanders. 'Anything will do: buckets, pots, pans. And form a line from the ford to pass them along. Well, do not just stand there like frightened rabbits! Move!'

The villagers raced off in every direction, appearing moments later with all manner of containers with which to scoop water from the river. Eltisley watched the scene distantly, as though it were a bad dream and he would wake up to find it had not happened. The man with the pig and the landlord of the Dog put their arms around his shoulders, and led him to sit on the grass away from the inferno. Nearby, Dame Eva was holding a cup of water to Mistress Eltisley's bloodless lips, comforting her in a low, kindly voice.

Bartholomew watched the villagers' feeble attempts to douse the towering flames that licked all over the rubble. Hot timbers hissed and spat as bucket upon bucket of water was hurled at them, but their labours were having little effect. Exasperated, and knowing that every passing moment was a lost chance to save Alcote's life, he ran toward the burning inn, shielding his face with his arm as the heat hit him like a physical blow. He tried to move closer, feeling his clothes start to smoulder and the flames sear his skin. Cynric darted after him, grasping his arm in an attempt to haul him away.

'It is unstable, boy. That wall will collapse at any moment!'

Three of the Half Moon's four walls had already toppled, while the last leaned outward at an angle that defied all natural laws, and with flames pouring from its blackened windows.

Bartholomew thrust Cynric away and moved still closer, scanning the burning plaster, wood and thatch for any sign of Alcote. His eyes smarted, and the heat was so intense that the rubble wavered and swam in front of him. He thought he glimpsed something white, and he inched further forward, bent almost double as the heat blasted out like that from a blacksmith's furnace. Unable to see properly, he stumbled over a piece of timber and fell flat on his face. At the same instant there was an ominous rumble, and the precarious wall began to teeter. He was helpless, lying full length on the ground at exactly the point where the wall would crash down. He felt himself hauled backward as it fell, and closed his eyes, lifting one hand in a futile effort to protect his head.

With a tremendous crash, the wall smashed to the ground. Pieces of plaster pattered over him, and he found himself completely enveloped in a dense cloud of choking dust. Someone grabbed his tabard again and the whiteness thinned, so that he found he was able to suck in great mouthfuls of clean air. When he could see, Michael was kneeling next to him, his black habit pale with plaster and both hands pressed to his chest as he hacked and wheezed.

Bartholomew sat up, eyes watering as he coughed the smoke from his lungs. The Half Moon was now completely unrecognisable as a building. All was engulfed in flames, and nothing surviving remotely resembled a door, or a window, or a piece of furniture.

'What were you thinking of?' gasped Michael furiously. 'You might have been killed, and if Alcote was in there when it . . . well, whatever happened to it, then he is dead. You sacrificing yourself will do nothing to help him now.'

'He was in there,' said Bartholomew in a hoarse whisper, turning a tear-streaked face towards the monk. 'I am certain I saw his hand before the wall fell.'

Michael was silent, green eyes fixed on the roaring, spitting heap that was now Alcote's pyre. Cynric stood next to him, gazing up at the pillar of smoke that blackened the sky and mingled with the clouds far above.

'You are a brave man, Brother,' said William, touching Michael on the shoulder. 'I thought you were both dead when you disappeared in that ball of dust. Matthew is lucky to have such a friend.'

'And lucky to have one so strong,' added Cynric, smiling at the monk in shy admiration. 'I could never have managed to drag him back as you did.'

Michael acknowledged this praise with a gracious inclination of his head. 'Thank you, Cynric. Perhaps you would keep an eye on him while I go and assist the villagers to douse the fire. Do not allow him to dive into the flames after corpses again.'

Wondering if he were in the depths of some hideous nightmare, Bartholomew watched the villagers struggling frantically to smother the flames. As Hamon had predicted, the wind had carried sparks to nearby houses, the thatches of which were already beginning to smoulder. People laboured furiously to spread wet blankets across them, while the nearest cottage had been deemed unsalvageable, and several men were hacking at the straw with long knives, struggling to tear the roof apart before it could ignite in earnest.

Everyone was battling with the blaze that threatened their settlement. Even Dame Eva and Isilia were busy, standing in the line of people who passed water containers from hand to hand. Tuddenham ran this way and that, encouraging the labouring villagers with promises of cool ale, while Hamon stood nearest the fire, directing where the water should be thrown to best effect. Wauncy was to one side, bony hands clasped in front of him and his deep-set eyes raised heavenward like one of the Four Horsemen of the Apocalypse, while Horsey knelt next to him, his hands folded in prayer, but his attention fixed on the greedy flames. Deynman was one of a group of young men who poked at the smouldering rubble with long sticks, trying to break it up to make it easier to douse, and William, Cynric and Michael were near the ford, using their brawn to help fill some of the larger vessels.

Unsteadily, Bartholomew went to join them, standing up to his knees in the river and filling buckets and pans as quickly as they could be passed to him. He lost count of the times he leaned down to scoop up water, trying to ignore the ever-increasing ache in his back. For a while, it seemed that the struggling villagers would lose the fight, and that the flames would spread to the other houses. Tuddenham seemed tireless, striding back and forth, and exhorting the villagers to work harder and faster, when most of them were so exhausted they were ready to give up and let the fire have their homes and belongings. Then they reached a stalemate, with the fire held at bay but still likely to send sparks flying toward the vulnerable houses at any moment. And then they began to win.

Hours later, when Bartholomew's arms were so tired he could barely lift them, Hamon shouted that he thought the fire was out. Bartholomew glanced up at the sky. It was afternoon and a slight drizzle was falling, depositing yet more water on the saturated remains of Eltisley's tavern. The villagers gave a feeble cheer, then flopped to the ground or sat in small groups in silence, too weary even to discuss what would be one of the most memorable events of their lives. Some nursed burns, many had inflamed eyes from the smoke, and everyone's clothes had been singed from the cinders that had rained down from the sky, like hail from hell.

'We need to look through the rubble for Alcote,' said Michael hoarsely, coming to stand next to Bartholomew. He walked stiffly, unused to so much exercise, and water and dust had made his habit appear as if it were smeared all over with mud.

Bartholomew joined Hamon, Stoate, William and Deynman, who were prising away some of the charred wood and plaster to begin the search. Eltisley lay on his back in the wet grass with his hands over his face, and Bartholomew saw that he was weeping. His wife, her white apron black with soot, sat near Dame Eva and Isilia, who seemed to be sharing a skin of wine with her. But Dame Eva was a practical, as well as a sympathetic, woman and Bartholomew saw that Mistress Eltisley already wore a cloak he knew belonged to the old lady, and her shaking hands clasped a small silver cross that he had seen Dame Eva wear.

Watched by the silent villagers, Bartholomew and the others levered and hauled at the hot embers. After a while, Deynman gave a cry and started backward, dropping the stick he had been using, as his hands flew to his mouth. Bartholomew scrambled toward him, and pulled away sooty plaster to reveal a body underneath.

'Is it him?' asked Deynman, looking everywhere but at the charred form Bartholomew exposed.

Bartholomew did not know: there was not enough left to be able to tell. Unlike the body of the hanged man, set alight to smoulder gently in the shepherd's hut, the tavern had been an inferno, and had burned with a heat sufficiently intense to destroy most of whoever had been trapped in the building, and certainly to obliterate any distinguishing features. Something scorched Bartholomew's finger, and he saw it was a blob of gold, turned molten and then re-set in an uneven disk.

'Alcote's cross,' whispered Michael, leaning down to pick it up and dropping it immediately when he found it was too hot to hold. 'He always wore a gold cross.'

'Is that all there is?' asked Hamon, gazing down at the body. 'Where is the rest of him?'

'Burned away,' said Bartholomew, taking the blanket proffered by Stoate to cover the body. He did not want to move it while it was still so hot: it would be better to wait until it had cooled a little.

'That is not him,' said Deynman with sudden certainty. 'It cannot be. Master Alcote is in Wergen Hall, or in the church praying. I will find him.'

Bartholomew caught his arm as he made to run away. 'If Master Alcote were alive, he would have come to see what was happening here,' he said gently. 'You will not find him elsewhere.'

Deynman started to cry, perhaps the only one who would ever do so, since Alcote had not been popular with his colleagues or the Michaelhouse students. While he stood awkwardly, with Deynman sobbing on his shoulder, Bartholomew called to Eltisley to ask if there had been anyone other than Alcote in the tavern when it had ignited.

Eltisley shook his head slowly, his eyes dull, answering that the tavern had been empty except for the scholars in the upper chamber.

'Thank God the rest of us were out,' said William, crossing himself vigorously.

'Norys warned us about this,' said Michael softly. 'He advised us to sleep with the windows open, in case Eltisley set the tavern alight with some mad experiment. It seems he was right.'

Bartholomew looked over to where Eltisley stood, and was seized with a sudden rage. Jostling Deynman out of the way, he jumped off the rubble and grabbed the landlord by the front of his apron, shaking him as hard as he could.

'You did this!' he shouted furiously. 'There were no gasses! You were playing around with one of your dangerous concoctions and now Alcote is dead.'

'I swear to you it was not me!' shrieked Eltisley in terror, as he struggled to free himself from the physician's powerful grip. 'I was in the kitchen cooking your meal.'

'Then you left something burning in your workshop,' accused Bartholomew, not relinquishing his hold on the landlord's apron. 'You ignited the tavern because you were careless.'

'Matt, let him go,' said Michael tiredly, trying to prise the physician's fingers loose. 'Eltisley has just lost his home, his livelihood and all his possessions. Have some compassion.'

'And Alcote has just lost his life!' Bartholomew yelled. He thrust Eltisley against the garden wall, further enraged by the landlord's pathetic fear of him. 'You are so arrogant, you think you can meddle with whatever you like, and you care nothing for the safety and well-being of others.'

'You are strangling him,' protested Stoate, joining in Michael's attempts to make Bartholomew release the terrified landlord.

Seeing their patron in trouble, some of Eltisley's surly customers uncoiled themselves from the grass near the stream, and advanced menacingly. Cynric unsheathed a wicked little sword from its scabbard and tensed, ready to act should they threaten Bartholomew.

'Matthew!' snapped William, sensing an unseemly brawl was in the making. 'Is it not enough that poor Alcote lies dead without compounding the tragedy by slaying the landlord? It was an accident, man!'

Eltisley's customers eyed Cynric uncertainly, not convinced that they could best the man who wielded his sword with such practised ease. Hamon stepped forward, trying to place himself between Cynric and the surly men, while Isilia, seeing her kinsman place himself in such dire danger simply to prevent a fight, gave a shrill shriek that brought her husband running from where he had been talking to Wauncy.

Bartholomew gave Eltisley another shake. 'How did you do it? What dangerous potions were you playing with in that workshop of yours? Saltpetre, sulphur and powdered charcoal?'

Eltisley gaped at him. 'How do you know of such things? You are just a physician!'

Bartholomew's temper finally snapped. He thumped Eltisley up against the wall again, intending to smash the superior, arrogant face to a pulp with his fists. He did not have the chance: Tuddenham had arrived. Eltisley's sullen customers slunk away to sit on the grass again, Cynric sheathed his sword, and William and Michael dragged Bartholomew away from Eltisley before the physician could land more than two ill-placed punches that did little harm.

'You are insane!' howled Bartholomew, as he struggled in the powerful grip of his colleagues, aware, even in the heat of his anger, that most of the village was probably thinking the same about him. 'You play with potions and substances about which you understand nothing! You are a feeble-minded lunatic, who should be locked away before you kill anyone else with your stupid, half-considered theories. You are a heretic!'

Bartholomew had never charged anyone with heresy before, although he had certainly been on the receiving end of more than one such accusation himself. He was surprised to find that hurling such a charge at someone was immensely satisfying – although not quite as much as pounding him into the ground would have been. William nodded approvingly, although Bartholomew did not for a moment consider William's support to mean much, given that the friar's definition of heresy was anything that did not conform to his own rigid beliefs.

Meanwhile, Eltisley regarded Bartholomew with loathing, rubbing the red marks on his neck where he had almost been throttled. 'I merely want to understand more of the nature of the world in which we live,' he said coldly. 'I pray for guidance every morning, and I do nothing contrary to God's will.'

'Do you think murdering Alcote is God's will?' yelled Bartholomew, still trying to free himself from William's restraining grip.

'Murdering Alcote?' asked Tuddenham, horrified. 'You believe Alcote was murdered?'

'Matt,' warned Michael under his breath. 'That is enough. Eltisley was cooking in the kitchen when the building ignited, and he did not cause this tragedy intentionally.'

Eltisley's intentions were irrelevant to Bartholomew, and doubtless to Alcote, too. The only fact that mattered to him was that Eltisley had been tampering with a combination of powders and ingredients that he clearly knew caused explosions. Whether he had ignited them deliberately, or whether they had somehow come together by mistake in his workshop was of no consequence. Eltisley's selfish desire to learn had brought about Alcote's death.

'What will happen to my advowson now?' asked Tuddenham dispiritedly. 'All Alcote's efforts will have been for nothing. We will have to start over again.'

'I do not believe so,' said Michael soothingly. 'Alcote is not the only one who can draft legal documents, you know. I, myself, have no small talent in that area, although Alcote was a master at it. I will come to Wergen Hall this evening, and we will see what still needs to be done.'

'There is no need for you to come quite so soon, Brother,' said Dame Eva reasonably. 'We are all tired after our exertions, and my son looks unwell. I would rather he rested, and that you worked on the thing together tomorrow.'

Tuddenham did indeed look ill. Bartholomew exchanged a concerned glance with Stoate, who whispered that he would visit the knight later to prescribe something to make him more comfortable.

'I would rather know where my advowson stands tonight,' said Tuddenham stubbornly. 'I am a little weary, but will be well enough after a short rest.'

'You are terribly pale,' said Isilia anxiously. 'Rest this evening. I will sing, and Master Wauncy can play his drum. You can pore over deeds tomorrow.'

'Tonight,' repeated Tuddenham, in a tone that indicated the discussion was over. 'Meanwhile, offer the villagers free ale, Hamon.'

Hamon raised his voice so that the villagers could hear. 'My uncle would like to show his appreciation to all of you who helped stop the fire from destroying our village. There will be free ale at the Dog. Spare no expense, landlord. You can present us with the bill tomorrow.'

The immediate, single-minded scramble reminded Bartholomew of the feast after the Pentecost Fair, and he was startled to see that, all of a sudden, none of the villagers seemed to be tired, and all were able to partake in the vicious pushing and shoving. William went with them, relinquishing his grip on Bartholomew's arm in his desire to slake his thirst with Tuddenham's ale, and Eltisley took advantage of the diversion to slink away to somewhere he hoped Bartholomew would not find him. Within moments, no one remained by the ruined tavern but Bartholomew, Cynric and Michael.

'Poor Alcote,' said Michael softly, watching the last of the villagers race toward the Dog. 'He was a nasty little man, but he did not deserve this.'

*   *   *

Bartholomew sat on a stool in Wergen Hall, and thrust his hands into the sides of his tabard to stop himself from rubbing eyes that itched from the after-effects of the smoke. His discomfort was not eased by the blaze in the hearth that spat and hissed as flames devoured wet wood, and added its own choking fumes to the already stuffy hall.

Sitting opposite him, Michael had coughed until his throat was sore, necessitating the swallowing of large amounts of soothing wine to remedy the matter. This example was grimly followed by William, who decided his throat hurt, too. The wine made him uncharacteristically amiable, and resulted in Tuddenham's startled household being entertained with a few colourfully embellished tales from his days with the Inquisition, after which the friar retired to the floor, where he sprawled with his mouth open and snored.

Hamon had been burned, and his hands were smothered with Bartholomew's ointment of chalk and burdock. Stoate had disagreed with this treatment, and had recommended to his patients a poultice of ground snails and mint mixed with cat grease. There was not a snail, and scarcely a cat, to be seen in Grundisburgh. Later, Bartholomew had been alarmed to learn that Stoate was advising that his poultice could also heal smoke-inflamed eyes, if applied thickly enough. Wrinkling his nose in disgust at the notion of rubbing squashed snails in his face, Tuddenham compelled Bartholomew to sell him all his chalk and burdock to be used for his own household.

Hamon gave his watering eyes a good, vigorous massage, disregarding Bartholomew's repeated advice that rubbing would make them worse. Dame Eva shook her head in exasperation at him, and turned back to her sewing. Isilia sat next to Tuddenham, humming softly and gently stroking his coarse grey hair. The exertion had not been good for the knight, and he had a slight fever. There was little

Bartholomew could do for him, except prescribe something to ease the pain and recommend that he spend the next few days resting. Hamon was blithely intolerant of his uncle's weakened state, urging him to go hunting the following day. On the other hand, Dame Eva and Isilia fretted and fussed over him, to the point where Bartholomew saw the knight was considering an outing with Hamon simply to escape from their cloying attentions.

'I understand Master Alcote was paid two shillings to say masses for a man he found dying on the Old Road,' said Walter Wauncy conversationally, raising his skull-like head from the book he had been perusing.

'Yes,' said Bartholomew, startled by the question. 'When he took the wrong road to Grundisburgh after we found the hanged man at Bond's Corner, he came across a party of travellers who had been attacked, and one of them had been fatally wounded. How did you know?'

'He told me,' said Wauncy. 'He was to say these masses at St Botolph's shrine at St Edmundsbury, but obviously he is not in a position to fulfil these obligations. Give me the two shillings, and I will say the masses instead.'

Bartholomew gazed at him in disbelief. 'You want us to give you Alcote's money?'

'Not his money,' corrected Wauncy reproachfully. 'Funds to rescue this unfortunate's soul from Purgatory. It is not fair to keep it for yourselves.'

Bartholomew made a disgusted sound, and declined to discuss the matter further. Not only had all Alcote's possessions been destroyed in the fire, but he was unimpressed that Wauncy should already be trying to earn a profit from Alcote's death.

'Is Horsey keeping vigil over poor Master Alcote?' whispered Isilia, looking up from her drowsing husband as Wauncy drew breath to argue.

Michael nodded. 'I will relieve him at midnight. If I live

that long.' He coughed meaningfully until his wine goblet was refilled by Siric.

'So, what have you decided about my deed,' asked Tuddenham, roused from his doze by their voices. 'Is all lost as we feared, or can you salvage something from Master Alcote's efforts?'

'I think the stars are against this deed of yours,' said Isilia. 'First Unwin is killed for the relic in his purse; then Doctor Bartholomew and his servant are attacked by Padfoot; and now poor Master Alcote lies dead on the very eve that the advowson was to have been completed.'

'I agree,' said Dame Eva with a shudder. 'This deed has been ill fated from beginning to end. It might be best to forget the whole business.'

'That will not be necessary,' said Michael smugly, holding aloft a piece of parchment. 'Alcote was a cautious man, and left a copy of the draft he made here last night. It is virtually complete, and only needs a few loose ends tying here and there. I will work on the final version tonight, Master Wauncy can check it tomorrow morning, and by noon we can have it signed and be on our way.'

That there was only one more night to spend in Grundisburgh cheered Bartholomew considerably. Had Alcote not been a cautious man, and had Michael deemed it necessary to begin work afresh on the complex legal documents, Bartholomew would have concurred with Dame Eva that the advowson was ill fated, and recommended that the surviving Michaelhouse scholars should escape the village while they still could.

'Good,' said Tuddenham with relief. 'It would have been dreadful if all this had been for nothing. Have it ready by dawn, Brother, and tomorrow Michaelhouse shall have its deed, and everything will be completed.'

Wearily, and looking pale and sick, he retired to bed, taking Isilia with him. Ill at ease with only his grandmother and the Michaelhouse scholars for company, Hamon was not long in following, and moments later Dame Eva also made her farewells and went to her own quarters. The Michaelhouse men were to sleep in Wergen Hall again that night, now that the Half Moon was out of commission, and Tuddenham's servants had been relegated to the kitchens and stables. Most of them, however, had elected to remain in the Dog for as long as the knight's generosity and the landlord's barrels lasted.

Exhausted by his efforts to extinguish the fire, and from resting so little the night before, Bartholomew lay on a mattress and was almost instantly asleep. But his dreams teemed with visions of Alcote's blackened body rising from the flames of the tavern, while Eltisley in a warlock's costume invoked all manner of pagan spirits. It was still dark when he awoke to find he was shaking, and he went to see if Michael had left any wine that would soothe his frayed nerves.

The monk still wrote by the unsteady light of a candle, while Bartholomew sipped his drink and stared into the embers of the fire, thinking about Eltisley and his experiments. Michael saw his brooding expression, and set down his pen, rubbing his eyes tiredly.

'What is wrong? Are you distressed over Alcote? You know, Matt, it would not surprise me to learn that the body we found in the rubble was not his at all, and that he staged his "death" so that no one would make any more attacks on him. He may, even now, be sitting in some inn laughing at how clever he has been. We would never know – the body was too charred for identification.'

'Eltisley,' said Bartholomew, still staring at the glowing logs. 'The more I think about him, the more I am certain that the fire in his tavern was no accident.'

Michael made an impatient sound at the back of his throat, and picked up his pen to begin writing again. 'You are as mad as he is, Matt. Think about it rationally. Do you really think he would destroy his home, all his possessions and his workshop deliberately?'

'I do,' said Bartholomew slowly. 'And I think his shock at seeing us had nothing to do with relief that we were still alive: I think he wanted us dead.'

'No,' said Michael firmly. 'No one – not even a lunatic like Eltisley – would commit murder by igniting his house and destroying his livelihood in the process.'

'I thought at first that the explosion – because that is what it was – had occurred in his workshop,' Bartholomew continued, ignoring the monk's scepticism, 'and that it happened because he had left some volatile compound too near a badly banked fire. But, had that been so, the workshop would have been more badly damaged than the tavern. And it was not.'

'It was burned to the ground,' said Michael, dipping his quill in the ink and shaking it over the rushes so that it would not blot.

'But only *after* the tavern was ablaze,' said Bartholomew. 'And Eltisley basically admitted to playing with a concoction of saltpetre, charcoal and sulphur, which anyone with even a passing knowledge of alchemy knows will ignite and explode. Furthermore, it is clear that he was not doing it in his workshop, he was doing it in the tavern.'

'That still does not mean that he deliberately killed Alcote, or that he intended the rest of us to die with him,' reasoned Michael, his attention fixed on his writing. 'You are letting your dislike of the man interfere with your judgement, Matt. You saw how devastated he was after the fire: he was a broken man, to be pitied and comforted, not accused of murder.'

'I am sure he was appalled at the destruction he caused,' said Bartholomew. 'I have no doubt he did not intend to blow up his entire domain and almost take the rest of the village with it. But I remain convinced that he set his powders to kill Alcote – and us, given that he believed we were changing our clothes in the upper chamber.'

'This is all too ridiculous,' said Michael. 'Why? Why should a lowly Suffolk taverner want to kill his customers and be prepared to destroy his inn? Tuddenham was paying him good money to look after us.'

'And there is another thing,' said Bartholomew. 'Because *he* survived to tell the tale suggests to me that he set the stuff to burn and then ran away. He made no attempt to shout a warning.'

'We cannot know that,' said Michael, looking up at him. 'No one else was in the tavern except Alcote, and he will not be telling anyone whether Eltisley shouted an alarm or not. You will never be able to prove that Eltisley simply ran away and left Alcote to die.'

'I think he broke that dish of gravy deliberately,' Bartholomew went on, piecing together scraps of information that he was sure were related. 'He wanted us upstairs in the bedchamber, changing our clothes, so that he could kill us all at once. It was an ideal time, because the tavern was empty of other guests, and he would not need to harm anyone else in the process.'

'I see,' said Michael, bending his head to his work. 'But you have not answered my question. Why should a landlord want to kill his guests?'

Bartholomew thought hard. 'Perhaps it is something to do with Tuddenham's deed. Perhaps Tuddenham paid Eltisley to kill Alcote, because Alcote found something dreadful in his household accounts. Alcote said he had uncovered irregularities, and that he was burning documents to hide them.'

'You are being inconsistent: on the one hand you are saying that Tuddenham wants the advowson completed with indecent haste; on the other you claim that Tuddenham ordered Alcote killed because he found peculiarities in his affairs. Tuddenham would not have allowed Alcote to examine his documents at all, if there had been secrets in them worth killing for.'

'But Alcote told us himself that Tuddenham's affairs were complex, and not wholly honest.'

'Whose affairs are, Matt? Go to sleep. You are tired and inclined to flights of fancy. In the cold light of day you will see Alcote's death for what it is – a horrible, tragic accident.'

Bartholomew sighed and Michael set down his pen, resting his fat elbows on the table and shaking his head at his friend's stubbornness.

'You are making an error you have made before, Matt: you are assuming that everything that happens to you, and everything you learn, is somehow connected. That is not the case here. Eltisley has absolutely nothing to do with Tuddenham's advowson, and the fact that Alcote died when he was working on it is simple chance. He might equally well have been eating his dinner.'

'But what if Alcote had found something in all those documents he read that Eltisley wanted no one else to know? What if Alcote confronted Eltisley, and tried to blackmail him? We both know that is the sort of thing Alcote might well have done.'

'Matthew!' admonished Michael softly. 'The man is barely cold in his grave – in fact he is probably still quite hot, given how you singed your hands getting him out of the rubble – and you are accusing him of rank dishonesty. His soul might be being weighed at this precise moment, and you are asking me if I think he was falsifying documents and blackmailing people.'

'I am sorry,' said Bartholomew. He rubbed a hand through his hair, genuinely contrite. 'I am.'

'He is probably bribing his way through Purgatory at this very moment,' said Michael with a nasty snigger. 'Or offering his services to the Devil in exchange for a more pleasant stay.'

'You should not jest about such things, either,' said Bartholomew, glancing down the hall. 'William can hear comments like that from across whole towns, let alone a silent room. He will accuse us both of heresy, and will harp on about it for weeks. But all this aside, I am still convinced that Eltisley killed Alcote deliberately.'

'Which brings us back to that awkward little question you have so cunningly managed to avoid: why?' said Michael. 'Can you offer a single scrap of evidence – hard evidence, Matt, not supposition and conjecture – why he should want to harm Alcote?'

'No,' said Bartholomew, after a moment of serious thinking. He glanced up to see Michael looking victorious. 'But that does not mean I am wrong. You said almost as soon as we arrived here that there was something odd happening in Grundisburgh. Well, I agree with you, and I think Eltisley lies at the centre of it.'

'He is just a taverner, Matt. If there is something odd happening, as you insist, then it is no conspiracy, but simply a madman whose inflated opinions of his abilities are rendered dangerous because his thriving inn provides him sufficient wealth to buy the ingredients for his experiments. Now, unless you want to be in this miserable place for ever, let me do some work. Go to sleep.'

Bartholomew was restless and unhappy. He had never particularly liked Alcote, but he had known him for years, and was distressed that he should die such a death. Each time he closed his eyes he could see the corpse he had extricated from the remains of the tavern, and could hear Deynman asking if that were all that was left. Deynman. Bartholomew walked to where the student slept, his dark hair tangled with straw from the mattress. Asleep, he looked young and vulnerable, and Bartholomew felt a sudden pang of fear for him. Deynman might not be the most able of students – and his behaviour in the affair of Agatha the laundress's teeth had been reprehensible to say the least – but Bartholomew had grown fond of him, and the notion of anyone stabbing him in a church or blowing him up in a tavern horrified him.

Making a decision, he crouched down, and touched the student's shoulder. Stirring sleepily, Deynman opened his eyes and immediately smiled when he saw Bartholomew. It was a spontaneous reaction, and one that made Bartholomew more certain than ever that he wanted Deynman away from Grundisburgh and its nasty secrets.

'Rob,' he whispered, as the student sat up rubbing his eyes. 'I need you to do something.'

'Anything,' said Deynman rashly. 'What is it? Do you want me to help you with an operation? I can do the sawing if it is an amputation, leaving you to stop all the bleeding.'

'No!' Bartholomew suppressed a shudder at the thought of Deynman wielding a saw over some unsuspecting patient. 'I want you to take Horsey to the leper hospital as soon as it is light.'

'Does he have the disease, then? It does not show.'

Bartholomew began to wonder whether his plan to place Deynman in charge of Horsey's welfare was such a good idea after all. 'I think neither of you is safe here. You must leave, and we will collect you when we return to Cambridge. You will be safe with the lepers.'

'You mean I should leave you here alone?' asked Deynman, appalled. 'But you might need me!'

'I do. I need you to take care of Horsey. Can you do it? Can you slip out of Grundisburgh with no one seeing you, and hide with Brother Peter until I come for you?'

'Of course.' Deynman's face was a mask of worry. 'But what about you?'

'As soon as Horsey returns from Alcote's vigil, I want you to go. Do not take anything with you – just make it appear as though you are going for a stroll. Do you need money? Take mine.'

Deynman looked in disdain at the handful of coins Bartholomew offered him. 'Perhaps I should lend you some. I have ten marks in my belt and two gold crowns in my boot.'

Bartholomew smiled, feeling foolish for imagining that his wealthy student would need his inconsequential pennies. 'Offer some to Brother Peter for the lepers. And please do not try to heal any of them – leprosy is incurable, and stripping some poor horse of its tail will not change that.'

Solemnly, Deynman held out his hand to Bartholomew. 'I am sure we shall meet again, but if not, I shall pay for masses to be said for your soul until we meet in heaven.'

Deynman was probably the only person Bartholomew knew, other than William, who confidently assumed that the natural progress of his immortal soul would be up, and not down to join all the other sinners.

'And I shall do the same for you.'

Deynman smiled. 'Do not worry about Horsey. I will look after him.'

Bartholomew left him to go back to sleep, feeling a certain weight of responsibility lifting from his shoulders. Deynman was drowsing again almost before Bartholomew left him, showing a lack of anxiety that Bartholomew envied.

He paced back and forth, oblivious to Michael's irritable glances as the draught he created caused the candle to leap and flicker, making it difficult for him to see. Unaware of the monk's disapproval, Bartholomew opened one of the window shutters, leaning out to inhale deeply of rich, clean air that was heavy with the scent of blossom. After a while, he closed it, and began to doze on the stone window-seat.

The only sounds in the room were the scratch of Michael's

quill and Father William's snoring. The embers in the hearth glowed a deep red, giving out little heat and virtually no light, so that the monk was hunched uncomfortably in the small yellow halo cast by a single candle that had been set in an inglenook. Eventually, he finished writing and looked up.

'It must be almost time for nocturn,' he whispered, shaking Bartholomew awake. 'One of us should go to relieve Horsey in the church.'

'I will go,' said Bartholomew, picking up his cloak. 'Ask William to come at dawn, and then you and I will sit over Wauncy while he reads that deed you have just written. Tuddenham will sign and seal it, and we will be on our way as soon as the wax has set.'

'That would be ungracious of us,' said Michael, smiling at the image Bartholomew had produced. 'It is not seemly to snatch the goods and run.'

'It is not seemly for Unwin to be murdered, for Alcote to die in a bizarre accident, and for Cynric and me to be chased through the forest by savage white dogs,' retorted Bartholomew.

'Perhaps you are right,' said Michael. 'But there is nothing we can do about it now. Of course, I would feel a lot happier if that loathsome pardoner were under lock and key: I do not feel safe with him on the loose. If you want a suspect for murder, Matt, there is your man.'

Bartholomew sighed. 'If I am being unreasonably bigoted about Eltisley, then you are just as bad over Norys. We should be ashamed of ourselves.'

'I shall leave the shame to you,' said Michael smugly. 'I have better things to do with my time – like going with you to relieve Horsey. If I accompany you to the church, I can walk back with Horsey, and no one will be out on his own in the dark. Alcote *was* attacked last night on this very path, after all.'

On their way out of the hall, Michael leaned over the

sleeping Cynric and muttered in his ear. Bartholomew saw something exchange hands, but was too engrossed in his own thoughts about Alcote to ask about it. Together, he and Michael left Wergen Hall, and began to walk quickly along the narrow track that led to the village. It was cloudy, and there was no light from the moon or the stars; all Bartholomew could see were the outlines of trees and the dark masses of houses. The village was quiet; not even a dog barked as they went past, and the only sounds were their own footsteps. As they reached the churchyard, the moon emerged from behind a cloud, bathing the village in a soft silver light.

'That is better,' said Michael, stepping forward with more confidence. He stopped suddenly, and peered through the trees. 'What in God's name is going on over there?'

Bartholomew could see something moving in the elms at the very back of the churchyard, near where Unwin was buried.

'It is probably Horsey,' he whispered. 'Praying over Unwin's grave.'

'Horsey would not leave Alcote unattended,' said Michael in a low, nervous voice. 'Nor would he creep about in dark graveyards at midnight. He is no fool, and neither are we. Come on, Matt, I have had enough of this.'

'Where are you going?'

'Into the church, where we will lock the door and wait for daybreak.'

'But there is someone by Unwin's grave. We cannot just ignore it.'

'We can, Matt! I want no white dogs materialising out of recently dug graves in front of me!'

'You have always claimed that you do not believe in Padfoot,' said Bartholomew, moving toward the grave. 'Come on, Brother. Where is your proctorial spirit of adventure and enquiry?'

'I left that in Cambridge,' muttered Michael, following him reluctantly. 'It is most definitely not with me here in Grundisburgh.'

As they neared the grave, they heard a low moan followed by a wavering call that sounded like a child crying. The blood in Bartholomew's veins ran as cold as ice, and Michael gripped his arm so hard it hurt. Another cry answered it, and then there was a hiss. Bartholomew closed his eyes in relief, and turned to Michael, smiling in the darkness.

'It is a pair of cats!'

'It is more than a pair,' said Michael, straining his eyes as he peered through the shadowy trees. 'It is a flock!'

He stepped out of the trees and headed toward the animals, making flapping movements with his hands as he tried to drive them away. But Bartholomew saw that the cats were not the only things moving in the dark.

'Michael! Behind you!'

His yell of warning came just in time. Michael spun round, and was just able to duck the savage blow from the spade that was aimed at his head. Another figure emerged from the darkness and struck out, sending Michael tumbling into the long grass. With a howl of anger, Bartholomew raced to the aid of his friend, bowling into the second attacker with such force that he sent him clean over the wall of the churchyard. Then there was a scraping noise to his left, a sound that Bartholomew had heard enough times to recognise as that of a sword being drawn from a leather scabbard.

A weapon whistled through the air, so close that Bartholomew felt it sever some hairs on the top of his head. Meanwhile, Michael had seized the spade, and wielded it like a staff until an expert slash by the sword broke the wooden handle in two. Horrified, the monk backed away, bumping into a third man, and knocking him to the ground. The attacker Bartholomew had propelled over the wall was climbing back again, to rejoin the affray.

Knowing he and Michael would stand little chance against three men, one of whom was armed with a sword, Bartholomew groped in his medicine bag, fingers fumbling for his surgical knife. He could not find it. Instead, his shaking fingers encountered something small, but heavy: it was Deblunville's cramp ring. He drew it out, and hurled it as hard as he could, hearing it strike the swordsman's face with a sickening crack. Without waiting to see the result, he leapt forward and dived at him, hoping to knock the sword from his hand.

They rolled over in the wet grass, Bartholomew struggling to prevent his opponent from using his weapon, his opponent trying to batter him with the hilt to force him to let go. He was stronger than Bartholomew had anticipated, and the physician sensed that the instant the man freed his sweaty wrist, the pommel of the sword would crash on to his head, and that would be that. With increasing desperation, Bartholomew concentrated on keeping his fingers tightly wrapped around the swordsman's arm, but the skin was clammy, and slid inexorably out of Bartholomew's grasp. And then suddenly, it was free. Bartholomew closed his eyes as the weapon glinted above his head, and then opened them again as a dreadful scream tore through the air.

There was a gasp of fright, followed by the sound of running footsteps. All at once, Michael's burly silhouette was looming above him, while behind, Cynric crouched, looking this way and that in the dark like a hunting animal. Of the swordsman, there was no sign.

'What happened? What was the dreadful yowl? Was it Padfoot?' Bartholomew sat up quickly, peering into the shadows to see if the white dog was there, biding its time for another attack.

'Something just as terrifying,' said Michael unsteadily, brushing leaves and wet grass from his habit. 'A good Welsh battle-cry.' He rubbed a shaking hand across his face. 'That was a close call, Matt! If Cynric had screeched a fraction of a moment later, we would be dead.'

Shyly, Cynric smiled. 'Perhaps I should have screamed to terrify Padfoot last week,' he said.

'But what are you doing here, Cynric?' asked Bartholomew. 'You are supposed to be asleep.'

'Old Cynric does not sleep when there is fighting to be done,' said Cynric reproachfully. 'Do you think I would leave you to do all this alone? I followed you from Wergen Hall, and saw those men in the graveyard long before you realised they were there.'

'A word of warning would not have gone amiss,' said Bartholomew curtly. 'We would not have disturbed them had we known they were so heavily armed.'

'You went after them before I could stop you,' objected Cynric. 'You always are incautious. How many times have I told you not to attack without first assessing what you are attacking?'

'We should not sit here chatting while these men escape,' said Bartholomew. 'We should catch them before they do any more mischief.'

'They are long gone,' said Cynric. 'I would go after them, but my bow is useless, and only a fool chases his enemy with only half his weapons.'

'What happened to it?' asked Michael. 'I suppose it was damaged by that potion Eltisley made?'

Cynric grimaced. 'Snapped my string clean in two the last time I tried to use it.'

'Do you know who those men were?' asked Bartholomew, climbing to his feet and looking around him uneasily. 'Did you recognise any of them?'

'I saw nothing but shadows lurching and weaving all around me,' said Michael. 'Did you see anything?' He sounded disappointed.

'Not really,' said Bartholomew, 'but one of them was an

expert swordsman. That should narrow down our list of suspects.'

'Why?' asked Michael.

'How many people in villages are trained to use swords?'

'Lots, Matt – we are officially at war with France. Lords of the manor are obliged by law to train villagers in the use of weapons, lest the King should need them as soldiers.'

'But this man used a sword with some skill, not like a country bumpkin with a stave.'

'You are no judge of such things,' said Cynric rudely. 'He was not so skilled, or he would have dispatched you with ease, and not allowed you to jump all over him as he did.'

'Would you believe that one of those louts had the audacity to hit me with the spade he had been using to excavate Unwin's grave?' said Michael, indignantly.

'Is that what were they doing?' asked Bartholomew, repelled. 'Are you sure?'

'See for yourself,' said Michael. There was a scrape of tinder, and light from a candle cast a dim circle around them. Something glinted in the grass, and Cynric stooped to retrieve it. It was the coffin ring.

'You would not want to lose that,' he said, handing it back to Bartholomew.

Unwin's grave was partly uncovered. The earth had been carefully piled to one side, almost as if the culprits were intending to fill it in again. Bartholomew took the candle and looked more closely, leaning into the shallow hole to brush away some of the soil.

'They were not digging up Unwin, Brother,' he said, looking at the fat monk in dismay. 'They were providing him with a little company. Because here is Norys – your absconded pardoner.'

CHAPTER 11

IN THE GLOOM OF THE CHURCH, PARTLY ILLUMINATED BY five tallow candles, Bartholomew leaned over Norys's body and began his examination. The parish coffin was already in use for what remained of Alcote, so Norys was relegated to a table borrowed from Walter Wauncy's kitchen – for a price. Horsey watched in horror as yet another body was laid out in the chancel, and Bartholomew sent him back to Wergen Hall with Cynric, who was also to inform Tuddenham that Norys had been found.

From the state of the corpse, Bartholomew judged that Norys had been dead for days, perhaps even since the Wednesday when he had last been seen. Whether Norys had first travelled to Ipswich, and then returned to visit Mistress Freeman and secure his alibi, was impossible to tell. Norys might have died on the Wednesday, but he might equally well have died a day or two later. The body smelled powerfully of decay, and gas swelled the stomach under the mud-stained clothes.

'His lips,' said Michael with a shudder. 'They are green.'

Bartholomew studied them closely. 'How curious. Perhaps it is something to do with where the body has been kept hidden all this time.'

'You mean in Unwin's grave?'

'No – he is too clean to have been buried there for long. It looks to me as though he has been stored somewhere, until he could be disposed of permanently.'

'I expect he killed Unwin and Mistress Freeman, and then

dispatched himself in a fit of remorse,' said Michael, looking down at the remains dispassionately.

'I expect so,' said Bartholomew. 'Then he hired those three louts to bury him several days later, in the churchyard on top of one of his victims.'

'How did he die? Can you tell?' asked Michael, ignoring Bartholomew's facetiousness.

Bartholomew shook his head. 'There is no wound that I can see. He was not hanged, stabbed, strangled or hit over the head.'

'Poisoned?' asked Michael. 'A coward such as Norys might well prefer poison as a painless way to launch himself down to the fires and brimstone of hell.'

'You sound like William,' said Bartholomew. 'And you should not jump to conclusions. Norys may not have killed himself at all – someone else may have done it.'

'How?' demanded Michael. 'You say there are no wounds, and he looks as though he may have died in his sleep.'

Bartholomew prised open Norys's mouth, and peered inside. 'Hold the candle closer,' he instructed. 'I cannot see.'

Michael looked away in revulsion as Bartholomew leaned towards the dead man's mouth. When the physician put his fingers inside it and began to feel around, Michael felt sick.

'Look at this,' said Bartholomew, sounding interested.

'No,' said Michael, studiously staring in the opposite direction. 'I do not want to see whatever it is. You can just tell me about it.'

'It is a piece of food that was trapped between his teeth,' said Bartholomew. Michael looked round in surprise, and saw a fairly large strand of something yellowish between the physician's fingers. Michael turned away quickly, feeling his gorge rise.

'So?' he asked, trying to dispel the image from his mind.

'I cannot be certain – it is too mangled and decayed – but it looks and smells like shellfish.'

Michael dropped the candle and charged outside. When Bartholomew found him, he was sitting on the wall of the churchyard looking off into the silent night.

'What is the matter with you? You are not so squeamish when you demand that I examine bodies in Cambridge.'

'That is not true,' said Michael unsteadily. 'I find the whole business repellent wherever we happen to be. But fishing bits of half-eaten food from the mouth of a rotting corpse is an impressively revolting thing to do, even for you.'

'But you realise what this means?' asked Bartholomew, holding the fragment of food up in the darkness. 'If this is indeed shellfish, it implies that Norys enjoyed a meal of mussels with Mistress Freeman before she died – before they died.'

'That sounds a little far-fetched,' objected Michael.

'It isn't, Brother,' said Bartholomew, certain facts coming together in his mind. 'I told you at the time that I thought Mistress Freeman might have died because she ate tainted mussels – I could smell vomit in her mouth, and I suggested that someone came after she was dead and cut her throat. Now we have Will Norys, dead from no obvious cause, but there is a strand of what looks to be mussel in his mouth. And then there was the dead cat in her garden.'

'I do not see the point you are trying to make,' said Michael irritably.

'The point is that Norys and Mistress Freeman ate mussels together, and that Norys had brought one of his cats – or, more likely, the cat followed him there. He gave it some, as owners of much-loved animals are wont to do – and so the cat died, too.'

'So?' asked Michael after a moment. 'This tells us nothing that we had not already considered.'

'It does,' said Bartholomew. 'It tells us that Mistress

Freeman probably did not commit suicide, and that Norys probably did not kill her.'

'How in God's name do you deduce that?' asked Michael tiredly.

'If Mistress Freeman had planned to poison herself with bad shellfish, she would not have given any to Norys. And if Norys had wanted to kill her with them, he would not have eaten any himself or given them to his pet.'

Michael shook his head. 'He may have brought the shell-fish as a means to inveigle his way into her house. He may have planned to kill her after they had eaten – if his transparent attempts to ingratiate himself and force her to lie for him about his alibi failed.'

'In that case, Mistress Freeman, Norys and the cat ate the mussels unaware that they were tainted, and all three died in or near the house. The only logical conclusion from this is that someone else found them before you ever discovered Mistress Freeman's body, and tried to make her death appear as murder. This same person must therefore have removed Norys, intending to dispose of him later in a place he would never be found – namely Unwin's grave. And finally, this person must have put the bloodstained clothes and Unwin's empty purse on Norys's roof, knowing that you would find them there and be convinced that it was Norys who killed Unwin.'

'I see,' said Michael flatly. 'And who might this cunning someone be?'

'It could be Eltisley,' said Bartholomew. 'Perhaps his murder of Alcote yesterday made him realise that he needed to destroy the evidence of his other crimes, and so forced him to dispose of Norys's corpse quickly. What better hiding place than in the tomb of the man Norys is accused of killing?'

'I do not think so, Matt. We have evidence that Norys killed Unwin *and* Mistress Freeman; we have nothing but your nasty accusations to show that Eltisley has killed anyone. And do not forget what Dame Eva said – Eltisley could not possibly have left his tavern during the Fair to harm Unwin, because there were people demanding ale and he would have been missed instantly. Perhaps the killer is someone we have not yet considered.'

'I suppose Deblunville might have killed Unwin to embarrass Tuddenham,' said Bartholomew, reluctantly trying to generate alternatives. 'The rumour about him killing his first wife seems to have had some truth, so murder was not wholly foreign to him. But Deblunville died yesterday, and so could not have been burying Norys tonight.'

'Hamon?' suggested Michael with a shrug. 'You said that whoever attacked us was proficient with a sword, and he *is* a lout.'

Bartholomew nodded slowly. 'He has a motive: the prevailing opinion is that Norys is Unwin's killer, and as long as Norys remains at large, Michaelhouse will decline to send another of its members to Grundisburgh like a lamb to the slaughter, and Hamon can therefore select his own priest when he inherits the estate from his uncle.'

'Tuddenham will live for years yet,' said Michael dismissively. 'And once Isilia's child is born, it will inherit the estates, not Hamon.'

But Bartholomew knew very well that Tuddenham would be cold in his grave long before Isilia's child made its appearance, and that if it were a girl, Hamon would inherit anyway. If it were a boy, Hamon would run the estates until the child was old enough to manage them himself – if he lived that long and if Hamon did not find some way to wrest them away from him in the meantime.

Michael sighed. 'It could equally well be Bardolf or Grosnold. None of these lords seem to like each other much. And there is the curious fact of Eltisley seeing Grosnold holding Unwin by the arm shortly before he died.'

'Eltisley *says* he saw Grosnold with Unwin,' said Bartholomew.

'But who is to say he is not lying about that in order to throw us off his own track?'

'True. But remember what Bardolf said about his fellow lords – that any of them might kill a priest who tried to promote peaceful relations when each has so much to lose. What a muddle!'

Bartholomew stood and stretched, looking at the sliver of mussel he still held. He walked to the stream that trickled across the village green, and bent down to release it into the persistent tug of the current, watching as it was swept away into the darkness.

When he returned, Michael was still sitting on the church-yard wall waiting for someone from Tuddenham's household to come and view Norys's body. The monk's head was tipped back, and he was gazing up at the glitter of stars in the black night sky, and at the wispy silver clouds that floated across the face of the moon.

'You know, Matt, we should review what we have learned, just to see if we can reason some sense from it.'

'Must we?' asked Bartholomew, sitting next to him. 'I am heartily sick of all this.'

'So am I,' said Michael. 'But we cannot leave later today unless we are certain that we know who killed Unwin. The Master would never forgive me if I had not done all I could to catch whoever killed Michaelhouse's best student. So, first we had the hanged man at Bond's Corner, clearly murdered and found half-burned in a shepherd's hut. We have no idea who he is, or who killed him and why, although we know he was wearing clothes stolen from Deblunville by Janelle.'

'No, Brother. First came Alice Quy and James Freemen, both dead in odd circumstances after claiming to have seen Padfoot. Second, we have the hanged man. Third, we have Unwin, stabbed – and his purse stolen, only to appear on Norys's roof minus its relic.'

'And we have two different descriptions of someone fleeing the church after his murder, and we have Grosnold seen talking surreptitiously with him just before his death. I remain certain Norys is responsible; you cannot see reason and are inclined to think the culprit was someone else.'

Bartholomew sighed. 'Fourth, we have Mistress Freeman, dying in her home because she ate tainted mussels – perhaps alone, but probably with Norys and his cat – and then the throat of her corpse slit because someone wanted her death to appear like murder. We do not know why, although it seems to me that someone wants us to believe that Norys murdered her because she declined to provide him with an alibi for Unwin's death.'

'Deblunville was fifth,' said Michael. 'He died of a wound to his head, which may or may not have been inflicted when he slipped on wet grass. But if someone did kill him, I doubt we will ever know who, given that you say half the county was out that night, looking for golden calves.'

'Alcote was sixth,' said Bartholomew. 'Killed by the explosion that destroyed Eltisley's tavern. I think it was deliberate; you believe it was an accident. And now seventh, we have Norys. Still, at least we know he did not kill Deblunville or Alcote – he was already dead by then.'

'What about his green lips?' asked Michael. 'Could they be a sign of poison?'

'They might, I suppose, although there is no blistering or burning. Perhaps the colour has something to do with the bad mussels.'

'But Mistress Freeman did not have green lips.'

'True, but Mistress Freeman did not remain out of her grave for a week. The real question is whether these seven deaths are related or isolated. I am sure that Alice Quy, James Freeman and the hanged man are connected, because of Padfoot. Unwin's murder may be a case of simple theft, although he saw Padfoot, too. Norys's and Mistress Freeman's are probably related to each other – if they both ate the same tainted mussels – and although neither was murdered, someone came and tampered with their corpses to make us believe that Norys killed Unwin.'

'And Alcote?' mused Michael thoughtfully. 'How does he fit into all this? He never saw Padfoot, as far as I know, and he is unlikely to be connected to Unwin's death, although I would not put theft past the man – he may have coveted Unwin's relic.'

Bartholomew shook his head in exasperation. 'I can see no pattern in all this. I am inclined to think Eltisley is the root of all evil, and you believe it is Norys. I do not like charlatans who dabble in medicine; you do not like pardoners. We are scarcely thinking like rational men, are we?'

'Speak for yourself,' said Michael. 'But I have a plan to see whether you are right and Alcote's death was no accident. We will see whether it works before we leave for Cambridge.'

'What is it?' asked Bartholomew nervously.

Michael assumed the infuriatingly secretive expression that he knew always antagonised the physician. 'You will have to wait and see. You did not confide in me over Mother Goodman's charm, and so I am not obliged to reveal my professional secrets to you.' He glanced up. 'Here comes Cynric with Tuddenham and his retinue – his mother, his wife, his nephew, his priest and his servants. I wonder he has not brought his hounds and his horses and his hawks.'

'I did not expect him to come himself,' said Bartholomew, worried about Tuddenham's failing health. 'He should have sent Hamon or Siric.'

'He probably does not trust them with something like this,' said Michael, standing to meet them.

Left alone, Bartholomew walked back to the river, listening to its faint gurgle and the hiss of the breeze through the nearby willows. Bats flitted in and out of the branches, hunting down insects that lived near the water, and somewhere an owl hooted, to be answered by another in the distance.

'Death seems to follow you around, Bartholomew.' Bartholomew jumped at the proximity of Hamon's voice. 'It is a curious trait for one who claims to heal the sick.'

Bartholomew studied him hard, trying to ascertain whether he was injured or sore from a recent tussle over Unwin's grave. Or whether he had a bruise on his face from the violently hurled coffin ring. But it was too dark to tell, and Hamon's step appeared steady enough. He seemed about to add something else, but Tuddenham called him, and the younger knight strode away to add his contribution to the indignant clamour of voices in the churchyard, as Michael explained where Norys had been found. After a while, Michael escaped and came to sit next to Bartholomew on the river bank.

'Your support would have been nice,' he said reproachfully. 'Tuddenham and his clan asked questions that made me wonder whether they suspect *me* of killing Norys and burying him in Unwin's grave.'

'Well, you have always been somewhat fanatical about the fact that Norys was Unwin's killer,' said Bartholomew tiredly. 'What do you expect them to think?'

'But I am not a killer myself,' Michael pointed out indignantly. 'I am a man of God, who has taken a vow to forswear violence wherever possible.'

'"Wherever possible"?' echoed Bartholomew, laughing softly. 'Do the Benedictines put such convenient clauses in their vows, then? Have you sworn to avoid physical relations with women "unless the occasion arises", or live a life free of material possessions "unless they happen to be available"?'

Michael gave him an unpleasant look in the darkness. 'My sacred vows are not something for you to mock,' he said. He jerked his thumb over his shoulder to where raised voices still issued from the church. 'Just listen to them! Quarrelling like a pack of dogs over what happened to Norys.'

'What are they saying?'

'Tuddenham and Wauncy believe that someone killed Norys to prevent him from revealing who really murdered Unwin; Isilia and Dame Eva think Norys committed suicide and hired the three louts to bury him over his victim because of some peculiar satanic ritual; and Hamon and Siric are convinced Deblunville's household is responsible, as some sort of revenge for their lord's death.'

They sat in silence for a while and eventually the voices died away. The church door was opened once and then closed, and then opened a second time a little later. Shadowy figures moved around the churchyard as Unwin's grave was inspected. Michael clambered inelegantly to his feet and went toward them while Bartholomew remained sitting on the river bank, disinclined to speak to Tuddenham or his family while suspicion and accusation seemed to be the order of the day.

Michael's sudden yell split the air like a crack of lightning. Bartholomew almost leapt out of his skin, and his feet skidded on the damp grass in his haste to run to Michael's rescue. By the time he arrived, the monk was sitting on the ground with his fat legs splayed in front of him and his habit rucked up to his thighs, looking more outraged than Bartholomew had ever seen him. Dame Eva and Isilia stood uncertainly together, while Hamon and Siric tried to help the monk to his feet. Tuddenham and Wauncy hurried from the thick yew trees at the rear of the churchyard.

'What happened?' asked Bartholomew, offering Michael his hand. Michael took it, brushing Hamon and Siric aside, and almost hauling Bartholomew on top of him as he proved more heavy than the physician had anticipated.

'Someone searched me!' said Michael, barely able to speak

from the extent of his indignation. 'Someone ran their hands all over my body! Me! A man of the cloth!'

Bartholomew bent to brush leaves from the monk's habit to hide his amusement. 'Why did you do nothing to prevent this affront to your dignity, Brother?' he asked.

'Because whoever did it knocked me from my feet first,' spat Michael. 'While I lay helpless with my arms pinned underneath me, someone searched my person.'

'Searched you for what?' asked Bartholomew. He supposed he should not find the situation amusing, given that someone might well have plans to kill each and every one of the scholars from Michaelhouse.

'I do not know,' said Michael stiffly. 'My purse, I suppose. But, being a poor monk with no earthly vices, I do not carry one.'

He most certainly did carry one, and it was heavier than any purse Bartholomew had ever owned. But Michael was not foolish enough to wear it where it could be seen: it was tucked out of sight among the voluminous folds of his habit, and the equally voluminous folds of his body.

'It was someone here,' said Michael, glaring accusingly at the assembled members of Tuddenham's household. 'It could not have been a passing vagrant, because he would not have been so rash as to attack a man of God while the churchyard was full of people.'

'But neither would we,' said Hamon, a smile plucking at the corners of his mouth. 'And I can assure you, Brother, that none of us would have derived any pleasure from running our hands over you, if that is what you are suggesting.'

'Well, one of you did,' snapped Michael. 'You were all very quick to reach me as soon as I was able to yell.'

'That is because we were all nearby,' protested Isilia. 'Dame Eva and I were examining Unwin's desecrated grave over there. Of course we came running as soon as we heard you shout.'

'I heard you from the church,' said Hamon. 'I was there looking at Norys's body with Siric.'

Siric nodded vigorously.

'Well, that just leaves me and Wauncy,' said Tuddenham. 'And we were inspecting the place where this swordsman is supposed to have attacked you, to see whether he had dropped anything that might identify him.'

'Then you would have seen your mother and your wife at Unwin's grave?' asked Bartholomew, wanting to be certain that everyone was telling the truth.

Tuddenham shrugged. 'I did not notice what they were doing. It is dark and shadowy, and difficult to see anything at all.'

'Then did you see your husband?' asked Bartholomew of Isilia.

She shook her head. 'As he said, it is dark, and, since I was not expecting to be asked to provide him with an alibi to prove he did not molest a monk under the elm trees, I did not watch what he and Wauncy were doing – or Hamon and Siric.'

'I did not notice, either,' said Dame Eva. 'I was concentrating on poor Unwin's grave.'

'I am afraid Siric's and my only witnesses are Norys and Master Alcote,' said Hamon in a serious voice, although Siric was forced to turn away to hide the humour that glinted in his eyes. 'And I fear they will not be quick to prove we were with them while someone manhandled Brother Michael.'

Seeing Michael was unharmed, and more amused than alarmed by the incident, they began to drift away. Cynric slipped up behind Bartholomew to mutter that he had seen no one else enter or leave the churchyard.

'So, unless your molester escaped across the fields behind the church, we must assume it is one of the six people here,' said Bartholomew, still smiling at the vision of Michael helpless on the ground while someone groped him, despite his best attempts to keep a straight face. 'Would you rather imagine yourself searched by Dame Eva or Walter Wauncy?'

'What would you say if I told you that whoever robbed me got what they wanted?' asked Michael coldly.

Bartholomew raised his eyebrows. 'A chance to see whether all that fat underneath your habit is actually real?'

'No,' said Michael shortly. 'The final draft of the advowson.'

Bartholomew gazed at Michael with a churning stomach, his amusement gone in a flash. Was it the advowson that lay at the heart of the matter after all? Was that why Alcote had been killed – to prevent it from being completed? His mind worked rapidly. Everyone in Tuddenham's household had been present at Wergen Hall when Michael had announced he could salvage Alcote's work: Tuddenham, Hamon, Dame Eva, Isilia, Wauncy and Siric. Any one of them could have given Michael a shove in the back to send him flying and then stolen the deed from him.

'So, it has gone?' he asked with a sinking heart. 'We will have to start all over again?'

'It has gone,' confirmed Michael. He gave a sudden smile in the darkness, revealing small yellow teeth. 'But it will do them little good, eh, Cynric?'

Cynric grinned back, while Bartholomew looked from one to the other in confusion. Michael's demeanour had changed from outrage to the smug complacency he always oozed when he thought he had done something clever.

'I hid the spare copy, just as you told me,' Cynric said to Michael. 'It is in a place where no one will think to look – not even you.'

So that was what Michael had been arranging with Cynric as they had left Wergen Hall to relieve Horsey's vigil, Bartholomew thought. Meanwhile, Michael looked intrigued. 'We will see about that, Cynric. This might prove an interesting diversion for my powers of deduction. Do not tell me where you hid it, I will guess.'

'You will not,' said Cynric with equal conviction.

'Matt's medicine bag?' asked Michael immediately.

Cynric shook his head.

'You were expecting something like this to happen,' Bartholomew said slowly. 'You made a point of mentioning that the deed could be completed in front of the whole Tuddenham household, specifically to pre-empt an attack on you, so that you would have a chance to ascertain whether Alcote was killed for the advowson or killed by accident. That was what you meant when you said you had a plan to solve the mystery.'

'More or less,' said Michael, pleased with himself.

'That was a dangerous thing to do. Whoever it is might have slipped a knife in between your ribs to get the deed, not just pushed you to the ground. Alcote was not simply searched, was he?'

Michael sighed softly. 'Actually, I mentioned it in front of the whole household because I imagined everyone would be glad to see the back of us and our deed tomorrow. It only occurred to me later that someone might attack me for it – hence I gave a spare copy to Cynric. Initially, I was sceptical about your claim that Alcote was murdered, but the more I worked on Tuddenham's documents last night, the more I realised there might have been some truth in what you suggested.'

'You mean because Tuddenham's affairs are so murky?'

Michael shook his head. 'Quite the contrary. We have allowed Alcote to mislead us. He told us that Tuddenham's affairs seethe with inconsistencies and dishonesties. Well, I found from my work last night that, although there is some question as to whether the Peche Hall land is his, there is virtually nothing in Tuddenham's business that is sinister or illegal.'

'Of course not. Alcote said he burned the deeds that proved that.'

'But Alcote was lying, to make us think he was working hard for the College. The priest, Wauncy, had made an inventory of all Tuddenham's documents before we arrived, and none of them is missing. If Alcote had burned anything, it was nothing important.'

'But why should Alcote lie?' asked Bartholomew, bewildered.

'Simple, Matt. He was pretending the deed was immensely difficult to write, so that when we return to Michaelhouse he could claim that his role was more important than it was. In reality, the whole business is so straightforward that even you could draft an advowson from it.'

'And that was why he refused our help?' said Bartholomew, ignoring the barb. 'Because if we had been allowed to see the documents we would have seen that he was lying about how complex the advowson was to write?'

Michael nodded, 'Precisely. But there was also something else. I found out that he was building a case to wrest a place called Gull Farm from Tuddenham's neighbour, John Bardolf, and hand it back to Tuddenham – for a commission, of course.'

'Gull Farm?' mused Bartholomew. 'At Unwin's funeral, Bardolf told me that his father had stolen that from the Tuddenhams thirty years ago. He openly acknowledged that it really belonged to Tuddenham, and just as openly said he was going to keep it because he was fond of it.'

'I see. Well, doubtless Tuddenham would have been delighted to have it back, although it seems to me that Alcote's case was based more on documents he had written himself than on ones that are genuine – showing us that Alcote was not an honest man. He was a liar and a cheat, and he played a game that was more dangerous than he realised: he told everyone that he was the only man who could write the advowson, and he died for his deception.'

'How could Alcote have been so stupid?' cried Bartholomew, suddenly angry at the Senior Fellow's selfish machinations. 'It has been clear from the start that things are not all they seem here. How could he risk his life for something so pointless?'

'And our lives,' said Michael. 'We would have left days ago, had he not kept us all waiting while he worked out how he could turn the situation to his own advantage. But to go back to yesterday, he was probably killed so that the deed – which he announced, quite openly, would be completed today – would never be finished.'

'So, you think the fire was aimed at Alcote alone?'

Michael shrugged. 'Probably, although had we been incinerated, too, it could only have helped the killer's cause. Michaelhouse does not have an inexhaustible supply of scholars to sacrifice, even for something as attractive as an advowson.'

'It all seems rather desperate,' said Bartholomew. 'The living of the church might mean a lot to our College, but it is only a small part of Tuddenham's estates. I do not understand why anyone should go to such lengths to keep it from us.'

'And that is precisely where our theory comes to a standstill,' said Michael. 'Who would gain from keeping the living in Tuddenham hands? Hamon, who would lose the right to appoint his own priest? Tuddenham himself? Wauncy will be the poorer when a Michaelhouse man comes to share the money he makes from saying masses for the plague-dead, while Dame Eva seems to dislike the notion of her husband's estates being less than they were in his time. Or was Norys right, and do we need to look outside the village – to Grosnold or Bardolf? Or perhaps the person behind all this is someone we have never met, directing events from afar.'

'You mean like the Bishop of Norwich or the Despenser family, who are overlords here?

'Why not? The Bishop of Norwich might not approve of Tuddenham giving the living of a church in his see to an institution where the Bishop of Ely holds power. Or perhaps the Despensers want the deed for themselves – a family like that does not rise to such infamy by allowing lucrative advowsons to slip through their fingers.'

They sat in silence on an ancient tomb, trying to think of a reason why someone should have taken against their College.

'William's psalter?' Michael asked the hovering Cynric suddenly, his mind returning to where the book-bearer might have hidden the document for safe keeping. 'He seldom bothers to look at it when he prays, and a slender piece of parchment could remain undetected there for weeks.'

Cynric shook his head. 'Do you think we are safe here?' he asked, looking around him. 'Will the person behind all this murder and mayhem try to attack us again tonight? Should we be inside the church with Tuddenham and his retinue, rather than relaxing here like sitting ducks?'

Michael shook his head. 'Now that the killer has what he believes to be the only copy, I believe we will experience no further problems until we present the other one later today. And I intend to do that with as many witnesses present as possible.'

'We would never leave Suffolk alive,' said Cynric. 'Keep it hidden until we reach St Edmundsbury Abbey, and then give it to the monks. Tuddenham can come to sign it at his leisure, and it can be forwarded to us later.'

Michael nodded approvingly. 'That is a good plan. It puts no one at risk and, if Tuddenham is behind all this, we will know when he fails to set his seal to the deed that will make the living ours. But at least we now have the answers to some of our questions: we know for certain that Alcote was murdered, and we know that his death relates to the advowson.'

'Do you think Alcote destroyed the tavern in an attempt to fake his own death?' asked Cynric.

'Deynman thinks so,' said Bartholomew. 'He cannot believe that we will never see him again. I know how he feels. Roger Alcote has been a part of Michaelhouse for so long that I cannot imagine the place without him.'

Michael sighed. 'Alcote is . . . was . . . a clever man, and all we have to prove that the corpse in the Half Moon was his is a melted cross. It would not surprise me in the slightest if he later appeared unharmed, having left us to deal with this dangerous business without him.' He was about to add more when there was a stricken cry from the church. It was Hamon's voice. Moments later, Siric raced out, looking for Bartholomew.

'Sir Thomas is took sick,' he gasped. 'Go to him, and I will fetch Master Stoate.'

Sir Thomas was indeed 'took sick'. He sat doubled over on one of the benches in the chancel, and clutched at his stomach, while Hamon knelt next to him anxiously and Isilia patted one of his hands. Dame Eva stood behind him, murmuring soothing words in his ear, although Wauncy was chanting the words of the mass for the dying, and was probably already calculating how many fourpences he would be able to claim from the bereaved family over the next few years.

'That will not be necessary,' said Bartholomew sharply, to the priest's clear disappointment. 'Sir Thomas is not going to die quite yet.'

'Leave us,' groaned Tuddenham to his family. 'All of you. Arrange for a litter to take me home. You go, too, Brother. I want only Bartholomew with me.'

When the door had thumped shut behind them, Tuddenham looked up at the physician with pain-filled eyes. 'Were you lying to my family as Stoate would have done?' he asked in a feeble voice. 'Am I to die now?'

'No,' said Bartholomew. 'I told you to rest, and this is what happens when you ignore good advice. You are not fit enough to pore over desecrated graves in the middle of the night.'

Tuddenham gave a wan smile. 'I would just as soon be in my bed. But did you keep your word? Have you told my household about my weakness?'

'Of course not,' said Bartholomew, offended that he should ask. 'But if you are taken ill like this again, your family will guess you are not as healthy as you would have them believe.'

'I will keep it from them a little longer,' said Tuddenham weakly. 'What excuse will you make for my sickness tonight? Stoate said he would claim I had an excess of bile in the innards if I was ill before I made the state of my health known – unpleasant, painful, frightening, but not fatal.'

Lying was not something Bartholomew did well, and he was sure he would be unable to convince a horde of anxious relatives that there was nothing wrong with Tuddenham, while knowing he would soon die – especially the astute Dame Eva. She would home in on his falsehood like an owl on a mouse, and she would know instantly that there was something he was not telling her.

'Stoate can tell them, then,' said Bartholomew. 'He is here now.'

Stoate raced up the nave. Dawn was still some way off, and the church was in total darkness except for the candles that stood around Alcote's coffin. In his haste to be at his patient's side, Stoate tripped up the chancel steps, and went sprawling. Bartholomew went to help him up.

'How clumsy,' said Stoate, embarrassed as he nodded his thanks to Bartholomew. He had dropped his medicine bag, and phials and charts rolled across the floor. Bartholomew collected them, replaced them in the bag, and handed it back to Stoate, who gave him a brief smile.

Wincing at a bruised knee, Stoate knelt next to Tuddenham, who had watched the physician's dramatic arrival with a weary expression. Bartholomew appreciated how he must feel: it was not a comforting thought that the man who was to nurse you through your final illness was unable to run through a church without falling over.

'The litter is coming,' said Stoate. He glanced at Bartholomew. 'Excess bile in the innards?'

'Apparently,' said Bartholomew, preparing a strong pain-killer. 'He should be taken back to bed, so he can rest. It is not advisable to allow him to be disturbed in the middle of the night.'

'Fortunately, we do not usually have guests in the village who dig up corpses at the witching hour,' said Stoate, not entirely pleasantly. 'I doubt this kind of thing will happen once you leave.'

'I hope not, for Sir Thomas's sake,' said Bartholomew, crouching to help Tuddenham sip the potion he had made.

'Will you bleed him?' asked Stoate. 'The evil humours in his body should be released.'

'They should not,' said Bartholomew. 'He should drink this, then rest.'

'He must be bled,' insisted Stoate. 'You dabble in surgery; you must bleed him.'

'I do not practise phlebotomy,' said Bartholomew firmly. 'And I think that in Sir Thomas's case, bleeding will simply cause him unnecessary discomfort.'

'But you must! The bad humours will build up in his body, and he will never be well.'

'You do it, then, if you deem it so vital,' said Bartholomew, watching Tuddenham drain the last few drops of the potion. 'I will not.'

Stoate shook his head. 'I do not let blood, either.'

'You do,' said Bartholomew, surprised at this assertion. 'Several people have told me that you prescribe blood-letting three times a year. Including yourself.'

'You must have misunderstood,' said Stoate. 'I do recommend blood-letting thrice yearly, but I do not offer to provide the service myself.'

'And which one of you am I supposed to believe?' asked Tuddenham, in a low voice heavy with irony. 'One says I should be bled, the other says I should not.'

'You should,' insisted Stoate.

'It is your decision,' said Bartholomew, refusing to argue any further. 'It will not kill you, but it will not make you better.'

'Well,' said Tuddenham with a faint smile, 'if it makes no difference, I think I will forgo the pleasure. But I am sure you bled my wife, Stoate, when she was first with child? She said you did.'

'I recommended that she be bled,' corrected Stoate. 'I did not do it myself. Mother Goodman probably did it. She has some skill in those matters.'

Bartholomew went to summon the litter-bearers, and saw Sir Thomas carried out of the church and back to Wergen Hall. The knight was already beginning to drowse from the strong potion Bartholomew had given him, and his face had regained some of its colour. Stoate went with him, holding Tuddenham's wrist as he made a show of testing the strength of his life-beat, although how he could do it with the litter bouncing up and down, Bartholomew could not begin to imagine.

'This has been quite a night,' said Michael, walking slowly into the church. 'We have been attacked by men wielding swords, found the body of a murder suspect, been searched most intimately for the advowson, and seen Tuddenham taken ill in his church. What was wrong with him? Guilty conscience for ordering the death of Alcote?'

'The night is not over yet, Brother,' said Bartholomew, crouching down to retrieve something from under the trestle table on which Norys lay. 'Here is Unwin's stolen relic.'

The morning was well advanced, with bright sunshine streaming in through the windows, when Bartholomew awoke in the church. He rubbed his eyes and stretched, realising that he had fallen asleep over his prayers. Michael had not, and was kneeling at the altar, although his preoccupied frown suggested that his mind was not on masses for Alcote's soul, but on the confusion of facts and theories they had amassed the previous night. There was a clank as the door was opened, and Bartholomew hastened to join him, so that William would not guess he had spent much of what remained of the night in an exhausted slumber rather than praying for the charcoaled mess that graced the parish coffin.

The Franciscan flopped on to his knees and glowered. 'May the Lord have mercy on the iniquitous soul of Robert Deynman and his evil ways,' he thundered.

'Why?' asked Bartholomew. Even half asleep, he realised the prayer was intended for his ears, and not the Almighty's.

'He refused to recite prime with me. He said he would rather go for a walk, and he insisted Horsey went with him. That boy will come to a bad end one day.'

But not, Bartholomew was relieved to hear, in Grundisburgh. William continued to grumble about how the two students had slunk down the Ipswich road, and that he strongly suspected they were up to no good. Hoping their journey would be uneventful, and that he would collect them safe and sound later that day, Bartholomew accompanied Michael to Wergen Hall, where the monk planned to correct one or two details on the deed before leaving Grundisburgh and its superstitions and secrets, never to return.

Tuddenham was sleeping, his face drawn and pale and his breathing shallow. He was beginning to look like a man with one foot in the grave, and Bartholomew knew that the astute Dame Eva sensed all was not as it should be. He was sorry for her, understanding that parents are seldom braced for the death of a child who has reached adulthood. She sat next to her son and held his hand, and it was not easy to persuade her to leave him to rest. Isilia was as bad, and it took some effort to dissuade her from delivering a large and carefully prepared breakfast to her ailing husband.

Eventually, Bartholomew prised them from the sickroom. They went slowly, as though they imagined Tuddenham might take a turn for the worse even as they walked to the door. Bartholomew instructed Siric to allow no one to disturb him, and then went to look for Michael.

Michael waved him away as he approached, working hard to complete what needed to be done before someone from Tuddenham's household guessed what he was doing. Bored and unsettled, Bartholomew went to wander aimlessly in the gardens, poking around in the stables, and looking with uninterest at the great destriers that were tethered there. Cynric had managed to obtain some bread and nuts, although Bartholomew hoped the episode with the beef had not given him a taste for the theft of food, and they ate them in Isilia's pretty herbal arbour.

Bartholomew was considering taking Michael something to eat, when he glimpsed Hamon slinking out of Wergen Hall in a manner that could only be described as furtive. With nothing better to do, and with Cynric back to normal and ready to engage in a little daytime stalking, they followed him along the path that wound down the hill, and then along a trackway that cut off to the east. Bartholomew was curious. Hamon was not a man who walked – knights rode, even short distances – and Bartholomew could not imagine what could be sufficiently important to make him resort to using his feet.

Every so often, Hamon would stop and look around to see whether he was being followed, but he was no match for Cynric; the Welshman knew exactly how close he could come without being seen and when to melt back into the shadows to avoid detection. At last they reached the river at a point where it flowed deep and swift before widening into a shallow pool fringed by willows. A set of irregular stepping stones stretched across it, and Hamon leapt inelegantly from one to another – falling in water to his knees when he misjudged one – and clambered up the bank on the other side. Cynric and Bartholomew followed a good deal more gracefully.

They were now on land that had been Deblunville's, and Bartholomew began to feel anxious, afraid that some nasty plot was in progress. Eventually, in a pretty, secluded grove well away from any houses or fields, Hamon stopped and paced impatiently, apparently waiting for someone to arrive. Bartholomew tried to imagine who. Someone from Burgh, who was helping Hamon plot against Tuddenham and the advowson? An accomplice, who had helped him kill Deblunville with a stone in the woods near Barchester? Or was it Bardolf, who seemed intelligent enough to persuade others to do what he did not want to do himself?

Before he had time to speculate further, Cynric tensed, and pointed to someone walking through the trees. Hamon, who had been gazing in that direction for a while, also stiffened.

'Janelle!' breathed Bartholomew, as the pretty woman stepped into the glade.

She regarded Hamon uncertainly, as if not quite sure what to do. He hesitated for a moment, then held out his hands, and with dainty steps she walked towards him and took them in hers. Bartholomew was confused. Surely Janelle could not be the mastermind behind all this evil, using Hamon as her instrument? He watched uncomfortably as Hamon kissed her gently on the lips.

'Come on,' he whispered to Cynric. 'We have seen enough.'

He turned to leave, but as he did so his bag caught on a twig that snapped sharply. Hamon moved faster than Bartholomew would have thought possible, and had the tip of his sword at the physician's throat before Bartholomew was able to take more than a few steps. Cynric had melted into the shadows, but Bartholomew knew one of the Welshman's daggers would be embedded in Hamon's body the instant Cynric considered his friend to be seriously at risk. Nevertheless, he did not much like the sensation of cold steel so near his neck, and hoped Cynric knew what he was doing. Hamon, however, seemed more dismayed than threatening when he recognised his uncle's guest.

'So, now you know,' he said, lowering his sword slightly.

'Know what?' asked Bartholomew in confusion, feeling he knew nothing at all.

'He saw only a brotherly kiss,' said Janelle quickly. 'What harm is there in that?'

'It was not brotherly!' proclaimed Hamon hotly. 'You know it was not.'

Janelle sighed in exasperation. 'Where are your wits, Hamon? We might have convinced him you were simply here to offer me your condolences for the tragic demise of my husband. Now, after your outburst, he would have to be an imbecile not to see that there is more to our relationship.'

'I have never hidden the fact that I adore you,' claimed Hamon vehemently. 'It would be like ... like denying that the Earth rotates!'

Janelle's irritation gave way to wry humour. 'I was always taught that it did not. Walter Wauncy argues most convincingly against such a mad notion.'

'Then he is wrong,' said Hamon loftily. 'I attended the debate at Wergen Hall, where it was proved, beyond the shadow of a doubt, that the Earth spins most of the time.'

He licked a finger and held it up. 'It is still now, of course, because there is no wind.'

Janelle looked from Hamon to Bartholomew in amused disbelief. 'Is that so? But academic disputes, however fascinating, will not help us decide what to do about Doctor Bartholomew, who, thanks to your indiscretion, now knows that we are . . . close.'

'I *will* marry you,' declared Hamon, his attention fully on Janelle, as he let the sword drop to his side. 'No man will steal you from me a second time.'

'No man stole me the first time,' said Janelle practically. 'It was my decision to marry Roland Deblunville, and mine alone. I know now that I made a terrible mistake – one that might have proved fatal for me – but up until our wedding day I thought he was the innocent victim of a hateful plan initiated by Tuddenham to spread lies about him. Foolishly, I believed that monster when he said there was nothing sinister about Pernel's death, but he was lying. He had smashed her head against the stone windowsill, and killed her.'

'It may have been an accident,' said Bartholomew cautiously.

'It was not,' said Janelle, with utter conviction. 'She was old enough to be his grandmother, and he pushed her, knowing she would fall. He married her for her land, and when Burgh was his, he killed her so he could marry me and have Clopton, too. I have no doubt that in time I would also have had an "accident" – he was already flirting with Lady Ann from Hasketon: he ogled her all through our wedding feast, although I am sure it was her dairy farm that he really wanted.'

'I told you that Deblunville killed old Pernel,' said Hamon, sheathing his sword. 'But you did not listen to me.'

'Deblunville was more persuasive than you, Hamon,' said Janelle, rather bitterly. She turned to Bartholomew for support. 'Who did you believe – the dashing and personable

Deblunville, or the oafish, inarticulate man who hates him because his uncle tells him to?'

Bartholomew did not like to answer. He felt he did not know Hamon or Deblunville well enough to tell who was the more truthful of the pair, and was not inclined to come down on the side of Deblunville anyway, with Hamon glowering at having been described as oafish.

'And Deblunville was obsessed with the search for the golden calf,' Janelle continued, when no reply was forthcoming. 'He was out every night, despite my attempts to keep him with me. He believed Hamon was close to discovering it, and wanted to get to it first.'

'I *am* close to finding it,' protested Hamon.

'How?' asked Bartholomew curiously. 'Have you discovered a clue, such as the foundations of the old chapel near which the calf is said to be buried?'

'Well, no,' admitted Hamon. 'Not yet. But I will.' He looked fondly at Janelle. 'And then I will be richer than Deblunville. I will have my uncle's estates, and you will have Clopton and Burgh. Together, we will be a powerful force in the county.'

'But Isilia's child will inherit your uncle's manors,' said Bartholomew, unable to stop himself.

Hamon regarded him coldly. 'We will see about that.' He turned back to Janelle. 'Marry me! Wait a week or two, until it is seemly, and then marry me. Our alliance will make us rich and powerful, and I think we are a couple who could get along nicely together.'

'That is true,' she said, considering. 'My brains and your strength will make us a formidable force. We could rule the whole of the Lark Valley.'

Hamon's eyes glittered with excitement, and he took her into his arms. Disconcerted by the display of naked ambition and craving for wealth, Bartholomew backed away.

'You will not tell my uncle about my betrothal to Janelle,'

ordered Hamon over his shoulder, more interested in his woman than in the retreating physician. 'I would rather tell him myself. I will kill you if you mention it before I am ready.'

'To start the rule of your kingdom as you mean to continue?' asked Bartholomew, who had reached the trees at the edge of the glade, and was sufficiently disgusted to feel like being rash.

Hamon ignored him, his attention wholly on Janelle. Janelle, however, was less sanguine.

'Can he be trusted?' she asked, regarding Bartholomew uncertainly. 'How do we know he will not go straight to your uncle and tell him of our plans?'

'He has an advowson to write,' said Hamon. 'Now Alcote is dead, the Michaelhouse men have to rewrite the whole thing. He will be far too busy to meddle in our affairs.'

'But he was not too busy to follow you here,' Janelle pointed out.

Hamon sighed, and turned to face Bartholomew. 'If you tell my uncle about me and Janelle, I will tell William that you stole Eltisley's beef and buried it under an oak tree at midnight to effect a charm against Padfoot. He will have you dismissed from your College for practising witchcraft.'

'How do you know about that?' asked Bartholomew, aghast that the jaunt he had sought so carefully to conceal was apparently common knowledge.

'This is the country, Doctor. There are few secrets here. I know that Deblunville's men encountered you in the woods near Barchester, that a piece of beef was stolen from Eltisley, that Brother Michael's new linen disappeared, and that your servant is suddenly cured of his malady. I am not stupid, you know. You used Mother Goodman's charm to break Padfoot's hold.'

Bartholomew gazed at him. It was certainly true that William would react immediately and uncompromisingly on hearing Bartholomew's role in effecting Cynric's recovery. And the fanatical friar might do much worse than having Bartholomew dismissed from Michaelhouse – he would call in his Franciscan inquisitors and have him tried as a warlock. Janelle was unfair when she intimated that she had all the brains: Hamon's method of ensuring Bartholomew's silence was a brilliant one, given William's outspoken views on the subject of heresy.

The lovers' voices drifted back to Bartholomew as he made his escape.

'And if Grosnold dies without an heir, we could persuade him to name my child his successor,' schemed Janelle.

'You mean the child Deblunville fathered?' asked Hamon, sounding startled.

As he glanced back, surprised at the suggestion himself, Bartholomew glimpsed Janelle's unreadable smile.

'I am not carrying Deblunville's child,' she said enigmatically. 'Despite what you may have heard, and what I may have allowed people to believe.'

'You see?' said Michael, looking at Unwin's relic – the twist of parchment with the cluster of ancient hairs inside it – that Bartholomew had found beneath Norys's body the night before. 'I was right all along. Norys *did* kill Unwin to steal his relic.'

They were sitting in the church together, in the small hours of the following night, and Michael was taking a rest from his labours with the deed to hear Bartholomew's story about Hamon. The monk had been overly optimistic about what he could achieve that day. Exhaustion had claimed him and he had slept all afternoon and much of the evening, too, and had decided to work through the night: not at Wergen Hall, but in the church where he could claim he was praying for Alcote's singed remains.

Bartholomew, who also had slept much of the previous

day, was keeping him company, while Cynric and William were at Wergen Hall, carefully packing the few belongings that had survived the fire in the Half Moon, so that they would be ready to leave the instant the deed was completed.

As far as Bartholomew was concerned, Hamon's rash infatuation with Janelle made him a stronger suspect for killing Alcote. Janelle was very interested in material possessions, and Hamon might well see preventing Michaelhouse from owning the living of the church as something that would persuade her of his devotion. Michael was more interested in discussing the murder of Unwin, remaining convinced that Norys somehow lay at the centre of that mystery.

'We know that whoever killed Unwin probably also stole his purse. The purse – minus the relic – was then found with the bloody clothes on Norys's roof. Now, just when Norys's body reappears, the relic falls from his clothing on to the floor beneath his body, to be found by you.'

'The relic was not in his clothing,' said Bartholomew. 'I looked for it there. And it was not under the table before Tuddenham and his retinue arrived.'

'How can you be sure?' demanded Michael. 'It is dark in here. I can barely see you, and you are standing right next to me.'

'I am sure because I looked very carefully before the Tuddenhams arrived. I wanted to make certain that nothing *had* dropped from Norys's clothes, so I checked. I am absolutely positive it was not there before Tuddenham and his household came.'

'Then any one of them might have dropped the relic, or left it there for us to find,' said Michael, closing his eyes tiredly. 'Tuddenham, Hamon, Dame Eva, Isilia, Wauncy, Siric. Damn!' He slammed his clenched fist on the windowsill in frustration. 'If only we had been more observant!'

'Yes,' said Bartholomew ruefully. 'Because we know that

the only way someone could be in possession of the relic would be if he had killed Unwin, or had some knowledge of his death. Therefore, whoever put the relic under Norys's body is the murderer.'

'I suppose this killer wanted us to think exactly what we did,' said Michael, disappointed to learn, yet again, that absolute evidence of Norys's guilt was lacking. 'That the relic fell from Norys's clothing, and is therefore confirmation of his guilt.'

'No!' exclaimed Bartholomew suddenly, his voice loud in the silent church. 'That is not what happened. It is not even what we are supposed to think, because it is not meant to be there at all. Stoate dropped it!'

'What?' asked Michael dubiously. 'How have you arrived at that conclusion?'

Bartholomew straightened from where he been leaning against the wall, and began to pace as he reasoned it out. 'Stoate was in such a hurry to reach the side of his most affluent patient that he tripped up the chancel steps in his haste. His bag came open and some of its contents spilled out. The relic must have fallen with them.'

'Stoate killed Unwin?' asked Michael in disbelief. 'But why? This makes no sense, Matt!'

'Oh, no!' groaned Bartholomew, putting his hands to his head as the whole affair became crystal clear in his mind. All the disjointed scraps of evidence suddenly snapped together to form a picture that was so obvious, he was appalled he had not seen it before. 'I see what happened. How could I have been so stupid?'

'You tell me,' said Michael.

'The night Unwin died, Stoate introduced himself in the tavern. We had a lengthy conversation about various aspects of medicine.'

'Yes,' said Michael, remembering. 'All of them highly unpleasant.'

'I am sure Stoate told me he practised surgery – mainly bleeding, from the sound of it.'

'Yes, he did,' said Michael. 'You were inappropriately delighted about the whole business.'

'He denied yesterday that he ever said so,' said Bartholomew. He flopped on to the bench next to Michael, and closed his eyes. 'He said that Mother Goodman does it if it is needed, but Mother Goodman has told me that *he* did it on at least two occasions, including once when she was present. She interrupted our conversation in the Half Moon the first night we stayed there, to tell us the prices Stoate charged for opening vessels in different parts of the body, and he did not contradict her.'

Michael nodded. 'I remember that. So, Stoate is a liar. However, that does not also make him a murderer or a thief. I do not see where all this is leading, Matt.'

'Unwin's body had an injury on the arm, near the elbow, and one sleeve was drenched in blood. I see exactly what happened. Unwin went to Stoate to be bled, and Stoate bled him to death!'

Michael gazed at him for a moment, and then gave a short laugh of disbelief. 'The fatal wound was the cut to the elbow and not the stab in the stomach?'

'Yes,' said Bartholomew. 'It is more easily done than you might think. If the incision made for phlebotomy is too deep, or the wrong vein is cut, a person can bleed to death very quickly if the surgeon does not know how to stop it. Stoate is not a surgeon, and has not been trained to practise phlebotomy. He killed Unwin with his ignorance and arrogance!'

'So you are not exaggerating when you say bleeding is bad for the health?' said Michael. 'You had me convinced long before all this happened, but now I can promise you that no barber with his bloody knives will ever come near my veins.'

'I wish none had come near Unwin's,' said Bartholomew

fervently. 'I suppose his anxiety for his new post made him feel a need to drain away the humours that were making him nervous.'

'And Stoate killed him outside the church where we found all that blood,' said Michael, scratching his head.

'That was why there was so much of it on Unwin's sleeve. How could I have missed it?' Bartholomew ran a hand through his hair in agitation. 'It did not escape William: he asked me why there was blood on Unwin's arm, and I made a bad assumption – that it had drained out of the stomach when he had been lying in a different position than the one in which we found him.'

'And now Stoate is busily denying that he practises phlebotomy, lest you associate the small cut on Unwin's elbow with a physician who dabbles in surgery.'

'But why did he not deny it from the start?' asked Bartholomew, rubbing his head. 'Why claim that night in the tavern – within a very short time of Unwin's death – that he *did* bleed people?'

'Two good reasons,' said Michael, considering. 'First, Mother Goodman was sitting near enough to hear every word; her position as village midwife means that she knows he bleeds people – and we have seen enough of that lady to guess she would not sit quietly knitting, while a physician she loathes lies about what he does. And second, you were very persistent with your questions, whether you appreciated it or not, and had the poor fellow scrambling to provide you with answers.'

'I did not!' protested Bartholomew. 'You make me sound like William in inquisitor mode.'

'You can be very intimidating, Matt, particularly to people who do not have your training. And on that subject, I can also say that I very much doubt Stoate has been to Paris and Bologna Universities as he claims. He is too young, and why should someone with those qualifications settle in a remote village like this? He would be in London or York or Norwich, making his fortune.'

'He certainly dispenses odd cures,' agreed Bartholomew. 'Like ground snails for sore eyes. Our eyes are better, but the eyes of everyone who slapped that paste on them are still inflamed.'

'So, crushed snails is not something that the mighty physicians of Paris recommend, then?' asked Michael with a smile. 'Nor do they teach bleeding?'

'They do not,' said Bartholomew. 'It is heartily denounced as something tradesmen do. But I cannot believe I was so blind about that cut on Unwin's elbow. After he had bled to death, Stoate must have dragged Unwin back into the church, and then stabbed the body and stole the purse to make it appear as though he had been murdered by an opportunistic thief for his belongings.'

'And it stands to reason that if Stoate stabbed Unwin's corpse to make his accidental death seem like murder, he also did the same to Mistress Freeman's throat. You were right all along, Matt. The killer heard that Norys had been accused of killing Unwin, and Mistress Freeman was desecrated to make us believe that was true.'

'So, what shall we do?' asked Bartholomew. 'Stoate is with Tuddenham at Wergen Hall now.'

'We must confront him,' said Michael. 'And the sooner, the better.'

They headed up the path toward Tuddenham's manor. Since dawn was only just beginning to lighten the sky, most of Wergen Hall's inhabitants were still in bed, and the house was in darkness. Eventually, Siric answered the door to Bartholomew's insistent hammering.

'What now?' he snapped. 'Sir Thomas is sleeping, and needs no more leeches tonight.'

'Is Stoate with him?' asked Michael.

Siric shook his head. 'Sir Thomas had a bad night, but

about an hour ago he started to sleep like a baby. I did not want a physician prodding him and disturbing his rest, so I sent Stoate home.'

While Cynric went to rouse William to continue the vigil for the charred remains in the church – feeling, no doubt, that the slippery Alcote needed all the prayers he could get – Bartholomew and Michael took the path back to the village, and made their way to Stoate's house. His horse, still tailless thanks to Deynman, was saddled, and weighted down with two hefty bags.

'It looks as though Stoate knows the game is up,' Michael whispered to Bartholomew. 'He is about to leave.'

There was a sharp click and both men swung round. Stoate stood behind them holding a loaded crossbow.

'Stay where you are,' he ordered sharply. 'I will use this if I have to.'

For a moment, no one said a word. Bartholomew and Michael gaped at Stoate's crossbow, while Stoate glared back challengingly. A gleam of desperation in his eyes suggested to Bartholomew that Stoate would indeed use the weapon if necessary – and perhaps even if it were not. Michael stepped forward.

'You might hit one of us,' he said calmly, 'but you will not have the time to reload before the other attacks. Michaelhouse men do not approve of charlatan physicians who kill with their ignorance and greed – you would not stand a chance.'

'Greed?' asked Stoate, startled.

'Yes, greed,' said Michael. 'Making a few extra pennies by bleeding poor villagers who do not know that you are no more a physician than I am.'

Stoate's finger tightened on the trigger of his crossbow. 'I studied in Paris and Bologna,' he said angrily. 'Ask anyone around here.'

'How would they know?' asked Bartholomew. 'They, like

us, only have your word for it.' He began to move away from Michael, making it impossible for Stoate to point his weapon at both of them at the same time.

'Stay where you are,' said Stoate, understanding what he was doing immediately. He waved the weapon at his house, and glanced up at the sky. 'Go inside and close the door.'

'Which do you want us to do?' asked Michael, deliberately aggravating. 'Stay where we are, or enter your charming home?'

'Move!' snapped Stoate. He glanced anxiously at the sky again. Rutted roads and recent rain meant that riding fast while it was still dark would be tantamount to suicide, yet he knew he needed to be away before people awoke and clogged the paths as they walked to the fields. Bartholomew took several steps and then hesitated, wondering how he might delay Stoate's departure until either he was prevented from making a speedy escape by the labourers on the roads, or Cynric realised that something was amiss and came to look for them.

'Do not try my patience, Bartholomew,' hissed Stoate. 'It will not be you I shoot, it will be your fat friend. I know you would never leave him while he is mortally wounded, and that will allow me to make a clean escape. Or you can move into my house, and no one need be hurt.'

Michael pushed open the door, and Bartholomew followed him inside. Stoate stood in the entrance, watching them minutely, his finger never leaving the trigger of his weapon.

'Now sit against that wall, and put your legs out in front of you.'

It was a position that would make any sudden lunge at Stoate virtually impossible – unless the lunger had no objection to being impaled by a crossbow quarrel. Stoate looked at the sky again.

'All this started with Unwin, did it not?' said Michael, trying to make himself comfortable on the floor. 'You bled him – at his request, probably – but you were careless, and he bled to death.'

'It was an accident,' said Stoate harshly. 'These things happen in medicine. I suppose I should not have left him once I had made the incision, but I had not wanted to attend him in the first place. Grosnold had found Unwin sick and shaking, and was concerned. He ordered me to bleed him, and Grosnold is not a man easily refused.'

'You made an incision in Unwin, and then left him unattended?' asked Bartholomew, appalled. 'What were you thinking of? That is one of the grossest cases of negligence I have ever heard!'

'He said he would be all right,' protested Stoate uneasily. 'When I came back – only moments later – he was stone dead and there was blood all over the ground. What else could I do but try to disguise his death? I moved him into the church – fortunately for me, most of the blood in his body had already leaked out, and so it was not as messy as it could have been – and made his death appear to be a murder by stabbing him and taking his purse.'

'Grosnold ordered you to bleed Unwin?' asked Bartholomew. 'What was he doing back in Grundisburgh after his spectacular departure across the village green?'

'I have no idea,' said Stoate, casting yet another anxious glance at the sky. 'I try not to become involved in the sinister affairs of the lords of the manor around here. They are not men to be trusted.'

'Unlike the physicians,' muttered Michael. He shook his head in wonderment. 'So, Eltisley really did see Grosnold with Unwin in the churchyard. But he was not holding Unwin's arm in a threatening manner as we all assumed; he was being solicitous, because Unwin's nervousness was making him unwell. Grosnold even sent for a physician to bleed him, and was doubtless "surreptitious" because Unwin told him Matt would not approve of phlebotomy.'

Stoate nodded. 'I was summoned because Unwin told him that Bartholomew would refuse. If only I had refused, too! Then none of this would have happened.'

'But why did Grosnold deny speaking to Unwin if he had nothing to hide?' asked Bartholomew.

Stoate shrugged. 'All I know is that he instructed me to say nothing about his meeting with Unwin. He gave me five marks for my silence. It seemed a good deal: I would say nothing about his role, therefore he would say nothing about mine.'

'So, what happened to Mistress Freeman?' asked Bartholomew. 'She did not die of a slit throat; she died from eating the mussels that were scattered all over her floor. As did Norys.'

'The mussels killed her?' asked Stoate in astonishment. 'They were tainted?'

'Were they a gift from you?' asked Bartholomew. 'To ensure she was at home when you came to kill her, and make it appear as though Norys had done it?'

Stoate gave a humourless laugh. 'Yes, they were a gift from me, and yes, they were to ensure she was home when I called. The plan was to share them with her, and then to convince her that it had been Norys we had seen together, running from the church.'

'But you saw no one running from the church,' said Michael. 'The cloaked figure was you.'

'I did see someone,' said Stoate earnestly. 'Everything I have told you is the truth, except the length of the cloak. I *did* speak to Mistress Freeman by the ford – Norys was not with her, and she told me that he had gone to fetch her shawl, because the evening was turning chilly – and we *did* see someone running out of the church. And whoever it was *was* rubbing his eyes.'

'Why lie about the length of the cloak?'

'Because the one I wore that night was short, very like that which I saw on the person running from the church. I realised that I needed to create confusion, if I did not want other witnesses to say the short-cloaked figure was me. So, I said he wore a long one.'

'So the cloaked figure you saw with Mistress Freeman was just someone who had innocently stumbled on the body you had deposited in the church, and who had fled lest he be accused of a murder he did not commit?' asked Michael. 'Two people ran from the church that day wearing cloaks – you and this other person?'

'So it would appear. But neither of us fled unnoticed: several people saw us – as your colleague Father William discovered when he practised his nasty Inquisition techniques on the village – and some may well have seen me, not the other person.'

He was right, thought Bartholomew. Some of the villagers William had browbeaten *had* claimed to have seen a man in a short cloak, not a long one: they had seen Stoate, the real killer of Unwin.

'But why were you wearing a cloak at all?' he asked, still puzzled. 'It was hot that day.'

'When one wears yellow hose, one does not sit on grass,' said Stoate impatiently. 'I took my cloak with me to spread on the ground, so that the village boys would not jeer at a green-stained seat. Little did I know how useful it would be: it also allowed me to carry Unwin back to the church without traces of blood seeping on to my best clothes.'

Michael shook his head unhappily. 'How do we know we can believe you? You have lied about everything else.'

'I have lied about nothing, except the length of the cloak,' said Stoate, most of his attention on the slowly brightening sky again. 'You never asked me whether I killed Unwin, and you have never questioned me about Mistress Freeman.'

'What about your medical qualifications, then?' demanded Michael. 'They are false.'

'They are not. My father took me to Paris when I was

fifteen, where I sat in a library and read Galen's *Tegni*. Two years later we went to Bologna, where I found another library and read it again. So, you see, I have not lied to you about that either. I told you I studied medicine in Paris and Bologna, and I have.'

'But that claim is grossly misleading,' objected Bartholomew. 'You know perfectly well that people will assume you mean you have studied properly, not just read a book that you could not have understood without also reading all the commentaries that go with it.'

'I do extremely well as a physician,' said Stoate smugly.

'By giving foxglove to treat Tuddenham's stomach disease?' demanded Bartholomew. 'By dispensing a foul ointment of cat grease and crushed snails for burns? By prescribing a potion containing betony and pennyroyal to the pregnant Janelle without cautioning her how to use it?'

Stoate wiped a bead of sweat from his face with his forefinger. He slapped his hand back on to the weapon again as Bartholomew tensed, weighing up the chances of reaching Stoate before he could fire. Michael gave him an agonised look, sensing that Stoate's nervousness might well lead him into shooting if Bartholomew gave the impression he was about to attack at any moment.

'I lose very few patients,' said Stoate coldly. 'Which is more than can be said of you, from what you have told me about your practice in Cambridge.'

'You will miss having a rich patient like Tuddenham,' said Michael, worried that Bartholomew might start an argument that would goad the nervous physician into shooting at them.

'I will not have him for much longer anyway,' said Stoate. 'Now is a good time to leave.' He peered at the ground, trying to ascertain whether the dawn was sufficiently advanced for riding.

'What do you mean?' asked Michael, realising they were running out of time. Stoate would not spend a moment longer than necessary before he made his escape, and Michael sensed that Stoate intended to shoot him anyway, just so that he would not be followed. 'Or have you left him a purge that will expel his soul from his body as well as his evil humours?'

Stoate pulled an unpleasant face at him, and declined to answer. He finished checking the ground and then squinted up at the sky, abruptly turning his attention to Michael when the monk raised a hand to scratch his head.

'So what happened in Mistress Freeman's house?' asked Michael, sweat breaking out on his forehead as he tried to think of something to say to delay what he knew was inevitable. 'You presented her with mussels. Then what?'

'I thought she could cook them for us to eat together, while I worked to convince her that it was Norys who killed Unwin – just as you believed.'

'And when you arrived you found that she had shared her mussels with Norys instead,' said Bartholomew. 'You were lucky. You would have died, too, had you eaten them.'

Stoate shook his head, his eyes distant. 'I had no idea what had happened – I will have a few strong words with that fishmonger when I next see him. There was no answer from her door, so I looked through the window, and there they were – Mistress Freeman and Norys, dead in each other's arms. I was afraid I would be blamed, since people know I call on her from time to time, so I slashed her throat. I knew you would assume Norys did it.'

Seeing him distracted by his memories, Bartholomew slipped his hand in his medicine bag, groping for one of his surgical knives. He eased it up his sleeve, and quickly withdrew his hand.

'But there was no blood, was there?' he said. 'Corpses do not bleed.'

'I had forgotten that. I knew that someone like you would be suspicious of a slit throat with no blood, so I fetched some from the slaughterhouse. Everyone knew a pig had been killed there for Hamon, so I guessed there would be blood in the vat.'

'But you used far too much of it,' said Bartholomew.

'I had to make it look convincing,' said Stoate. 'Then I took some old clothes, dipped them in the blood, wrapped them in a long cloak that I found in my attic – along with Unwin's purse – and flung the whole lot on Norys's roof, where I knew someone would see them.'

'But you kept the relic,' said Michael, removing it from his scrip and waving it at Stoate. 'That was what told us who had really killed Unwin. It fell out of your bag when you tripped up the chancel steps in the dark, rushing to help Tuddenham when he was ill.'

In a lightning-quick movement, Stoate darted across the room and snatched it from Michael's hand. He had the crossbow pointed at the monk again before Bartholomew could do more than let the knife slip from his sleeve into the palm of his hand.

'I will sell this when I reach somewhere it will not be recognised,' said Stoate, pleased. 'What is it exactly? A lock of the Virgin's hair?'

'It is St Botolph's beard,' said Michael, shocked. 'What kind of hair did you think our Blessed Virgin had, man?'

Stoate looked quickly at the sky, then glanced along the road. Bartholomew's fingers tightened on the knife, trying not to think about what might happen if he missed, and if Stoate were startled or angered into firing the crossbow. Stoate, however, was no fool.

'Sit still,' he ordered sharply. 'And put your hands in front of you, where I can see them.'

While Michael sighed and puffed at the indignity, Bartholomew shoved the knife under his leg, and rested his empty hands in his lap, cursing himself for hesitating when he should have hurled the weapon.

'And what did you do with Norys's body?' asked Michael. 'Pay three louts to bury it in Unwin's grave for you?'

'No,' said Stoate, still watching Bartholomew for hints of trickery. 'That had nothing to do with me. I left his body in the woods near Barchester, and I have no idea how he managed to arrive in Unwin's tomb. I do not desecrate graves.'

'Just the corpses that lie in them,' said Bartholomew, seeing Stoate glance up at the sky once more. It was now quite pale, and Bartholomew could make out individual leaves on the trees. A good horseman would be able to make reasonable time, if he were careful. Stoate took a deep breath and tightened his finger on the trigger, while Bartholomew let one of his hands drop to the floor, easing it toward the knife that pressed into his leg.

'But I killed no one,' insisted Stoate. 'Unwin, Mistress Freeman and Norys were accidents – as it seems to me you had already reasoned anyway.'

'But what about the man hanging at Bond's Corner?' asked Michael, desperately playing for time. 'Did you kill him? And what about Alcote, or was that an accident too?'

'I know nothing about Alcote or any hanged men,' said Stoate, glancing up at the sky for the last time. 'Now, gentlemen, pleasant though your company has been, it is time for me to be on my way.'

Before Bartholomew could grab the knife, Stoate had pulled the trigger on the crossbow, aiming at Michael. There was a click that sounded sickeningly loud. With a sharp intake of breath, Bartholomew gazed at Michael in horror. Michael stared at Stoate, then gave a bellow of anger, struggling to stand while Stoate looked stupidly at the jammed mechanism on his weapon. Bartholomew snatched up his knife and hurled it before Stoate could recover his wits. The wicked little blade sliced cleanly through one of Stoate's flowing sleeves, and impaled itself in the door jamb, vibrating with the force of the throw.

Startled into action, Stoate heaved the crossbow at Michael. There was a whir and a snap as the mechanism unfouled, and the bolt was loosed. Michael dropped to the floor with a howl of pain. Seeing the monk fall, Stoate darted out of the door, and Bartholomew heard something thump against it as it was blocked from the outside. Stomach churning, Bartholomew scrambled to Michael, who lay clutching his chest.

'I am hit, Matt!' he groaned. 'Murdered by a physician!'

'Where?' shouted Bartholomew, searching frantically for a wound, but finding none. He heard a clatter of hooves outside as Stoate mounted his horse.

Michael's hand fluttered weakly over his side, but Bartholomew could still see nothing, not even a tear in his habit where the quarrel had sliced through it. Then his shaking hands encountered something hard, and Michael gave a gasp. He pushed his hand down the front of Michael's gown, anticipating some dreadful injury, but then saw the crossbow bolt embedded in the wall above his head. With a sigh of relief, he sat back on his heels, and rubbed a trembling hand through his hair. Michael regarded him with frightened eyes.

'Is it a mortal wound?' he whispered.

'You fell on your purse,' said Bartholomew. 'The quarrel missed you altogether. You are only bruised. That will teach you to carry so much gold.'

Michael sat up and prodded himself carefully. 'Stoate is escaping!' he exclaimed, when a quick examination convinced him he was unharmed.

He scrambled to his feet and joined Bartholomew at the barred door, jostling the physician out of the way to hit it with a tremendous crash that ripped the entire frame from the wall. Bartholomew raced out into the road to see Stoate disappearing round the corner in a thunder of hooves.

'You will never catch him!' yelled Michael as Bartholomew began to give chase. 'I am going to Tuddenham.'

In the distance Michael spotted Cynric, who had been searching for them. He shouted for the Welshman to follow Bartholomew, while he ran in the opposite direction to fetch help.

Bartholomew tore down the path Stoate had taken, running as hard as he could. As he rounded the corner, he could see the horse in front of him, galloping down the narrow track with its saddle bags bouncing behind it, and Stoate clinging on for dear life. Bartholomew ran harder, feeling the blood pound in his head and his lungs pump as though they would burst. Stoate turned another bend, and Bartholomew shot after him, hurling his medicine bag away when it threatened to slow him down. When he rounded the next corner, Stoate was out of sight. It was hopeless – he could never catch a horse on foot. Gradually, he stopped, breath sobbing in his chest as he fought for air.

'He is long gone,' said Cynric, appearing beside him, panting hard. 'He will be in Ipswich before we can organise a chase, and then he will be on a ship bound for France or the Low Countries.' He kicked at the ground furiously. 'That damned Eltisley! Stoate would not have escaped if he had not damaged my bow.'

'What has Stoate done to warrant shooting him down in cold blood?' came Eltisley's smooth voice from behind them. Bartholomew and Cynric spun round, and saw the landlord standing there with a bow of his own, flanked by three of his sullen customers, who looked a good deal more proficient with their weapons than he did.

'You will not catch him on foot,' said Bartholomew, thinking that Eltisley meant to help arrest a killer and a desecrator of corpses.

'I have no intention of catching him at all,' said Eltisley softly. 'It is you I want.'

CHAPTER 12

ELTISLEY SCRATCHED HIS BLISTERED FACE – STILL smeared with Stoate's paste of crushed snails and mint in cat grease – with his free hand, and jabbed his sword into the small of Bartholomew's back to make him walk faster. It was still not fully light, and Eltisley and three friends – those Bartholomew had seen hunched sullenly over their ale in the Half Moon – had directed Bartholomew and Cynric away from the village on a path that led west. Cynric had been stripped of his arsenal, and Bartholomew had no weapons anyway, not even the surgical knives that he carried in his medicine bag, which was now lying in the bushes on the Ipswich road. Eltisley bragged to his men about how he had the foresight to damage Cynric's bow with one of his potions.

'Do you have any of your medicine for blisters?' he queried, scrubbing vigorously at a cheek that was red and running. 'That remedy Stoate suggested does not seem to be working.'

'You can ask him for another,' said Bartholomew, 'when you meet your partner in crime later.'

'I do not know what you are talking about,' said Eltisley. 'I have no partner – and if I did, I would not choose a physician. Whatever caused Stoate to flee the village has nothing to do with me.'

'He killed Unwin,' said Bartholomew. 'He opened a vein and allowed him to bleed to death.'

'That was careless,' said Eltisley. 'So Norys did not kill the friar, as everyone believes? It was Stoate? Well, I never! But do you have any of your lotion or not? My burns are itching and driving me to distraction.'

'No, but I imagined you would have a remedy of your own,' Bartholomew said, hoping that Eltisley would use one of his evil concoctions and make himself ill.

'All my potions were destroyed with the Half Moon. It is a dreadful loss to the village.'

'How did you manage to blow up your tavern without killing yourself?' asked Bartholomew, stumbling as Eltisley poked him again. 'Lay a trail of inflammable powder on the ground, so that you could light it from a safe distance?'

'I experimented with that the other night, but it did not work. So, I invented another way – I soaked a piece of twine in saltpetre and lit it. Saltpetre is one of the ingredients I used to create my little bang – along with charcoal and sulphur, as you surmised. It was all rather more dramatic than I intended, however. I did not mean it to destroy my entire tavern.'

'Just poor Alcote on the upper floor?' asked Bartholomew coldly.

'Now that was a waste. If I had to lose my tavern, I would have preferred that all you Michaelhouse scholars had gone with it, not just one. You were beginning to make nuisances of yourselves, with your near-completed advowsons and your meddling in village affairs. Still, I have you now.'

'What is this all about?' demanded Bartholomew, stopping and turning to face him. 'I do not see why we should make killing us easier for you by walking somewhere conveniently secluded.'

'At the moment, I am prepared to allow that dreadful friar to go free – he is not intelligent enough to pose a threat to me and my affairs. But if you make life difficult, I shall change my mind. The choice is yours.'

Bartholomew turned and began to trudge along the path again, Cynric following. He was thankful he had sent Deynman and Horsey away to safety, and only wished he had done the same for the others.

It was a dismal morning, with low, grey clouds and a wetness in the air that made everything foggy and dull. Bartholomew tried to piece together the mess of facts that had accumulated to make sense out of his present predicament. Although he had always suspected that Eltisley was not all he seemed, to be captured by him and his henchmen at arrow-point so soon after the encounter with Stoate was still a shock, and he could not imagine what he and his colleagues had done to warrant Eltisley's determination to kill them all.

'What will you do now that you have lost your tavern and your workshop?' he asked, initiating a conversation to see what he might learn. 'Where will you perform your experiments?'

'Another tavern will be provided,' Eltisley said confidently. 'I am too valuable to lose.'

'Provided by whom?' asked Bartholomew. 'Tuddenham? Hamon? Or is it one of the other lords of the manor, such as Bardolf or Grosnold?'

Eltisley smiled gloatingly. 'You do not have the wits to work it out, despite the fact that you have all the information at your fingertips.'

'Such as what?' asked Bartholomew, racking his brains. Eltisley, however, declined to answer and they trudged along in silence. Once they turned down a little-used trackway that cut north, Bartholomew knew exactly where Eltisley was taking them, and it did not surprise him in the least.

'Barchester,' he muttered to Cynric. 'We are going to Barchester.'

Cynric faltered, and Eltisley gave him an encouraging poke with a dagger. Cynric spun round fast and had ripped it from Eltisley's hands before the taverner realised what was happening. His men, however, were not so easily taken unawares, and had their bows raised and their arrows pointed at Cynric before the Welshman could take a single step toward the trees that would mask his escape.

Eltisley snatched the dagger back, and pushed Cynric forward again. 'That is exactly the kind of behaviour I recommend you avoid if you do not want William sent back to Cambridge in a wooden box. And your students – I will track them down and kill them, too. Now move, and no talking.'

Cynric began to walk again, his face expressionless, although Bartholomew knew he was seething with rage. One of the men, who carried a sword at his side, sported a painful-looking bruise on one cheekbone. It looked to Bartholomew exactly the kind of injury that might have been caused by a hurled heavy metal ring, and Bartholomew could only assume that it had been Eltisley and his henchmen who had been burying Norys in Unwin's gave. But why? The pardoner was already dead, and had been dumped in the woods by Stoate.

'If there is another chance, run,' he muttered to Cynric, when Eltisley fell back to say something to his friends. 'Get the others, and take them as far away from this place as you can.'

Cynric said nothing.

'Please, Cynric,' pleaded Bartholomew in a desperate whisper, when he realised Cynric had no intention of leaving him. 'Eltisley intends to kill us anyway. This nonsense about letting William go free is just a ploy to gain our co-operation.'

'No talking.' Eltisley jabbed at Bartholomew with his dagger. Cynric spun round, his face dark with anger, but Bartholomew pulled him on, knowing that it would take very little for the unstable Eltisley to order his companions to shoot, and they looked like the kind of men to do it.

Eventually the tattered roofs of Barchester came into view,

sticking forlornly through their veil of trees. In the grey light of the overcast morning, with low, dirty clouds overhead, the deserted village looked even more miserable than usual with its broken doors, unstable walls and ruined thatches. Bartholomew walked cautiously, alert for the sinister growls and unearthly screeches that would precede the old woman and her mad dog hurtling out of the undergrowth to attack them. The woods, however, were as silent and as still as the fog that swathed them.

'You are looking for Padfoot,' said Eltisley, watching him. 'You need not fear – he is not here today. Even spectres have business of their own to attend.'

'What nonsense are you speaking?' said Bartholomew, irritated that the man should take him for a fool. 'Padfoot is no more spectre than you are. It is the crone's tame dog. Do you pay her to stay here and frighten travellers so that they will not linger?' He snapped his fingers as realisation dawned. 'Of course you do! I found a bright new penny in one of the huts when we first came here.'

'Mad Megin likes shiny things,' said Eltisley. 'Especially coins.'

Bartholomew continued, as certain things became clear. 'When we first arrived, Tuddenham told us that it was you who discovered Mad Megin's drowned body in the river last winter, and you who buried her in the churchyard. I see now that she is not buried at all.'

Eltisley smiled. 'But I did find her drowned in the river. I brought her back to life, and now she is my servant.'

'You did what?' asked Bartholomew, startled despite himself.

Eltisley made an impatient sound. 'I brought her back to life. I took her out of the river, pressed the water from her lungs, and gave her a few drops of one of my potions. Within moments, she was gasping for breath, and her life-beat was strong and sure.'

'Then she was probably not dead in the first place,' said Bartholomew.

'She was dead,' said Eltisley with absolute conviction. 'She was not breathing when I first found her. And her experience changed her. She is not the same woman now as she was before she died – she does not even remember her name.'

'You damaged her, then,' said Bartholomew. 'I have heard of cases where people have been dragged back from the brink of death and unless it is done immediately, the mind is impaired. It would have been kinder to let her die.'

'You believe death is better than life?' asked Eltisley, astonished. 'But all my work has been devoted to prolonging life – creating potions to cure diseases, making wines that repel the evil miasmas that bring summer agues, concocting remedies to prevent shaking fevers and palsies. Life is always better than death.'

'And how well did these potions work against the plague?' asked Bartholomew.

'Two in three survived thanks to my mixtures,' said Eltisley. 'Almost everyone who took Stoate's red arsenic and lead died, but my boiled-snake and primrose water was far more successful.'

'A third was about what most villages and towns lost,' Bartholomew pointed out. 'Your potion made no difference at all.'

'That is not true,' said Eltisley, nettled. 'Many villages were completely wiped out, like Barchester, and most religious communities lost more than a third of their number. That Grundisburgh only lost a hundred souls to the Death was entirely due to me.'

'Is that the essence of your experiments, then?' asked Bartholomew. 'To combat diseases?'

'Not entirely. I am searching for the element that will raise the dead from their graves.'

'What do you mean?' asked Bartholomew uneasily.

Eltisley smiled at him as though he were a wayward and not particularly intelligent child. 'I am going to find a cure for death.'

'And did you succeed with that poor animal you had in your workshop the other night?' asked Bartholomew, once he had recovered from his shock, recalling Eltisley with the dead dog the night Cynric stole the beef.

Eltisley frowned absently. 'No, but I have made some adjustments, and I believe the balance of elements is correct now. Of course, I realise that a dog is different from a human – it is always better to experiment on humans. I was successful with Mad Megin, and I intend to continue my work until I have all the people in Grundisburgh churchyard walking among us.'

Bartholomew shuddered at the image. 'But most of them will be nothing but bones. Will your potion restore their flesh, too?'

'I can apply my mind to that little problem later,' said Eltisley dismissively.

'But do you want Grundisburgh to be full of people like Megin?' asked Bartholomew, repelled.

'Megin has served me well,' said Eltisley carelessly. 'If Padfoot does not succeed in chasing away intruders, she does it for me. Or my friends here. They go out at night wearing masks, and rob people on the Old Road – there is nothing like rumours of outlaws to deter unwanted visitors.'

'They do more than deter,' objected Bartholomew. 'They kill. Alcote came across a group of travellers who had been attacked the day we arrived in Grundisburgh, and one of them was dying. He paid Alcote to say masses for his soul at St Edmundsbury.'

Eltisley sniggered nastily. 'Alcote should have said them for himself. But there is no problem with the occasional traveller being dispatched on the Old Road – it merely means that the danger is taken more seriously. They attacked you, I understand, when you first came here.'

'And I shot one in the arm,' said Cynric with satisfaction. 'They fled into the bushes like frightened deer when they encountered a real fighting man.'

'I know why you are keen to prevent people coming here,' said Bartholomew quickly, before Cynric could incite the surly men to anger. 'Barchester is where you conduct your experiments on the dead. Although I looked in the houses, and saw nothing unusual, I did not look in the church.'

'Well, now is your chance,' said Eltisley, gesturing that they should ascend the incline on which the church stood.

There was no sign of Mad Megin or her white dog as they walked up the rise. The building stood as still and silent as ever, with ivy darkening its walls and weaving through the broken tiles of its roof. Eltisley made his way to the small door Bartholomew had been about to enter when Megin had made her appearance, and pushed it open. It creaked on unsteady leather hinges, and sagged against the wall. He stood back, and indicated that Bartholomew and Cynric were to enter.

Inside, wooden benches held more phials, jugs, bottles and pots than Bartholomew could count. They were all around the walls, and more of them stood on the altar that had been dragged from its eastern end to the middle of the nave. Dark streaks up the walls and across the paved floor suggested accidents and miscalculations galore, and the whole church had a metallic, burned smell to it. Bartholomew was certain it could not be healthy.

Eltisley struggled with a ring set in a heavy stone slab in the chancel. With a spray of dirt, it came free, revealing a sinister black hole.

'Perhaps you would wait in there,' said Eltisley. 'It is as secure a place as I know, and no one will hear you shouting for help – except Mad Megin, I suppose, but she will do nothing about it.'

'What is it?' asked Bartholomew, glancing down at the pitch darkness with a distinct lack of enthusiasm.

'It is the old crypt, where the lords of Barchester and their families were buried before the plague ended their line,' said Eltisley cheerfully. 'They will reward me handsomely when they rise from the dead to reclaim their manor.'

'Is that why you are doing all this?' asked Bartholomew, looking around at the phials and bottles that lined the room. 'You want to be rewarded for your efforts by the dead?'

'I will be the richest man alive,' said Eltisley gleefully. 'And all those who have helped me will also reap the benefits. I can be a very generous man.'

'And who has helped you?' asked Bartholomew. 'Tuddenham? Grosnold? Hamon?'

Eltisley smiled. 'You can work that out while you wait. It will give you something to do.'

'We cannot go into a tomb with victims of the plague,' said Bartholomew, aghast. 'Even opening this vault might cause the disease to spread again. Are you totally insane?'

Eltisley regarded him coldly. 'I am not in the slightest insane. And no one who died of the plague is down there. Mad Megin buried all of those in a pit in the churchyard. Now, hurry up. Do not be afraid if you hear rustlings and voices, by the way. I have given the corpses several doses of my potions, and I anticipate some of them will show signs of life soon.'

Sceptical though he was about Eltisley's talents in that area, sitting in a tomb with long-dead corpses that were expected soon to come alive was not the way Bartholomew fancied spending his morning.

'No,' he said firmly, folding his arms.

One of the sullen drinkers stepped forward quickly, and gave him a push that knocked him off balance. Eltisley stuck out a foot, and Bartholomew found himself tumbling into the blackness. He opened his mouth to yell, but had landed before he could make a sound, thumping down a set of cold, damp steps into a musty chamber veiled in cobwebs. Cynric followed him moments later, and the trap-door thudded shut. There was a rumbling sound as something was dragged over it so that they could not escape, and then silence. They sat absolutely still in the darkness.

Bartholomew looked around him, straining his eyes in the pitch black to try to make out what kind of place they were in. He could see nothing at all, and could not even hear the voices of Eltisley and his friends in the church above. It was indeed as silent as the grave. He shivered. It was cold, too, and smelled of wet bones, worms and rotting grave-clothes. He heard a faint rustle, and leapt to his feet, banging his head on the roof as he did so.

'What was that?' whispered Cynric shakily.

The rustle came again, slightly louder, and then something ran across Bartholomew's foot. He forced himself not to shout, and scrambled up the steps to where he thought Cynric was sitting.

'Just a mouse.' He coughed. 'We will suffocate in here.'

'No,' said Cynric. 'I can see daylight around the edges of the slab. We will not lack fresh air.'

'This is horrible,' said Bartholomew, trying to move further up the stairs, away from the ominous scrabbling that came from the floor of the vault. 'I am sorry, Cynric. I have dragged you into something dreadful yet again.'

'You certainly have,' agreed Cynric. 'More dreadful than anything I could have imagined. How are we going to escape?'

Bartholomew glanced to the thin rectangle of light that outlined the trap-door. 'We could open that.'

Cynric tried first, then Bartholomew, then both together,

but the slab was heavy, and whatever had been placed over it rendered it totally immovable. Cynric slumped down, and Bartholomew could see his dejected silhouette in the faint light that filtered around the slab.

'That mad landlord intends to use us for his vile experiments,' he said in a low voice. 'He will kill us, and then try to raise us from the dead. I do not know which I fear more.'

Bartholomew could think of nothing to say. He sat quietly, listening to the rustling growing louder, closer and more confident, and once he thought he heard a squeak. He thought about what Eltisley had told him, and tried to make sense of it all. Some details became clearer, but he was certain Eltisley was not the sole power behind the evil dealings at Grundisburgh, and that someone was leading him, encouraging him and providing him with the funds to continue his work.

Although it felt like an age, not much time had passed before there was a rumble from above, and they heard someone struggling to lift the slab once again. Cynric tensed, and flung himself out of the vault the moment the gap was large enough. He was so fast that he had overpowered Eltisley before the landlord realised what was happening. Bartholomew reached out and seized the foot of one of the henchmen, pulling him off balance, and clambered quickly out of the hole to help Cynric wrestle with another. To one side he heard a yell, and saw Michael struggling between another two of Eltisley's surly customers.

A crossbow quarrel snapped loudly as it hit the floor, bouncing off to disappear into the blackness of the vault. Bartholomew could hear Eltisley screaming in anger and frustration, and Michael fighting to free himself from his captors. But it was an unequal battle. Eltisley's men had swords and daggers, and one of them was already rewinding his crossbow for another shot. Cynric was brought up short by a dagger at his throat, while Bartholomew lost his balance and was toppled back down into the vault by one of Eltisley's wild pushes. Moments later, Cynric was thrust in after him, and then Michael, tumbling in a flurry of flailing arms and legs to land heavily on Bartholomew. The slab fell into place, and there was a rumble as it was secured once more.

'That was lucky,' said Michael, sitting up. 'You broke my fall.'

'And you broke my legs,' mumbled Bartholomew, squirming to free himself of the monk's immense weight. 'Stand up, Brother. I cannot breathe!'

Cynric darted back to the steps, to sit as far away from the floor of the vault as he could. Michael picked himself up, and peered around him.

'Now what?' he asked.

'We cannot escape,' said Cynric gloomily from his perch. 'What you just saw was our only chance. They will not allow us to take them by surprise again. We are doomed.'

'We are not,' said Michael firmly. 'I will not be dispatched by a loathsome maniac like Eltisley. If I am to die because another takes my life, it will be a worthy adversary, and not some madman who believes he can bring people back from the dead.'

'He told you all that, did he?' asked Bartholomew. 'All about the riches he hopes to gain from granting dead people an unexpected new lease of life?'

Michael made a dismissive sound. 'The man is a fool! The dead do not keep their earthly riches after they die – that is all inherited by the next of kin. What he will have is a lot of paupers, with nothing to give him but the rags in which they were buried.'

'Did you explain that to him?' asked Bartholomew. He started backward when he touched Michael's hand in the darkness. It was cold and clammy, and felt like that of a corpse.

'I did not bother,' said Michael loftily. 'Still, it would make for some intriguing legal precedents about the question of ownership.'

'We should be thinking about how we can escape, not speculating on points of law,' said Bartholomew, moving up the steps as the rustling began again.

'What was that?' demanded Michael, looking about him wildly. 'I heard something. Is there someone in here with us? Has Eltisley succeeded in his ambitions, and raised Barchester's dead?'

'Do not be ridiculous, Brother,' said Bartholomew, sitting with Cynric as far as possible up the steps. 'Eltisley will never make the dead walk again. It is beyond the laws of nature.'

'That man is beyond the laws of nature.' Michael suddenly shot up the steps with an impressive spurt of speed for a man of his size. 'Something touched my foot,' he explained shakily.

'Just a mouse,' said Bartholomew.

'A rat, boy,' said Cynric ominously. 'Rats live in tombs, not mice.'

Michael bowled Bartholomew and Cynric out of the way, and began heaving at the trap-door. It moved very slightly. Encouraged, Bartholomew helped, but although they could raise the slab the width of a finger, whatever was placed over the top of it was simply too heavy to move. Michael sat down, disheartened.

'Did you manage to tell Tuddenham about Stoate?' asked Bartholomew, to take his mind off a situation that was growing more alarming by the moment.

'I met William by the church, and sent *him* to tell Tuddenham, because I was anxious about you. Then I ran into a couple of those loutish brutes who are always hunched over their ale at the Half Moon, and they brought me here.'

Bartholomew sat on one of the cold, damp steps. 'Eltisley is threatening to kill William. But he will not get the students – I sent them away yesterday morning.'

'Thank God!' said Michael. 'I wish you had sent William away, too. I suspect Eltisley will kill him, whether we comply with his wishes or not.'

'So there is no hope of rescue, then?' asked Cynric, stricken. 'You sent William to Tuddenham with a message to chase Stoate, but no one knows we are here?'

'I thought Stoate was all we needed to worry about,' protested Michael. 'He confessed to killing Unwin, and I was not anticipating being abducted by another murderer this morning.'

'Do you have your candle?' Bartholomew asked Cynric, trying to think of something he could do, other than wait for the mad landlord to kill the rest of the deputation from Michaelhouse. 'There may be another way out of here.'

Michael chuckled humourlessly in the dark. 'Church-builders always put an alternative exit in vaults,' he said. 'The dead do not like to feel trapped.'

Cynric produced his stub, and fiddled about with a tinder until the wick was alight. Hot wax spilled on to Bartholomew's fingers as he eased his way down the steps. The ground moved, and Bartholomew saw with horror that there were dozens of rats there, large brown ones with scaly tails and glittering eyes. He hesitated.

'Go on,' encouraged Michael. 'They will not bite you as long as you keep moving.'

'You go, then,' said Bartholomew, thrusting the candle at him and climbing back up the steps.

Michael gave a long-suffering sigh and walked down to the floor. The rats inched away, and he began to pick his way to the back of the chamber. It comprised an elongated room with three shelves along each side and a tiny altar at the far end. Four bodies were placed end to end along each shelf, so that there were twelve on the left and twelve on the right. With the rats scurrying about his bare ankles, Michael moved forward, peering at the shrouded figures in their niches.

'Nothing,' he said, returning a few moments later. 'The whole thing is made of solid stone.'

'What about the altar?' asked Bartholomew. 'Perhaps there is something behind that.'

'Be my guest,' said Michael, handing him the stub. 'Those vermin are beginning to lose their nervousness, and it will not be long before they want to try sinking those sharp yellow teeth into something a little fresher than their usual fare.'

Before he could think too much about what he was doing, Bartholomew strode briskly to the back of the vault, sending furry bodies scattering in alarm. The altar was a simple wooden table, covered with an ancient cloth that was thick with dust. He pulled it off and peered underneath. The floor was solidly paved with slabs of stone sealed with mortar, while the wall behind the altar was made of unevenly hewn lumps of rock. He pushed at a few of them, but they were the foundation stones for the church, and the builders had intended them to last. When the building collapsed, as Bartholomew sensed it would do soon, the vault would remain intact.

He began to walk back toward the steps, breaking into a run when he trod on one of the rats and made it scream. He felt its sharp teeth dig into his boot, and was grateful he was not wearing sandals like Michael. When he reached the stairs again, his hand was shaking. He dropped the light, and the chamber was plunged into darkness.

'I do not have another candle,' said Cynric in the dark vault. Michael simply sighed. After a moment, their eyes grew used to the gloom again.

'We will have to try to overpower Eltisley when he comes,' said Bartholomew, trying to think positively.

'With what?' asked Cynric. 'We have no weapons, and you do not even have your bag with you to take a swing at them with.'

'We have that crossbow quarrel,' said Bartholomew. 'During

our last struggle, one of the men fired a crossbow bolt at us, and I saw it fall down here.'

'Go and fetch it, then,' said Michael. 'And retrieve the candle while you are at it.'

That idea did not much appeal to Bartholomew while rats milled about on the floor. He tried to think of a better idea, but failed. 'All right, then. But if we all go, you two can drive them off while I feel around on the floor.'

It was not a plan that filled anyone with much enthusiasm, but in the absence of an alternative, they inched down the stairs and stepped gingerly on the floor. Feeling that caution was the wrong approach, Michael suddenly began stamping his feet and spinning around like some crazed Oriental dancer. While Cynric did likewise, Bartholomew dropped to his hands and knees and began groping around for the quarrel, trying to ignore the cold, wet patches and mysterious lumps that his fingers encountered.

Michael's breath came in laboured gasps from the vigour of his exercise, and Cynric was already edging toward the steps. Bartholomew knew they would not maintain their rat-scaring act for much longer, and his search became more erratic. Just when he thought he would have to think of something else, he found the bolt. He snatched it up with a triumphant yell, and vied with the others to be first up the stairs.

'Give it to me,' said Cynric, feeling for it in the darkness. He nodded. 'It will do. Did you find the candle?'

There was a disappointed silence when Bartholomew did not reply.

'We should try to think out answers to all this,' said Michael, after a moment. 'It might give us some kind of bargaining power, if Cynric's attempt to free us fails.'

'Eltisley said we have all the facts,' said Bartholomew. 'So we should be able to work out at least part of it. I have been thinking hard, and I think I know the identity of the hanged man.'

'Then who is it?' asked Michael.

'James Freeman.'

'You mean the husband of the poor woman Stoate poisoned with his neighbourly dish of mussels? The man who died of a slit throat two weeks before we arrived in the village? How in God's name did you come up with that?'

'Mother Goodman told me that one of the first people at the scene of James Freeman's death was Eltisley, and Eltisley later bragged about that fact himself – he went into some detail about the box he had designed to carry Freeman to his grave. But no one *saw* the body except Eltisley, not even Mother Goodman, who usually lays out the dead. All anyone saw were bloodstained clothes.'

'But Dame Eva found the body. Obviously she saw it.'

'I doubt she stayed long and studied it,' said Bartholomew. 'Anyway, she is old and frail. She probably glimpsed someone lying there all covered in blood – probably one of Eltisley's henchmen playing dead – and made the assumption that it was Freeman, because he was in Freeman's home.'

Michael scratched his chin thoughtfully. 'Eltisley did make a good deal of fuss about the coffin he produced – telling us how he designed it specially for the occasion.'

'Quite,' said Bartholomew. 'And he designed it so that it would leak blood, and that would be what everyone would remember. No one would ask to look inside the coffin with that stuff dribbling out all over the place. And there is another thing: corpses do not bleed. So, Freeman's body should not have been bleeding at all, gaping throat wound or no.'

'But why should Freeman be the hanged man, as opposed to some lone traveller who stumbled on Eltisley's evil empire by mistake?'

'Eltisley believes he can raise the dead. By faking Freeman's death, I imagine he saw an opportunity to avail himself of a living human subject. Then, he could add credence to the legend that anyone who sees Padfoot will die a violent death – thus keeping people away from Barchester where he conducts his experiments – *and* procure someone to kill at his own convenience and then try to bring back to life.'

'So, you are saying that there was never a body with a slit throat, and that the blood dripping from Eltisley's box had nothing to do with a corpse?' asked Michael. Bartholomew nodded, but the monk was not convinced. 'But why was the hanged man – Freeman – wearing Deblunville's clothes?' He kicked out at a rat, braver than the rest, that was edging upwards.

'Oh, that is easy. Janelle said she stole them from Deblunville for her father. She left them near the Grundisburgh parish boundary, but someone else found them before they could be collected. Since Freeman's clothes had been soaked in blood to convince everyone he had died a gruesome death, Eltisley would have needed another set. Doubtless he or one of his henchmen found Janelle's bundle, and gave them to Freeman to wear while they kept him prisoner.'

'But Norys told us that whoever ran from the church was wearing Deblunville's clothes,' Michael pointed out. 'How do you explain that?'

Bartholomew scratched his head. 'I do not know, but the dagger we saw on the hanged man was the same as the one under the smouldering corpse in the shepherd's hut.'

'God's blood, Matt!' said Michael. 'These rats are climbing the stairs.'

Bartholomew swallowed. 'They will become bolder the longer we stay here. Kick them away.'

Michael gripped Bartholomew's arm and flailed about with his legs. 'There,' he said with satisfaction. 'That should make them think twice about tangling with me.'

'They will be back,' said Cynric.

'Think of something else,' said Bartholomew. 'James Freeman had to die because he claimed he had seen Padfoot – no one lives who has set eyes on Padfoot. It was the same with Alice Quy, dead of childbirth fever six months after having her last child. I will wager you anything you like that both had been out on one of Hamon's nocturnal expeditions, looking for the golden calf. Either by design or by chance, they ended up at Barchester and encountered Mad Megin and her dog, who were guarding the village for Eltisley.'

'Yes,' said Michael. 'You are right. And we were foolish, you know. We allowed ourselves to be misled by Deblunville's false assumptions – that it was Tuddenham who was promoting the Padfoot legend to provide an excuse for his people trespassing on his neighbours' land while searching for buried treasure.'

Bartholomew nodded slowly. 'But, of course, had we really thought about that, we would have seen it made no sense: the only two people to have availed themselves of this excuse – James Freeman and Alice Quy – were killed almost immediately. Why go to all the trouble of inventing an excuse if you plan to kill anyone who uses it? Eltisley, not Tuddenham, killed the two villagers.'

'Mother Goodman told you that Eltisley had sent Alice Quy a harmless potion because she could not pay Master Stoate's inflated prices for medicine.' Michael tried to ease higher up the stairs.

'It was supposed to contain feverfew and honeyed wine,' said Bartholomew, 'an appropriate remedy for such disorders. But, of course, all that was wrong with her was fear, because she had set eyes on this so-called phantom. By the time she had taken a few draughts of Eltisley's potion, her fate was sealed. Her death proved to the villagers that no one sets eyes on Padfoot and lives.'

'And then there was Deblunville,' said Michael. 'He, too, was supposed to have seen Padfoot – although he claimed it was a wolf. Eltisley must have bashed him over the head in the woods. We know he was experimenting with how he was going to kill us that night – you saw flames shooting out of his workshop – and then he went to Barchester to continue because he had been unsuccessful at home. He must have come across Deblunville, conveniently separated from his archers, and decided it was too good an opportunity to miss.'

'Grosnold's man told me that Padfoot had been heard sniffing around Wergen Hall, but that people were too afraid to open the window to look. It was probably a fox, but you can see how Eltisley has the whole village terrified over this Padfoot nonsense.'

'And it has worked brilliantly. You said that even Grosnold took the path that leads around the edge of the village, not through the middle, and he is a knight.'

'We walked through it the first time,' said Cynric. 'Nothing happened to us then – except for Unwin seeing the white dog.'

'Eltisley must have been delighted with the story that Unwin saw that thing,' said Michael bitterly. 'Stoate unwittingly gave credence to the lie that all who see Padfoot die.'

'And to the same end, Eltisley made a flagrant attack on Cynric when he felt he was under the same curse,' said Bartholomew. 'He tried to give him dog mercury.'

Cynric said nothing, but made a stabbing motion with the crossbow quarrel, and there was a sharp squeal. He shook it in disgust, and they heard the soft thump of a body as it landed somewhere on the floor. There was an immediate and ominous scurry.

'Occasional travellers through Barchester present no problem because they leave,' continued Bartholomew, trying not to imagine the rats chasing after the corpse of one of their own. 'What Eltisley does not want is people from the village seeing him here, and wanting to know what he is doing. He needs privacy. There is no one in Barchester except Mad Megin, who serves to keep visitors away with her white dog. It was no ghost you saw, Cynric: it is a gigantic hoax, perpetrated by Eltisley to keep people so frightened that they will not interfere with him.'

'Maybe,' said Cynric cautiously, in such a way that Bartholomew was sure the Welshman remained convinced that Padfoot was real.

'We saw a light the night we were attacked,' Bartholomew went on. 'I thought it was a traveller seeking shelter, but no traveller would ever stay – be allowed to stay – in Barchester. That was Eltisley working over his potions.'

Michael sighed. 'Eltisley might believe he is a veritable genius, and that he has intellectual powers to rival the likes of Roger Bacon, but he is sadly mistaken. Someone else is involved in all this – someone who has enough money to buy Eltisley all he needs for his experiments, and someone who does not want us to have our advowson.'

'Somehow, the deed seems to pale into insignificance when all this is considered,' said Bartholomew, jerking backward as something nosed at his hand.

'But someone stole it from me in the churchyard. It *is* important. It must be something to do with the fact that someone in Tuddenham's family does not want a representative from Michaelhouse to be the executor of his will.'

'I forgot about the will,' said Bartholomew, not very interested, but wanting to keep Michael talking so that they would not be sitting in silence in the tomb with only the rustle of rats for company. 'That was one of the terms Alcote agreed with Tuddenham, was it not?'

'It was the one Tuddenham was most insistent upon,' said Michael. 'It is a good decision: he will have an executor who is completely independent, should there be any unpleasantness, and his heirs will save a good deal on legal fees.'

'Why should there be unpleasantness?' asked Bartholomew. 'The line of inheritance is clear: if Isilia's child is a boy, he will inherit; if it is a girl, Hamon will inherit.'

'There will only be difficulties if Tuddenham dies before the child is born,' said Michael, 'because his will stipulates that no child born after his death can inherit. But this is all irrelevant since Tuddenham is in good health.'

Bartholomew gazed at him in the darkness. He considered keeping his silence, but the promise had been to keep the knight's illness from his family, not from Michael. 'But Tuddenham has a mortal illness, and will not live to see himself a father again.'

Michael let out his breath in a long sigh. 'Why did you not mention this before? Now it begins to make sense. Now I understand why Tuddenham is so desperate to have the advowson signed and sealed before we go. He wants Hamon to inherit, not his unborn child.'

'But he could stipulate that in his will anyway,' said Bartholomew. 'He does not need Michaelhouse's help to do that.'

'But Michaelhouse will see his wishes fulfilled in a way that few other executors will be able to do. We have no vested interest in who inherits and who does not – the living of the church is ours whatever happens – and we have the power of the Church behind us, not to mention some of the best legal minds in the country. The real issue is that there are ancient laws that might override Tuddenham's choice of heirs – a son is a son. Even Henry the Second was obliged to leave his kingdom to his hated oldest son, and not his favourite younger child. Hamon will need our expertise if he is to inherit Tuddenham's estates.'

'But what does Tuddenham have against his unborn

child?' asked Bartholomew, kicking out and feeling something soft fly away from his foot. 'He seems happy with Isilia. Unless . . . ' He trailed off, thinking.

'Unless what, Matt?' asked Michael. 'I beg you, if you have any more information, please do not keep it to yourself. Small things that seem unimportant to you might make a great deal of difference to the law.'

Bartholomew took a deep breath. 'It is probably not his child that Isilia is carrying.'

Bartholomew could imagine the expression on the monk's sardonic face. 'And how are you party to that intimate little detail?'

'The disease he has tends to take away the ability to father children. I was surprised by the fact that Isilia was pregnant when I first learned of his illness, but he probably knows Isilia's child is not his. Do you think that would give him cause enough to insist so vehemently that we finish our business here, and leave with the documents that will allow Hamon to inherit?'

'I do indeed,' said Michael. 'And it would give Hamon good reason for wanting the advowson signed quickly, too. But who would oppose it?'

'Isilia, for one,' said Bartholomew. He drew his hand up with a sharp intake of breath, when something grazed it with what felt like teeth. He continued, somewhat unsteadily, rubbing his wrist. 'Also, Dame Eva does not seem to like Hamon very much, while Wauncy might not approve of Hamon inheriting over Isilia's offspring.'

'But we have no evidence to connect Eltisley with any of these people,' said Michael. 'And I am wearing sandals, and I can feel fur and scrabbling claws all over my feet!'

'The person behind all this must be Isilia,' said Bartholomew, not wanting to think about scaly rat feet climbing on Michael's bare toes. 'No one else would know the child was not Tuddenham's. All her caring attentions towards him must be an act – he knows this and he does not want her to see he is ill until the deed appointing Michaelhouse as his executor is safely in Cambridge.'

'You are right,' said Michael, trying to sit with his feet in the air. 'Well, she had me fooled, too, with her lovely, innocent face and her touching concern for the husband old enough to be her father. She probably did not want to marry him in the first place. And who can blame her? He is like a horse, with all those long teeth.'

'But there is also the father of the child,' said Bartholomew. 'He would have an interest in it inheriting over Hamon, and might try to prevent the advowson from being completed.'

'Do you know who that might be?' asked Michael. 'It cannot be Hamon, or none of this would be an issue. Is it Grosnold, do you think? Or Wauncy?'

'Or Eltisley?' asked Bartholomew in distaste.

'Eltisley has killed four times,' said Cynric. 'Alice Quy, James Freeman, Deblunville and Alcote. He will not hesitate to do so again.'

'I suspect, with hindsight, that he also tried to poison us with that brown sludge the first night we stayed at the Half Moon, given how insistent he was that we finish the bottle,' said Bartholomew. 'He was pleased when he saw the bottle was empty, not knowing that Deynman had spilled it on the floor. Alcote drank a little, and was quite ill.'

'And then, once it became clear that Alcote was the man writing the deed and that the rest of us were mere onlookers, attempts were made on Alcote alone,' said Michael. 'He was unwell most of the time he was here, suggesting that some insidious poison was in the food he ate – or in the copious amounts of raisins he devoured – and then there was the attack on him the night before he died.'

Cynric leapt to his feet and began kicking out furiously. There were several squeals, and something soft thumped into Bartholomew, who thrust it away from him with a shudder.

'Eltisley thinks he is beyond the law,' said Michael. 'Sit down, Cynric! You keep kicking these things into my lap. Why Isilia should consider forming an alliance with Eltisley is beyond me. He is likely to kill her, to see if she can be resurrected.'

'I do not see how they are connected, though,' said Cynric. 'Isilia and Eltisley. She is sweet and kind, and he is a maniac.'

'Do not let appearances deceive you, Cynric,' said Michael sagely. 'Behind that lovely face lies a mind as strong and cunning as a rat trap – which I would give a good deal to have one of right now. She must have paid him to destroy his tavern with Alcote in it, and snatched the copy of the will from me in the churchyard.'

'What if— ?' began Bartholomew. He stopped as a screech from above heralded the opening of the trap-door. There was a flood of light, and the rats slunk away into the shadows.

Bartholomew saw Cynric braced to pounce and tensed himself, waiting for an opportunity to launch a bid for escape. It never came. More wary this time, one of the surly men immediately kicked out at Cynric's hands, and the crossbow quarrel went skittering down the steps to the floor below. Michael let out a cry of dismay, while Cynric only gazed at it in horror.

'All is ready,' said Eltisley pleasantly. 'I would like you to come out, Brother. I have an elixir I would like you to taste. And that Welshman, too. The monk might prove too fat for what I have in mind, but the servant should do nicely. I will save Bartholomew to help me later – I might be forced to call upon his expertise, if this does not work.'

'What would you say if I told you to try your elixir on yourself?' asked Michael, as he stepped out of the vault. The landlord seemed surprised by Michael's hostility.

'I would say that your students and the friar will test it in your stead. At the moment, I am still prepared to let them return to Michaelhouse.'

'You do not have them,' shouted Bartholomew desperately. 'They have gone away.'

'To the leper hospital,' said Eltisley. He beamed at Bartholomew's shock. 'I overheard that slow-witted student of yours telling the handsome one where they were headed, as they fled along the Ipswich road yesterday. It was clever of you to try to spirit them away.'

Bartholomew's heart sank.

'Well, where are they, then?' asked Michael.

Eltisley hesitated. 'They have not arrived at the leper hospital yet.' He shrugged absently. 'Perhaps they have been waylaid. Or lost. That stupid student is capable of getting lost on a straight road, I am sure.'

Bartholomew was uncertain whether to be relieved they had escaped Eltisley's clutches, or concerned that they might have fallen into someone else's. He could only hope that Horsey had realised the danger they were in, and had come up with an alternative plan.

'And we will catch that friar, too,' said Eltisley. 'He will not be able to hide from me for long.'

Bartholomew was confused. Was William hiding from Eltisley? He did not know that he should, and would be under the impression that Stoate, hastily riding towards Ipswich, was the villain of the piece. So where was William, and what was he doing so that Eltisley could not find him? Bartholomew's heart sank further when he realised that William, headstrong and keen to prove himself, might have decided to tackle Stoate alone. Perhaps he was even now pursuing the killer physician on horseback, or had confronted him and was lying in some roadside bush with a crossbow quarrel in him.

Eltisley's attention was on Michael. 'I have been working on a rather clever idea that you will test for me. You see, not everyone likes the time in which they live, so I have invented a potion that kills temporarily. Then, at a later date, my other elixir – the one that raises people from the dead – can be taken, and the person can be restored to life at a time of his choosing.'

'But that is monstrous!' exclaimed Michael. 'The time in which we live is the one granted to us by God, and it is not natural to decide you do not like it, and exchange it for another.'

'People will pay handsomely to do it, monstrous or not,' said Eltisley, oblivious to Michael's revulsion. 'You would be surprised how many men would like to lie low for a few years.'

'Murderers, thieves, rapists, arsonists and a whole host of other felons, I should imagine,' said Michael scathingly. 'You have invented an elixir to allow criminals to evade justice.'

Eltisley's face hardened. 'You will take my potion, and you are not a criminal.'

The slab was slammed shut, almost landing on Bartholomew's head. On reflection, as the physician crouched in the darkness listening to the rustles as the rats began to move again, he decided that having his brains dashed out might be a better way to die than being eaten alive by rodents, or downing one of Eltisley's hideous concoctions. Michael's voice echoed down to him, and he strained to hear what was being said.

'My colleague believes that you killed James Freeman,' came Michael's voice conversationally. 'He thinks you hanged him, so that you could test your potion, and that he was wearing clothes from a bundle you found near the Grundisburgh parish boundary.'

'He is right,' said Eltisley. 'Someone had abandoned those clothes – I found them when I was walking and thinking up new theories as we philosophers are wont to do. Since I needed some for James Freeman – to replace the ones I had bloodied to convince people of his death – I gave them to him, and he wore them when I hanged him at Bond's Corner. Unfortunately, you chose that moment to cut him down.'

'My apologies,' said Michael.

Eltisley made an irritable sound. 'You have no idea how frustrating it was to watch Bartholomew's attempts to revive him, when I knew a few drops of my potion would work! But I thought that if I made my appearance from the bushes, you would assume I had hanged him.'

'You had,' Michael pointed out.

Bartholomew kicked away a rat that was clawing its way up his leg. It landed with a soggy thump on the floor below.

'But not with any intention to kill,' protested Eltisley. 'He would have been alive today, had you not come by and interfered. Then I was left with a body to dispose of.'

'Why did you not test your elixir on him after we had gone?' asked Michael.

Eltisley sighed. 'I did, but that particular elixir was designed to raise people who had only just died, and the delay caused by your meddling meant it did not work.'

Bartholomew knew students who always had an excuse as to why they had not completed some task he had set them, or why an experiment he had asked them to undertake was unsuccessful. It was never their fault; someone else was always to blame. Eltisley was just like them.

'Then what did you do?' asked Michael.

'I could not have James Freeman's body discovered, or people would be asking me who I had buried in his specially constructed coffin. It was quite a problem for me. Have you ever tried to dispose of a corpse?'

'Not lately,' replied Michael.

'It is no mean task, I can assure you. I tried to burn it, but it smouldered for days and I was still left with a sizeable chunk. I had to chop it into small pieces, and leave it out for Padfoot – although he did not seem to be very interested.'

'Probably prefers his human corpses raw,' suggested Michael.

Eltisley continued. 'Anyway, after he died, I took the clothes off Freeman, donned them along with some potions to disguise my face and went into Grundisburgh church, intending to have a conversation with Walter Wauncy. My ingenious plan was that Wauncy would say he had seen the hanged man alive and well, and your story would be dismissed as fantasy – drunken scholars reeling from a night in the taverns, claiming to find a dead man who was later seen in a church by our priest. Who would question the word of a priest?'

'But instead of Wauncy, you found Unwin, who was dead,' said Michael, 'so you ran away.'

'I tried to give him some of my potion, but in my excitement at finding a subject so unexpectedly, I spilled it. Vapours wafted into my eyes, and I could barely see what I was doing. I decided to abandon the experiment before someone accused me of a murder I did not commit. I ran away across the fields behind the church, although the shoes were too small: they slopped, and made haste difficult.'

So, Stoate had been telling the truth, thought Bartholomew. He *had* seen a man running from the church rubbing his eyes. And Norys had seen him wearing Freeman's shoes and belt – recently stolen from Deblunville by Janelle. Deblunville's shoes had not fitted Eltisley, and they had slopped, something peculiar enough to lodge in Norys's mind.

'Norys saw you,' said Michael. 'He described the belt and shoes – but not the dagger, because you left that with James Freeman's body.'

'I was impressed by Norys's observing powers,' said Eltisley. 'Although I was relieved that he did not recognise anything else. For a dreadful moment, I thought he was going to come to help disentangle my cloak from the tree it snagged on. I ripped it pulling myself free.'

'And how did you manage to take the afternoon away from your tavern to conduct your experiments during the Fair?' asked Michael. 'Did people not demand to know where you were?'

'I have a wife,' said Eltisley loftily. 'I have better things to do with my time than selling ale to peasants. But later I was arrested for the priest's murder anyway, because of that bloody knife.'

'I suppose the knife was the one you used to kill an animal – to provide the blood you needed to make Freeman's "death" appear convincing.'

'Exactly,' said Eltisley. 'Ironic, do you not think? But you were kind enough to come to my rescue, and provide evidence that Norys was the culprit, not me, so I was free to continue my work.'

Bartholomew rested his head against the cool stone and felt sick. He did not stay still for long. Something furry bumped up against his leg, forcing him to push it away. How much longer could he repel the things? Would they get him first, or would Eltisley?

'And who is it who is financing these great experiments of yours?' asked Michael. 'Isilia?'

Bartholomew heard Eltisley clap his hands in delight. 'At last you have reasoned it out! Mistress Isilia does not want that loutish Hamon to inherit Tuddenham's estates over her brat, as is likely to be stipulated in Tuddenham's will. She asked me to relieve her of your presence so that the will cannot be written, and since I was running a little low on funds, I agreed.'

'And is there anyone else who pays you?' asked Michael.

'You seem to possess a great deal of equipment and supplies, and Isilia cannot give you that much money – Tuddenham would be suspicious of her spending too much.'

'Many people are interested in my work,' said Eltisley blithely. 'Everyone has a loved one they would like to see again. I have even been paid by priests, who want me to raise a saint for them.'

'There is not much left of most saints to raise,' said Michael. 'Bones, hair, teeth, nails, fingers and beard have been scattered all over the country as relics.'

'That will be dealt with when the time comes,' said Eltisley grandly.

Their voices faded away into silence. In a brief moment of hope, Bartholomew thought they had forgotten to replace the chest that held down the slab, but there was a rumble and a thump, and that was that. He sat with his head resting on his knees, wondering how he had ever become embroiled in the whole mess, and fervently wishing that he had never left Cambridge in the first place. He thought of Unwin, dead because he had been foolish enough to let Stoate bleed him, and Alcote, dead because Isilia did not want Hamon to inherit Tuddenham's estates. And then he thought about Michael, Cynric, Horsey, Deynman and William – who would go the same way. He was angry enough to beat his fists uselessly on the stone slab to vent his frustration.

It was not long before the rats intruded into his thoughts. One of them started to scramble up his back, while a scaly tail slid across his arm. He stood and shook them off, hearing them tumble down the stairs. Then it occurred to him that the rats could not possibly have squeezed themselves through the tiny gap around the edges of the trap-door, and that he must have been right in his original assumption, scoffed at by Michael, that there was another way in – and out.

But he was in almost complete darkness and surrounded by rats. How was he to find it? He groped around on the step, and found Cynric's tinder. Now all he needed to do was to locate the stub of candle he had dropped when he had stepped on his first rat – assuming they had not already eaten it. It took all his courage and self-control to make his way down the steps in the gloom and feel about among the milling rats on the floor.

Immediately, he found the crossbow quarrel that Eltisley's henchman had kicked from Cynric's hand, and used it to stab randomly while he searched with his other hand for the stub. Expecting to be bitten at any moment, he forced himself to feel around until his cold fingers finally encountered it. It had been chewed, but was still functional. With unsteady hands, he scraped the tinder until it caught, and watched leaping shadows fill the vault. Some of the rats slunk away. But not all of them.

Hoping that the stub would not sputter into nothing as it burned down, he began his search, watching the rats to see if he could tell whether they were coming or going in any particular direction. The rats, however, seemed as interested in him as he was in them, and their beady eyes were fixed unswervingly on his feet. His first exploration of the vault told him nothing, other than it was solidly built – something he already knew. He poked at every stone near the altar, then paced the floor to see if there were rings in the paving slabs that might lead to another chamber. There was nothing.

Trying to hold the candle still, he next concentrated his attention on the shelves and their sombre contents. As gently as he could, he moved the shrouded shapes to peer at the wall behind, looking for hidden doors. He coughed as the mouldering bodies began to crumble. The ones on the upper shelves released clouds of dust, while those on the lower ones broke apart because they were damp. They smelled of ancient bone and rotting material, and Bartholomew felt himself becoming nauseous from the lack of clean air.

Just as he was about to give up, the final stack of bodies revealed what he had been looking for. The lords of Barchester had apparently been running out of space for their dead, and the most recent additions to the vault had been placed on shelves that were newer than the rest – and that rested against a blocked door. A rat eased through the rotting wood at the bottom of it even as he watched. He leaned down and grabbed at one of the broken timbers, relieved to feel it break off in his hand as he pulled. But there were three ancient corpses in the way.

With distaste, he eased the first one out of its niche and laid it on the floor. It was lighter than he had expected and smaller, suggesting it had probably been a child. He reached for another, revolted by the way a skeletal hand dangled out to touch him, some of the little bones clattering to the floor in a puff of dust. Coughing, he laid it next to the first, and reached for the last one. This was large and dense and, as he pulled, its shroud caught fast on the corner of the shelf. He tugged harder, struggling to support its weight. Nothing happened. With growing urgency, he hauled as hard as he could and, with a ripping sound, it tore out of its shroud and landed on top of him, so that its grinning head was no more than the width of his hand away from his face. He gave a yell and tried to thrust it away from him, but it was too heavy. Horrified, Bartholomew saw the mouth opening wider and wider until the jaw dropped clean from the skull.

Revulsion gave him the strength he needed, and with an almighty thrust he sent the thing flying away from him, so that it landed with a sickening smash against the wall near the altar. For a few moments he was able to do nothing but stand in the gloom, and try to control his trembling. But time was of the essence if he wanted to help Cynric and Michael, and he thrust his disgust to the back of his mind and began to prise the wooden shelves away from the door. When it was clear, he hacked at the door itself. The rotten wood yielded quickly, and he soon had it open. With lurching disappointment, he saw that the passageway beyond was blocked by a pile of rubble.

Bartholomew closed his eyes and leaned back against the wall, almost oblivious to the rats that swirled around his legs and gnawed inquisitively at his boots. All he could think of was that he had failed. He opened his eyes, and saw a rat clamber over the top of the pile of masonry, and make its way into the vault. He frowned and scrambled up it, to try to peer through the gap between rubble and roof. Gingerly, he thrust the candle through it, and saw that the fall was not a large one, and that there was a flight of stairs beyond. Scarcely daring to hope, he began to claw away the rubble, until there was a space large enough for him to squeeze through.

Ignoring the way his clothes snagged on the sharp edges of stones, he squirmed over until he was on the far side, heart thumping in panic when he thought at one point that he might have misjudged, and trapped himself between the rubble and the roof. Then he was through, and skidding down the other side. His candle fizzled and went out.

There was nothing he could do but grope his way forward in the darkness, tripping and stumbling up the uneven steps, and flinching when his hands encountered something furry and warm rather than damp and smooth. Eventually, he reached another door. He felt it blindly, trying to locate the handle. Rats clawed at his boots as he grasped the metal and turned. Nothing happened. It was locked from the outside.

He forced himself to run his hands over the wood methodically to see if he could find the lock. What he found was a latch. Lifting it he pulled again, but the door remained firmly closed. About to give up in despair, it occurred to him to lift the latch and turn the handle at the same time. With a sudden creak, the door began to open. With profound relief, he stepped out into the church.

He was in the chancel, having emerged through a small door that stood to one side of the altar. He could hear the voices of Eltisley and his henchmen further down the building, and hoped that did not mean that Michael and Cynric had swallowed whatever potion Eltisley had given them, and were already dead. Clutching the crossbow quarrel, he inched toward the screen that divided the nave from the chancel, and peered round it.

Eltisley was standing at one of his benches with Isilia by his side, while Michael and Cynric, white faced and nervous, were sitting together on stools. Eltisley's friends − five of them − were ranged behind them, three with their swords drawn, lest Cynric should try to escape.

'And who is the father of your brat, madam?' Michael was saying. 'Some village lad? Or do your tastes run to lords of the manor? Grosnold, perhaps, or Deblunville?'

'That is none of your affair,' said Isilia, shocked. 'Hurry up, Eltisley. Sir Thomas will wonder where I am if I am here much longer, and I wish to ensure that these meddlesome scholars are dispatched once and for all. I do not want them writing the deed that will give Hamon the estates that rightly belong to my children − I have not lived three years with that old man to end up with nothing.'

'Science takes time, my lady,' said Eltisley, busily mixing something that smoked with something green. 'I am working as quickly as I can, but this will not be rushed.'

The potion was green! And Norys's lips had been green! Had Eltisley tried his brew on the pardoner, too? Bartholomew tried to think rationally. Stoate had found Norys and Mistress Freeman dead from eating bad mussels, and had dumped Norys in some trees near Barchester. Someone had later moved him. Since few people, other than Eltisley, frequented Barchester, it stood to reason that the landlord had found the body, and stained its lips green in an attempt to test his elixir. Having experienced problems with burning and chopping up Freeman's body, Eltisley had decided to bury Norys in the churchyard – and what more secure place than in the grave of the man Norys was accused of killing?

Eltisley was almost ready, and, judging from the thick gloves the landlord wore to protect his hands, once they had swallowed his concoction there would be very little Bartholomew could do for Cynric or Michael. He had to think quickly. He glanced around him. He was evidently in that part of the church where Eltisley kept his more volatile compounds. Large pots, crudely labelled, stood well apart from each other.

'Do not pester him, Isilia,' came another voice from the shadows of the nave. 'Let him work in peace.'

Bartholomew froze as he recognised it. He heard Michael's gasp of shock. 'Dame Eva?'

The church was silent as Michael and Cynric gazed at the old lady in horror. In the chancel, Bartholomew's mind whirled with unanswered questions and disconnected fragments of information. Eventually, Dame Eva spoke, amused by the monk's shock at seeing her.

'Of course it is me. Do you think Isilia could have managed this alone?'

'But Eltisley . . .'

'Eltisley does as I tell him. How do you think he finances his experiments? By selling ale to the local peasantry?'

'I see,' said Michael slowly. 'That is why you ordered his release so quickly after Tuddenham arrested him for Unwin's murder. You let him out so that he could continue to work for you.'

And that, thought Bartholomew, was why Dame Eva had

been so solicitous toward the landlord's wife after the tavern had ignited. It had not been simple compassion that had prompted the old lady to give Mistress Eltisley her cloak and cross; it had been remuneration for damage done in her service.

Bartholomew crouched near the screen, and saw the old lady standing in front of Michael. A steely flint in her eye suggested that Eltisley would not be allowed to fail her by letting the Michaelhouse scholars escape a second time. Bartholomew needed to act fast if he wanted his friends to live. He moved back, and began reading the labels on Eltisley's powders and potions.

'So, it was you,' said Michael to Dame Eva. 'You stole the draft of the advowson from me in the churchyard; you ordered Alcote murdered; you told Eltisley to tamper with Cynric's bow; you arranged for Mad Megin and her dog to live here, and frighten the living daylights out of any passers-by; you told Eltisley to kill Alice Quy with one of his potions, and stage Freeman's death to strengthen the villagers' fear of the Padfoot legend; and you killed Deblunville.'

'I did not touch Deblunville. That was Eltisley acting on his own initiative.'

Eltisley gave his peculiar beaming smile. 'I took a stone and replaced it carefully after I had brained him, so that it would appear that he had fallen and hit his head. You see, setting eyes on Padfoot does not mean people are murdered, it means they die in mysterious accidents.'

'Deblunville did not think he saw Padfoot,' said Michael. 'He thought he saw a wolf.'

'It did not matter what *he* thought he saw,' said Dame Eva. 'It mattered what other people thought he saw, and that he was seen to die because of it.'

'Then it was you who attacked Alcote the night before the tavern exploded?' asked Michael. 'It could not have been Eltisley, because he was out killing Deblunville.'

'Isilia and I tried to rid the world of the vile little man together. But one elderly woman and one pregnant one are not ideally suited for ambushing, and Alcote was stronger than he looked. We had intended to stab him, but Isilia dropped her knife, and I could not get a clear hit. In short, we made a mess of the whole business. My husband always said it was better to employ someone to do that sort of thing for you, and now I understand what he meant.'

Expecting to be discovered at any moment, Bartholomew found an empty barrel and dumped all the yellow powder into it that was in a smallish pot labelled salfar, hoping it really was sulphur, and not just something Eltisley had created. He looked around for charcoal, his mind refusing to face the possibility that anything he might do to harm Dame Eva and her cabal might also harm Michael and Cynric.

'I told Eltisley to kill Freeman, not keep him alive to test his theories on,' said Dame Eva giving Eltisley a reproving stare. 'That was a mistake which might have proved costly. Fortunately, it turned out well in the end.'

'But why?' asked Michael, shaking his head. 'What can you hope to gain from all this? What does it matter to *you* who inherits your son's estates?'

Bartholomew found the charcoal powder, and poured it on the sulphur. He was about to stir it with a pewter spoon when he realised that the metal might produce sparks as it encountered the volatile mixture, so he looked around for something else to use. All he could find was a reed that had fallen from the roof. Immediately it snapped, and he froze with horror, expecting Eltisley's men to come rushing in and catch him. But nothing happened, and the old lady continued to regale Michael with a list of her reasons for causing such chaos and misery in the village she called her home.

'Hamon does not have the intelligence to run a large estate like this,' she said. 'He cannot even manage Peche

Hall properly, and that is tiny. If he had any sense at all, he would have killed Deblunville to prevent him from making a claim on our land in the courts.'

'Is that why you consider Hamon inadequate?' asked Michael. 'Because he would not murder Deblunville for land?'

The old lady's eyes became gimlet hard. 'Is that not reason enough? How does he hope to keep his inheritance if he will not fight for it? And he is dallying with that manipulative Janelle again, now Deblunville is dead. Fool!'

'He will keep his inheritance by using the law,' said Michael. 'That is why it is there.'

'But he might lose his case.'

'He might have lost his life, if he had tried to murder Deblunville. And then an estate would have been neither here nor there to him.'

The old lady made a sound of exasperation, and flounced towards the screen. Bartholomew, about to add saltpetre to his mixture, ducked back though the door to the vault, hoping his sudden movement had not been seen. The old lady walked into the chancel, and looked around her.

'I told you not to tamper with these powders again,' she said, seeing Bartholomew's barrel in the middle of the chancel floor. 'Last time, you destroyed the tavern – the tavern my husband had built – when it would have been easier and cheaper to slip some poison into the scholars' food.'

'I have not been tampering with them,' said Eltisley sulkily.

'Then get rid of them,' she snapped. She kicked at Bartholomew's barrel with her foot. 'Or you will have us all gone the same way as that despicable Alcote. Did I tell you I caught him burning some of Thomas's documents? Not important ones, true, but that is beside the point.'

'I need those powders,' protested Eltisley. 'I will not bring back the dead with crushed flowers and honey, you know.

To combat a powerful force like death requires potent compounds.'

'You said you would have that potion before the beginning of the summer,' said Dame Eva, moving out of the chancel and heading back towards Eltisley in the nave. 'You promised.'

'I am almost there,' said Eltisley eagerly. 'In fact, I am about to perform an experiment on the fat monk and his servant. This elixir will temporarily deprive them of life, and then I will bring them back again with another potion.'

At that point, two more of Eltisley's surly customers entered the church, looking nervous. It was clear they had failed to do something they had been ordered to do. Dame Eva's eyes narrowed.

'Where is he?' she demanded. 'You said you could find him.'

'The friar has disappeared,' said one of them, swallowing hard. 'We looked everywhere, but he is no longer in the village. He must have fled.'

'Damn!' muttered Eltisley. 'He would have made a good subject. What about the students?'

The man shook his head. 'They never reached the leper hospital. We cannot find them, either.'

Dame Eva sighed impatiently. 'I am surrounded by incompetents! Still, I suppose it does not matter – the friar is far too fixed on seeing heresy in the god-fearing to make sense of what he has learned here, and the students do not have the intelligence. I do not see that an institution like your University will survive long, given the kind of person it attracts. And I hear Oxford is worse.'

Bartholomew wondered where William and the students could possibly be, but there was no time for speculation. He eased out of the doorway, and located the saltpetre, an evil-smelling whitish substance that could be dangerous in the wrong hands. Closing his eyes, and expecting to be blown sky high at any moment, he dumped it on top of the charcoal and sulphur, giving it a very cautious stir with his reed and fervently hoping he had remembered his alchemy lessons correctly, and had the proportions right – three parts saltpetre to one part charcoal and sulphur. In the nave, Eltisley was heading toward Michael.

'And who is it that you would like brought back from the dead?' asked the monk of Dame Eva, in a futile attempt to delay the process. 'A loved child? Your husband? A lover?'

'I never needed any lover!' the old lady spat. 'My husband was all I ever wanted.'

Bartholomew scratched his head as he considered how he could ignite his concoction without blowing up Michael and Cynric, as well as Eltisley and his cronies. He had to put it somewhere it would cause sufficient damage to allow him to help his friends, but not enough to bring down the already fragile church roof. The powder needed to be placed in a confined space, where the explosion would give him a few moments to act – perhaps to grab a sword and create havoc. But where? He was beginning to despair, when his eye fell on the piscina in the chancel. Piscinas were sinks with drains that allowed holy water to be poured away into the foundations, mainly so that unscrupulous people could not steal it to sell.

He found a wooden bowl, and began to scoop the powder down the hole. Sweat broke out on his forehead when the bowl bumped against the stone sill of the piscina, making the conversation in the nave falter for a moment, until Michael restarted it with yet another question. As the level of powder in the barrel fell with agonising slowness, Bartholomew saw a length of carefully coiled twine on one of Eltisley's benches. It was white and crusted, and Bartholomew supposed that it was one of the pieces that Eltisley had soaked in saltpetre and used as a slow-burning fuse to ignite the tavern in the blast that had killed Alcote. He picked it up carefully, and inspected it. He was right. He hefted up the barrel, now less than half full, and continued to empty its volatile contents into the drain.

'Do you think this half-mad landlord will bring you your husband back?' Michael was asking Dame Eva incredulously. 'Is that what all this is about?'

Hands shaking, Bartholomew began to unravel Eltisley's twine, hoping it, unlike most of the landlord's devices, would work properly. One of the men who leaned against the wall ambled toward the screen, and began to pick idly at the peeling paint. Bartholomew ducked back into the chancel door, willing the man to go away. He could not light the fuse with him there – it would hiss and splutter and attract his attention, at which point Eltisley could extinguish it by stepping on it. Bored, the man blew out his cheeks in a sigh, and gazed at the patches of yellow-grey powder on the chancel floor that Bartholomew had accidentally spilled.

'Eltisley will succeed,' said Dame Eva, as though failure was not an option. 'And then all will be as it was when we were lord and lady of the manor. Hamon and my son will be dispatched to the wars in France, and our heir will be the child Isilia carries.'

'But you do not know who the father of that child is,' Michael pointed out, jerking his head away as Eltisley made a grab for him. He tried to stand, but two of the men stepped forward, and held him down. Cynric was similarly secured. There was nothing for the man near the chancel to do, so he stayed where he was, watching the scene without interest, still picking at the peeling paint, while Bartholomew fretted.

'You are lying to worm your way out of this,' said Dame Eva. 'Isilia carries Thomas's child.'

Isilia looked distinctly uneasy, although Dame Eva did not seem to notice. She continued.

'And he will be better than Thomas or Hamon with

their squeamish principles, and their silly notion of giving lucrative livings away to greedy men in distant Colleges.'

'Thomas believes Michaelhouse will pay for a mass-priest to pray for his soul,' said Isilia scornfully, glad to change the subject from that of the father of her child.

'He thinks their clever minds will prevent my grandson from inheriting what he wants Hamon to have,' said the old lady. 'The deed Alcote wrote had a clause saying that a Michaelhouse Fellow was to be the executor of his will. Thomas expects you to outwit any lawyers we can hire to act on behalf of the child. He is probably right. And I have recently come to think that he is not so healthy as he would have us believe. Since his will stipulates that no child of Isilia's born after his death will inherit, I cannot allow it to be written.'

'But there will be no advowson now,' said Isilia with satisfaction. 'Michaelhouse will take nothing from the village that killed every last member of its scholarly deputation.'

'You are wrong there, madam,' said Michael, struggling furiously. 'Michaelhouse will take anything it can get its hands on.'

The man near the screen finally moved away, and went to help his friends hold Michael. Bartholomew darted out from his doorway, and finished uncoiling the twine. Now what? he thought. How could he distract everyone from the hissing long enough to allow the powder in the piscina to ignite? He had deliberately cut a short fuse, but it would still take several moments to burn.

Meanwhile, Eltisley had succeeded in pinning Michael down, and was tipping the green potion toward his mouth.

'I will not drink that,' gasped Michael defiantly, through clenched teeth. 'I do not allow things that are green to pass my lips.'

'You have no choice,' said Eltisley, swearing under his

breath as some of the liquid spilled on to his own tunic. Smoke appeared as the stuff burned through the fabric.

It was too late for caution. Bartholomew crouched down and struck Cynric's tinder over a small pile of dried leaves and reeds from the roof.

'What was that?' demanded Dame Eva sharply, glancing towards the chancel.

Bartholomew struck the tinder again, but it was damp and refused to ignite. Sweat broke out on his forehead in oily beads.

'Someone else is in here,' said Dame Eva, pointing at the screen. 'Eltisley!'

'No!' yelled Michael, as Eltisley tipped his flask towards his face. Green liquid slopped from it.

Bartholomew's tinder finally struck, and the spark ignited the pile of grass. He blew on it, and hurled the burning handful on to Eltisley's twine. There was a hiss like a furious cat, and nothing happened. Dame Eva glared in the direction of the chancel, and began to walk purposefully toward it herself. In desperation, Bartholomew grabbed a pot and hurled it as hard as he could at the fragile ceiling. It smacked into the rotting thatch, and fell to the ground in a shower of reeds and dust, landing just behind Eltisley, and making the landlord jump in alarm. Dame Eva changed direction, peering toward the back of the church.

'I tell you, there is someone in here!' she shouted. 'Do not just stand there. Go and look.'

Bartholomew lit the fuse a second time, filling the chancel with a sharp hissing and the stench of burning. And then it went out again. Bartholomew gazed at it in dismay, cursing Eltisley for his dismal inventions. Dame Eva swung back toward it, eyes narrowed.

'No, not there,' she yelled at Eltisley's men, who were busily searching the back of the church. 'In the chancel!'

She began to hobble towards it, moving faster than Bartholomew would have thought possible for someone who had always seemed so frail.

'Bartholomew!' she exclaimed, seeing him kneeling on the ground.

Behind her, two men stepped forward to seize him.

Bartholomew gazed at the fuse in resigned disgust, realising that he had come very close to foiling the women's attempts to kill him and his friends. But, with two of Eltisley's sullen customers already pushing their way past Dame Eva to get at him, he saw that his feeble rebellion was finally over.

Suddenly, the twine fizzed into life again. Startled, Bartholomew scrambled to his feet, and flung himself into the passage that led down to the vault. There was an insane whistling sound, and then the loudest bang Bartholomew had ever heard as the powder sought to expand in the confined hollow in the wall. One moment he was on his feet, the next he was flat on his back, surrounded by swirling smoke. Dust and pieces of plaster crashed down from the ceiling, and he sensed the whole thing was about to fall. He picked himself up, and raced into what remained of the chancel. Dame Eva and the two men were nowhere to be seen. The screen had gone completely, and where there had been a roof of sorts, was now grey sky. The remains of the rotten thatch in the chancel had caught fire, and were burning furiously.

'Michael!' he yelled, clambering over the rubble into the nave. A cold fear gripped him. Had he used too much of the powder when Michael and Cynric were sitting so close? Had he done exactly what he had accused Eltisley of doing with Alcote, and used a mallet to crush a snail?

The nave roof had collapsed, and he could see nothing moving. Frantically, he began to tear the smouldering thatch away, trying to remember exactly where it was that his friends had been seated. He saw a leg in the rubble, and hauled it free, half-relieved and half-disappointed to see it was not Michael. It was Eltisley, his eyes wide and sightless, and a piece of wood piercing him clean through. He looked surprised, as if death was not something he imagined would ever happen to him. Beside him was one of his surly cronies, also dead, while to one side lay the severed foot of another.

'Matt!' A flabby white hand waved at him from further back. Weak with relief, Bartholomew grasped it, and hauled the monk from the wreckage. Michael was covered in fragments of reed and white dust from the plaster, but he was basically unscathed.

'Eltisley was standing in front of me, and I think he saved my life,' said Michael, looking around him wildly. 'He is as dead as I would have been, had he not protected me from the blast. Where is Cynric?'

'Here, boy,' said Cynric, emerging from under a large piece of thatch, his face black with soot. 'I realised what you were doing, and threw myself backward just in time.' He glanced up, and grabbed Michael's arm. 'Come on! This old church will not stand a shock like this.'

As if to prove the truth of his words, there was a groan, and what had once been a fine wooden gallery at the back of the building collapsed, sending a puff of dust and smoke rolling down the nave. The fire in what remained of the roof burned ever more fiercely, dropping pieces of blazing thatch all around them. Cynric led the way out, leaping over piles of rubble and hauling Michael behind him. Bartholomew followed, but then stopped as the south wall of the church began to teeter inward.

'No!' he yelled to Cynric. 'That is going to topple. Come this way.'

Cynric glanced up, and wrenched Michael back as the top part of the wall tumbled slowly, depositing great slabs of stone in the nave to smash the tiles. Bartholomew scrambled back the way they had come, heading for a window in the north wall that was less choked with weeds than the others. Cynric pushed him on, slapping a piece of burning thatch away as it landed on his shoulder.

With a rending groan, the south wall eased further inward, sending Eltisley's potions and bottles crashing to the ground. More stones fell, landing with ear-splitting crashes, so close behind him that Bartholomew could feel their draught on the back of his neck. He reached the window and stopped to help Michael, heaving and shoving at the monk's heavy body for all he was worth. It was taking far too long. More masonry fell, closer this time, and the south wall tipped further.

Finally, Michael was through, and Cynric was after him like a rabbit into a bolt-hole. Bartholomew glanced at the south wall. It was now falling in earnest, moving slowly at first, then picking up speed as the whole thing toppled toward him. He saw Michael's hands reaching in through the window, and jumped toward them, his toes scrabbling against the peeling plaster as he fought to gain a foothold. For a heart-stopping moment, he thought he would not make it, and he felt something strike the sole of his foot as it fell. And then he was through, hauled unceremoniously across the sill and out into the long grass and bushes behind.

Gasping for breath, he scrambled to his feet and followed the others through the bushes, aiming to get as far away from the collapsing church as possible. There was an agonised screech of tearing timbers, and the south wall finally fell, smashing forward to land heavily on the north wall opposite. That, too, began to collapse. Hindered by the dense bushes, Bartholomew began to fight his way to safety, feeling as though he was moving far too slowly. He glanced up and saw that he was still in the wall's shadow, and that it was already falling.

At last he was out of the undergrowth, and into the area of long grass that formed the churchyard. He was about to run across it, when there was an ominous growl. Cynric had stopped dead and Bartholomew barrelled into the back of him.

'Padfoot!' gasped Cynric in horror, gazing at the great white shape that blocked his path.

The choice between being savaged by Padfoot or crushed by masonry was not one Bartholomew had anticipated. But the wall gave another sinister rumble, and the animal looked old, mangy and rather pathetic in the cold light of day. Shoving Cynric out of the way, he snatched up a piece of stick and raced toward it. The animal opened its mouth in a toothless roar of surprise, and gave a half-hearted swipe as he ran past, its pink eyes watering in the glare from the fire. A sharp snap from the flames startled it and it cowered backward, sniffing at the air with a snout that was battered and balding. It looked more bewildered than frightening.

'Come on!' Bartholomew howled to the others.

Seeing him unharmed, Cynric followed with Michael at his heels. There was another tearing groan and the north wall finally gave way, landing in the bushes with a thunder of falling stones, ancient mortar and blackened timber. The shabby beast that had been Padfoot was enveloped in a cloud of swirling dust from which it did not emerge.

'What in God's name was that?' panted Michael, snatching at Bartholomew's arm to make him stop. Together they looked back at the column of smoke that was pouring from the building and the pall of white dust that splattered the trees as if it were snowing.

'It was a bear,' said Bartholomew. 'Just an ancient bear with no teeth and no claws. If I had ever managed to get a good look at it, I would have seen it for what it was – a poor, harmless thing.'

'Bears are not white,' gasped Michael. 'They are black or brown.'

'Some can be born white with pink eyes, just like cats, dogs or people. It probably escaped from a band of entertainers during the plague.'

'It did.' Tuddenham's voice so close behind them made them all spin around, and Cynric flourished a knife he had somehow managed to grab from one of the men who had been holding him. With Tuddenham were Grosnold, Walter Wauncy and Father William. Hamon was there, too, with the pregnant Janelle grabbing possessively at his arm. The young knight looked proud and pleased, and almost handsome. Bartholomew hoped he knew what he was letting himself in for with Janelle.

Tuddenham continued. 'It was a dancing bear that belonged to a troupe of actors who sometimes passed this way. One of them came to ask if we had seen it a few months ago, but I did not connect the missing white bear to the legends of Padfoot, until now.'

'Your mother did,' said Bartholomew shakily. 'She used it to ensure your villagers stayed away from where Eltisley was conducting his vile experiments.'

'I know,' said Tuddenham. His face was white and one hand gripped his stomach. He nodded at the burning rubble that had been the church. 'I heard everything that was said in there.'

'But what are you doing here?' Michael demanded. 'How did you know where we were?' He looked at William. 'The last I saw of you was when you went to tell Tuddenham about Stoate.'

'Hamon summoned us here,' said William. 'He was taking a pre-dawn stroll nearby – accompanied by half a dozen men, for some unaccountable reason – and he saw lights burning in the church. When he saw Eltisley arrive with you and Cynric at arrow-point, he returned to Grundisburgh to fetch help.'

'I would have mounted a rescue there and then,' said

Hamon apologetically, 'but none of us were armed with more than our spades, and it seemed more prudent to fetch reinforcements than to attempt something that stood a good chance of failing.'

Dame Eva and Janelle had been wrong about Hamon, Bartholomew thought. He was not as simple as everyone seemed to believe.

'Have you seen Deynman and Horsey?' he asked anxiously. 'I sent them to the leper hospital for safety, but when Eltisley's men went to collect them, they had not arrived.'

'A leper hospital?' queried William distastefully. 'Hardly to be recommended as a place of safety, Matthew. They may have escaped Eltisley, but what if they catch the disease?'

'It is not that easy to catch leprosy,' said Bartholomew. 'But it is irrelevant anyway, considering that they are not there. Do you think they were attacked on the Old Road and robbed?'

'I think they have probably found some tavern,' said Michael, 'and are happily dicing together, oblivious to the fact that the likes of Eltisley have been scouring the country-side looking for them.' He turned to William. 'So, how did you escape Eltisley's men all morning?'

William looked furtive. 'I was here and there,' he said evasively. 'Doing what I could.'

Hamon gave a snort of laughter. 'He was in the latrine,' he said, relishing the friar's embarrassment. 'Ever since dawn, just after he delivered your message about Stoate to my uncle.'

'Are you ill?' asked Bartholomew. Latrines, even splendid ones with doors like those in Grundisburgh, were not places where the sane liked to linger.

William pursed his lips, but confessed. 'It was that wretched device of Eltisley's again. It jammed on me a second time, and I could not free myself for love nor money. I was locked in until Master Wauncy answered my cries for help.'

Michael gave a humourless smile. 'It seems the failure of one of Eltisley's inventions actually saved your life. Had that lock not prevented you from leaving, you might well have found yourself with a mouthful of his green elixir.'

'So I gathered,' said William. 'As Sir Thomas said, we overheard much of what was said in the church.'

'Then why did you not come to our rescue?' demanded Michael. 'That madman almost had me drinking a brew that would have killed me "temporarily".'

'We were coming,' said William indignantly. 'Have patience, Brother! Hamon was halfway in through the window with his sword drawn, and I was behind him with a cudgel, when that terrible explosion occurred. It blew Hamon right over me and out into the bushes.' He shook his head disapprovingly. 'That Eltisley was an agent of the Devil, and the Devil rose up from hell and snatched him away. What we saw was a glimpse into the fiery depths.'

'What we saw was Matt using Eltisley's powders to save us,' said Michael tartly. He turned to Tuddenham. 'You really heard it all?'

Tuddenham nodded, and Hamon came to stand at his side, a hand on his shoulder in a gruff expression of sympathy and support. 'I heard that my wife and mother were plotting against me, and that it was not my child that Isilia was carrying. I suspected all that, of course, and I knew that they might try to prevent the deed being signed.'

'You might have mentioned it to us,' said Michael accusingly. 'Then we could have been on our guard, and Alcote need not have died.'

'But then you might have decided not to draw up the advowson, and Isilia's brat would have inherited my estate over Hamon.'

'It could have been your child,' said Bartholomew. 'It is unlikely, but not impossible.'

Tuddenham shook his head. 'I always knew it was not mine.'

'So, who was the father, then?' asked Michael, intrigued.

'That is not the kind of question a gentleman should ask of a dead lady,' said Tuddenham softly. 'But I do know, and her secret will die with me.'

'And did you know what Eltisley was doing on your manor?' asked Bartholomew, angry that the knight might have turned a blind eye to such practices.

Tuddenham gave a brief nod. 'I knew that my mother was supporting Eltisley in some ridiculous experiment, because she was desperate to have my father back, but, like you, I did not take seriously Eltisley's claim that he could raise the dead. And I cannot think why my mother wanted to resurrect my father anyway – the man was a brute, and a poor manager of our estates. He let Bardolf's father steal Gull Farm from him without even attempting to wrest it back. After his death, she lavished more and more praise on him, accrediting him with a goodness that he never expressed in life. She, like Eltisley, was not entirely sane in her own way.'

'And all this is about who will inherit your estates?' asked Michael. 'You did not want Isilia's child as heir, because he is not yours?'

'Essentially,' said Tuddenham. 'But I never imagined Isilia, or my mother, would sink to such depths of evil to accomplish what they wanted.'

'She seemed so angelic,' said Bartholomew, almost to himself, thinking of the lovely Isilia and her green eyes and fresh skin. 'How could such treachery come from such loveliness?'

Tuddenham glanced sharply at him.

'You suspected it, though,' said Michael quickly, before the knight could infer too much from Bartholomew's words. 'That was why you tried to keep your illness a secret – so that we would be safely back in Cambridge before they realised you were dying and that they would need to destroy the advowson if they wanted your estates for themselves.'

'I knew my mother was employing delaying tactics – trying to make more work for you, to slow the process down,' said Tuddenham tiredly. 'For example, last week she produced that huge chest of irrelevant household accounts, knowing you would have to read them, and that to do so would waste your time. I just thought she was trying to wear you down, not that she was biding her time for murder.'

'Really,' said William, folding his arms, clearly unconvinced.

'Yes, really!' snapped Tuddenham. 'But my mother is a cautious woman, and it seems she did not want to chance my having an accident before the birth of Isilia's child – you may have noticed how solicitous they both were of my health – so, she must have decided that the deed should not be completed at any cost.'

'She almost succeeded,' said Michael. 'She tried several times to have Alcote poisoned – once with Eltisley's digestive tonic, and again with raisins – and she even attempted to stab him before Eltisley took matters in hand.'

'Did any of them escape?' asked Cynric, gesturing to the burning church. 'You would not want the likes of those ladies and that Eltisley roaming the country with revenge in their hearts.'

'Indeed not,' said Tuddenham. He nodded toward Siric, who was guarding three of Eltisley's surly drinkers, all sitting on the grass and covered in white plaster. Next to them lay a row of unmoving figures, their faces covered with a hastily gathered assortment of garments. From under Tuddenham's russet cloak poked the hem of Isilia's velvet dress, while Hamon's boiled-leather hauberk hid most of Dame Eva from view. Eltisley lay next to her, identifiable by his green-stained apron.

'You will check, when the fire dies down?' asked Michael.

'Look in the vault, too, in case one of them managed to crawl to safety.'

'We will,' said Hamon quietly. He gazed at Eltisley's body with revulsion. 'That madman will stay this way, I hope. Do you think he had taken some concoction that will allow him to rise from the grave, and come to haunt us?'

Bartholomew shook his head. 'Sir Thomas was right. There was no chance of Eltisley's potions working to raise the dead. It is against the basic laws of nature.' He gestured to the black knight, who had come to stand with Tuddenham and Hamon. 'And is Sir Robert Grosnold also aware of what has happened here?'

'He is a good friend and a loyal ally,' said Tuddenham, smiling wanly at his neighbour. 'He slipped back to the village to warn me that my mother and wife were plotting against you the day Unwin died.'

'I overheard Dame Eva and Isilia talking to Eltisley just before the feast started,' said Grosnold. 'You see, I rode my destrier too hard across the village green and he damaged a leg. I was forced to stop and attend to it: it was then that I heard the three of them plotting. I walked back to inform Tuddenham, and was about to go home when I saw that poor friar, Unwin, all weak and shaking. I dispatched the physician Stoate to bleed him, but it seems it did him no good.'

'No good at all,' agreed Bartholomew. 'But why did you not tell us you were with Unwin just before he died? We thought you had a hand in his death when you denied meeting him.'

Grosnold did not look pleased. 'I am a knight. I do not slay priests unless absolutely necessary.'

'Quite so. But why did you say you did not return to Grundisburgh, when you had?' pressed Michael.

'Because I did not want half the village to know I had returned to warn Tuddenham about treachery in his own household,' snapped Grosnold. 'I had no idea whether I could trust you to be discreet, as I could Stoate and Unwin. And regrettable though Unwin's death was, it was over and done with, while the matter of Dame Eva and Isilia was still very much alive. So, like a good soldier, I considered my priorities. And there were appearances to be taken into account: I did not want the villagers seeing that I had driven my destrier lame in my demonstration of equestrian skills, either.'

'Anyway, he had no reason to suspect Stoate played a part in Unwin's death,' said Tuddenham. 'As far as he was concerned, Stoate had bled Unwin to improve the balance of his humours, and then Unwin had been murdered in the church for his purse.'

'But it was not the first time you had spoken secretly to Unwin,' said Bartholomew. 'You met him before we ever arrived in Grundisburgh. I saw you talking to him in your bailey.'

'True,' said Grosnold. 'I asked for his blessing because I had been hunting on a feast day, and needed absolution. He gave it to me.'

So that was it, thought Bartholomew, recalling the student emerging from Grosnold's bailey that night. And because Grosnold had made a confession, Unwin could not break his silence to tell Bartholomew what had transpired. It was all purely innocent after all.

'I know you suspected me of ambushing you here after you did my astrological consultation,' Grosnold continued. 'You thought I wanted to ensure your silence regarding the deed you found about who gave me my manor . . .'

'What deed is this?' asked Hamon, interested.

'A deed that is none of your affair,' said Tuddenham softly. He exchanged a look with Grosnold that told Bartholomew that it was a secret that he had known for many years, and that it would be a secret kept.

' . . . or that I had something to hide regarding Unwin's death,' Grosnold finished.

'Well, you did,' said Bartholomew. 'You denied meeting him, and confused us with lies.'

'But not with malicious intent,' said Tuddenham defensively. 'Grosnold sought only to protect me.' He smiled at his neighbour. 'And if Alcote had possessed a friend half as loyal he might be here now, not lying in his coffin in the church.'

'Just a moment,' began Michael indignantly. 'We have—'

Tuddenham held up a hand. 'You did not like him, Brother. None of you did. You did not grieve for him, as that nice young Horsey did for Unwin. You were angry and indignant at his murder, but none of you will miss him much.'

'Do you really think he is dead?' asked Bartholomew, remembering the fussy little scholar. 'I keep expecting him to walk up to us, and announce that there has been some dreadful mistake.'

'Yes, it would not surprise me to learn that he had persuaded some other unfortunate to take his place in Eltisley's inferno,' said Michael. 'It would be the kind of thing he would do.'

'Or perhaps he did die, but his angry spirit will not let his body rest,' whispered Hamon, looking at the forlorn hovels of the deserted village. 'Perhaps he will join the plague-dead here, in Barchester, and wander through the houses wailing and gnashing his teeth.'

It was not a pleasant image, and Bartholomew found himself glancing behind him, in the direction in which Hamon was gazing so fearfully. He pulled himself together irritably, refusing to be drawn into yet more superstitious tales and pagan beliefs. Padfoot, which had held the village in such terror, was nothing but a toothless performing bear, and the happenings at Barchester were sinister enough, but there was nothing supernatural about them.

'Alcote's time had come, and he was called,' said William in the tone of voice he usually reserved for preaching to people he considered heretics. 'Although called by whom, I should not like to guess.'

'It is the will of God that he is gone,' said Wauncy. His eyes, glittering in his skull-like face, took on a predatory gleam. 'But if you are genuinely concerned for the state of his soul, you might consider making a donation for a few masses to reduce his time in Purgatory. Unfortunately, owing to the sudden increase in demand for my services, I have been forced to raise my prices: sixpence a mass.'

'God's blood!' spat Michael, outraged. 'Your taverner murders our colleagues, and you charge us extra for requiem masses?'

'Master Wauncy will say a mass free of charge every day for a month, for Master Alcote and for Unwin,' said Tuddenham, ignoring the gasp of fiscal indignation from his cadaverous priest. 'I am sorry for all the wrong that has been perpetrated against Michaelhouse on my manor, and will make amends. I not only propose to give the living of the church to your College, but will build the new vicar – the replacement sent for Unwin – a fine new house. If you are still willing to accept the advowson, that is.'

'We are,' said Michael, before anyone could decline. 'It is what Alcote would have wanted.'

Bartholomew looked at the forlorn row of corpses that lay in the long grass, his gaze lingering on Eltisley's green apron. 'Well, at least now poor Alcote is avenged.'

Michael shivered suddenly as a chill breeze hissed through the dead village and made the flames on the burning church dance and flicker. 'Then let us hope he is also at rest,' he whispered.

epilogue

Cambridge, June 1353

THE SUN SLANTED GOLDEN AND SOFT THROUGH THE branches of the fruit trees in the orchard at the back of Michaelhouse where Bartholomew and Michael sat side by side on the trunk of an old apple tree that had fallen many years before. The air was still and warm, and was full of the familiar aromas of the town: the sweet scent of flowers, the rich smell of cut grass and the sulphurous stench of the river and its myriad of ditches that criss-crossed the countryside.

'So, it is done,' said Michael in satisfaction, stretching his legs out in front of him, and folding his hands across his stomach. 'Today, in Cambridge, the deed granting Michaelhouse the living of the Church of Our Lady in Grundisburgh was formally signed by Walter Wauncy on behalf of Thomas Tuddenham, in front of the Chancellor of the University and the Master and Fellows of the College.'

'But at what cost?' asked Bartholomew. 'It brought about terrible suffering, and led to so much evil being done.'

'Yes,' said Michael. He gave a sudden grin. 'I suppose it was what you might call a wicked deed. But Michaelhouse gained from it. It has all been worthwhile.'

'Roger Alcote would not agree,' said Bartholomew. 'Nor would Unwin. Not to mention Will Norys, the Freemans,

Alice Quy, Roland Deblunville, Dame Eva, Isilia, Tobias Eltisley and Eltisley's men.'

'But some good has come of this,' protested Michael mildly. 'Horsey is now parish priest of Grundisburgh, and we will never need to concern ourselves about his welfare again. And he will make a much better parish priest than Unwin ever would have done.'

'Why did he volunteer to do that, do you think?' asked Bartholomew. 'The rest of us were only too keen to leave Suffolk and return to Cambridge.'

'I think his few days in the leper hospital with Deynman may have swayed him. There is always the possibility in the Franciscan Order that he might be sent to work in one, and I think he thought a job as a priest in a pretty rural village like Grundisburgh was far preferable. He will be well paid – especially with all those masses for the dead to say – and relatively safe from diseases.'

Bartholomew did not reply. He had been concerned when there had been no sign of Deynman and Horsey at Brother Peter's leper hospital, and had spent some days traipsing across the county with Cynric searching for them. They were finally unearthed at a leper hospital in Ipswich. Somehow – although Bartholomew could not imagine how, given that the Old Road was almost completely straight – Deynman had managed to lose his way. Unconcerned, he had merely made the decision that one leper hospital was very much like another, selected a suitable institution in Ipswich, and settled in comfortably to wait for Bartholomew to collect him.

Unlike Horsey, who had apparently had doubts about the venture from the very beginning, Deynman had not been in the least surprised when Bartholomew eventually tracked them down, although his teacher's exasperation had clearly puzzled him. But it had been one of the few times when Deynman's inability to complete even the most basic of tasks had worked to his advantage.

Michael was still talking about Horsey. 'Or perhaps it was some kind of calling. Some priests do have a vocation to make the lives of others better, you know, despite what you think of us monks and friars. I once knew a Benedictine who was prepared to work three months of every year among the poor.'

'Really?' asked Bartholomew dryly. 'That must have caused some consternation about his mental health.'

Michael glanced at him quizzically, but then went on to other matters. 'William tells me you settled Mad Megin with Brother Peter in the leper hospital.'

Bartholomew nodded, 'He will look after her, and she can help him in the laundry. No one else would take her – Eltisley took too long to revive her when she tried to drown herself, and her mind was impaired. She was grief-stricken over the death of the performing bear and distress is making her act more oddly than ever.'

'And you healed her sore eyes?'

Bartholomew nodded again. 'Eltisley had been experimenting on her with his potions. What kind of man takes a sick old woman and uses her like some kind of animal to test wild theories?'

'A man like Eltisley,' said Michael with a shrug. He leaned back, and a slow, comfortable smile spread across his flabby face. 'I have the answers to two outstanding questions about this mess. Guess what they are.'

'I have learned more than I ever wanted to know about this miserable affair,' said Bartholomew, refusing to take the monk's bait. 'The best thing we can do now is put the whole thing behind us, and concentrate on our teaching.'

'You will want to know this,' said Michael, gloating.

'Well, come on then,' said Bartholomew irritably. 'All that fuss over the formal signing of the advowson today has left me exhausted. I am going to bed soon.'

'The father of Isilia's child,' said Michael. 'I know who he is.'

'How?' asked Bartholomew suspiciously. 'Tuddenham would not tell us, and no one else seemed to know.'

'Mother Goodman knew,' said Michael, infuriatingly smug. 'She said she would tell me if I gave her your Suffolk cramp ring.'

'So that is what happened to it,' said Bartholomew. 'I have been looking for that. Cynric wanted it to present to Rachel Atkin as a betrothal gift.'

'It is the kind of thing that would appeal to Cynric and his superstitious mind,' said Michael. 'Speaking of whom, has he told you where he hid the copy of that deed yet?'

'Yes,' said Bartholomew, smiling. 'And I also know he has wagered you a shilling that you will not guess where he put it. So, do not think I will tell you where it is, so you can claim his money.'

'This is a matter of honour, Matt, not money,' said Michael reproachfully. 'You cannot allow a servant to outwit one of us scholars.'

'Then you had better do some serious thinking,' said Bartholomew.

'I have,' said Michael. 'But he has me completely confounded. I would hate that man to be on the wrong side of the University, and become an adversary rather than an ally.'

'Give him his shilling, then,' said Bartholomew, laughing. 'And do not try to cheat him by trying to worm the answer out of me.'

'Give me a clue. Is it somewhere logical? Is it somewhere I will be angry at myself for not guessing?'

'No, Brother,' said Bartholomew. 'You will never guess – just as Cynric said.'

'We will see about that,' said Michael, stiffly. 'But to go back to what we were discussing: the father of Isilia's child was Walter Wauncy.'

'I do not believe you,' said Bartholomew, too amused to be surprised. 'The man looks like a corpse, and is as old as her husband. Mother Goodman was spinning you improbable yarns to entertain the villagers with later.'

'That is what I thought,' said Michael. 'But apparently he has fathered a number of children in the village – strange for a man who is supposed to be celibate. He is said to be something of a devil for pretty girls.'

Bartholomew laughed out loud. 'So he might regard himself, but I doubt any of the village women would agree. There is no earthly way a man like Wauncy could inveigle himself an invitation to the room of a beautiful woman like Isilia.'

'He has distinctive ears – large and transparent,' said Michael. 'When I looked at some of the village children, I counted at least five with the same feature. None of their fathers seemed to have ears like that. Anyway, Isilia told Mother Goodman about Wauncy herself. It happened one day when Tuddenham was out, and Isilia was becoming rather desperate for manly attentions.'

'Desperate is the word,' said Bartholomew, still laughing. 'But I suppose Tuddenham's condition might have made it difficult for him to provide his wife with these "manly attentions", as you put it.' He frowned, recalling something else. 'I went to see Mother Goodman before we left, to write down some of her remedies for teething. She told me that Wauncy was the father of Janelle's child, despite the commonly held rumour that it is Deblunville's.'

'And that was why Wauncy was willing to marry her for three pennies less than the Burgh priest charged,' said Michael, nodding. 'He would not want her revealing that little indiscretion. And now he has married her to Hamon. She was more than willing to wed Hamon now that he, and not Isilia's brat, will inherit Tuddenham's estates.'

'The course of true love,' said Bartholomew.

'Love is all very well, but riches are better for a successful marriage,' said Michael knowledgeably. 'And Janelle and Hamon will have plenty of those with Tuddenham's estates as well as the manors of Burgh and Clopton. If they ever find that golden calf, they will be wealthy beyond their wildest dreams.'

'They will never find that, Brother. It is a legend, like Padfoot. It does not really exist.'

'Do not be so sure,' said Michael. 'Anyway, Hamon intends to continue to look – on all his manors.'

Bartholomew shook his head, thinking about Isilia's and Janelle's choice of lover. 'It is ironic that Tuddenham went to all this trouble to prevent Isilia's illegitimate child from inheriting his estates, but now Janelle's child will – and it will have the same father.' He shrugged. 'Perhaps it is true, Brother. Perhaps Wauncy is a rogue among the ladies.'

'Well, better the child should have Wauncy's flapping ears than Tuddenham's teeth,' said Michael, 'although I shall pray most heartily that it does not inherit his cadaverous face. But Wauncy is not returning to Grundisburgh now that the advowson is signed. Tuddenham has dispatched him to a new parish at Wyverston near Stowmarket, so Horsey will begin his duties as Grundisburgh's priest immediately. I think it is Tuddenham's way of informing Wauncy that he provided him with an heir he did not want.'

Bartholomew sighed. 'I suppose Hamon will do well enough as lord of the manor when Tuddenham dies. Between them, he and Horsey will take care of Grundisburgh.'

'Look.' Michael held something out to him, and Bartholomew saw it was a small twist of parchment containing a few innocuous hairs. St Botolph's relic.

'Where did that come from?' asked Bartholomew wearily, having last seen it in Stoate's possession. 'Did your Bishop send his agents out after Stoate at your request, and drown him in the Seine as he was reading his Galen for the third time? Or did the boat in which he crossed the Channel mysteriously sink with the loss of all lives?'

'You do have a lurid imagination, Matt,' said Michael reprovingly. 'You should eat fewer vegetables and more bread and meat. Stoate himself gave me this relic, as a matter of fact.'

Bartholomew sat upright. 'Stoate? How? He will have fled the country by now!'

'Apparently not,' said Michael, infuriatingly smug. 'According to him, he is sorry for the deceptions he embarked upon, but he knows he did no serious wrong – he still maintains the death of Unwin was a dreadful accident while Norys's and Mistress Freeman's desecrated corpses came to no harm, because they were properly buried afterwards. And the tainted mussels that killed them, of course, were not his fault at all.'

'Of course,' said Bartholomew. 'So when did he tell you all this? Where did you meet him?'

'He sought me out after the signing ceremony today,' said Michael. 'I confess I was a little startled to see him in Cambridge, particularly since he was wearing the habit of a Carmelite.'

'He has become a friar,' said Bartholomew heavily. 'So, he escapes justice after all.'

'I hardly think so, Matt,' said Michael in a superior tone. 'Can you imagine what living hell the life of a friar must be? Allowed to own nothing, begging for his food, and at the beck and call of every squalid peasant in the parish.' He shuddered. 'Such a life would be Purgatory itself! He is going today to join a community near Grimsby.' He shuddered again. 'I barely know where that is, but Stoate assures me that it will be far enough away, so that no one will know him and he can make amends for his mistakes in peace.'

'Somewhere he can parade as an honest man seeking

to devote his life to God, you mean,' said Bartholomew bitterly. 'He will be accepted into the Carmelite Order on a deception, and no one will ever know what a lying, cheating, vile desecrator they have in their midst. He may think he has killed no one, but what about all the patients who might have lived had he not prescribed his false cures? What about Norys, who he was happy to see hanged in his place?'

'He will not be accepted on those terms,' said Michael, gloating somewhat. 'As soon as Stoate had gone on his way, I mentioned the matter to my Bishop. He will send a letter to the Prior of the House Stoate intends to join in a month or two, mentioning the fact that he is not all he appears. Your charlatan physician will not be allowed to forget his past crimes – indeed, he will atone for them in ways only a mendicant Order can dream up.'

'Your Bishop has an astonishingly long arm when it comes to these sorts of things,' said Bartholomew, rather distastefully. 'God forbid that I should ever come under the scrutiny of his beady eye, or within reach of his vindictive fingers.'

'Do not worry about that,' said Michael with a peaceful sigh. 'He knows how much you have done for the University and the College over the last few years. My lord the Bishop might not let a wrong go unpunished, but he does not forget those who have helped him, either. If ever you decide to become a Benedictine, Matt, he will find you a pleasantly lucrative position somewhere. Physician-priest to some lord perhaps, or even at the King's court.'

'No, thank you,' said Bartholomew in horror. 'The University is bad enough for politics and intrigue, but court must be even worse!'

'I do not think so,' said Michael with a happy beam of satisfaction. 'In fact, I know so.' He took a deep breath of river-tainted air, and settled back against the sun-warmed stones of the orchard wall. 'And it is good to be back, Matt!'

hISTORICAL NOTE

O N 6 MAY 1353 A LICENCE WAS GRANTED TO MICHAEL-
house to appropriate the living of the Church
of Our Lady at Grundisburgh. The final advowson was granted on 1 June 1353 by Walter Wauncy, and a
copy of the document is in the Muniments Room at Trinity
College, Cambridge, Michaelhouse's successor. By this time,
Michaelhouse held four other advowsons – Cheadle in Stafford-
shire, Tittleshall in Norfolk, Barrington near Cambridge, and,
of course, St Michael's Church in Cambridge.

Records show that Wauncy's term of office as rector came
to an end in 1353, and he was replaced by a man called
John de Horsey, who remained until 1361. It is likely that
Horsey was a Michaelhouse man, and that the College was
practising its newly acquired rights by appointing a vicar of
its own choosing to Grundisburgh. Wauncy, meanwhile, was
associated with several court cases in Suffolk, one of which
involved a manor at Wyverston near Stowmarket.

The reason the advowson was granted is not known,
although they were popular ways of making friends and
influencing people in medieval times. Whoever had the
living of a parish church was entitled to collect the tithes
– and Grundisburgh was a large village with a number of
freemen who would be eligible to pay – and was permitted

to donate two thirds of the revenue to the charity of his choice. Such a charity might well include a College, so the advowson would allow Michaelhouse to provide 'jobs for the boys' as well as making a handsome profit. The living of Grundisburgh remained in Michaelhouse's hands until Henry VIII incorporated Michaelhouse into his new foundation of Trinity College.

In 1353, the Tuddenham family were lords of the manor, probably living in Wergen Hall, which is thought to have stood on or near the site of the present Grundisburgh Hall. There was a second manor in the village, possibly centring on a house called Bast's. A document of 1339 records that a Robert Tuddenham, aged twelve, was Thomas Tuddenham's heir, although it is not known who, if either, survived the plague.

In the neighbouring villages, several documents just pre-dating the Black Death say that Roland Deblunville was lord of the manor in Burgh, while the knight Sir John Bardolf was lord of the manor of Clopton. A man called Robert Grosnold lived in Otley during the fourteenth century, although his dates are uncertain. One of the manors at Otley was called Nether Hall.

Stories and legends in this part of Suffolk abound. The Benedictine monks of St Edmundsbury Abbey did acquire the bones of St Botolph from a chapel thought to have been located in Grundisburgh in the eleventh century (one manuscript gives a date of 1095, although it probably occurred earlier than this), and there is a story that a golden calf was buried by the villagers near the site of the chapel for safe keeping. Legend also has it that the calf is still there. Unfortunately, St Botolph's relics were cremated by a devastating fire that swept through the monastery in 1465.

There is also a story that a mysterious white dog called Padfoot is occasionally seen in the village, as a prelude to a great personal disaster. It is said that the last person to have seen the ghostly hound was an American airman during World War II, the night before his plane was shot down. Rings made from coffin handles were believed to prevent cramps, while setting the ninth pea in a pod on a lintel was supposed to secure a husband for unmarried village maidens.

Many villages were abandoned after the Black Death, and there are references to a nearby settlement called Barchester in some documents, although no trace of it survives today. Others, such as Coates in Lincolnshire and Thorpe-in-the-Glebe in Nottinghamshire survive as lumps and bumps in fields, known to archaeologists as DMVs (deserted medieval villages).

There was an inn called the Half Moon in Grundisburgh, which was still selling beer in the early twentieth century, but is now a private house, while the Dog – a pleasant and welcoming place – thought to be named after the spectral hound (although the current inn sign portrays a beagle), still looks across the attractive green to the church. There is no record that either of these taverns existed before the seventeenth century, but a village of Grundisburgh's size and importance would have had at least one.

The church at Grundisburgh has been largely rebuilt since the fourteenth century, and has been provided with a startling eighteenth-century red-brick tower. However, the fourteenth-century wall painting of St Margaret still looks down from the chancel wall, and the piscina dates from Bartholomew's time. The church looks over a village green that is thought to date from when a charter was granted for a Tuesday market and a Pentecost Week fair in 1285. A stream still trickles through the middle of it, although there are footbridges provided for those not wishing to brave the fords. It is a peaceful village with friendly inhabitants. Whether scholars from Michaelhouse ever visited in 1353, to secure the advowson for their College, is not known, but there is no reason to suppose they did not.